# To the Ends of the Earth

## June Wyndham Davies

PIATKUS

For Maud and Wyndham Davies

and
to the memory of
the Wooburn exiles of 1831

## Acknowledgements

My thanks for their support and expert knowledge go to Keith Chatfield, Jane Conway Gordon, R W Finch of SOGAT 82, Ann McGarel-Groves, Louisa-Anne Meredith, Mike Molloy of the GPMU, Derek and Julia Parker, Carole Rivett, Helen Sharman & Philip Sheahan.

First published in Great Britain in 1996 by
Judy Piatkus (Publishers) Ltd of
5 Windmill Street, London W1

*A catalogue record for this book is available
from the British Library*

ISBN 0–7499–0331–7

Set in 10½ / 11½ pt Times by
Create Publishing Services Ltd
Printed and bound in Great Britain by
Biddles Ltd, Guildford & King's Lynn

# Prologue

It was an unusually hot spring day in October when the owner of Lacey's Creek came into town to buy a convict. When the swirling dust had settled she alighted from the carriage, shaking out her crushed skirts. The stocky man on the driving seat looped the reins, jumped down and reached back into the gig to hand her the parasol.

'You ought to have brought Meggie with you,' he grumbled, setting the battered hat on his sandy crop.

'I'm quite capable of putting up my own parasol, Mr Garvey,' she said briskly, suiting the action to the words. 'Besides, this place isn't safe for a young girl, not on Auction Day.'

Garvey looked in disbelief at the youthful face of his employer and started to say something, then thought better of it, but by the twitching of her lips he could tell she was not unaware of the irony of her own words.

Out on the sparkling waters of the Harbour, fifty or more ships of the line rode at anchor, ropes creaking and chains rattling as they waited for a free berth alongside the warehouses that lined Sydney Cove, to load or discharge their cargoes of flax, pine, whale oil, sandalwood, sealskins and livestock onto the quayside. One, the *Perseus*, anchored at the government quay below Fort Macquarie, had brought across the ocean a grimmer cargo of livestock: under the watchful eye of the New South Wales Corps in their tall, black hats and bright-scarlet coats, gangs of newly arrived convicts, having sweated to unload the hold of the vessel that had brought them halfway across the world, were squatting in chains on the dockside under the pitiless sun.

'Fools that they are!' hissed the woman furiously. 'Do they think they'll get a better price for them by leaving them on the quays in the noon sun?'

'Easy now, missus,' said the foreman in a subdued whisper. 'You lose your temper and we won't be gettin' what we wanted, will we?'

He watched her closely, waiting for a reaction as her eyes flew

1

anxiously along the line of convicts, but there was no sharp intake of breath, no start of recognition.

'Hard to tell from this distance,' he said as her shoulders slumped.

She shook her head wearily. 'I don't think he's there,' she said, drawing the veil over her face.

This was the third time in less than a fortnight that they'd dashed in from Lacey's Creek, when the signal station on South Head sent the news to Parramatta that a new convict ship had passed through the Heads and was beating its way up the Harbour to Sydney Cove, and Garvey had run out of comforting words. He could have given her many reasons why the one she was waiting for had not arrived – most of them deadly.

They were bringing up the women and children from the hold, a sight which never did much for his stomach. He averted his gaze. Some of the men back at the farm would have given anything for a day in Sydney, with its grogshops and its high concentration of the colony's pitifully few women, but he could never be quite at ease in the town, with its strange mixture of elegant new sandstone buildings cheek by jowl with the squalor of the convicts' huts.

They were standing below Government House, close by Cadman's Cottage at the foot of the Rocks, the finger of land that jutted out between Darling Harbour and Sydney Cove, where the first convict settlement had started. Beyond the unloading point for the convict ships was Limeburner's Point, where the early convicts, to provide the mortar for the infant town, had burned the mollusc shells abandoned in heaps by the blacks who had lived here long before the arrival of Captain Cook or the First Fleet; to the right, beyond Government House, was the wide green expanse of the Domain, part still wild, part a magnificent new botanic park. Looking out with narrowed eyes over the sparkling waters of the many bays that formed the vast natural harbour, sheltered between the protective headlands of North and South Head, his gaze was brought up short by the conical peak of Pinchgut Island, where in recent memory the more recalcitrant of the transported convicts had been marooned alone with starvation rations to learn an even harder lesson than that already learned by separation from family and home.

He shivered and turned away. 'Come on, missus,' he said bracingly. 'If we're to get you into the auction, it's time we went.'

They drove across the little stone bridge over the Tank Stream and left behind them the convict road gangs labouring under the whip to hack out with their pickaxes the new roads which would connect the airy upper slopes of the Rocks with the waterside below, and spare the residents of the smart new villas the inconvenience of passing through the slums that lined the quays. Just before the Wynyard

Barracks, Garvey turned the carriage into the courtyard of a commodious hotel and handed the reins to the convict ostler, with a command to make sure the horses were rubbed down and baited.

'Do you think the new arrivals will be up here in time for the auction?' she asked huskily as he handed her down.

'Sure to be, missus,' he reassured her. 'While the cat's away the mice will play, an' the new governor will be here before too long. Samson an' his crooked clerks will want to get every last bit of commission on convict assignments before the new governor puts a stop to their little games.'

He pretended a fascination with the view up to the windmills on Church Hill while keeping a careful watch on her from the corner of his eye. God send she didn't come over faint again, as she had in the convict barracks this morning – aye, and all the other mornings she had made him drive her to Hyde Park Barracks when they had failed to find the one she sought on the quayside. A barracks full of wretched convicts was no fit sight for a young lady, that was for certain, any more than what she was about to see in the auction rooms was fit. He cleared his throat and turned his gaze to the white sails of a three-master tacking across the Heads. 'If ye want to stay in the carriage, missus, I'm more than willing – '

She cut him off. 'No. Thank you, Mr Garvey, but this is something I have to do for myself.' This time, she couldn't explain why, she felt she had to be at the auction in person. She shook out her skirts and adjusted her veil; then she took a deep breath and stepped up to the verandah.

The lobby between bar and auction room was full of men waiting for the auction to start, indulging in a bumper or two of rum and discussing the proposals for a loyal address to the new governor, and the practicalities of illuminating the town to welcome him. As she walked in, a shock wave seemed to run around the hotel. Within seconds, more men were spilling out of the main rooms into the lobby, and there was much tipping of hats and jostling to greet her. She was vexed to see how little the veil helped to disguise her.

'What did you expect?' hissed Garvey. He looked at the collection of merchants and farmers hurrying eagerly from the bar, the Merinos taking care not to mix with the Emancipists; most of them could identify her at half a mile, he reckoned, even without sight of that pale hair.

Everyone wanted to ask after her wellbeing and enquire if she would do them the honour to join them at dinner, but she excused herself gracefully, conscious that the appreciative looks from some were balanced by stiff disapproval from others. A decent woman was such a rarity out here that neither poor looks nor meagre fortune

3

would disqualify her as a potential wife of one of the rich settlers, even the Merinos, who traced their lineage back to the non-convict landowners who had made their fortunes from sheep or rum. It was their misfortune that one of the few women in the Bay District with youth, looks and money had turned out to be so eccentric that she had not only refused all suitors to date but even insisted on conducting her own business affairs without any male support beyond a farm bailiff.

The auctioneer, equally disapproving but mindful of the purchasing power of the Lacey's Creek holdings, found her a quiet corner at the back behind a jumble of packing cases and a fancy carved screen waiting to be collected by the new governor's convict servants. Not yet awhile, though. It was in everyone's interests that the administration should continue to turn a blind eye to the existence of such auctions – the interest of everyone except the convicts, that is, and the poor Emancipist settlers in the outback, and who had ever taken any notice of them?

By law those convicts not required for the government service – such as the skilled artisans needed to work on civic buildings – should have been assigned on the basis of need to the dungaree settlers hacking new farms out of the bush. Instead, palms were regularly greased to ensure that every fresh boatload of convicts, en route from the dockside to the barracks, was brought first to Samson's auction rooms, so that prosperous settlers might take their pick, before even the government had made its choice.

She sat impatiently through the first part of the auction, her body stiff with tension as Samson extolled the virtues of cases of Bathurst cheeses, hogsheads of Taylor's double stout from the *Vibillia*, or the finer points of fat rams, Timor ponies and Cape cattle just landed from the *Bengal*. Garvey joined in the bidding from time to time, as much as anything to take away from the singularity of any bidding they might do later, for he knew full well that the Merino landowners would already have had their pick of the best goods that came off the ships.

By the time they reached the second half of the auction she felt as though she could hardly breathe, and not solely owing to the smell of stale rum. Through the pierced screen her eyes were riveted on the doorway through which the convicts slowly stumbled, still uncertain on land after their long months at sea, but urged on by barked orders from the redcoats. The first few were half naked, dressed only in the remains of tattered breeches and sea-rotted shirts; they would not get their 'canary suits' of grey and yellow worsted until they reported to the Hyde Park convict barracks. Some of them bore on their pallid and grimy backs the mark of the cat, the vicious lash with which the

4

sea captains kept discipline among the rabble of thieves, murderers and rioters who filled the hold on the long haul from the mother country.

Her stomach lurched with fear. What if Captain Hurvine had been unable – or unwilling – to carry out her instructions?

A huge bear of a man with an almost square skull shambled into the room, his face blistered from the hot sun. He paused in the doorway, his small eyes darting round the room, taking in the crowds. A rifle butt struck his shoulder and he moved up into the room and onto the platform. She drew her breath in sharply as she caught sight of his back, crisscrossed with scars old and new; what wasn't scarred was blistered and sunburnt.

And then her eyes moved past him and she saw the one she had been waiting for.

'Easy now,' warned Garvey, putting a restraining hand on hers. 'At a guess I'd say it's the last man we'll be wantin'?' he went on softly. 'Don't be starin' at him now, or Samson'll see our interest and push the price up just for the hell of annoyin' ye.'

She nodded, dragging her eyes away from the shuffling figure bringing up the rear of the sorry procession.

Garvey walked up to the front of the auction stand with the rest of the prospective purchasers; under pretext of examining the men in the chain he took a good look at the one on the end of the line. Tall, quite slender, a little grey under the tan he'd acquired on the crossing, holding one shoulder hunched, one arm somewhat stiffly at his side. His dark hair curled damply over his brow and his face was half-hidden by a dark, curly beard. He wore a halfway decent jacket, stained and worn, but enough to keep the worst of the sun's glare from burning him.

He wasn't the youngest, nor yet the fittest, and Garvey wouldn't have picked him as first choice. He joined in the bidding on several of the others, just for the look of it, but his bids were low and he was outbid each time. He had a notion to bid seriously for Calderson, the big man with the square skull, but when his list of violent crimes was read out, many of those looking for brawny manpower backed off. Out in the bush and on the smaller farms a man lived pretty much cheek by jowl with his servants, and who wanted to find themselves bedding down under the same roof as a ruffian like him, one who had probably escaped the gallows only by the merest of chances? Samson, the burly auctioneer who took a percentage on each sale, was unwilling to admit defeat, but there were no bids. He placed a blue mark against the convict's name; having been flogged on board ship he would be for the chain gangs building the new roads beyond the Blue

Mountains, where convict police and convict overseers could keep him under control.

A half-dozen more, mostly Irish politicals with a few English agricultural rioters among them, came under the hammer. A sad-looking group of men, one or two hardened by the violence of the voyage, most of them lost and forlorn, wondering what folly had brought them here, so far from their families. Shorn of the drink- or rhetoric-induced bravado that had diverted them from their mundane life of plodding survival, few looked capable of harming a fly. 'Can plough' or 'knows horses' was sufficient to encourage bids from farmers and land agents, who would rather line Samson's pockets than be assigned the skinny town rats from the London slums and rookeries who, experience had taught them, would be totally bemused by a bush farm.

The auctioneer moved on to the last man, pushed forward from the shadows to stand in the shaft of sunlight that slanted down from the high windows. 'Machine-breaker,' intoned the soldier, reading from the list in his hands. 'Transported for life.' In spite of the chains the man straightened his shoulders and held his head up proudly, his brown eyes surveying the crowd below the platform.

'Looks like the machines broke him!' guffawed one of the farmers from the back. 'Fellow's a cripple!'

'Nonsense, sir!' said the auctioneer, prodding the unfortunate man in the ribs. 'Fine figure of a man.'

'Git him to lift his arms!' demanded another.

'Arms above yer 'ead!' bellowed the escorting officer, raising the lash threateningly.

She wanted to look away, but she couldn't. With a contemptuous glare at the officer the convict raised his left arm, but his right, despite the chain that joined them, would not go above shoulder height, and even that much effort turned his face ashen and made the sweat break out on his lip.

'Excellent houseman,' said the auctioneer in some desperation. 'Reads an' writes a good hand. Make you a fine convict tutor. Now, who'll start the bidding?'

But no one was much interested. The last ship had brought in a number of Irish revolutionaries, some of their leaders from the minor gentry, and they had temporarily glutted the market for convict tutors. There was a clanking and a shuffling behind the man standing stiffly in the shaft of sunlight, and eyes were already straying past him to the chain of women being lined up in the shadows behind him.

Samson knew he'd lost the initiative. The bidding was over in a moment. 'At a knockdown price to Mr Garvey, Lacey's Creek,' said the auctioneer mournfully, bringing his hammer down on the barrel.

6

# Part I

# Machinations

The mills of God grind slowly,
    yet they grind exceeding small...
        Friedrich von Logan

# Chapter One

A shaft of sunlight fell through the slender beech trees, picking out the girl and the kitten on the plaid rug, an island of pattern in the haze of bluebells that carpeted the wood. The kitten stirred from sleep and rubbed its dazzled eyes.

The girl leaned over to shade it from the sun. One of her ringlets had come loose from the ribbon that confined it and the kitten raised its tiny paws, claws carefully sheathed, and batted it playfully from paw to paw until it tangled and caught.

'Ouch!' The tug on the hair as the kitten tried to suspend its weight from the lock was painful enough to make her eyes water. She reached down and tried to disentangle the silky, fair hair from the tiny claws. Released from its makeshift swing, the kitten fell back among the bluebells and rolled over and over down the slope.

She scrambled to her feet and hurried after it. 'Oh, you poor little thing!' she exclaimed, as she picked up the little body and felt it carefully all over, letting her breath out on a sigh of relief when she was convinced that nothing was damaged.

The kitten was the weakling of the litter that the old mill cat had unexpectedly produced and when the old ratter died soon after, she had raised the litter by hand. She loved them all, but this undersized little creature was her favourite.

She buried her face in the fluffy grey fur and the kitten began to purr softly. She gave a little laugh, part joy, part relief, and purred back at it.

Overhead a bird began to sing and she put her head on one side, listening to it. It was so peaceful here, one of the few places in the Wye Valley where you could escape the creaking of the mill wheels and the incessant thumping and pounding of the machinery. A little way down valley and the air would be trembling with the pounding of rag-beaters at the paper mill and the thumping of heavy stamp hammers at the new wire mill; Hedge Mill upstream and Glory Mill downstream beat out the same ear-shattering rhythm.

9

But in this little hollow, tucked away not far from where the Maidenhead road branched away from the Oxford turnpike to follow the line of the river Wye down to the Thames, you could forget that you lived by the mills and listen to the sounds of the countryside. It was their own secret place, hers and Dickon's, but Dickon, fortunate Dickon, had been sent to London.

There had been no question of her going with him, even though she would have enjoyed the bargaining with the Stationers' merchants far more than he – and made a better job of it too! But Father would not hear of it, threatening to whip her if she spoke of it again. Not that he had whipped her for six months now, not since Lady Isabelle had almost fallen into hysterics on hearing that Ezekiel Revel still personally administered his daughter's physical punishment. Lady Isabelle's threat to wash her hands of the Revels entirely had been sufficient to frighten her father off, and her life had been a deal more peaceful since that day. Not that she was complacent: with Ezekiel Revel one could never be sure which way he would jump next and there were many men, from Wycombe to London, who rued the day they had set themselves up against him. But for the moment he was content to bow to Lady Isabelle.

She lay back and closed her eyes, feeling the warmth of the sunlight on her eyelids. She sighed. Lady Isabelle might be irritating, but without her and her nieces – and Dickon – time hung heavy on her hands.

She must have dozed a little in the warm sun, the kitten lying curled up on her soft robe of delicate myrtle green. As she stirred she heard, from the road on the far side of the bluebell woods, the rumble of heavy wheels.

She jerked her head up in alarm. It couldn't be the Oxford mail; it *couldn't* be! So much time could not possibly have passed! Her breath caught at the back of her throat and even the kitten seemed to freeze as she waited and listened.

The wheels slowed as the coach began the long pull up the London road towards Beaconsfield, up White Hill and past Cut-Throat Woods. And then the postillion sounded his horn.

In a panic she grabbed the basket, scooped the plaid shawl and the kitten into it and, with wobbly knees that threatened to give way beneath her, scrambled her way up the bank.

As she came in sight of the holding ponds, she saw that the sun was dipping towards Hog Pen Hill and knew she was too late. Her heart pounded, not with the running, but with terror. Her father in a rage was enough to unman the strongest of his rivals; every fibre and muscle of her body shrank from contemplation of what awaited her.

She skirted the rag houses, covering her mouth and nose with her kerchief against the unhealthy stench that emanated from them. She had a stitch in her side and her breath was coming in gasps as she went past the coach house, doubling round to the back gate where she ducked into the shrubbery and picked her way down the secret path, back through the ornamental bushes to the kitchen door. With her hair out of its ribbon and the hem of her dress marked by her hasty progress through the fields, she knew she dared not present herself at the front of the house for fear that his important visitors might not yet have gone.

Her lips tightened as she heard the sound of sobbing through the open upper windows. So Father had already turned his rage on Aunt Lucy.

She glanced around to make sure that the way was clear. There was no sign of Cook, who had a tendency to disappear into the cellars when trouble started. A wooden bucket was sitting on the path, just outside the kitchen door. A tiny frown appeared between her eyes. Monday was Phoebe's day for the washing and she had seen no linen blowing in the drying yard. She emerged from the shrubbery, glancing down at the bucket as she passed.

Out of the mass of waterlogged grey fur, one little pointed face looked sightlessly up at her.

Joshua Delahaye crossed the little bridge across the Wye, stooping to check that the sluices were clear of any debris, washed down by the prolonged heavy rains, that might back up the flow of water in the narrow river or clog the great wheels of the paper mill. Rising, he shielded his keen brown eyes against the sun hanging like a red ball of flame on the crest of Northern Woods and setting the walls of Clapton Revel aglow.

The graceful red brick house had been the home of the owners of Clapton Mills since the time of William and Mary. It was spoken of as the 'big house' by the families in the huddle of cottages that formed the hamlet of Upper Moor, but although it was set in its own acres, it could not bear comparison with country houses such as Cliveden and Bosingham House.

Rumour had it that the house had been built by a Dutchman, and it was a rumour Joshua was quite prepared to give credence to, for though the estate, set in the winding and wooded valley, was certainly large enough to have taken a decent manor house, set well back from the road, with perhaps a couple of wings and an elegant frontage, the builder had turned his back on the wide acres and had built a tall, narrow house right on the turnpike road, hemmed in by the river and the mill, just like the pictures Joshua had seen of the narrow town houses that edged the canals of Amsterdam.

11

The house was set above the hamlet, on a gentle incline where the land sloped away to the river, giving three storeys in front and four behind. It was a pretty house, but built far too close to the mill and the drying houses, with only the coach houses and the little bridge over the sluice between them.

Successive owners had altered the house but little, although one of the mill ponds had been dug out to form an ornamental lake. Revel, finding the accommodation too small, had built on an extra wing to the left of the portico; at its lowest level the new wing had furnished a morning room alongside the kitchens, with a delightful view of the lake, but from the approach it had totally destroyed the symmetry of the house front.

Joshua breathed deeply of the cool evening air, driving the stench of alkali and wet paper out of his lungs. Every evening when he turned his horse towards Upper Moor and the little bridge across the Wye, he congratulated himself anew that he had not taken the mill manager's house that lay just above the mill, between Clapton Farm and Clapton Revel. Even in winter when the rain or the snow soaked him through, he never begrudged the extra mile to Wooburn Green. It was worth it not to be at Revel's beck and call.

When the village children saw him leaving the paper mill on his big bay mare, they laid aside their slings and left their bird-scaring at the edge of the barley fields to hurry to the gate. There was usually a friendly word from the mill manager to break up the long day, and more often than not a small treat – a ginger snap from Beck's bakery or a mint humbug, sometimes even a farthing apiece to add to the ha'pennies the farmer paid them for keeping the birds from the crops – but today, to their disappointment, he rode straight on without a word.

On the far side of the field the stooped figure of Bernard the Walker plodded towards Lower Moor. The old man had lost his work at the mills some years ago when rheumatism attacked him and now he made his living by walking from hamlet to hamlet carrying messages and small items in a sack on his back. Bernard was a prime source of village gossip, but today Joshua deliberately kept to his path along the riverbank, barely acknowledging the old man's greeting, his mind and his eyes on the piece of paper he had drawn from his pocket.

He'd known for some time that there was discontent in the valley, among field workers and mill workers alike. After a succession of severe winters, 1830 had already seen great suffering among the poor, yet feelings that had run high in the winter had died down again, even though this had been the wettest spring anyone could recall. Wooburn was still an agricultural area, despite the mills, and the prospect of another poor harvest, together with the new threshing machines,

12

which would push even more field workers onto the parish by taking away their winter work, was bound to stir matters up once more. Journeymen papermakers on the tramp from the Kent mills had even talked of a mysterious Captain Swing banding together the malcontents and leading them to rebellion, but Joshua had dismissed that as scaremongering. Until today.

There was little he could do about the farm labourers; his concern was much more with the mill hands.

The Wye Valley depended on its mills. For centuries the valley had taken London rags, brought up the Thames to Hedsor Wharf on the barges, and turned them into paper. Skilled work it was too, work that the journeymen papermakers had been proud of the length of the river, from Wycombe to Bone End, through Loudwater and Wooburn and Hedsor, but today the centuries-old skills of the vat man, who produced the finest of handmade paper, were no longer so prized. There was already a Fourdrinier machine at Clapton that could do the work of twenty vat men and now there was talk of doubling the number of Fourdriniers and setting in Hollander rag-grinders alongside, to keep up the supply of pulped rags for the extra machines. That would mean an end to employment for the women and older children who worked in the rag rooms, removing buttons, slitting hems and cutting the rags into small strips ready to dust and pulp. He'd tried to persuade Revel to slow down the changes, but Revel had turned on him, his violent temper bubbling even closer to the surface than usual.

'Not buy more machines?' he yelled. 'Why the devil not?'

'At least till agriculture picks up again, Mr Revel,' he suggested mildly. He heard himself modulating his vowels, flattening them as he always did when he spoke to Revel, and hated himself for it. 'Then, when there is some other work for the men to fall back on – '

'What are you, some damned Radical?' his employer accused furiously, his face darkening and the veins standing out on his forehead. 'Some damned Jacobin? Been listening to that fellow Cobbett? Eh? Eh?' He jabbed his finger angrily at his foreman, emphasising each word. 'It's not enough that I've to leave us short-handed by sending the children home nights – '

'Which has meant we've not lost one tired child in the machinery, unlike – '

'You start sowing any more fancy ideas in the men's heads an' I'll put you out on the road, mister, same as Bosingham did with yer father! Aye, that's where all this comes from, acourse. That father o'yourn...'

Joshua felt the back of his neck stiffening, as it always did when Revel threw his father's reputation in his face. 'My father has his

13

views, Mr Revel,' he said as evenly as he could manage, 'and I have mine. My aim is to ease relations and try to avoid trouble between the mill and the men. I – '

'Trouble? Trouble?' screeched Revel. 'What have the mill hands to say to *relations* and *trouble*?' He deliberately clipped his words in a parody of Joshua's accent. 'What have hands to say to anythin', mister? Eh? Eh?'

'There is still a market for the fine handmade papers, Mr Revel. We could still keep the vat men at Clapton, alongside the machines, then – '

'Teach me my business, would yer, mister?'

'No, Mr Revel.'

'Good. Then you'll write to Cazelle and tell him I'd be obleeged if he'd send me another of Donkin's Fourdriniers.'

Joshua sighed heavily as he turned over the tattered piece of paper, eyes screwed up against the lowering sun to decipher the scrawl. Not that he needed to read it, for he already knew it by heart.

> Who sent for the machines? [it asked rhetorically]. Who sent to put honest men out of their work and their babes to cry to the Lord in their hunger? Whosoever done it shall not be long on this earth, nor yet his property, which is got through roguery. Dellehay, your blood shall atone for your rashness if en ye do not relent and right soon. Prepare for a certain and sad end if en ye heed not this warning.
> Signed of the agents of Captain Swing.

Underneath was a crude drawing of a dagger with blood dripping from its blade.

Delahaye closed his fist on the paper. His horse, unbidden, turned into the narrow lane that led across the little bridge. Captain Swing be damned! he thought angrily. Richard Jessop it was, for certain. Jessop was a skilled vat man, one of the few who had not been apprenticed to the paper trade as a child, but had gone first to the village lace school where Dame Savage taught the children their letters in exchange for a few pennies and the strips of edging lace they so laboriously produced. An elder of one of the breakaway Methodist groups, Jessop's fondness for reading the fire-and-brimstone passages of the Bible reflected as much in this scrawl as in the man's everyday speech.

Deep in thought, he let the reins lie slack on the mare's neck as she picked her way past Moor Meadow and along the deeply rutted Glory Lane. If he had been paying more attention, he would have noticed the mare pricking up her ears, but his mind was still back at the mill, wrestling with the problem of Jessop and the machines.

As they turned out of the lane he thought he heard a rustling in the bushes; his head jerked up sharply and in spite of himself he found his hand going to his waist where he carried a small but sharp knife. Even as the slim blade slid out of the leather sheath he berated himself for an idiot: it would be a foolhardy mill hand who tried to attack him while he was on horseback. Quite apart from giving him the advantage of height, the bay mare was known to be one of the best mounts in the district and if trouble threatened, she could show the fleetest attacker a clean pair of heels. With a deprecatory smile he sheathed the knife and leaned forward to quieten the mare, just as a small figure shot out through the hedge, tripped and fell almost under the horse's hooves.

It took all his strength to turn the mare aside, her hooves pawing the air above the fallen body. She reared in the air, almost dancing on her hind legs as he brought her around, forcing her to sidestep around the prone body.

'What the hell do you think you're about?' he exclaimed wrathfully, sliding out of the saddle as soon as the horse was clear and hurrying to the figure lying huddled across the rutted surface of the lane. His stomach turned over as he saw beneath the cloud of dust stirred up by the horse's hooves the still, small figure of a woman – or a child? – lying in a tangle of shawl.

For a long, awful moment he thought that he had killed her. He fell on his knees at her side and lifted the shawl – silk, so it was none of the village girls! – dreading what he might see. There was no blood, no hideous head wound, but his heart skipped a beat as he saw the golden ringlets – the colour of apricot silk, Tarquin had once said.

A pulse beat dizzily in his temple as the words rang in his head. Oh, God, he thought, praying as he had not since he was a little child. Oh, God, don't let me have killed her! Don't let me have killed Kattrin! His hand trembled as he began to pat her pale limbs, looking for signs of injury.

There was a sharp intake of breath and gold-green eyes looked up at him from beneath a tangle of dusty ringlets. 'Oh, Joshua!' she gasped. 'I thought I'd missed you!'

'Missed me!' he yelled wrathfully, hauling her unceremoniously up off the ground. '*Missed* me? I damned nearly didn't miss you, my girl! Don't you realise how close you came to being trampled to death under my horse's hooves, you little fool?' He caught her by the shoulders, almost shaking her as relief mixed with anger.

'Oh, Joshua, don't be so cross with me!' Two large tears chased down her cheeks, washing a rivulet through the dirt. 'It's just ... the

15

kitten – and my father – I went to the mill but you'd gone and . . .' She lost herself in the tangle of words. Suddenly, realising the danger she had put herself in, she began shaking from head to foot. 'I – I was frightened and . . .'

Without thinking what he was doing he jerked her into his arms and held her there a moment, his face buried in her dusty hair. 'Not near as frightened as I was when I thought I'd killed you,' he groaned.

They might have stood there an age, uncertain which of them was supporting which, but the mare, restless and whinnying, came up behind to nudge him and recall him to his senses.

'We can't stand here in the lane like this,' he said shakily. He forced himself to release her and step back, holding her arm to steady her. She looked up at him, her gold-specked eyes wider than ever, then with a sniff she wiped the tears from her face with a dusty hand, leaving two large smears across her pale cheeks.

He turned to untangle the mare's reins and while his back was turned she dived into the hedge to retrieve the basket. Taking her firmly by the arm, he caught the mare's reins and walked them slowly down to the riverbank.

He looped the reins around an old willow stump and went down the bank to dip his handkerchief into the water. 'Better clean your face up, Miss Revel. If Lady Isabelle were to see you . . .'

'Don't call me "Miss Revel" in that horrid stuffy way,' she said, pulling a face. 'Otherwise I'll know you really are furious with me.'

Joshua didn't trust himself to answer. Until very recently he had thought of her and her twin brother as children still: two young and restless children, constantly tumbling around the gardens of Clapton Revel like a pair of kittens, or underfoot in the mill, where they had learned from the craftsmen everything there was to know about paper from the rag kettles in the dusting room to the rattling machinery in the salle. He had always called her Kat, for the kitten she so much resembled, with her wide eyes set in a slender oval face, but she was no longer a child, and such presumption would not go down at all well with Lady Isabelle. Miss Revel it would have to be. He caught her chin, turned her face towards the setting sun and gently began to wipe the worst of the dirt from her face.

She smiled trustingly up at him as he worked and for an instant he found himself returning the smile, gazing down into her wide hazel eyes; today, because of the green dress, they showed more green than gold, with a scattering of bronze flecks around the iris and the curious golden horseshoe-shaped rim below. After a moment the smile vanished from his firm-lipped mouth.

'I haven't, have I?' she said anxiously.

16

'What?' He spoke as if he had just come back from a long way away. 'Haven't what?'

'Offended you?'

'Frightened me out of my skin, you mean!' he said, turning away with a brusque laugh. 'By rights I ought to beat you, leaping out of the hedge at me like that!'

It was a ridiculous thing to say. As if he could ever have lifted a finger against Kattrin! Or her brother! In the seven years since he had come to Wooburn he had watched them grow from children through gawky adolescence to handsome adulthood and done his best to shelter them from their father's wrath. Dickon, reluctantly leaving for London, had begged him to keep an eye on his twin, for which duty Joshua had needed no second bidding.

'No need to beat me,' she said, her shoulders sagging as she sat on the fallen tree trunk. 'Father will surely do it for you.'

He cursed himself for his thoughtlessness. 'I did but jest,' he said quietly, coming up behind her and putting his hand on her shoulder. 'You know I would not – '

'I know.' She sighed and leaned back against him. 'You jested. But he will not.'

At the feel of her body against his Joshua froze, not wanting to move, yet fearful of staying in the same position. Beneath the lace fichu, slightly disarranged in the recent accident, he could see the gentle rise and fall of her pale bosom. He had only to move the hand on her shoulder a fraction and –

'I cannot think he will,' he said unsteadily. 'Why, this is no worse than when you and Drusilla locked the governess in the pantry at Bosingham House!' He dropped his hand and deliberately drew away from her. 'He did not beat you then.'

'Only because Lady Isabelle had forbidden it.'

'And will surely do so again.'

'I think this time he will not listen to Lady Isabelle,' she said with a shrug. 'And perhaps she would not blame him. I should have been there to receive his visitors. It was unforgivable to be so late.'

He had been aware that important visitors had been expected, for a number of the mill hands were related to the indoor servants at Clapton Revel, but so caught up had he been with the Swing letter and the new machines that for once he had made no effort to find out more.

'I dine at Bosingham House this evening,' he said sombrely. 'Should you wish me to speak to Lady Isabelle for you?'

'Better not,' she said gravely. 'If Father found out, he would only turn his wrath on you, and it was, after all, my fault.' She bit her lip, struggling to put a brave face on it. 'I don't mind what he does to me,'

17

she said after a moment, tossing her head defiantly. Then the façade cracked. 'But he shouldn't have drowned the kittens,' she said forlornly.

'Is that you, Joshua?' called a thin voice as Joshua eased off his boots and entered the kitchen.

'Who else were you expecting, Father?' He crossed to the table, freshly scrubbed that day, and put the basket down on it. He sniffed the air appreciatively; something savoury was cooking in the oven set in the wall over the hearth.

'Who else are you offering?' There was a shuffling as Will Delahaye tapped his way out of the parlour and across the wooden floor of the hall, his leg dragging on the floor between the crutches.

Father and son exchanged a brief smile, then Will's glance fell to the covered basket.

'What's this?' he asked, suspicion writ large on his lined face. He hopped over to the table and pulled the blanket off.

'It's a kitten,' said Joshua.

'I can tell it's a kitten,' snapped his father. 'Doesn't mean I'm blind because I'm a cripple!' A muscle twitched in his son's jaw but Joshua stayed silent. 'What the devil would we be wanting with a kitten?'

'Court of last appeal,' said Joshua wryly. 'Revel had drowned its brothers and sisters and had an execution warrant out on this one, and – '

'You need tell me no more,' said Will Delahaye, rolling his eyes heavenwards. 'With Kattrin Revel's soft heart and your even softer head...'

Joshua pulled a face. 'I never intended to let her talk me into it.'

'Then why did you?'

'Father, she'd been weeping over the others and – '

'Weeping!' he exclaimed scornfully, pushing the basket angrily away and nearly overbalancing himself as he did so. 'Weeping? What has she to weep over?' He shook off his son's steadying hand and hopped angrily away into the hall. 'Are you as touched in the head as she is? There are women weeping over dying babes that they can't feed, and you and she are to weep over drowned kittens?'

Joshua bit back the angry retort that rose to his lips. He knew it was just the pain talking, but once his father had worked himself up into this mood, there was no reasoning with him. Better to give him his head and let him get it all off his chest.

'Oh, there'll be a time coming, a time of reckoning for the likes of Miss Kattrin Revel,' said Will, leaning breathlessly against the parlour door jamb, his voice rising higher as he grew more angry. 'A time when we shall have no more masters and men. When the tax-eaters

18

and the mortgage men and the fund-holders shall be forced to work for their wages, like the rest of us! When the orphans and the widows shall rise up and say, "No more! No more shall we starve to put fine clothes on the backs of the dainty ladies, for the Miss Revels of this world to sit by in idleness!" Oh, there shall be a reckoning then, my boy, mark my words!'

'Mark them, Father?' said Joshua with a glimmer of a smile. 'I could give you your words back, verbatim! Chapter and verse – more readily even than my catechism!'

'You may mock now, my boy, but – '

'I know: ". . . but heads will roll".'

'Aye, that they will,' he growled, hopping down the hall and into the parlour and subsiding angrily in his chair by the window. 'Look what happened in France not thirty year since . . .'

Joshua took up the flint box and struck until a spark fell on the kindling and caught. He thrust a brimstone match into the smouldering rag and as he held the flame against the kindling in the parlour hearth, he looked quizzically over his shoulder. 'If ever we go down the same road as France, Father, which heaven forbid, your head will be one of the first to roll. You're like Danton: no self-respecting revolutionary would put up with you!'

With that he turned on his heel and stalked back out to the stables to see to the mare. She had come to no visible harm in the recent accident, but he wanted to put some salve on her mouth where the bit had jibbed. After that it would be back to the kitchen, to see to the dinner that Widow Beck set in the oven every day, when she came in from the next cottage to bring Will his midday meal. His father really needed more care, but he had always refused to acknowledge the extent of his disability. Besides, it would be quite against Will Delahaye's principles to have servants in the house.

And yet it was really far too large a house for the two of them to run by themselves. A handsome brick house with a spacious yard and its own stabling, it was set slightly back from the thatched wattle-and-daub cottages that clustered round the edge of the village green. It was newer than the rest, with airy high-ceilinged rooms – fortunate, for the Delahayes were a tall breed of men and Joshua always came out of the other cottages with a crick in his neck from stooping.

Will Delahaye liked to believe he kept house for his son, but in truth in the last year it had become more the other way round as Will became increasingly confined to the front parlour overlooking the green. It was often midday before he felt strong enough to leave the bed which had been installed there for him when he became unable to manage the stairs.

When Joshua came in from the yard he found his father sitting in his customary seat in the window, his leg propped up in front of him and the kitten on his lap, darting tiny paws at the piece of string he was dangling in front of it.

'Why did Revel drown them?' he said gruffly. 'Good ratting stock. Clapton mill cats always were. Waymon at the Red Lion would have taken them.'

'Wanted to punish his daughter. She'd hand reared them, so he knew it would strike her hard to lose them. And in such a manner.'

Will Delahaye raised one eyebrow. 'What had she done to deserve that?'

'She'd lost track of the time, and he had visitors she should have been entertaining.'

'He's a man can always find his victim's weak spot.' Will nodded. 'But it's her aunt should be entertaining visitors, not an unmarried young girl like her.'

Joshua suppressed a smile with difficulty. For all his egalitarian principles, his father was really quite old-fashioned in his attitude to women.

'Revel won't see it that way,' he said, moving around the room and setting the place to rights. 'And as for the aunt – well, you and I know she's not the hostess she should be.'

'Bit like Shakespeare's Prince of Denmark, that one,' remarked Will Delahaye, looking at his son from under bushy eyebrows. 'Only mad north-northwest.'

'When it suits her, you mean?' It was an idea that had not previously occurred to his son.

'Still, you'd think the girl would have welcomed the visitors,' Will went on, as if Joshua had not spoken. 'All the way from London – might have brought news of her brother. Stationers' Company men. Come about the new machines, I'll warrant.'

'How is it, father, that you hear all the news before anyone else?' he said in some exasperation.

Will shrugged. 'All I can do is sit here and hope the world comes to me. I can't go out to it.'

And come they did, mused Joshua, returning to the kitchen to serve up the dinner. His father reminded him of a spider – benevolent, but none the less a spider – sitting at the centre of his web drawing in news along every intertwining strand.

He could hardly remember the time when it hadn't been so. But of course eleven years ago he had been at school: those had been the good times, when his father had been estate manager to Lord Bosingham and Joshua was sent to Eton alongside Bosingham's stepson Tarquin, half scholarship boy, half at favour of the Bosinghams. There had even been talk of university, if Joshua were willing to take

20

the Thirty-Nine Articles and proclaim himself a true member of the Church of England. And he would have done. But then his father had lost his leg in the accident. He'd been ill for so long, and when the Bosinghams let their sponsorship lapse, the last of the family money from the Garnetts, Joshua's mother's family, had gone to keep Joshua at Eton.

It had soon run out and Joshua had had to leave school and find work to support them both. He'd started off at one of the Wycombe mills, but when the mill owner had sold out, Revel had been happy enough to take Joshua along with the mill. None of his competitors boasted an educated, scientific mill manager who understood the new machines so well and could keep them running so efficiently. Hedge and Glory had to send to London for one of the few skilled engineers if their machines threw a fault, and lose days of production waiting their turn on Donkin's precious time, but Revel had Joshua, who could turn his hand to anything.

'You're not eating?' asked his father as he stumped across to the table, where only one place was set.

'I'm bidden to dine at the Bosinghams',' he said.

'Maybe you'll see those visitors.'

'From London? Maybe.' He ladled out a generous portion of Widow Beck's beef stew and crossed to the pantry. 'And did these mysterious visitors bring news of Dickon?' he called over his shoulder as he tapped off a tankard of ale from the barrel.

'Ask them. They dine at the Bosinghams too. Or ask Miss Revel, seeing as the two of you are such bosom friends,' he said sarcastically.

'She's to be there?' His father didn't answer. 'Maybe she'll be spared the beating then.'

'Beating?'

'Aye. She went off home in the certainty of a beating. For missing the visitors. You mock at her for weeping over the kittens, Father – aye, and damned near got herself killed shooting out of the hedge under my horse's hooves to save this one – but she shed not a tear for herself.'

'A beating never did anyone any lasting harm,' said Will unconvincingly. 'Spare the rod and – '

'– and spoil the child. And yet you never raised a hand to me.'

'No. I promised her . . .' His voice trailed away and for a moment he was lost in thoughts of Joshua's mother. 'You might have felt my hand a few times if it hadn't been for that promise,' he said, more robustly.

'Your hand, aye. But Revel, he uses his riding crop.' He remembered Nonie's words last year when he had driven Kat over to Cookham to see her. 'That's a fiend in human clothing, that one is,

21

Master Joshua,' she'd said, more heated than he'd ever heard her. 'Doesn't think he's done his duty unless he leaves scars to show for it.'

He'd heard Kattrin and Dickon talking in the summerhouse after one particularly harrowing session. 'I don't know how you bear it,' Dickon had said, his lip quivering and his eyes filling with tears even though on this occasion he had escaped his father's wrath. 'How can you hold out against him?'

'I couldn't give in,' she said, wincing as she tried to move. 'I couldn't say I was wrong when I wasn't. He was being horrid to Aunt Lucy, and someone has to stand up for her.'

'It shouldn't have to be us!'

'Who else is there, Dickon?' she said, her bottom lip trembling. 'You know she can't stand up for herself.'

'But you know what he wants. Why can't you – '

'What? Howl? Beg him to stop?' She gritted her teeth. 'I won't give him that satisfaction.'

'When he starts on me, I say whatever he wants me to say,' said Dickon wretchedly. 'I'd say black was white and the devil lived in heaven just to make him stop.'

'You could stand out against him if you put your mind to it,' she urged him. 'Be strong. Be firm.'

But firmness was not in Dickon's nature, or he would not have been in London, a city he loathed, haggling over business he detested. A sensitive lad, all his life cowed by his father, he had been prey for all the bullies at Eton. Particularly Tarquin's cronies. A weakling himself, Bosingham's stepson, by using his stepfather's money and influence, had gathered around himself a group of ruffians to do his bidding. And the more frightened Dickon became, the more they had made him their target. Joshua smiled grimly as he remembered the day he had thrashed Harris, Tarquin's chief bully. 'Lay another finger on Dickon Revel and you'll answer to me,' he'd said, blowing on his bleeding knuckles.

Ironic that Joshua had ended up as foreman to Dickon's father; doubly ironic that they would both be dining this evening with Tarquin's family.

'You going as a guest or a musician?' asked his father angrily, looking at the leather flute box. 'It's a disgrace that Bosingham should take such advantage of you!' He struck the arm of his chair with a clenched fist. 'Why, he treats you as no better than old Avenal, playing the fiddle for pennies outside the Feathers!'

Joshua raised his eyebrows. 'He no more takes advantage of me than he does of his stepdaughter,' he said mildly. 'I imagine Philomena and I will both play for the guests.' He smiled down at his father. 'I rather enjoy it, you know. Much easier than sitting with all the old tabbies! Don't wait up for me this evening,' he went on, turning back the quilt on the couch. 'The Bosinghams usually make a long night of it and you're looking rather tired.'

'Don't fuss so!' said his father irritably. 'Pity to crumple your cravat,' he said then, more gently, admiring his son in the well-tied cravat and silk brocade waistcoat. With his broad shoulders and well-made figure, he would certainly make his mark among the dandies and red-faced squires of Bosingham's country set. 'She would have been proud of you,' he said softly.

Joshua looked at his father and waited, holding his breath, hoping that he would say more, but, as ever, he was disappointed. He began to say something himself, then thought better of it and turned back to the couch to plump up the pillows.

'Leave that, I told you!' snapped his father. 'Jem can see to it. He promised to bring me in my ale later on.'

That meant a meeting, with Will Dandridge the shoemaker, Josiah Blinks the butcher, Tom Wingrove from the Rose and Crown, Jem, the tapster from the Red Cow, William Blake the bricklayer and a handful of the other villagers coming in for one of his father's readings, from Tom Paine's *Rights of Man* or William Cobbett's *Register*, or possibly something even more radical; even for those few who could read, most newspapers and journals were out of reach because of the swingeing newspaper taxes imposed by Wellington's government. Joshua had chosen to live on the green because it would give his father more company, but the only company Will chose to encourage was that of the independent small tradesmen and the alehouse keepers, Radicals and freethinkers all of them. He turned away with a sigh.

Will caught at his son's arm. 'Take care, Joshua!' he said urgently.

Joshua looked at him with a frown between his eyes. 'Care?' he said, puzzled. 'I'm only going up to Hedsor.'

'A man in your position should take care who he mixes with in these days.'

'These days, Father? You mean, the days of Captain Swing?' He rummaged through his coat pocket trying to find the letter. 'Someone should tell Jessop to take care,' he said heavily. 'An Aylesbury man was transported for just such a threat not so long ago. Anyone reading this would have no hesitation in turning Jessop in to the magistrates.'

'Anyone?' asked his father, looking at him steadily. 'Does that include you? After all, Bosingham is a magistrate.'

Anger flooded Joshua's face and he did not trust himself to speak. After a long pause he turned away to trim the Argand lamp. When it

23

was done to his satisfaction he took an incandescent spill from the little tin on the shelf and stroked it between the sandpaper sheets, taking care not to let any sparks fall on his clothes. When it caught, he set it to the wick, watched the pale flame catch and run around, then set the chimney over it. 'Take care you know what you're doing, Father, stirring them up in this way,' he said at last, replacing the green glass shade carefully. 'You cannot care for their families if they are in Botany Bay.'

'And you can?'

Joshua shrugged.

'If Jessop loses his work,' said his father sombrely, 'whether it be to the machines or for sedition, he cannot care for them either.'

'I know.' His voice was low and vibrant. 'Father, I can't turn the world around tomorrow. I do what I can.'

'I'll have no special pleading!' said his father harshly. 'Can I say to them, "Yes, turn out the masters – but not my son"?'

'I am not of the masters!' cried Joshua. 'I do but stand between the spark and the powder, between them and an explosion. You – *you* lead them on to what they cannot achieve!' He struggled to check his anger. 'You hold out an Eden to them that they can never gain!' He turned away from the fire, his face all sharp planes in the flickering light, his dark-brown eyes glowing, and looked down at his father. 'I won't take to skulking in hedgerows, Father, fearful of my own shadow,' he said, more calmly. 'If they are determined to murder me, they may do so.' He checked his cravat in the mirror. 'But they should think carefully first – if they look to kill me, be sure I'll take a few of them with me.' He shrugged himself into the close fitting dark-blue evening coat and looked at his father a moment longer. 'And have they thought who Revel would put in my place?'

After leaving Joshua at the river with the kitten, Kattrin had hoped to slip back into the house unnoticed. She passed unchallenged through the kitchens, putting a finger to her lips to stay Phoebe's questions; pausing a moment to look around the hall, she slid out of the door and was halfway to the staircase when her father loomed out of the shadows.

'Dupe me, would you?' he snarled, catching her by the wrist with one hand and slamming her painfully against the panelled wall. He took in her dishevelled appearance. 'Crawling in here like some little slut from the cottages! How dare you? Eh? Eh?' He slapped her deliberately across the face with the open palm of his hand, then brought it back to strike the other side with the back of his hand. Her head snapped first to one side and then back again as he raised his hand to repeat the blow.

24

'Ezekiel, no!' gasped Aunt Lucy, cowering halfway up the stairs, a sodden handkerchief pressed to her lips.

'Keep out of this, woman!' snarled Revel. 'I'm her father and, by God, I'll discipline her yet!' He turned back to Kattrin, his eyes narrowed in fury. 'Where have ye been, eh? Eh?' He shook her violently and as her head jerked back, it struck against the staircase; one of the hair pins holding her ringlets in place skewered into her scalp and she cried out in pain.

She blinked back the scalding tears, willing them not to fall. Best to admit the fault and hope that a soft answer might turn away wrath. 'I'm sorry I was not here for your visitors, Father,' she gasped. 'I was out walking and I forgot the time. I – '

He shook her until her teeth rattled. 'I'll give ye "forgot the time"!' he raged. 'Important visitors from London and you out walking in the woods, unchaperoned. Made a fool of me, damn you! You little slut, who were you meeting?' he roared, raising his hand to her once more.

'The Bosinghams,' Aunt Lucy moaned from her vantage point at the bend of the stairs.

Revel froze, his hand in midair. 'She was meeting the Bosinghams?' he demanded incredulously.

'The dinner, Ezekiel,' said Lucy hoarsely. 'The Bosinghams' dinner. Tonight. Her face ... the guests...'

'Ah!' He lowered his right hand, but never slackened the grip on his daughter's wrist. 'That wouldn't do, would it? We want young Louis to see her at her best, don't we, sister?' He smiled unpleasantly up at Lucy, but she had already scuttled off.

'I'm truly sorry, Father,' whispered Kattrin wretchedly, fighting back the tears as he tightened his grip on her wrist. 'I never meant to – aaah!'

He gave her wrist one last squeeze, until she thought her bones would crack, and pushed her contemptuously away.

'I can wait,' he said with a thin smile. 'Tomorrow, next week or next month. It matters not a jot to me, my dear. But you will be punished.'

And that in itself was part of the punishment, she thought miserably, not knowing where – or when – the axe was going to fall. Only that it would.

Anger was still churning Joshua's stomach as he snatched up his greatcoat, his flute and, after a moment's hesitation, his cane, and went out of the house. He had declined the offer of a ride in Revel's carriage, preferring to hire a post chaise from the stables behind the Red Lion. His stern expression faded as he saw Cridden, the grizzled

25

coachman, standing whip in hand, holding the door open. The old soldier always took pride in his appearance and for this occasion wore a decent approximation of a uniform; he was unlikely to abuse the hospitality of Bosingham's servants' hall and end up drunk on the box, as some of Waymon's younger men had been known to do.

'Evening, Thomas,' said Joshua as he climbed into the post chaise, taking care not to brush his clothes against the panels of the door.

'Evenin' to you, Mr Joshua. Been a hot an' dusty day, so it have, but a welcome change after all that rain.'

'Family all well?'

'There's well and well, sir,' said the old man with a shrug. 'Young James, as is married to our Sarey, has lost his employ up by 'Oltspur.'

'I'm sorry to hear it.'

'Hard times ahead for him,' said Thomas sombrely. 'Tied cottage, see. Mr Dupré have give him a sennight's grace, which is somethin', I reckon. But if he don't find another place soon, I can see as how they might have to come live with us.'

'But how will you find the space?' Cridden's ancient cottage between the forge and Waymon's stables was already cramped, with the old man, his wife and two unmarried daughters and two orphan boys besides, paid for from the parish poor rates, whom they took in to help with the rent.

Cridden scratched his head. 'Dunno, Mr Joshua, an' that's a fact. But I'll not stand by and see them go on the parish. An' Sarey with another young 'un on the way ... Course, if we'd still had the farmhouse,' he said, his eyes lighting up for a brief moment, '"twouldn't have been no problem.'

But the Criddens, like so many of the villagers, had lost their tenant farm in the enclosures, when the high price of corn made it profitable to clear the roughest of waste land and plough it for crops. Unable to find the money for hedging and drainage of the rough commons where they had grazed their animals for as long as anyone could remember, they had been forced to sell out, only to see the land enclosed by the rich landowners and the old farmstead left uninhabited to go to rack and ruin. All through the Thames Valley small farmers who had survived for centuries – the good years and the lean – by growing their own vegetables and crops on their strips of the common field, and by grazing a pig on the common waste, had sold their rights for a payment that had seemed good at the time; once they had to buy in the necessities they had previously produced for themselves, however, the money had soon been spent.

Their self-sufficiency gone, they had had no choice but to hire themselves out as day labourers on the very land they had once lived off. While the wars kept labour scarce they were fairly paid, but in the

26

fifteen years since the peace, farming had slumped and within a generation the smallholding farmer had vanished from the face of the English earth like snow in summer.

'If you do hear of anythin', Mr Joshua, sir?' said Cridden. 'Sarey's man's a good worker, can turn his hand to anythin'...'

'I'll keep an eye out,' said Joshua heavily. But with even skilled journeymen papermakers tramping the country in the hope of work, it would be out of the question to set anyone else on at the paper mills, and the wire mill needed to cut its men.

'That'd be right good of you, Mr Joshua,' said Cridden, closing the door on him. The gentle thud of the carriage door was echoed by a louder noise as the gates of the Wooburn workhouse on the far side of the green were closed with a sonorous clang and the heavy bolts and bars slid into place. 'Us'll just have to count our blessings,' said Cridden, pushing his old-fashioned tricorne back on his head with a sigh. 'Come what may, we're still better off than them poor devils in the workhouse.'

A clear three-quarter moon silvered the surface of the ornamental lake by the manor house as Cridden set off at a steady pace. No light showed; Dupré's new tenant must be away in London again. It did no good having the squire living elsewhere, even though it was only in Beaconsfield; the deterioration of the village in the last few decades under its absentee landlord was visible in slowly collapsing thatch and falling fences, and its invisible effects could be just as disheartening, for the squire was often the only source of financial assistance to villagers in hard times and a mere tenant would never be as fruitful a source of charity.

Joshua leaned back against the worn hammercloth and dozed his way through the town, past the dark and neglected church which under its absentee vicar, Dupré's youngest son, seemed as dead as the graves that surrounded it, and on through Cores End where the Nonconformists were coming out of the evening meeting at Bethel Chapel, bidding each other a fare-thee-well as they set off to their homes.

Cridden nursed his horses up Hawks Hill, past Hedsor Wharf and the long walled gardens of Cliveden, where Frederick, Prince of Wales, grandfather of the present king, had once held summer court, drawing the Bosinghams and others of the newer nobility to build themselves large houses nearby.

The moment the hired post chaise turned in at the elaborate wrought-iron gates of Bosingham House, Joshua realised that his idea of a quiet dinner had been mistaken. On the panels of the carriages making their way along the drive he could see the coats of arms of a number of the leading families from Beaconsfield, Burn-

27

ham and Wycombe. He hoped Revel had not misled him: the invitation had come indirectly and he would not put it past his employer to 'forget' to tell him if Bosingham – who, after all, owed his present prosperity to his father's position as equerry in court attendance on the late king, poor mad George III – had stipulated knee breeches. Revel was always on the alert for an opportunity to belittle his mill manager, but Joshua was not in the least reliant on his employer for his entrée into society: through his mother's family he was as well connected as the Bosinghams, for all he worked for his living, and Bosingham still had a soft spot for Joshua, in spite of Tarquin's enmity.

At the last curve in the drive Joshua saw the Revel carriage draw up in front of the grand portico and Revel and his party alight. Suppressing a yawn with difficulty, he put his head out of the window. His employer, who, to give him his due, had been up and about every bit as long as Joshua, would be, as he always was, as fresh as a daisy.

He craned his neck trying to see if Kat had accompanied her father, but by the time his chaise reached the portico, the Revels had already passed into the house.

He alighted under the haughty gaze of the butler, who, to show his disapproval of anyone who did not keep his own carriage, gave him an infinitesimal bow and passed him on to the footman. Relieved of his coat and his cane, Joshua progressed into the inner hall where he greeted his host – not, he was pleased to see, wearing formal court dress – and made his bow to Lady Isabelle, a commanding figure in crimson brocade, with her hair dressed impossibly high à la giraffe and decorated with ribbons, rosettes and an imposing aigrette of ostrich feathers. At least she had not succumbed to the latest fashion for broad evening hats: he knew from bitter experience that, for a tall man like himself, conversation with a short woman in a large hat was nigh on impossible. Behind her stood the two simpering Bosingham girls, whom he never could tell one from the other for all they were only half sisters. If they had not been wearing gloves he might have made the distinction, for Philomena had pale hands with long, slender pianist's fingers, whereas Drusilla, who spent her time in the saddle or helping the gardener in the new conservatory, had redder and rougher hands. They were more modestly coiffed than their aunt with their hair dressed high over Apollo hoops and held only with clusters and twirls of ribbons. He exchanged polite nothings with them before passing on into the crowded saloon.

It was one of Bosingham's mixed receptions, the kind Lady Isabelle deplored, where her brother's cronies from town mingled with the more presentable of his country neighbours. But Lady

Isabelle was not one to shirk her responsibilities: King George IV would surely not last out the year, which meant an election, and in election time all sorts and degrees of men not normally socialised with must be wooed and treated. For the few men who had the vote, be they farmers or blacksmiths, almost nothing was too good in an election year – provided they would pledge themselves against Reform and against any tinkering with the Poor Laws or the Corn Laws. And the aldermen and burgesses – be they brewers or mill owners, or bought-in London merchants who never saw Wycombe save on election day – must be made to feel at home in the houses of the rich and influential, even if that meant inviting them for a day's hunting. As she had said to her brother only that morning, one simply had to hope that they would be sufficiently overawed to hang back at the rear and avoid the cardinal error of riding before the master, or overriding the hounds.

Looking round the room, Joshua recognised several London merchants, a couple of mill owners and a prosperous London stationer, one of the many families of Huguenot descent in the paper trade, with whom Joshua had often done business for his employer. What had brought Cazelle so far from London?

Most of the men were properly dressed for evening in the required uniform of close-fitting trousers and pumps with silk socks. Apart from one or two farmers who stood out in snuff coloured coats, old-fashioned cravats and breeches, and the occasional young dandy in the extreme kick of fashion with wide trousers and a tight coat, the only individuality was shown in the tying of the cravat and the cloth of the waistcoat, which varied in its extravagance according to the age of the wearer and the degree of his addiction to the Romantic movement.

Their wives and daughters showed more variety: barely a female in the room had not been affected by the fashion for Sir Walter Scott and all the young ladies wanted to look like Young Di or Amy Robsart, while the more mature had clearly taken Maria Stuart as their model. Lace-edged bodices were cut low and wide, tapering to a point above bell-shaped skirts over layers of petticoats. The pastel shades so beloved since the turn of the century were scarcely to be seen, even in so provincial a gathering, and the room was bright with golds, cerises, purples and acid greens. There were even some tartans, though probably none that a self-respecting Highlander would recognise.

Tiny waists of course were all the rage and those ladies who had had to resort to tight lacing fanned themselves vigorously, their heaving bosoms and the flushed complexions beneath the over-elaborate hairstyles and broad evening hats revealing the extent of their discomfort.

Joshua took a glass from a footman and moved through the crowd, exchanging greetings. At one stage he thought he caught sight of Kat's golden curls over by the windows, the ringlets all drawn to one side in the latest style, but the room was too crowded for him to reach her. He hoped that Tarquin would leave her in peace this evening; for a while Revel had seemed positively to be pushing the two of them together. Even Bosingham had appeared to approve of Tarquin's pursuit of the girl, though the connection of a viscount, even if only a stepson, could look much higher than a mill owner's daughter.

He turned away from conversation with Waller of Hall Barn and Zachary Allnutt, the young master of Marsh Green Mill, and found himself next to Revel, who gave him a brief nod of recognition.

'Mr Revel.' His nod in return was timed to a nicety to combine the minimum of deference with the maximum of good manners. Kat and her aunt stood nearby and he bowed to them. 'Miss Thornton. Miss Revel. I trust I see you both well.' In truth he thought neither looked in fine bloom. Lucy's wide hazel eyes were red-rimmed, though that was not unusual, and her silver-gilt hair had been arranged in an unflattering coiffure. Since Kat was standing half behind her aunt and half behind her father's bulk, Joshua was unable to see any more than that she was attired in a robe of jonquil silk with a laced corsage that was excessively low-cut, even by the standards of the day, and that she looked exceptionally pale.

Before he could speak to her, Dickon joined them, exclaiming, 'Joshua! How are you?' and shaking his hand enthusiastically.

'Well, I thank you. And how was your visit to town?'

Dickon shrugged. 'London was as dirty and unpleasant as ever,' he said, oblivious to the scowl on his father's face. 'I don't believe you've met Louis Cazelle.' He indicated the willowy young man at his side, wearing pale yellow trousers – rather tighter than his thin shanks could carry – an exceedingly loud waistcoat and shirt points so high under his elaborately tied blue satin cravat that he could hardly turn his head.

The two young men took each other's measure with a swift glance; neither seemed pleased by what he saw. They exchanged stiff bows.

'Servant, sir,' said Louis Cazelle in a studied drawl.

'Yours, sir,' returned Joshua, suppressing a smile as he took in the overlong hair, one lock drawn down to rest in artless fashion on the pale brow, the chin – in imitation of the late Lord Byron – neither clean-shaven nor bearded, and the attempt at the cynical smile of the poet which, allied to wide doe eyes instead of a piercing gaze, gave

30

him somewhat the appearance of a startled fawn. Just then his father, a stocky, broad-shouldered man in his early sixties, came up to join the group.

'Servant, Cazelle,' said Revel, bowing low enough for a duke. By the time Joshua had been introduced and had made his compliments to the older man, who was here to be sworn in as one of the Wycombe burgesses, Cazelle's son had gone off with Kattrin.

The banqueting room was lit by hundreds of wax candles in wall sconces and huge tinkling chandeliers, each adding its share to the stifling heat. Lady Isabelle abominated a draught and not the tiniest movement of air disturbed the flames. Joshua was down to take in an elderly dowager and as he held her chair for her, narrowly avoiding poking his eye out on the gilded arrow which transfixed the forlorn remains of a bird of paradise to her enormous evening hat, he caught sight of Kat on the far side of the table, passing down the room on young Cazelle's arm. There was something about her tonight, perhaps just the way she held herself, that was not natural, though it might just have been the evening dress, its extreme décolleté and shortened ankle-revealing skirts in marked contrast to the almost Quakerish gowns Revel normally insisted she wear. As he took his place he strained to catch her eye, but she was seated further up the room than he, and separated from him by a huge silver epergne full of grapes and nectarines from Lord Bosingham's hothouses.

With a sigh Joshua prepared to divide his attention between his dinner and his neighbours. To one side was Kat's aunt Lucy, in a robe of Navarino-smoke satin, picking at her food and barely eating enough to keep a sparrow alive, and on the other the elderly and very obese dowager in that startlingly broad hat, ladling food into her capacious maw as if it were her last meal, and, between mouthfuls, haranguing the banker on her far side over the iniquitously low rates of interest from the funds.

'If they fall any further,' she said comfortably, bending her head towards him and causing him to flinch away from the threatening arrow and the nodding feathers, 'we shall all be ruined. Quite ruined.' She gestured for the footman to replenish her plate.

There was ruined and ruined, thought Joshua wryly, thinking of the scraps doled out to the poor in the workhouse; it really depended on where you were starting from.

Kattrin, seated halfway down the room between Louis Cazelle and the vicar of Mapledurham, fanned herself vigorously as the footman removed one almost untouched plate after another from in front of her. She was having a perfectly horrible evening.

Partly to blame for it was the dress, of course. She had always

31

envied Drusilla and Philomena their fashionable robes, and resigned herself to being always more plainly dressed even than the governess, but it had come as a great shock to find herself without any warning in so extreme a robe as this, cut so low over the bosom that she felt in imminent danger of spilling out of it, and without so much as a fichu or even a scrap of lace for modesty.

Even Lady Isabelle, who had been telling Revel in her forthright way for months that he dressed his daughter as the veriest dowd, had pronounced herself shocked.

'I don't know what to make of the dratted man!' she'd said to Miss Selby, her elderly companion. 'I took him on one side and told him she could not possibly dine in company looking like that. Far too immodest. Quite unsuitable for such a young girl! I even offered to fetch a lace pelerine collar for her.'

'So good,' bleated Miss Selby. 'One can always rely on you, Lady Isabelle, to show proper feeling in the face of – '

'And do you know what he said?'

'I dare not hazard a – '

'He said, "Let Cazelle see what he's getting." And his laugh, my dear Selby, his laugh! So cynical!' She shuddered artistically. 'It quite made my blood run cold!'

Truth to tell, it was no more than she had come to expect from the man. She had never been happy in Revel's company and it was a mystery to her why her brother kept up the connection, unequal as it must be between a prosperous aristocratic landowner and a mill owner whose nouveau riche pretensions did not include mending his manners. But on the rare occasions when she had attempted to raise the matter, Bosingham had become alarmingly heated, huffing and puffing and refusing to discuss it.

'Very well. I bow to your decision in this,' she had told him icily. 'But if we must associate with these people, we had better be sure that they do not reflect too badly on us. The father I must leave to you, and the mad aunt may prove too much of a challenge even for me, but at least the girl can be moulded. I shall arrange for her to take her lessons with Drusilla and Philomena.'

'That poor child!' sighed Miss Selby, draining her glass.

'Poor child indeed! Well, I did my best, but I tell you, Selby,' said Lady Isabelle dramatically, the loops of hair at the height of the wire frames trembling, 'if it were not for m'brother, I swear I'd wash my hands of the whole family, 'deed I would.'

Down the table the 'poor child' turned a pettish shoulder on Louis Cazelle and his endless stammered compliments and turned with relief to the vicar of Mapledurham on her other side; at least a clerical gentleman could be relied on to keep his eyes on his plate, unlike

32

Louis, whose burning gaze seemed to her to be permanently riveted to the top edge of her dress.

To make matters worse she had a horrid feeling that the footman behind the next chair was John Hewson, though it was hard to be sure under the powdered short wig. It wasn't the first time she had come across one of her erstwhile classmates thus: service in the big houses in these days of unemployment was the height of many villagers' ambitions for their children. She had always prided herself on dealing tactfully with the situation, but in the days before her father had begun to buy the mills, she and Johnny had sat side by side in Dame Savage's lace school, learning their letters and their lace patterns together. She did not believe she had imagined the enmity in his dark eyes but tonight she could not cope with it; her head was throbbing and she would have liked nothing more than to slip away and curl up in a corner.

She found herself fiddling with the splendid diamond bracelet on her wrist. According to her aunt it had been her mother's, a rare present, given when Ezekiel Revel bought into his first mill. Kattrin had been unaware of its existence, but her father had reluctantly produced it that evening just before they set off for Hedsor. It was so wide that it covered the bruising on her wrist. The matching earrings, though equally splendid, could not draw attention from the swollen jaw which had failed to yield to a whole jar of Rowland's Alsana Extract; when her friend Drusilla Bosingham remarked on it, Kat had been forced to pretend a slight toothache.

A voice on her left brought her back to the present.

'You ride, dear lady?' asked the vicar of Mapledurham between mouthfuls. 'Do I recall seeing you at the meet? I don't think so . . . I told Bosingham, the hunting here don't compare with Leicester. Too many trees!' he said in the tone of a man who doesn't expect to be contradicted. 'Whoever called it Buckinghamshire had the wrong end on't. Ought to've called it Beechenhamshire. Damned trees grow like weeds here. Can't put up a good fox with all these damned trees! Even a hare – '

'I ride, but not to hounds,' she said, painfully aware of Lady Isabelle and her father, further up the table, both lending an ear to her conversation while pursuing their own. In truth she rode very badly: she hated the side-saddle, which Lady Isabelle insisted upon, for it made her feel most precariously ill-balanced. Her only experience of riding before coming to Bosingham House had been astride Dickon's pony, whenever her father was away.

'One of these fine ladies who'd rather have a play than a kill, eh?' said the cleric comfortably. He held up his quizzing glass and looked at her rather more closely than was really polite, his bright-blue, bulbous eyes straying appreciatively down to her low neckline. She could feel the blush coming all the way up from her satin slippers. 'Don't recall ever seeing you in town,' he said, suppressing a belch with difficulty. 'And I'm sure I'd never forget a pretty – ah – face like yours, m'dear.'

'I am rarely in town, sir,' she replied. Not that she had not been invited to return with Lady Isabelle and her nieces, but after the first visit, when an impecunious young baronet whose face she could not even recall had had the audacity to offer for her hand, her father had always seemed to find some reason why she should not go. 'We – '

'Seen Fanny Kemble?' he demanded in the rather explosive style of speech that characterised him. 'Perfect little actress, though not quite the equal of her aunt,' he went on without waiting for her reply. 'The divine Sarah, o'course. You should come up to town, m'dear. Join my party at the theatre.' He winked roguishly at her in a way that sat ill with his clerical garb. 'I've got connections in the theatre, y'know. Oh, the highest connections, m'dear!'

'Th-thank you, sir,' she said, and wondered why all the gentlemen within earshot burst out into the most impolite cracks of laughter.

Further up the table Bosingham was discussing the day's proceedings in the House of Lords with a fellow peer, but as the business of their lordships was at present the particularly juicy divorce case of Lord Ellenborough, Lady Isabelle swiftly intervened to provide a more fitting topic.

'What news from the Commons, Sir John?' she demanded, turning to the local Member of Parliament.

Sir John, startled, spluttered in his wine. Having spent the day in the saddle, he had been relying on his clerks to bring him up to date with the business of the House when next he saw them. But it would not do to say so to Lady Isabelle. 'Tying up the Emancipation Bill,' he said hastily.

'Bad enough that they have given the Catholics the vote!' Lady Isabelle exclaimed, scandalised. 'Now the Jews too! Before we know it we shall have that dreadful Israel man expecting to be invited to dine!'

'You mean old Isaac d'Israeli? Fellow from Bradenham Manor?' said Sir John. 'Dined with him only the other week at Gifford's, ma'am.'

'Interestin' old cove,' said one of the younger men further down the table. 'Son's an author, ain't he?'

'Damn dandy!' exclaimed another.

Lady Isabelle turned a basilisk gaze on Sir John, who knew his duty and muttered something about Lord Winchilsea's Reforming Bill. It was not a fortunate choice.

'I cannot believe that they have let that see the light of day!' said Squire Marsham, his face an unbecoming shade of puce.

'Absolutely appalled,' said Sir Lewis Higham, raising his head from his well-filled plate.

'Do we not already pay enough, with all these taxes?' his neighbour chipped in. 'As for the poor rates, I do not believe any other parish has been assessed so high. Quite out of all proportion, sir!'

'If the men received a more fitting wage for their labour,' said Allnutt softly, 'we would not have so many on the poor rates.'

'No, no, Allnutt!' protested Lord Carrington's son, who was standing for election and had briefly returned to Wycombe Abbey – or Loakes Farm, as the town persisted in calling Wyatt's Gothic pile, for which 'Abbot' Carrington had paid half his fortune to the fashionable architect. 'Wrong end of the stick entirely, my dear fellow! If the farmers had not to pay so much on the poor rates, they'd be able to pay their men more.'

'But if they paid the men more, then fewer of them would be on the poor rates!'

Joshua sighed. Here they were once more, locked into the same old circle of argument. What did they know, sitting there with their plump, ruddy, self-satisfied faces, dining off the fat of the land – what could they know of the downward spiral that the poor were locked into since the commons had been enclosed and the men thrown out of work by the machines.

'Where do all these sturdy beggars come from?' demanded Sir Lewis. He darted a venomous glance at Revel and Allnutt. 'If the paper mills brought in fewer outsiders to fall on the parish charge, we wouldn't have such iniquitously high poor rates, don't you see?'

'The papermakers don't fall on parish charges, Sir Lewis,' said Joshua quietly. 'The Society of Papermakers looks after the travelling journeymen – '

'Now thass a strange thing,' said Sir Lewis's son, who sat for one of the pocket boroughs in the next county which was in Bosingham's gift, and was often to be found drinking heavily at his table. He struggled to get his words out unslurred. 'Sounds to me like – like a combination, sir! And combinations are illegal, sir! Transh- Transh- Dammit! Transportable!'

'Not since twenty-four, sir,' said Joshua, suppressing his anger. 'The government – '

He found himself cut off in midspeech by his host. 'This plan of Winchilsea's for changes in the poor rate...' He shook his head. 'I told Sir John,"vote against them," I said,"if you want to please our people." Because our fellows don't want the changes, you know,' he

35

said, emphasising the point with a stubby finger. 'They don't like them at all.'

'If you mean the electors, sir, or the larger farmers,' said Joshua, 'then I dare say you are right.' They were the men with comfortable incomes who paid their labourers a nominal rate of eight or nine shillings a week, knowing that under the Speenhamland system of poor relief, the employers need actually pay only three shillings of the nine, and could look to the poor rates to make up the rest. 'But I think the villagers, sir, and the smaller farmers, who you will remember do not have the vote, on the whole support Lord Winchilsea's proposals.'

Why would they not? Even those who ran small family farms on their own still had to pay the poor rates, so that essentially they were subsidising the more prosperous farmers and landowners.

'Bosingham, really!' exclaimed Lady Isabelle, fanning herself vigorously. Again the conversation had not taken the turn she had hoped for. 'The villagers? Sturdy beggars? At dinner? Must we?'

Joshua bit back an angry retort. Having long ago decided that he could achieve more inside society than outside it, he could not afford to offend his erstwhile sponsor – and as Lady Isabelle was the dominant force at Bosingham House, even less could he afford to offend her.

'Never fear, Lady Isabelle,' said Sir Lewis comfortably. 'Wellington will squash Winchilsea most firmly.'

'Next thing they'll be demanding Reform!' complained the older Cazelle.

'It surely must come soon!' said Allnutt. 'Can it make sense that the new industrial centres are all unrepresented: for Birmingham, Manchester and Leeds, with all their manufactories and a good half million inhabitants, not a single Member in Parliament? And there's Cornwall with hardly anyone living there – and sends forty-four Members!'

'If you wish to talk of inequities, you need look no further than Wycombe,' grumbled his neighbour, who had recently failed to be elected to the town council. 'Besides the burgesses and the aldermen – and half of them don't even live in the town! – only seven of us have the vote.'

'I have it on the highest authority that Wellington will not have parliamentary or electoral reform at any price,' said Sir Lewis.

'But Wellington won't last any longer than the King,' Dupré observed shrewdly.

'And that won't be too long!'

'It's to be hoped he thinks it was all worth it!' said Bosingham with a hearty laugh.

'The Duke, my lord?' Miss Venn, the lanky heiress to whom Bosingham had recently been paying court, under orders from her father to bear her part in the conversation, snapped her heavy brows together in a vain attempt to follow it.

Bosingham bellowed with laughter. 'Not Wellington, ma'am! Prinney, of course! Our esteemed monarch, King George the Fourth.'

Miss Venn looked quite blank, but smiled dutifully. Heiress or no, she was no longer in her first flush and unattached viscounts did not grow on trees.

'It's a wonder he's lasted as long as he has,' Bosingham went on with a knowing smile. 'It's a brave man would take on Mrs Fitzherbert *and* Princess Caroline! For me, I have to say, one wife was quite bad enough for my health!'

There was a burst of laughter, hastily suppressed by those of his cronies who caught sight of Lady Isabelle's disapproving face. General Venn scowled blackly across the table at his daughter.

'Is that right, Fitz?' Captain Heston of the Guards, ignoring convention, appealed across the board to the man at Kattrin's side. 'They really have given up bleeding him?'

'Not so! Not so! Still cupping him reg'larly,' chuckled the vicar of Mapledurham, the one Heston had addressed as Fitz. 'Got his weight down from twenty-four stone to twenty, they tell me. But now they're diggin' holes in the soles of his feet as well. Tappin' water off the old fellow by the quart!'

'Sir!' Lady Isabelle was outraged. She remembered George before he had become Regent.

'The first gentleman of Europe' they had called him then, and 'Prince Florizel', and like all the young ladies at the time, young Isabelle Bosingham had been secretly in love with him. Hard to equate handsome Florizel with the bloated figure of fun he had become.

'Oh, you may look daggers at me, Lady Isabelle,' said the vicar of Mapledurham, leaning back in his chair with an engaging smile in his blue pop-eyes, 'but it's the truth. Georgy-Porgy's turned quite black, y'know! I'll lay odds we have King Billy before the month's out.'

'Fitz, King Billy and Reform!' shouted Captain Heston drunkenly.

Lady Isabelle's eyes had an alarmingly glazed look as she surged to her feet. 'Ladies!' she said in ringing tones, and even though the mouth-watering desserts had barely been set on the table, all the ladies rose obediently to follow her out of the room, while those men who were sufficiently sober rose to draw out their chairs for them — no mean feat for those sandwiched between two ladies both wearing evening hats.

# Chapter Two

The sun was streaming in through the window. With a groan Kattrin rubbed her eyes and sat up, wrinkling her nose as she caught the perfume of chocolate. The noise of the mill wheels and the hammers pounded in her brain. Her head ached appallingly where her father had cracked it against the panelled wall and last night she had drunk far too much wine and eaten far too little. This morning the very idea of food or drink nauseated her.

She wondered for a fleeting moment whether she could pour the thick, glutinous liquid out of the window. She picked up the chocolate cup from the silver tray on the night table and had one foot out of the bedclothes when Mary came back in.

'Time you were shiftin' yourself,' said the maid in her strong Buckinghamshire accent. 'Master's wishful to see you at breakfast. Best hurry, or you'll be late.' The buxom maid began to move around the room, picking up ribbons and shifts and shaking out petticoats, showing no signs of leaving.

Hopeless to think she could enlist her help: Mary's loyalty would always be to the person with the power and the money. Whatever Kattrin did would always be reported back to her father, even so small a matter as refusing her morning chocolate. And then questions would be asked and answers might be found unsatisfactory.

She sat at the dressing table while Mary pinned up her hair, dragging the brush painfully over her tender scalp. From outside came the clatter of the rag girls' clogs as they passed down the lane to the coach house, where a wagonload of stinking sacks of London rags brought up from Hedsor Wharf was waiting to be unloaded and carried across to the rag houses. It was a rare moment of liberty for the girls and they made the most of it, laughing and chattering until Mary went out to the landing window and bade them sharply get back to their work.

Kattrin envied them their companionship – and at the same time she found a ghost of a laugh curving her lips at the thought of what

38

Lady Isabelle would say to that! There were so many times like these, when she felt herself torn between two worlds, between Bosingham House, where she went to be taught to be a lady, and the world of the villagers, the world that had so nearly been hers.

Joshua, whose own life had known so many reverses, was the only person who seemed to understand. She had felt such a need to talk to him the previous night, but, if she was honest, not entirely because of the nonsense that Bosingham and his friends had been talking about the villagers; even more she had wanted just to be with him, to see his reactions to her in a grown-up dress, and above all to try to come to terms with the strange feelings she had experienced when he had picked her up and dusted her down in the lane.

It was far from the first time that she had found herself in his arms, for he had often helped her and Dickon out of their scrapes. Kattrin had always joined in all Dickon's sports and games – in fact, she had more often initiated them, for Dickon was a more timid soul and would much rather have been in his study, poring over his books and classifying his plant and insect collections. But he would always stick with his sister and Joshua, five years their senior and already in a position of importance in the mill, had picked them up when they fell over, mopped and bandaged cut legs and bruised hands and kept them from their father's wrath.

She had rarely been alone with him, apart from one occasion when she had hidden herself next to Dickon's trunk when Joshua drove him back to Eton, and those few times when Joshua had spirited her off to see Nonie, who had been his nurse in better days, and lived now in Cookham with her John, hiring out teams of horses to the water-men to pull the barges upriver against the rapids. But on those occasions she had been a child and he had treated her as a child. The way she had felt yesterday in the lane was quite different and if she could just talk to him about it, she might be able to understand why.

It had been just one added frustration that she had spent most of the evening apart from him.

Kattrin tapped her fingers on the dressing table, wondering why it was taking Mary so long to fetch her morning dress. It would be a pleasure to wear one of her comfortable old gowns again after the embarrassment of the jonquil evening dress. She had done her best to be a perfect lady the night before, but that wretched gown and Louis Cazelle had conspired to make her feel uncomfortable; then, when the ladies had withdrawn so abruptly, leaving the gentlemen to their port, Philomena had gone out of her way, as always, to make her feel gauche and out of place.

'Step-aunt Isabelle won't be very pleased with you,' she had gloated, pale-blue eyes flashing spitefully as she poured tea for

Kattrin and Miss Selby to hand round. 'She was counting on you to keep Fitzclarence under control.'

'Don't mind her.' Gentle Drusilla drew her companion across to the window embrasure. It was strange, thought Kattrin, that the two half-sisters, so alike in looks with their raven hair and blue eyes, should be so different in nature. 'Once Fitzclarence is in his cups, it's beyond anyone to rein him in. Even Aunt Isabelle. I swear they drained their flasks three times over at the meet today. Papa too.' In spite of her gentle nature, Drusilla was a bruising rider to hounds, unlike her half-sister. 'But I warrant Papa will sober up fast enough tonight when Aunt Isabelle gives him his curtain lecture for not keeping his friends under control. I wouldn't like to be in his shoes!'

The two girls giggled at the thought of Lady Isabelle giving her formidable brother a dressing-down. 'Of course everyone makes allowances for Augustus Fitzclarence,' said Drusilla, 'but to speak of his father the way he did – '

'His father?' said Kattrin, who had just seen the gentlemen coming in and had let her attention stray, wondering whether she would have a moment to speak to Joshua. 'I don't believe I know the elder Mr Fitzclarence.'

'Augustus's father isn't *Mr* Fitzclarence,' said Drusilla. 'He's the *Duke* of Clarence, you goose. Our next king.'

'But the Duke has no children. Princess Adelaide's babies all died, did they not?'

Drusilla brought her fan up to her face and giggled nervously behind it. 'Fie, Kattrin,' she chided. 'You really cannot be so innocent?'

Before she could ask Drusilla what she meant, Louis Cazelle had hurried across to her side and stayed there, composing poems to her eyes, for the rest of the evening. She had looked in vain for rescue from Joshua; flute in hand he had been swept across to the pianoforte and for the rest of the evening he and Philomena had entertained the company with their music.

Kattrin's attention had wandered from the foolish, vacuous young dandy to Joshua, playing his flute with a dreamy look in his eye as if the music had taken him to a far distant land that only he could imagine. As he finished on a long, haunting note, there was a flurry of polite applause and the faraway look faded, to be replaced by a warm smile that lit up his face.

'Goodness, isn't he handsome!' exclaimed a young lady sitting behind them.

Yes, he is, thought Kattrin. And wondered why she had never seen it before.

40

Her father, aunt and brother were already at the breakfast table when Kattrin hurried into the morning room. Her father had placed his pocket watch beside his plate and was drumming his fingers on the table, always a bad sign. Dickon flashed his sister a nervous smile and rose to pull out her chair.

'Leave that!' Revel barked, and Dickon scurried back to his own seat. Revel turned on Kattrin. 'You are thirteen minutes late!' he exploded.

She caught her breath, fighting the temptation to look him straight in the eye. She dropped her head meekly, gripping the chairback until her knuckles showed white. 'Your pardon, Father,' she said, in a voice that betrayed none of her inner turmoil.

'If I state a time, then that is the time I mean, not a quarter after, or even five!'

'Then you had much better give Kattrin her own maid,' said Aunt Lucy, looking up from rapt contemplation of the pale green tendrils painted on the delicate china plate. 'Mary cannot attend on two of us at the same time.'

The intervention was so unexpected that everyone, even Susan hovering by the door with a silver chafing dish of kidneys, seemed to hold their breath.

'What's that you say, sister?' Revel's voice was dangerously calm.

But Lucy had turned away from him, her eyes taking on once more the vague and cloudy look that was habitual to her. Singing under her breath, she began to shred her bread and butter into tiny strips.

For as long as Kattrin could remember, Aunt Lucy had been like this. When they were children everyone had danced delicately around the issue, telling them that they must not agitate their aunt when she was 'disturbed'. Fond as she was of her aunt, Kat had recently begun to wonder whether Lucy's illnesses were not sometimes orchestrated by Lucy herself, slipping in and out of her own private world whenever matters at Clapton Revel became threatening. Recalling the occasions when her aunt had abandoned them to their father's rage, she found it difficult not to be bitter.

But years of protecting her aunt and her brother from Revel had left their mark and she heard herself asking, 'What was it you wanted to say to me, Father?'

'What?' He turned away from Lucy with a snarl.

'Mary said you wished to speak to me,' she said quietly.

Flinging his napkin down on the table and pushing his chair back with a violence that caused coffee to slop out of the heavily chased silver pot, he leaned across the table and caught her chin, wrenching her head up until she was forced to look him in the eye. 'Hold yourself

41

ready for visitors this morning,' he said, grinding the words out between his teeth.

She blinked in surprise. Morning callers were a rarity at Clapton Revel. Apart from Lizzie Allnutt, who had once accompanied her husband when he called on mill business, only Lady Isabelle had ever called and expected to be entertained. She had called quite unannounced: 'Just looking in on you, to see how you are going on.' She'd swept through the hall, the feathers in her turban nodding, and by the time she had looked into all the rooms, found fault with their aspects and criticised their dispositions, Lucy had retreated in panic, leaving Kattrin to cope alone. She had done her best, ringing the bell for the maid to fetch tea and cakes to the parlour.

'Drawing room, Miss Revel,' Lady Isabelle corrected her sharply as the maid left the room. 'Farmhouses, or the better order of cottages, may have a parlour.' She examined the old-fashioned furniture through a lorgnette. 'Clapton Revel, however – ah – antiquated, has a drawing room.'

Then the maid had come in with a message from the kitchen that 'Cook was too busy for such fal-lals, and besides, she'd had no orders from the master about tea and cakes and if Miss Kattrin wanted any such, she could just come to the kitchen for them herself.'

Lady Isabelle, bristling at the insult, had assembled the servants in the hall and made it quite clear to them what their duties were and that in future they would take any orders they were given, unless they had tired of their positions. There had been no more trouble with the staff, but there had been no other morning callers either.

Revel, growing impatient with his daughter's silence, dug his fingers into her cheeks. 'Well?' he demanded.

'M-morning visitors, Father?' she stammered.

'Aye. The Cazelles.'

'Indeed?'

'Indeed.' He released his grip so suddenly that she staggered back. 'And you can change that dowdy gown as soon as you like!' he said, looking her over from head to toe. 'There's a blue dress come from the dressmaker, pretty much like the one you wore last night. Mary knows the one. You'll make sure to wear it.'

She looked in dismay from his angry face to the modest morning dress, which she had often worn for her lessons with Drusilla and Philomena; with its heavily ruffled hem and wrist-length gauze over muslin puff sleeves it was pretty enough for the most demanding of morning callers. Certainly more suitable than the low-cut evening robes which had recently made an unexpected appearance in her closet.

'But Papa,' she protested, 'I cannot wear such a gown for a morning call!'

'When I've shown Henry Cazelle round the mills I'll be back,' said her father, ignoring her protests. 'Do as you're bid, or you'll be sorry for it.' His eyes narrowed. 'Don't think I've forgotten your disobedience yesterday.'

Revel turned his attention to Lucy. 'Mark this,' he snapped as she cringed away from him. 'Young Cazelle has my permission to see her alone. So none of your namby-pamby nonsense. Keep out of the way. Understand?' Without waiting for an answer he turned back to his daughter. 'Louis is to make his addresses to you,' he said, stabbing the air emphatically with his finger. 'The two of you are to be married by the year's end.' He rounded on Dickon. 'At the mill, boy. Five minutes. Sharp.'

So shocked was Kattrin that her father was gone before she could gather her wits. She had wondered what all the changes had been leading up to and now she knew: it had all been leading up to Louis Cazelle.

'Kat! Kattrin!' Dickon's voice penetrated the haze in her brain and she turned to look at him. 'Close your mouth,' he said wearily. 'You look like a fish.'

'I feel like one,' she said unsteadily. 'I feel like a fish – drowning.' Across the room the door closed behind Lucy.

Dickon poured half a cup of coffee – for Susan had long since melted away – and thrust it into her unresisting hand. 'Drink this. Might make you feel a little better.'

She took a few sips, then pushed the cup away angrily, adding to the stains on the exquisite damask cloth. 'The only thing that will make me feel better is being told I just imagined all that,' she said.

'Can't be done, m'dear. He's decided on a course for you and me and as far as he's concerned it's settled.'

She jerked her head up from contemplation of the spreading stain. 'You and me?'

'Yes. The son and heir isn't to be forgotten, however much of a disappointment he may be.'

'He said that?'

'I've always known he thought it, but it was a bit of a blow to have it spelled out quite so brutally.' He smiled, but the smile went awry.

'Dickon, what's going on?'

'He's gone into partnership with Cazelle. Together they've been fixing the price of the best rags – the fines and the superfines – and leaving the others with nothing but the outshots. Inferior rags make inferior paper, and when the mill owner goes bankrupt, they buy him up at a bargain. But Wooburn's no longer big enough for Father.

43

He's after bigger fish, in a bigger pond. London.' He sipped his coffee, but it had gone cold. 'They might do it, too – get the monopoly there. Cazelle already has shares in the machinery manufacturers. Oh, it's all very clever...'

'And you and I? Where do we come into his plans?'

'Cazelle has a daughter, Sarah.' He gazed blindly out across the lawns to the lake, sparkling in the morning sunshine. 'She's older than us – quite a bit older. Daughters need dowries, which takes money and shares out of the business. By marrying you to Louis and me to Sarah, they keep it all in the partnership. Good business sense.'

'But I've no intention of marrying Louis Cazelle!'

'I doubt you'll have any choice. But he's not such a bad fellow. Take my word, m'dear, you have got the best of the bargain.'

'Dickon! You have agreed to all this?'

He shrugged.

'But what of all your plans? He promised Lord Bosingham that if you worked with him a year, he'd let you go on the voyage.'

'He won't do it!' His face twisted with pain. 'I suppose I always knew there was no hope.' He pushed his chair aside and ran out of the room, but not before she had seen his eyes brimming with unshed tears.

She was almost more furious with her father on Dickon's account than on her own. Her brother had spent much of the previous summer corresponding with an eminent professor at Oxford, had applied and been accepted to study under him and then, to cap his success, had been invited to accompany the professor's son on a forthcoming voyage of exploration, as junior scientific officer. Any other man would have been proud, but Revel had insisted that no son of his would become either a bookworm or a sailor.

For the only time in his life Dickon had rebelled, but the rebellion had been short-lived. Dickon had not the strength of character or will to oppose his father. When Revel made a bonfire of his carefully labelled specimen cases of insects and butterflies, the last of the fight went out of him. Bosingham, soothing troubled waters, had suggested that Dickon should work with his father and review the matter in a year. But it was clear that Revel had never had any intention of letting his son go.

When Mary hurried her away to change, dismissing her protests that the low-cut blue dress was quite unsuitable for the occasion, Aunt Lucy, true to form, was nowhere to be seen. Kattrin, dispirited, had little choice but to do Mary's bidding.

'What you got to moan about?' demanded the maid, briskly tying the laces. 'Many a girl 'ud be happy to have such a dress.'

Kat bit off the response that sprang to her lips, drawing the gown up to cover a little more of her bosom until Mary slapped her hand away. Kat played her last card. 'Lady Isabelle would think it most improper to receive morning callers in such a gown,' she said mutinously.

'That's as may be, but she an't callin' the tune this mornin', is she?'

No, thought Kat. You think you are. And little incidents began to fall into place: Mary on the corridor that led only to her father's room and the maid's recent absence during her father's visit to London. So that was the way the wind blew!

The sound of the bell brought her sharply out of her reverie. 'The Cazelles,' said Mary, and the flat of her hand between Kat's shoulder blades propelled the girl across the room.

It was unforgivable of her father to put her in such a situation! Kat fumed, as the door closed behind him and Henry Cazelle. She flounced over to the fireplace, determined not to be the first to break the uncomfortable silence.

Louis cleared his throat. In the gilded mirror she saw a flush rise from behind his ridiculously high shirt points. Could he possibly be as uncomfortable about this as she was? Last night he had seemed so confident, so sure of himself as he leered down at her. But then last night he had drunk a great deal of wine. She must be fair: for a man, too, such a proposal to order must be less easy when sober, in the cold light of day.

She was searching for some witty remark to lighten the atmosphere when Louis reached her side. He had the fixed silly smile on his face once more and she wondered how she could ever have imagined that he was ill at ease; as he bent his head towards her she wrinkled her nose and wondered how she could ever have imagined he was sober!

'Miss Revel,' he began, absently fingering the curls on his forehead, 'your father has given me his permission to – '

She could not bear it; she had to interrupt him.

'Are you come from Bosingham House?' she asked, her voice artificially bright. For the first time in her life she found a use for the fan hanging idly from her wrist and fluttered it before her face in what she fervently hoped was an artless manner. 'And how is Lady Isabelle today? And Miss Bosingham and Miss Drusilla?'

'Send their compliments to you, Miss Revel.' He was rather annoyed that she should have interrupted his well-rehearsed speech. 'Not only do I have your father's permission to approach you, but I may say that Lady Isabelle has encouraged me to pay you my addresses.'

Kattrin could have screamed. There went her main ally.

She should have been warned; after all, she had always known that

Lady Isabelle, a widow of many years' standing, saw marriage as the only purpose in women's lives. Philomena, of course, was already spoken for; she would marry her stepfather's distant cousin on whom the Bosingham estate and title, in the absence of any sons, was entailed, although the cousin did not seem in any great hurry to press his suit. Drusilla, who had sworn never to marry, had recently become engaged to Edwin, the heir to Lord Dunster, a hearty young man entirely in Drusilla's style, being fonder of hunting, shooting and fishing than of the pleasures of the ballroom. Kat, delighted for her friend, had not realised that this had left their aunt free to turn her attention to her other protégée.

She should have realised which way the wind was blowing when she overheard Lady Isabelle taking her father to task one day. 'If you wish to see your daughter marry well, then we will have some semblance of quality in this house,' Lady Isabelle had snapped at Revel. 'Wealth is all very well, but it can never substitute for good breeding. Your son, of course, has had the advantages of Eton, but as for your daughter...' Peeping through the banisters, Kat saw her raise her eyes to heaven. 'However, I do not despair,' she concluded. 'If I have a free hand I have every hope we may marry Katherine off well. If not...' She left the rest delicately in the air as she swept off to inspect the kitchens, to examine Cook closely about mealtimes and inform her that in future Clapton Revel would keep to the fashionable hours for dinner.

Like a fool, Kat had considered that her father had met his match in Lady Isabelle, and rejoiced at it. It had never occurred to her that the two of them might one day join forces against her.

She was tempted to turn on her heel there and then, but she had promised Dickon she would hear Louis out. She would be calm, not act without thought, as Joshua said she too often did.

Joshua. If only she could ask his advice! But no. She could not think about Joshua today. Not while she had Louis Cazelle to deal with. And how *was* she to deal with him? He was going to propose that they spend the rest of their lives together, yet what did she know of him? Nothing. And how did you tell whether you wanted to spend your life with someone? She had so little experience of men: not until she had begun to visit at Bosingham had she met any man other than her father, her brother, the occasional mill owner and Joshua. Even the information that the impecunious young baronet had shown an interest had come as a complete surprise. It was scarcely enough to build a future on.

She wished that she had someone to turn to.

Charlotte!

Her eyes sparkled as she remembered Drusilla's sophisticated

London cousin telling her and Drusilla about her debut, in the racier years of the Regency.

'I was to inherit a considerable India fortune from my godfather, my dears,' Charlotte had explained, 'so when I first came out, I was made a great deal of by my father's cronies. They divided quite clearly into three groups: bums, heads and the rest.'

'Charlotte!' Drusilla had been mildly scandalised.

Charlotte, product of more robust attitudes under the Regent, had been quite unperturbed. 'With the padded skirts you don't get so many bum maulers these days,' she went on. 'When I was a girl, there was but a thin layer of muslin. Sometimes not even a petticoat! But the theory still holds, I believe. The hands will slide somewhere, and if they slide all over you on a short acquaintance, then they will slide just as boldly over other women throughout your married life. Some wives might welcome that kind of attention going elsewhere, but 'twould surely not suit me.'

Drusilla was fascinated. 'And heads?' she asked.

'Ah, the head patters!' Charlotte smiled. 'Ask them a question and they will bid you not to trouble your pretty little head about such matters. A cunning woman could twist one of them round her little finger, but frankly, my dears, I've never thought it worth the effort.'

And if it had worked with Regency rakes, why should it not with today's young society men?

'Mr Cazelle,' said Kattrin, favouring him with a dazzling smile, 'I am so glad that we have had this opportunity to talk.'

'Really?' He straightened his shoulders and his chest puffed up like a turkey cock. 'By Jove, Miss Revel, I – '

'You are a man of the world, Mr Cazelle.'

'Very kind of you t'say – '

'So you can tell me all about the vicar of Mapledurham.'

'Mapledurham? Ah, you mean Fitzclarence. Yes, by Jove. By all means.' He paused in his preening and looked down at her with a puzzled frown. 'What was it you wanted to know?'

'What did he mean when he said he had influence in the theatre?'

'What wit, eh, Miss Revel? I must say!' His face lit up. 'Influence in the theatre! B'Gad! I should dashed well say he has influence!'

She smiled encouragingly and tried to look as though she were hanging on his every word.

'Old Duke of Clarence, y'see,' Cazelle chuckled, 'bathed in the river Jordan, as we say in London!' He giggled. He was vaguely aware that he should not have been talking about such matters to a young lady. If only he had not had that brandy ... two brandies, really, for his father, unaware, had pressed another on him to give him Dutch courage for the task ahead. 'Well, I *say* the Duke. Could be the King by now, of course,' he said, considering the matter. 'Though out here, in these benighted woods, how you ever get any news is beyond me.'

'I knew I could depend on you to explain it,' she said, fluttering her eyelashes in a way that Philomena, who had struggled to obey her aunt's orders to 'make that wretched child into a lady of fashion', would have been proud of. 'A man of the world like you – and of course, in London, one is so much more *au fait* with what is happening in society...'

This was easy, she thought, suppressing a small smile of victory. All you had to do was flatter him a little and he was so fond of the sound of his own voice he'd probably go on for ever. She prompted him. 'Bathed in the river Jordan, you said?'

'Dora Jordan. The actress. Clarence lived with her this age. At least, till the Regent's daughter died. Poor Charlotte! And then all the princes had to go out and marry German princesses. Or had he already broken with Dora by then?' He frowned and shook his head. 'Before my time, of course, but I remember m'father saying ... Anyway, Augustus Fitzclarence – vicar of Mapledurham – he's their son. Darlin' Irish Dora and the Duke of Clarence.' He grew very serious. 'If old Georgie goes – and it can only be a matter of days – then you, Miss Revel, will have been sitting next to the son of a king.'

She wrinkled her brow. 'But I don't understand? Why would a prince want to be a vicar?'

'Not a prince, my dear Miss Revel. Dear Augustus may be the son of a king, but he'll never be a prince!' He saw the frown on her forehead. Innocent child, he thought. I like that! 'Wrong side of the blanket. Out of wedlock.' He tapped the side of his nose in a knowing sort of way. 'Ten Fitzclarences in all. Imagine, ten by-blows with his actress, but he only managed the one – the brat that died – with Madame Saxe-Meiningen!'

'Madame – ?'

'That's what we call her in London,' he said airily, as if he spent his days exchanging witticisms at court. 'Princess Adelaide.'

'Who may even be queen by now?'

'No wonder the poor old king went mad,' he went on, as if she had not spoken. 'Not this one. Old George the Third. Imagine, fifteen children he had, but out of all the dozens of grandchildren, only ones in line and on the right side of the blanket were both females!' He counted them up on his fingers. 'When the Regent's daughter died young, that just left Kent's daughter Drina. I met her once: boring little brat she was then. Don't suppose she's changed. Alexandrina Victoria – suppose she must be about twelve now. I doubt if Clarence will breed any more, for he's asthmatic as they come and not much younger than his brother.' He pondered his words a moment and looked up in some surprise. 'Upon my soul, we could have Queen Alexandrina on the throne any day!'

She led him on, without much difficulty, to talk of the court and the fashions in London, feigning an interest. Anything to keep him from remembering what he was here to do. She was discovering how very amusing it was to be the manipulator for once, instead of always the manipulated. When Cazelle began to flag she crossed the room and poured him a glass of her father's best sherry wine. As she poured, she desperately searched her mind for some other subject to keep him talking until the others returned. If all else failed, she would have to fall back on paper: not for nothing had she haunted the mills since childhood!

In the event it was not a fortunate choice. Stationer's son though he was, he knew much less about the new Fourdrinier machines than she did, and it was not part of her plan to lecture him, especially when he was so fond of the sound of his own voice. She had to resort to the wine again and was pouring him a second glass when she heard her father's unmistakable heavy footfall in the hall. Her stomach lurched as the door opened and he and Henry Cazelle came into the room, with Dickon trailing reluctantly behind them.

'Well, well!' said Cazelle, rubbing his hands together in satisfaction. 'I'll take a glass of sherry with you, Revel, while we hear how these young people have been getting on in our absence.'

Kattrin watched her father cross to pour the wine, a look of satisfaction on his face.

'Well, well!' repeated Cazelle. 'So you have fixed it all between you, have you?' he asked, clapping his son heartily on the shoulder. 'Can't tell you how delighted I am to be welcoming you and Dickon into our family,' he went on, raising his glass to Kattrin.

'I beg your pardon, sir?' She tried for a look of innocent astonishment.

Cazelle and Revel turned as one to look at Louis with remarkably similar expressions and the London man-about-town disappeared as if he had never been. With a hunted look in his eyes, Louis showed a strong resemblance to a small animal desperately seeking a hole, with the sound of the huntsman's horn drawing ever closer.

He tried to bluster it out. 'Fact of the matter is, sir, we – er – I enjoyed chatting to Miss Revel so much ... the other matter ... plenty of time for that, Father. Fact is, getting acquainted, don't you know? So we – I – never got round to – '

'Never got round to it?' exclaimed Revel, the cords in his neck standing out. 'Why, you – '

Cazelle, who reserved to himself the right to castigate his own son, was beginning to look rather hot under the collar when Dickon intervened.

'I believe we are expected at the Bosinghams', Father.'

'Of course, of course,' said Cazelle eagerly. 'To see the lawyers about – '

'Quite.' Revel cut his guest off short. He had no intention of discussing his business in front of women, with their notorious addiction to gossip, though he rather thought that in this instance young Louis might just have the slacker tongue.

The little French gilt clock on the mantel tinkled the hour. 'It will not do to keep Lord Bosingham waiting,' said Dickon.

Kattrin could hardly refrain from a sigh of relief as she watched the four men climb into the carriage, though she knew the reprieve would be short-lived. She wondered whether her father's business with the lawyers was anything to do with Hall Barn; Lady Isabelle had been pressing her father to make the Wallers an offer ever since she heard that they were seeking a buyer. Kat's feelings on the prospective move to Beaconsfield were very mixed; Hall Barn was an altogether grander house than Clapton Revel and they would need far more servants – perhaps even a butler, like the formidable figure at Bosingham House. And how would her father – not to mention Aunt Lucy! – deal with someone like that?

She sat alone in the morning room, a thin muslin shawl covering the deep décolleté of the blue dress, picking absently at the luncheon that the servants had set on the table, racking her brain for a solution.

'Miss!'

She froze, her hand halfway to her mouth, wondering if she had imagined that urgent whisper.

'Miss Kattrin!'

So gaunt and hollow-cheeked was the girl at the window that Kattrin hardly recognised her, but the hand that held the shawl close round her head had the swollen knuckles and blackened finger ends of the rag sorter.

'Why, is it – Emmy?'

'Sshh, missie!' The girl looked apprehensively over her shoulder. 'If Cook sees me here she'll kill me!'

Kat crossed the room and pushed the sash window up. 'What is it, Emmy?'

'Oh, miss, please help me,' said the girl, dragging her eyes reluctantly from the feast spread out on the table. 'We're starvin', Miss Kattrin. Starvin'. Since Pa's been out of work we've naught to eat. An' the children – they're not goin' to last much longer if I can't get them food. Already the babe – '

50

'But I don't understand,' said Kattrin in confusion. 'You and your sisters – you all have work...'

'Had. When Pa spoke out 'gainst the machines, we all had to go.' A wry smile flitted briefly over her wasted features and Kat had a sudden memory of Emmy and Agnes and the other sisters, going home up the lane late one summer's evening, arm in arm, calling out something cheeky to the apprentice boys. 'I'd never have got this close to the house, Miss Kattrin, if 'n I'd still been workin' in the rag houses! Cook'd have smelled me comin' a hundred yards off.'

If Kat had not had so much else on her mind she would have noticed the lack of the rag girl's stench, a stench they absorbed from sorting out clothes too tattered for even the poorest of the London poor. Sorting and cutting the rags was a filthy job and one that had wrecked many a country girl's constitution; quite apart from the dust that settled on the lungs, the rags often carried disease, having ended up doing service as dressings or poultices. It was not unusual to come across a gangrenous toe or mummified finger; once they had even found a dead baby wrapped in a filthy old cloak.

'I don't miss the stink and the dust, miss,' said Emmy, 'but, oh!' She wrapped her skinny arms round her stomach, struggling to suppress a groan. 'Oh, that were steady work and it do come hard to starve.'

'You should ask at the kitchen door,' said Kattrin with a frown. 'Cook has instructions to give – '

'Not to us, missie,' said Emmy simply.

'Because your father spoke out?' Kattrin's hazel eyes sparkled in anger. 'I won't have that! I'll speak to Cook myself and – '

Emmy rolled her eyes in panic. 'Don't you do that, miss!' she begged. 'If your father hears I've troubled you, he'll have us put out of our cottage.'

'But will not the papermakers help?'

'The Society only helps the skilled men, miss. And Pa were never that. He went north after a position. They do say as they're so short of men up there that you can get work in the mills there without a settlement certificate from your parish.' She shrugged. 'What else could he do once your father had put the black on him in the valley? There won't any mill owner stand out against Revel now. And so many men waitin' for the few jobs, why should they?'

'But surely your father will send back money for you and – '

'We an't heard from him these three months. Mother wanted us to follow him, but then the babe come early and we'd to wait till she'd her strength back, but God knows when that'll be. An' now she an't able to feed the babe no more and . . . I di'n't know where else to turn, Miss Kattrin.'

51

'I will do what I can. But I have no money. What about the parish?'

'Pays the rent, thank God. We had hopes of outdoor relief, but who'll give us women work in the fields or on the roadmaking when there's a dozen men for every task? Even the bird-scarin' don't pay n'more, fer there's so few birds left. Last time our Charlie got a farthin' for a sparrer was more'n a month gone.' As a way of protecting the seed crop, the parish officer paid children a farthing for every sparrow's head they presented, the rest of the bird going as a welcome addition to the pot, but three hard winters had left few hedge birds. 'Just the memory of that sparrer pie...' muttered Emmy, a distant look in her eyes. 'We tried magpie, but it made us all sick. Oh, the neighbours tried to help, but now there's that many out of a job...' She bit her lip. 'We can't live on nettles much longer. Us'll just have to pray for a good harvest.'

But they only had to look at the fields to know that 1830 would see but a thin harvest. Five months of persistent rain and driving storms had rotted the early sowings and flattened the surviving crops. The early summer sun was shining strongly now, but only a few weeks ago much of the Thames Valley had still been under flood water. Up at Flackwell Heath, on the top road to Wycombe, where the orchards were usually sheltered from the unseasonable frosts and the inhabitants proudly boasted that they came 'from Frackle, sir, where the best cherries come from', most of the fruit had failed to set. There would be no cherry-picking holidays in the Flackwell orchards for the mill workers this year and so few baskets of fruit picked that it would hardly be worth the cost of sending them to London. This year the Heathens would own to being 'from Frackle, sir, God help us.'

There must be some way of helping, thought Kattrin. Where could she turn? Whom could she ask? And then Emmy clutched her stomach and groaned.

The sound spurred Kattrin on. Action first, thought later, she told herself sternly, and turned hastily back to the table. One eye on the door, she gathered up the bread and the cold meats and some of the fruit and cheese and wrapped it in her shawl.

'God bless you, missie,' breathed Emmy.

'Come again tomorrow, at about this time, if you can.'

'If I can?' said Emmy with the ghost of a chuckle. 'Wild horses wouldn't stop me!'

'Not here. Where the shrubbery runs alongside the lane. I shall be – '

On the other side of the house a door opened and there was the noise of water hitting the cobbled yard. Footsteps sounded on the back stairs and Kat looked anxiously over her shoulder. When she turned back, Emmy, like a wraith, had simply vanished.

Kat took what little food was left, spread it out on a large silver tray to make it look more and took it upstairs to her aunt's room, more than a little shocked at her own deception.

She wasn't best pleased to be stopped outside her aunt's room by Mary. 'What you doin' up here?' the maid asked aggressively.

Kattrin bit off the sharp words that sprang to her lips, for it was no part of her plan to antagonise the woman. 'I've brought Aunt Lucy something to eat,' she said brightly.

'She's asleep,' came the curt response.

'I'll waken her,' said Kattrin with a sunny smile. 'She must eat.'

'Leave her be! See for yerself – she's deep asleep.' Her eyes lit on the wine. 'But you can leave the tray. For later.'

Through the crack Kat saw her aunt, dwarfed by the vast wooden bed and the mound of lace-trimmed snowy white quilts, lying on her back, snoring softly. Her face hardened as she saw the small brown bottle on the side table: Mary was giving Lucy laudanum again. And yet whom could she complain to? She ground her teeth in frustration – a habit Revel thought he had beaten out of her when she was ten.

Idly she wondered what the men were doing at Bosingham House. In the light of what Dickon had told her, they were probably drawing up favourable terms for Cazelle's Stationers' Company to buy their paper. Once her father would have discussed such matters in front of her, but over the years, as she had shown more interest in papermaking than Dickon ever would, her father had deliberately shut her out. Still, it was odd that they had not thought to take her; Papa rarely missed an opportunity to insinuate her into the company at Bosingham House. She pouted. Today, when she felt an overwhelming urge for company – Drusilla's for preference, although even Lady Isabelle's would have done – the afternoon stretched ahead of her, long and dull.

It had been such a disjointed day and she found herself quite unable to settle. She picked up a book and laid it aside again; she thought of walking across to the mill, but apart from the risk of running into her father and the Cazelles, there was the greater risk of running into Joshua. Usually he would be the first she would turn to in troubled times but she was aware, deep inside, that her attitude to him had undergone a subtle change in the last few days; quite what it was and why it had happened she didn't really understand. She would have to sit down and work it out some time, but not yet. While there was Louis Cazelle and her father to deal with, she really could not cope with anything else.

She knew what she needed to soothe her mind and calm her spirits; if only she dared! She normally only risked that when she knew her father was safely away in London, but today she decided she had to indulge herself. If Father ever found out that she was still at the lace work, he would be furious, she knew. He had made it clear to Aunt Lucy years ago that lacemaking was beneath Miss Revel of Clapton Revel; it might once have been a ladies' occupation – the unlikely legend was that it had been taught to the English ladies by Queen Catherine of Aragon – but now it was a cottage industry, fit only for the village girls. Why else, he demanded, had he taken her and Dickon away from the lace school? That she had become, like her mother and aunt before her, one of the most skilful lacemakers in the area, an expert in the finest Buckingham point lace, would mollify his rage not one jot. As a child she'd thought his opposition to her lacemaking was because it was an unbearable memory of his dead wife, but she had left such self-deception behind years ago. She could never forget, however, the promise she had made to Aunt Lucy that her father would never find out from her that they had gone against him.

It had been much easier before Mary came to Clapton Revel. Becky had been full of admiration for their skills and had often watched open-mouthed as Kattrin and Aunt Lucy sat at their cushions, their nimble fingers crossing the threads around the pin pattern, the carved bobbins rattling against each other. But Papa had taken against Becky for some reason, and when she had married one of the skilled papermakers he had turned them both off. Becky and her husband had had to pack their traps and travel up to Wendover to the canal boats that would carry them to the mills in the north.

Tiptoeing past her aunt's chamber, she saw Mary seated at Lucy's satinwood dressing table, rummaging through the drawers. She couldn't imagine what Mary was looking for, but with the chaotic state in which her aunt kept everything, Kat reckoned the maid would be busy for some time!

Hoisting her skirts in a most unladylike manner, she stepped over the stair that creaked and crept along the passageway, past her own room and up to the attic floor, unused now except for the little cubbyhole that served as bedroom for Aggie, the little skivvy from the workhouse.

The nursery had long ago been stripped of its few toys and was used only as a storage room, but Aunt Lucy ensured that it was kept clean. Tomorrow or the next day, when her aunt emerged from her seclusion, she would embark, as she always did, on one of her frantic orgies of scrubbing and cleaning and the whole house would be turned upside down until her aunt had worked off whatever demons drove her.

Kattrin jammed the latch with a little wedge of wood and crossed the room to the fireplace. Sensitive fingers slid along the wig recess, where long-dead mill owners and their wives had stood dressed wigs to dry and set, until she found the place where the two sections of panelling had shrunk away from each other and pulled out a tiny key. Unlocking the chest that stood in the window, she lifted out an elaborately carved box.

A soft smile curved her mouth as from the box she took out the plump blue lace cushion, a strip of pattern she had pricked out on parchment the previous week and a small heart-shaped pincushion studded with a selection of bugles, the fine brass lace pins ornamented with tiny beads. The carved bobbins were in a separate inlaid box and she ran her fingers lovingly over them as she drew them out. Neither Aunt Lucy nor Mistress Savage in the lace school had favoured the heavier undecorated local bobbins known as thumpers, both preferring for the finer Bucks point work the more slender bobbins. As she sorted them through, selecting the trolley bobbins with their loose pewter jingles for the gimp thread, she held them up to the light like a child, delighting in the play of light on the glass spangles at the end. The crudely carved apple-and pear-wood bobbins had been passed down from her grandmother and great-grandmother; the ivory bobbins wound with silver wire were from more prosperous times. As her jangled nerves grew calmer she found she could visualise the finished lace – which was to form the lappets and trimming for a new morning cap for Drusilla's trousseau – quite clearly in her mind; she secured the parchment to the cushion by its eaches and began to set out the pins in the lace cushion in a pattern of her own devising.

She had only intended to mark the pattern and set the bobbins, but lost herself completely in her work, quite oblivious to the passage of time. Her concentration was entirely on her slender fingers, busily weaving the bobbins to pass the threads around the pattern pins, when above the clacking of the wood and ivory she heard the crunch of carriage wheels on the gravelled drive.

In a panic she drew the drawter over the finished lace, wrapped the lace cushion hastily in its hindcloth and thrust it back into its box. As she hurried down the corridor, straightening the embroidered muslin shawl she had wrapped defiantly over the low neckline of the blue dress, the clock in the hall struck the hour. She forced a welcoming smile onto her face and descended the stairs to find her father and the Cazelles standing in the hall.

She returned the Cazelles' bows with a modest inclination of the head. 'Good afternoon to you, gentlemen. Would you care to take tea?' she asked, determined to show the normal courtesies, even though in all likelihood her father would snap her head off and take the men into his room where the brandy was kept.

55

'In the drawing room,' said her father, quite taking the wind out of her sails. She led the way down the corridor and rang the bell.

Under her father's stern eye she served the tea, her own gaze demurely lowered. Louis looked perfectly at home, but both his father and hers looked ill at ease, the delicate teacups lost in their large hands. They soon gave up all pretence of polite conversation and turned instead to a discussion of the London markets and the effects on stocks and shares of the current agitation for Reform and the uncertainty over the King's health.

She listened with only half an ear, for she knew her father's views on Reform off by heart and had no reason to believe that Henry Cazelle's pronouncements would be much different. She was eager to find out whether Louis had any opinions on the matter and observed him surreptitiously while she handed round thinly sliced bread and butter and delicate ratafia biscuits.

If she had hoped for any surprises, she was to be disappointed. He was an ineffectual young man, and rather too prone to parroting the views of others. Louis, she realised gloomily, would do exactly what his father and hers told him to do.

Knowing that her father would have no interest in her views on anything to do with business or politics, she took advantage of a lull in the conversation to talk to Louis about London in the hope that he might have some more pronounced ideas in his head about fashion and theatre, but even there he had nothing original to say.

After a while the two older men left their talk of markets and put in the odd remark to keep the rather laboured conversation between their offspring from flagging. She was amazed that her father managed to control his impatience with some of the nonsense that Louis was talking, but at last it was too much even for him and he rose abruptly to his feet.

'You don't want any more of this muck,' he said. 'Rot your guts, that will. Come and see my racing curricle.'

'That the one Bosingham was talking about?' said Henry Cazelle, rising not at all unwillingly to his feet.

'Aye. Raced him from London to Salt Hill last month. For a wager. We do it every year. Every year he thinks he can beat me, but he's yet to manage it,' he crowed.

'I hear it's built to your own specifications?'

'Designed my first one, oh, must be over a dozen year ago,' said Revel, his chest swelling with pride. 'Had it built for me. Don't have the original any more, but I've always stuck to the same design. Never seen it bettered since, d'ye see.'

Kattrin shuddered. How could he bear to speak so coolly about the racing curricle when it had been the cause of her mother's death?

She felt a sudden pang for the barely remembered woman, so like Lucy and yet so unlike her, who had died when she and Dickon were still small, and seemed to have left so little trace behind her.

The door closed behind them, leaving her alone once more with Louis.

'More tea?' she offered nervously. 'Or would you like to – '

'You know we've better things to talk about than tea,' said Louis, rising and leaning on the mantel in a studied pose. Lord Byron, she rather thought, recalling an engraving she had seen in one of Lady Isabelle's magazines.

'Mr Cazelle, I – '

'Miss Revel – Katherine – please let me speak.' He took a deep breath. 'I've – you see it's – I have your father's permission to address you,' he blurted out. 'To – to ask for your hand in marriage, and I don't intend to leave here until I have your answer.' He heaved a sigh of relief as he got the words out.

There was no way around it: he had asked and she would have to answer him. 'I am honoured by your proposal, sir,' she said softly, 'but I really do not think that we would suit.'

'Oh, fie, Miss Revel,' he said with a high-pitched laugh. 'Suit? What is there to suit? I must marry someone . . .' He realised this was not the most flattering thing to say and hastened to make amends. 'You're a close one, Miss Revel, and no mistake!' he said with a shake of his head. 'Still, you're a deal prettier than I had been led to expect.'

'Why, sir, such compliments!' she exclaimed, lowering her eyes to hide the spurt of anger.

He was beginning to look mulish. 'No, that's not it!' he muttered. 'You can be as awkward as you like, but it's settled and there's not much you or I can do about it! They want an heir for this new partnership, and as Sarah's getting a little long in the tooth to breed, it'll probably have to be you – that is, us.'

'Sir, you are most kind, and I thank you for your flattering offer,' she said with a flash of sarcasm, 'but the truth of it is that I don't wish to marry.'

'But your father and mine – '

'Are entering on a partnership,' she snapped, rising to her feet. 'I fail to see how that involves me!'

'Well, you may wish to defy your father,' he said frankly, 'but I've no desire to go against mine!'

In her agitation she had moved out from the shelter of the tea table and Louis, seeing his chance, lunged at her and began, rather inexpertly, to rain kisses on her face. She twisted and turned in his embrace, desperately seeking to avoid his questing mouth, but as the shawl fell in a tangle between them, trapping her arm, he caught one

57

hand in her loose ringlets, just where her father had knocked her into the wall. As she winced he took advantage of the moment and kissed her full on the lips. For a moment she could not move her head for the pain shooting through her; he took her lack of opposition for approval and fastened his slack mouth on hers to kiss her again. Then, emboldened by his success, he let his free hand slide down over her exposed shoulder to her breast.

It was too much. Kattrin, recalling the time at the village lace school when she had watched an older girl deal decisively with an importunate swain, brought her knee sharply up into his groin.

She was too hampered by voluminous skirts and petticoats to do him much damage, but the impact was sufficient to make Louis's eyes water. With a startled oath he released his grip on her and collapsed, winded, in the chair.

'There is your answer, sir,' she said, gathering up her shawl and stalking across the room.

'But what am I to tell your father?' he croaked.

'That you proposed and I declined,' she said crisply. 'And there's an end to the matter.'

'I wish to God it was that simple,' groaned Louis.

# Chapter Three

The figure clung to the weathered brick wall, arms and legs outstretched like an insect frozen in midflight, as a piece of the worn sill broke off and fell lazily through the still night air. The figure scrabbled desperately for a new handhold and the bundle, tied up in a shawl, slid round to one side, threatening the fragile equilibrium. The falling stone grazed the balustrade that ran around the top of the new wing, ricocheted off and fell two storeys more before plunging into the sea of pearly grey mist that washed around the base of the house.

The legs in the dark velveteen britches hung suspended a few tantalising inches above the balustrade, fingers clinging to the sill for dear life, the arms in the short black jacket straining to take the weight. She could not hang there for ever; she would have to make a move before her arms came out of their sockets. But which way? Behind her the house, her father's rage, Louis Cazelle; ahead of her the descent to the crumbling portico, the risk of a fall, the terror of the unknown.

She bit her lip until it hurt, the voice in her head lashing her cowardice. Wasn't this the same wall that she and Dickon had so often climbed down? Wasn't the prospect of a warm and welcoming embrace at the end of her journey more appealing than the certainty of her father's terrifying rage?

Heart thudding, she let herself down gingerly onto the balustrade, letting out a sobbing breath as the stonework held steady beneath her feet. But it couldn't bear her weight for long and, groping through the mist till her hands found a firm grip on the iron drainpipe, she launched herself out into the dark void. The metal burned her hands as she slid down and she almost cried out as she came to an abrupt halt against the bracket, bruising her knuckles painfully. She knew she was only a few feet above the ground now, a shorter drop than it had been when she and Dickon had so blithely taken it all those years before.

Her heart was hammering in her throat as she let go and she landed with a thump in the flowerbed, her legs in the air. The bundle had twisted behind her as she fell, causing folds of cloth to slide up over her throat, putting her in imminent danger of strangulation. As she reached up to unknot the shawl, it occurred to her that she must look rather like an upturned June beetle, the kind Dickon used to mount on boards for his collection. Under other circumstances she might even have smiled.

But it hadn't been a day for smiling. In spite of her brave parting words to Louis, Kattrin had been shaking inside when she left the drawing room. Seeking out the housemaid, she told her that she had the migraine and cravenly retired to her bed.

As she lay in the darkened room with the spirits of vinegar in her hand, she had thought over the events of the day. Louis was right, of course. Sooner or later her father would wear her down.

In the middle of the night she had heard footsteps passing down the corridor. Quietly she sat up and watched the flickering candle-light show beneath the door. Tiptoeing across, she opened the door a crack and saw Mary passing into the corridor that led only to her father's rooms.

No help there. No help from anyone in the house, not from Lucy, sleeping away her drugged sleep, nor even from Dickon, who seemed already to have accepted his fate. She was on her own.

There was no choice, she realised. She would have to run away.

She sat bolt upright in bed, appalled at her own temerity, her arms cradling her knees as she struggled to put some order into the thoughts racing madly through her head. The prospect of running away terrified her, but the prospect of staying and marrying Louis appalled her even more.

She had lain awake for hours trying desperately to think where she could go. There was no obvious answer: the family had for too long isolated itself and she could think of nobody she could turn to.

The servants and the villagers she dismissed out of hand: even if she had known any of them well enough, it would scarcely be fair to ask them for help when it would surely cost them their livelihood. Lady Isabelle was the only woman with the courage to stand up to her father, but on this occasion, that redoubtable lady appeared to have allied herself with him and the Cazelles. And that meant Kat could not turn to Drusilla either. She chewed on her fingernail as she racked her brains to think of somewhere.

In the dark hour just before the dawn it came to her. Nonie.

Kattrin had still been a child, no more than twelve or thirteen, when Joshua had first taken her to see his friend Nonie, a plump, motherly woman who lived in a neat cottage between Hedsor and Cookham.

It still made Kat squirm with embarrassment when she remembered how Joshua had found her that day in the summerhouse. She had been in a terrible state. Dickon was away at school, her father in London on business, Becky on her way up north and Lucy shut away in her bedroom in one of her intermittent depressions. Kat remembered telling Joshua that she had been about to come and find him, to say goodbye. When he'd enquired where she was going, she'd explained, oh so earnestly, that she was dying. She blushed even now when she remembered the questions he had asked her and how heartlessly he'd laughed at her talk of dying: only the good died young, he'd said, so she was in no danger! Then he'd grown more serious and offered to take her to see Sarah Blaikie, one of the mill hands: there were things she needed to know, and Sarah would explain it all much better than he could. But halfway to the mill he'd changed his mind and without further ado had driven her to Cookham in the gig.

Normally she would have revelled in the journey – having Joshua all to herself, and crossing the river on the ferry – but so convinced was she that she was dying that the excitement she would normally have felt had quite passed her by. And then Nonie had explained the facts of female life to her. She'd felt such a fool – and sworn she'd never again be able to look Joshua in the face.

'Think no more about it,' Nonie had said. '*He* won't.' And Joshua, to give him his due, never had teased her about it.

'Ah, he's turned out a fine young man, though I say it myself as shouldn't,' said Nonie, her bosom swelling with pride as she looked down the garden that sloped away to the sparkling waters of the Thames, to where Joshua was chatting with the bargemen beyond the carefully tended vegetable garden. She turned back into the room and her smile broadened as she took in the expression of puzzlement on Kattrin's face. 'Did he never tell you I was his nurse? No?' The smile wavered. 'Brought him up, I did, when his mother...' She pressed her lips together and Kat had the awful feeling for the briefest moment that Nonie had been about to cry. Then it passed and she smiled again. 'Ah, well, his father and me, we didn't do too badly when all's said and done.'

Kat had sat by the fire, warm and cosseted, sipping a herbal infusion that swiftly relieved her cramps, until Joshua came back from the river with John, to announce, with regret, that it was time they left.

'If ever you've a problem, child, don't brood on it,' Nonie had said, wrapping up warm griddle cakes in a napkin for them to eat on the journey back. 'You've no one in your family to turn to, so come

61

across to me any time you're worried. Master Joshua will bring you over here; you've only to give him the word.'

That had been the first of several visits. Nonie couldn't always find such an easy solution to her problems, but just talking them through with her had usually helped Kat to see what was the best way to deal with them. 'Remember, child,' Nonie had told her on the last visit, 'any time it gets beyond you to cope with, you get yourself over here. There'll always be a chair at our table for you.'

But this time she couldn't ask Joshua to get involved. She couldn't expose someone else to her father's rage; this time she had to do what needed doing for herself.

She pulled the shawl away from her neck, wriggled free of the bundle, picked it up and ran, heading first for the coach houses, then ducking over the bridge towards the mill. Once safely beyond the drying houses she squatted down below the bushes to catch her breath and rubbed her bruised throat with a gentle hand.

Dickon's cap had come off her head in the fall and she tried to ram it back on over curls which had sprung loose from the knot in which she had confined them; as she struggled with her hair, his shirt pulled tight across her bosom and there was an ominous sound of tearing at the seam. Regretfully she abandoned the idea of finishing the journey in her brother's clothes; as soon as she reached the copse beyond the settling ponds she would have to change.

She found her way in the half light: even if she had not known it like the back of her hand, she would have found the pond by the smell.

She picked her way carefully round the edge, the shawl drawn carefully over her mouth and nose. Aunt Lucy always said that the early mist was a danger to the health; early mist around the reeking settling ponds would be twice as dangerous.

In the shelter of the trees she spread out her bundle on a pile of dry bracken, drew out her skirt and began to haul it on over the britches. As she was securing the last hook at the waist, somewhere over to her left she sensed something move in the mist.

Her knees began to buckle beneath her. Surely her father wasn't out looking for her already? There had been a time, not so long ago, when fear of her father had been so great that she had almost credited him with the power to see into her mind; now that same feeling of dread and powerlessness washed over her once more.

She stood motionless, so tense that she could no longer feel any sensation in her fingertips where they still gripped the hooks of her skirt. She stared into the mist as if willing it to part like a curtain and after a moment she was quite sure that something – or someone – was there.

It was only the vaguest of shapes in the greyness, but surely too small to be a man. Her breathing slowed to a more regular rhythm. Could it be a dog, she wondered, or a fox, sitting in the reeds waiting for some water bird to come past and present it with breakfast? But what water bird would choose to land on that filthy water?

Then it groaned. In that sound there was an echo of Emmy: the misery, the hunger, the desperation.

'Who's there?' she whispered, no longer afraid.

Again that same desolate groan. She took three steps forwards.

The skinny little boy gasped and backed away, feebly trying to ward her off with arms so painfully thin that they were like kindling sticks. 'You come for me too, angel?' he gasped, the terror strong in his voice. 'Oh, angel, don't come for me yet,' he begged. 'Not till I've found her. I'll find her, I swear it. I promised Mama I'd look after Becca. An' if you got to take us, you got to take us together.' He repeated it like a litany. 'You got to take us together.' He dropped to his knees and began to search frantically in the long grass that edged the stinking ponds. 'And I will look after her. 'Cos I promised . . .' He reached out to part a clump of reeds, caught his breath painfully, clutched his arms across his stomach and fell forward on his face.

She hurried to his side and bent over him. Gently she turned him over, patting him to see where he was injured. There was so little covering to the bones that it was like stroking a skeleton. Over at the mill a door slammed and voices called out to each other as the night men made ready for the day workers; raising her head she saw that the thin line of grey that edged the hills had become noticeably paler since she left the house. Her father would soon be stirring and it was past time that she was gone.

She dragged the boy away from the pond's edge, out of immediate danger, and made a quick circuit of the ponds; finding nothing, she convinced herself that 'Becca' was a product of the child's delirious ramblings. Meanwhile the sky was growing paler yet.

Every moment she hesitated made it less likely that she would get away. The insistent voice in her head told her to take up her bundle and head for Cookham, to leave the problem of the child to those better suited than herself to deal with it, but she could not do it. If the boy were to come round and start searching again he might fall in the holding ponds, where the acid water would finish what hunger had begun.

Her first instinct was to fetch Parkins, the night master, from the mill, but he was a man of no initiative and would be bound to send for her father. And her father would send the boy to the workhouse or put him out on the road. To die.

63

The boy was so thin that she hardly noticed the weight as she picked him up and carried him back across the bridge.

'Joshua!'

Will Delahaye, woken abruptly by the furious knocking on the front door, struggled to swing his leg over the side of the bed and failed. He cursed under his breath as he heard his son singing loudly down the hall.

'Joshua!' he shouted again, frustration sharpening his voice. 'Joshua!'

Joshua emerged from the dressing room, a towel over one shoulder, an open razor in one hand, a leather strop in the other and his chin half soaped. 'Did you call, Father?'

'Door!' growled his father. 'Likely the baker's boy.'

'Simeon?' Joshua raised an eyebrow. 'Either he's early, or I'm devilish late! And what the deuce he's doing at the front door ...'

He was heading down the hall when the knocking stopped as suddenly as it had started. Footsteps ran round the side of the house to the back gate.

'I'll be with you in a moment, Father,' said Joshua, frowning. He hurried through the kitchen and opened the back door just as a slim figure in black velvet britches and a boy's cap erupted into the stableyard.

Not Simeon, that was for certain. Looked more like a schoolboy out for a lark. And yet vaguely familiar.

'What is it, boy?' he demanded, absent mindedly catching up the corner of the towel to pat the drips that ran off his chin and down onto his chest. He was caught totally off balance as the figure threw itself at him, narrowly avoiding the sharp cut-throat razor he still held.

'Oh, Joshua! I thought you'd never answer the door!'

The razor fell on the floor with a clatter as Joshua instinctively put his hand out to catch the panting figure. Blinking in the bright light of the early sun that had just topped Beggars Hill, he could have sworn that he held a young Dickon in his arms. But Dickon had not been that size for some years. And Dickon had never had those curious horseshoe rims to the iris of the eye.

'What the devil – *Kat*?' He coloured as he became aware of his half naked body separated from hers only by a thin shirt – Dickon's school shirt, at a guess – and the effect it was having on him. He fumbled blindly for the towel, endeavouring to cover himself up.

Kattrin, having run all the way from Clapton Revel, was too busy trying to catch her breath and control her wobbling legs to be aware of his embarrassment.

64

'Oh, Joshua!' she gasped as he looked wildly round for his shirt, 'I thought I'd never get here!'

He almost hauled her across the room and pushed her into a chair, into which she subsided with great relief, leaning forward, her elbows on her knees, as her lungs fought for air. After a moment she had her breathing under control once more and looked up at him. 'Joshua, I need – your help,' she gasped. Then her eyes widened as she took in the state of him. 'Joshua, I need you *now!*' she said indignantly. 'You might at least have got dressed!'

'Hurry!' said Joshua, tying the mare up outside the mill. 'I'll be across in a few moments.'

'But – '

He had only meant to hurry her along, but his hand caught her on her hip, slid round and came to rest on the velvet britches drawn tight over her buttocks. In spite of himself he found his fingers curving to cup the firm flesh beneath the taut cloth, drawing her closer until they were only inches apart.

She looked up into his pale face and it was like looking at a stranger. He opened his mouth and she thought he spoke, but she could not hear the words for the blood drumming in her ears.

'Joshua?' Her voice broke the spell and he stepped back from her abruptly, his hands falling to his sides as if touching her would burn them.

'Two minutes,' he said harshly. 'I'll have the men with me, so you'd better be dressed.'

He forced himself to turn away and head for the mill. As he unlatched the heavy door, he looked over his shoulder and saw her still rooted to the spot. 'Hurry!' he mouthed at her, and she turned and sped back across the bridge.

When Joshua put his head round the door of the office, Parkins looked up from the accounts he was casting and rubbed his red-rimmed eyes. A man of small ambition and fewer skills, he made no objection when Joshua wanted to take Greenaway and Bedford out of the machine room.

Joshua sent the hands for wooden rakes and paddles; as they clumped across the little bridge over the sluices, he ran ahead to the summerhouse where he found Kat, dressed once more in her skirt, her shawl drawn tightly over her head to hide the betraying curls, holding a ragged boy gently in her arms and leaning over him, straining to make out his muttered words.

She looked anxiously up at Joshua as he came in. 'His name is Tom,' she said softly, smoothing the matted hair from the lad's cold forehead with an unsteady hand. 'He's awfully weak. I left him my supplies when I came to fetch you.' She nodded at the bundle, its contents spread out across the black and white tiles of the summer-house floor next to the cushions that she'd dragged from the stone benches for the boy to lie against. 'But he – I think he lacks the strength to eat.'

'Hello, young Tom,' said Joshua, taking the boy gently from her. He looked at the rags and tried to push the thought of lice and fleas and infections out of his mind as he unscrewed the lid of his flask and held it to the child's lips. He'd taken the milk that had been warming by the fire for his father's morning gruel and mixed it with a little brandy. 'Try to swallow some of this, old fellow. It will warm you.'

At first the liquid ran out of the corner of the boy's mouth, but Joshua tipped his head further back and tried again.

'He's from London,' said Kat softly as the boy choked, coughed and finally swallowed some of the contents of the flask. 'His father's dead. They came to Wycombe looking for his uncle, but they couldn't find him. The mother fell ill and they tried to find shelter until she was well enough to travel again. He says the workhouses turned them away. All of them! One after another!' she exclaimed indignantly. 'How could they do that?'

'Because they were out of their parish,' explained Joshua. 'Without a parish certificate, no workhouse is obliged to take them in for more than one night.'

'I think it's a disgrace!' she cried. Then, as the boy cringed away, she bit her lip, trying to control her indignation. 'They kept sending them on to the next parish,' she said unsteadily. 'Wycombe, Marlow, Little Marlow, Wooburn too. And then Wycombe again. The mother died on the road and all he could think of was to get back to London. And I told you about his baby sister...' She pressed her hand to her mouth and swallowed hard. 'I looked before I set off, but I couldn't find her anywhere!'

'Me arms were dead, see,' muttered the lad gruffly, 'so I di'n't see right off that Becca weren't in me arms n'more.'

'Gently now,' said Joshua. 'I've sent the men to – '

Greenaway appeared in the doorway. If he was surprised to see a woman in the summerhouse with the mill supervisor, he didn't show it.

'Mr Joshua,' he muttered. 'Best come out, sir, and take a look at this.'

Joshua laid the boy back against the cushions. 'Stay with him,' he said softly to Kat, and stepped outside.

The boy moved faster than either of them had expected, given his feebleness; ducking under Joshua's arm he rushed out with a hoarse cry to where Bedford stood, an expression of appalled horror on his normally lugubrious face, looking down at the little bundle of rags that lay, streaming water, on the muddy bank next to the wooden rake.

Joshua tried to put out his hand to stop the boy, but his arm would not move from his side; he and Greenaway seemed both rooted to the spot, quite incapable of moving. It was Kat who caught the child and held him, his face turned in and buried in the folds of her skirts.

Joshua tried to speak, but the words caught in his throat and only a hoarse croak came out. He felt the vomit rise in his throat as he saw what the pitiless water of the holding ponds had done to the baby, and it was as much as he could do to hold it back, not to disgrace himself before his men. He stood helplessly by as Kat – Kat who had grown up around the mills and knew what the acid water could do to flesh – fell to her knees in front of the boy, cupping his face in her hands, refusing to let him look. She spoke to him without cease, a relentless torrent of words, coaxing him to remember his mother and sister as they had been; she held him close to her, turned away from the terrible sight, until at last he crumpled in her arms, his head on her shoulders, his wasted body racked with sobs and she rose and carried him back into the summerhouse.

Joshua wrenched his shoulders away from the wall where he had slumped, and sent Greenaway to the mill for a wooden box for the pathetic little corpse. He felt like an old, old man.

'D'ye think the babe was – '

'Dead?'

'Aye. Before she . . .' Bedford, himself the father of a young family, could not bring himself to say it.

'Before she fell in the stinking bloody pond? How should I know?' demanded Joshua savagely. 'D'you think I'm God?'

Bedford blinked and took a hasty step back. 'But you'll tell the lad she was already – '

'Yes.' Joshua passed his hand over his eyes, struggling for control. 'Yes. Of course I'll tell him.' And Kat too, he reminded himself.

# Chapter Four

'There!' said Mary, pulling the last red tassel into place on the heavy white wool robe. 'Look at that, then. En't no other gel at the costume ball goin' to look as good as that, I'll wager! Your father won't have aught to complain about there!'

She held the lamp high for Kattrin to see in the mirror, but the girl, her face as white as the cloth of her Albanian tunic, didn't look up. All she could see was that moment a week ago when she had emerged from the summerhouse into bright daylight and heard Mary calling.

'Mr Cazelle says as there's only two in the whole country, Lord Byron's own, acourse, an' this 'un he sent back for one of his lady friends, so there won't no one else be wearin' one. She must have been very short, though,' she went on, frowning at the hem of the nether part of the garments which came a good six inches above Kat's ankles. 'Indecent, that's what it is!' Then, as the girl continued to sit, head bowed, restlessly clasping and unclasping her hands, the maid's patience snapped. 'Look 'ee here!' she said angrily. 'You've gone through the last week like a sleepwalker, and I've had just enough of it! I've slaved to get this bleddy costume sorted an' I get as much thanks out of you as out of a stone statue!'

Kat opened her mouth to speak but her words were lost in a sharp intake of breath as Mary fetched her a buffet across the shoulders, almost knocking her off her seat. Before Kat could recover, Mary dragged her across the room, her fingers digging cruelly into the soft flesh of her arm.

'If I say you'll look in the mirror, my girl, you'll look!' hissed Mary. But as she pulled the reluctant girl in front of the cheval mirror, there was a tearing sound and they both looked down in horror at the broad sleeve which now gaped, ragged-edged, away from the body of the robe.

Mary swore furiously. 'Now look what you've made me do!'

'What *I've* made you do!' said Kat, showing the first sign of spirit since that moment in the summerhouse when she had been forced to accept that Tom's salvation had been at the sacrifice of her own, delaying her too long to make her escape. 'Did I ask you to pull me about?'

'Don't you give me no lip!' Mary's hand shot out and slapped her across the cheek. By her father's standards it was not a heavy blow, but the shock was greater, being quite unexpected, and against her abnormally pale skin the mark stood out twice as red. 'There!' gloated Mary. 'That'll put some colour back in your cheeks!'

She jerked Kat's head round and Kat blinked at the stranger looking dully out at her from the mirror. It was like looking at a ghost: white face beneath a white cap, white high-necked tunic, white kilt skimming halfway between her knees and the white Albanian slippers, and exposing far too much white-stockinged leg. The only touches of colour beside the marks on her cheeks were the scarlet bobbles and tassels that hung from the bonnet and bounced on the slippers and decorated every fold and tuck in the tunic and the kilt. She stifled a sigh as Mary began to pin the sleeve back on the tunic. It might not seem quite so indecent once she was at the costume ball; after all, Drusilla's dress – she was going as Summer – was quite as short as this, and low-cut too. She wondered whether she'd be able to keep a straight face when she saw Louis, who was going as Romeo, in tights. But it could have been worse: she was to have gone as Juliet.

She'd tried everything she knew not to attend the Bosinghams' costume ball, but every ploy had failed, as she had known in her heart that it would.

'But I cannot go, Papa,' she'd said, 'I don't have a costume. You won't let me drive to the dressmaker's by myself and Aunt Lucy is not well enough to – '

His face suffused with colour. 'Not well enough?' he ranted. 'For two pins I'd have her put away! The woman's gone insane!'

Kat bit her lip. She had done nothing to stop her aunt's demented scrubbing of the house from top to bottom; it was what Lucy always did when she emerged from a fit of melancholy and it served no purpose to stop her, simply made her worse.

Only this time, when the house was shining like a new pin, Lucy had turned on herself She had taken one of Cook's kitchen brushes and with it had scrubbed her hands and arms until they bled. She had only been prevented from doing further harm to herself by Phoebe, whose hysterical screams had brought Cook puffing up from her basement kingdom.

'God wants me to make it all clean again,' Lucy had whispered, looking at them pleadingly as they took the brush away from her. The doctor, sent for from Wycombe, had dosed her heavily with chloral and put her to bed. Kat, unable to bring herself to turn her back on the sick woman, finally gave up all thought of escape.

By the time Lady Isabelle realised that Kattrin had not yet acquired a costume for the Bosinghams' masked ball and ordered a reluctant Miss Gibbons to escort her into Wycombe, Miss Chloë had so much work on her hands that she was quite unable to fit another in at so late a date, even to oblige Lady Isabelle. Hope had risen once more in Kat's breast, but then her father had gone to London and come back with this, and Kat, who had put every last ounce of determination and energy into the failed effort to run away, now had no more left to resist him any further.

The Cazelles were late. They were staying with friends in Penn and arrangements had been made for them to take Revel and his daughter up in their carriage on the way to Bosingham House. Kattrin was well aware that her arrival at the ball in company with the Cazelles would give the gossips food for speculation, and would almost certainly be the cue for a declaration of betrothal; while her father paced angrily up and down she sent up prayers that the Cazelles had been stricken with some illness that would necessitate their absence from polite society for at least six weeks – or as long as it would take her to summon up her courage to run away once more. She had to suppress a sigh of relief when her father, with an impatient oath, drew out his watch and chain, checked it angrily against the longcase clock in the hall and sent Aggie scurrying for the coachman.

'We shall be late!' he fumed, looking more like a turkey cock than ever in his red plaid Scottish trowsers and cloak. 'Come on, girl!' he barked at Phoebe. 'Miss Revel's cloak! And quick about it!' He turned away from the clock, the muscles in his face working furiously, and stopped abruptly in front of his daughter.

'What's that mark on your face?' he demanded.

She was so busy working out a speech in which she would explain to Lady Isabelle why she did not wish to marry Louis Cazelle, that she answered without thinking, 'Mary slapped me.'

'She did *what*?'

Kat shrugged. 'I assumed she had your blessing,' she said tiredly. 'Or is that a monopoly you reserve to yourself?'

He ground his teeth. 'Get in the carriage!'

'But the Cazelles – '

'I'll wait no longer for them. They must make their own way.'

It was the coachman's curse that woke Joshua from his doze, cutting across the still air of the summer's night.

He looked about him in something of a daze, thinking in the first

70

confused seconds of wakening that his father had called out for him, but Will, unable to bring his usual crowd of cronies into the house with the invalid there, had allowed himself to be driven to the Red Cow in Jem's cart.

Rubbing his tired red-rimmed eyes, Joshua drew the curtain aside and looked out across the green. A carriage, cornering too sharply, had come to rest with its rear wheel in the large pothole opposite the bakery. He smiled grimly to himself and hoped that it might be one of the local gentry who had refused to allow the men breaking stones on parish relief to mend the local roads, persuading the Parish Board instead to send them up to the Oxford coach road to fill in the potholes there. A moment's reflection, however, reminded him that none of the local gentry was likely to be out tonight.

The speaker at the Red Cow must be a real rouser, he mused, for no one had emerged to earn themselves a coin by helping the sweating coachman to push the wheel out. On the far side of the carriage one of the passengers had gone to the horses' heads and on the nearside Joshua could see the blur of a pale face at the carriage window. He decided, with a reluctant sigh, that he would have to go out and offer his assistance.

As he reached the door, a thin voice said, 'What's 'appenin', mister?'

Joshua was back across the room in a few strides. 'Tom?' he said softly.

The pale eyelids flickered and then opened, cringing against the light.

'Who's that a-cursin', mister?' muttered the boy, so softly that Joshua had to stoop to catch the words. 'They a-throwin' us out again? We goin' to have to go back on the road?'

Joshua interposed himself between the bed and the light to shade Tom's eyes. 'You'll never have to go on the road again, Tom,' he said, bending down to brush the damp hair from the lad's brow. 'Never again. I swear it.'

A sharp spasm crossed Tom's face and he closed his eyes tightly. Two fat tears squeezed from beneath his eyelids and ran down the sunken cheeks. When he opened his eyes again there was a different kind of pain in them, pain and a knowledge that made him look far older than his years.

'I remember now,' he said in a voice that was artificially calm. 'Ma's dead, in't she? An' Becca too. The angel come and took her . . .' He blinked rapidly. 'An' God. In a big hat. Funny that,' he said hoarsely. 'Allus thought God 'ud have a big beard.'

'That was the doctor, Tom,' said Joshua with a smile. 'And it wasn't an angel either. It was Miss Revel.' It fretted him that he still

71

did not know what was so bad that it had driven her from the house so early in the morning, dressed in her brother's clothes.

'She was like an angel,' the boy objected, unwilling to be robbed of his heavenly visitation.

'Something like, Tom. But she is quite human, I promise you. She saved your life. She tried to save Rebecca's too, but it was too late.' He wrung out a cloth in a basin of aromatic liquid and wiped it across the boy's forehead. 'Try to sleep now, Tom,' he said softly. 'We'll talk again tomorrow.'

Tom's eyes closed and Joshua lowered the lamp. A glance out of the window showed that the carriage had gone, so he drew the chair up to the bedside and settled down for another night's vigil.

No sooner had he shut his eyes than the boy spoke again, rather more gruffly this time. 'Mister? You still there?'

'Yes, Tom.'

'Mister?'

'What is it?'

'If they . . .' The voice wavered and there was a defiant sniff. 'When they find Ma, they'll bury her proper, won't they? See, I didn't want to leave her there, but she made me promise. For – for Becca's sake, see.' He swallowed hard. 'I knows her soul will go to heaven, 'cos she was allus good and kind, but – '

'We found her, old fellow,' said Joshua; there was a blur in his voice and he was grateful for the dimmed light. He reached out awkwardly and caught at Tom's thin hand lying on top of the gaily coloured patchwork quilt.

'Was she – was it . . .?'

'She looked very peaceful, Tom. We brought her to the village and she – ' He swallowed hard. 'We buried her in St Paul's, in the churchyard, with Becca beside her.' He wiped a tear from his cheek. Strange that he, who had never been able to weep for his own lost mother, should now be weeping for a woman he had never known.

'You wouldn't lie to me, mister?'

'No, Tom. They're together in the graveyard, in the shade of a beautiful chestnut tree.' He thought grimly of the fight he had had to induce Charsley, the Wycombe coroner, and the vestry, to permit the burial of an out-of-parish pauper, and swiftly put it out of his mind again lest his anger show through to Tom. 'When you're quite well again I will take you there, and you shall say what is to be put on the stone. Only first you must rest and grow strong.'

Something was not right.

The carriage wheels rumbled over the gravel drive and drew up in

72

front of the porch – but where were the other carriages? Where were the footmen with flambeaux to light their way?

'Father, do you think we ought – '

'What the devil's Bosingham thinking of, leaving us sitting out here like this!' exploded Revel, whose temper had been sore tested by the mishap on the green. 'Leave that, Royston!' he commanded the coachman, who was setting the steps in place and preparing to hand them out of the carriage. 'Knock on the door!' He left his daughter to make her own way out of the carriage and strode up the steps to stand, bemused, in front of the closed doors.

Bosingham himself was crossing the hall as the butler opened the door and when she saw the look on his face, Kattrin would happily have turned and fled.

'What the devil – ' began Bosingham, as the butler said, 'I regret that her ladyship is not receiving – '

'Come in, come in, man, don't stand on the doorstep,' said Bosingham testily. He caught sight of his stepson at the back of the hall. 'Tarquin! Where the devil is your aunt?' He turned back to the door. 'Can't think what the devil you're doin' here, Revel, but since you are here – '

'We're here because you invited us!' said Revel furiously.

'Eh?' Bosingham looked at them and saw for the first time their costumes. 'Good God, man, we cancelled the costume ball!' he exclaimed. 'Couldn't hold a costume ball under the circumstances.'

Revel looked as though he were about to go off in an apoplexy.

'What circumstances?' asked Kattrin quietly.

'The King's death!' said Bosingham impatiently. 'Dammit, I sent messengers out. Tarquin, you were to ride to Clapton and – '

'I said I *might* be going that way,' said Tarquin. 'But I didn't.' He couldn't conceal the smirk on his face as he looked from Revel to Bosingham. 'Naturally I assumed you'd at least send a messenger . . .'

Bosingham, put so clearly in the wrong, coloured angrily and muttered something gruffly under his breath about relying on Delahaye. 'That father of his generally hears the news before anyone else.'

'Delahaye hasn't seen fit to honour us with his presence,' said Revel wrathfully. 'Took a week's absence without even a by-your-leave! Damned good mind to give the fellow his notice!'

'Understand your indignation, my dear fellow,' said Bosingham, taking his uninvited guest by the arm as the butler glided stately as a swan before them to open the doors to the drawing room. 'Of course there'd be a queue of mill owners waiting to take him on – no one else in the valley knows the machines like him. Even Donkin says so. Told me once young Delahaye could walk into a position at any of the big mills, here or in the north.' He turned to murmur something to the butler. 'Since you are here, Revel, you'll dine with us?' He took their agreement for granted. 'Just a family dinner, of course. Some business to tie up first with m'London agent, y'see. Few things to decide before he leaves; I'm sure he'd appreciate your opinion. Tarquin, you'll take Miss Revel to find your aunt.'

'I believe her ladyship is in the conservatory,' murmured a footman, appearing as if by magic at Tarquin's elbow.

Tarquin inclined his head. 'Katherine?' He offered her his arm. 'We won't need you, Lawson.'

She was not very happy to be left alone with Tarquin, but as her father and Bosingham left the hall without a backward glance, muttering about a run on the market and problems with the funds, she had no choice but to go with him.

She knew Bosingham House well enough to realise very quickly that Tarquin was deliberately taking her the long way round. She found she was holding her breath, waiting for him to make a move towards her, and felt a sudden wave of anger that he should make her feel so helpless. It was one thing to be frightened of her father, but she was damned if she was going to pay this feeble young man the same compliment!

She turned to face him, her head held high. 'Revenge is sweet, is it not?' she asked softly.

Tarquin looked at her, an expression of puzzlement on his round face.

'You deliberately failed to bring the message, didn't you?'

Tarquin coloured up. 'As if I would do such a thing,' he protested.

'You always enjoy making my father look a fool in front of yours,' she said. 'But tonight you've made a fool of me too and I'm angry, Tarquin!'

'Serves you right!' He sounded like a spoilt child instead of a grown man of three and twenty. 'You and your father. You laughed at me. For wanting to wed you.'

The beaded tassels on her costume jerked and rattled as she came to an abrupt halt in front of the Gainsborough portrait of the first Lady Bosingham, one of the beauties of the Cliveden set.

'You wanted to – '

'Marry you. And you laughed at me. Don't pretend you didn't.'

'I didn't know,' she began to say, but his voice overrode hers. It was as if the words, so long unspoken, could no longer be held back, and broke forth in a torrent of rage.

'You laughed at me!' he said accusingly, the muscle beneath his left eye twitching furiously. 'I, the grandson of an earl, offered honourable marriage to the daughter of an unknown mill owner, and he threw my offer back in my face.'

'I – '

'And yet your father encouraged me when he thought I was Bosingham's heir.'

'I didn't – '

'But Bosingham's *stepson*, the son of a failed gambler, was not good enough for Miss Revel's husband.' There was a hurt expression in his eyes behind the rage.

She stopped abruptly. 'Tarquin! I knew nothing of this!'

'We went along so well at first. But you changed so completely towards me after you found out.'

'No!' She realised she was shouting and lowered her voice. 'Tarquin, my father may have thought you the heir, but I knew from the first you were not.' Drusilla had explained to her the complex family relationships soon after she came to Bosingham House. She remembered how at ease she had felt with him then, believing they had something in common, having both lost a mother. 'I thought you dealt admirably with a difficult situation. And truth to tell, I envied you.'

'Envied *me*?' He looked at her in disbelief.

'I'd rather have a stepfather who loved me, than a father who – '

'Who beats you?' She raised her eyebrows. 'Dru told me.'

So her friend had not been deceived by talk of toothache and falls on the stairs.

'You're right about Stepfather,' Tarquin went on. 'He's always been kind to me and Phil. But I don't understand. If that was not the reason ... Why did you change?'

'Because *you* changed. You ceased to be a friend to me.' She remembered all those moments in darkened corners when he had tried to kiss her, the hand that had brushed her breast in the corridor when no one was looking, the fear of finding herself left in a room alone with him. 'I'd trusted you, but then you began to be cruel and I never knew why.'

'But you *can* trust me!' he protested, his dark eyes sparkling. 'I know you don't love Cazelle. Run away with me, Katherine. I'll look after you.'

He snatched at her hands and she backed away from him in alarm. 'But Tarquin – I don't love you.'

'Love has nothing to do with it,' he said bitterly. 'My mother ran away with my father for love. Deuce knows what would have happened to her – and me and Philomena – if Bosingham hadn't come along.'

Kattrin was not sorry when Lady Isabelle appeared in the doorway with exclamations over all the confusion. When her father came hurrying after her, they joined the company in the conservatory that

75

Lord Bosingham had had built on to the back of the house. Philomena and Drusilla were already there, promenading up and down the black and white tiles with two men, the shorter of whom was Gifford Stratton, Bosingham's distant cousin and heir and Philomena's betrothed, the other a distinguished looking man in his early thirties whose classic features were somewhat forbidding.

'Stratton you have already met, Katherine,' said Lady Isabelle, performing the introductions. 'Gifford, you remember Miss Revel?' There was a calculating look in Stratton's eye as he looked her over rather in the manner of a hawk assessing the better points of a sparrow.

'And her father. Mr Revel is an – ah – acquaintance of my brother's, and a neighbour.' Lady Isabelle had the knack of always interposing a little sigh when she spoke of the mill owner, as if to emphasise that she herself claimed no such acquaintance and, indeed, wished the listener to understand that she took no responsibility whatever for the introduction.

Stratton bowed over Kattrin's hand, his eyes fixed on her costume, which seemed doubly indecent here where everyone else was properly and modestly attired in dark mourning colours. After a moment's hesitation he honoured her father with an equally measured bow. She had the feeling that Stratton was someone who had studied from an early age the exact degree of obeisance suitable to each recipient.

'And Godstowe, a connection of my late husband. William is attached to the Foreign Office. He is but recently returned from the continent.'

'From Greece, to be exact.' He bowed low over her hand and when he raised his head there was a warmer light in his smoky grey eyes. He drew her aside under the pretext of showing her a particularly splendid floral specimen which he had brought back for his aunt. 'May I say how much more credit you do the costume than Lord Byron ever did – or the man it was originally made for,' he murmured.

Her eyes widened in surprise. 'But surely it is a woman's costume?' she exclaimed.

'A man's, ma'am, I assure you,' he said, with a wicked grin that quite dispelled the classical severity of his looks. 'In that part of the world the men wear the skirts; the women wear nothing but the most dreary black from head to toe.'

Somewhere in the depths of the house a gong sounded. Tarquin leaped out of the chair in which he was sprawled, only to find his way to Kattrin's side blocked by his sisters and Stratton.

'William, what are you saying to make Miss Revel blush so?' enquired Lady Isabelle.

'Nothing, Aunt,' Godstowe assured her. 'Miss Revel, let us go in. I know my aunt will not wish to stand on ceremony.'

Philomena took Stratton's arm and stood aside for her aunt, leaving Tarquin to offer his arm to his half-sister, which he did with ill grace. Lady Isabelle found herself forced to go in on Revel's arm.

Godstowe appeared to have a great deal of freedom with his formidable aunt and, insisting that no one wished to stand on ceremony at a simple family dinner, succeeded in manoeuvring himself to sit next to Kat. For his part he was both surprised and delighted to have found so attractive a dinner partner in what he had anticipated, after the cancellation of the costume ball, would be a boring family dinner. He had a wide knowledge of the customs and intricate politics of the Balkans and at her prompting he talked to her of Greece and Albania, of the Greek struggle for independence, and of the court of the Sultan of Turkey. Accustomed to being treated as a brainless female by her father, she blossomed in the sunlight of Godstowe's admiration and from a disastrous beginning the evening very soon began to pick up.

With all the tact of a natural diplomat he made sure to include Tarquin, who was marooned on his other side owing to the uneven numbers at table, and had at first shown every inclination to resent his more worldly relative, but Kat, while she did her duty with Stratton, was eager to turn back to Godstowe, who continued to pay her assiduous attention throughout the dinner in spite of her father's frowns.

'But enough of the Greeks,' said Godstowe as the desserts were set on the table. 'I am starved for news of London after so long away. Tell me all the *on dits*! Is it true that Madame Vestris has opened her own company? And Miss Eden, is she really to marry Melbourne?'

'You must forgive me, Mr Godstowe,' she said with a half-smile. 'I am only a country girl. I rarely have the opportunity to go up to London.'

'I dare say we could take you up in the carriage with us next week, Katherine,' said Lady Isabelle. 'Though with court mourning it will be a quiet visit. No public parties, of course, and the theatres will all be closed . . .'

'Then you had much better go to Bath, ma'am,' said Godstowe. 'Or Brighton. Yes, by Jove! If you went to Brighton – '

'You could ride across from your estates?'

'What an inspired suggestion, Aunt,' said Godstowe with the ghost of a smile.

Lady Isabelle sighed. 'I don't know that I could bear Brighton now. It was the King who made Brighton – oh, in the days when he was Regent, of course. And without him . . . No, I believe we will hold to our plan to visit London. And Katherine must come with us.'

'She won't be going anywhere next week,' said her father harshly. 'Next week, I'd remind you, m'lady, we are announcing her betrothal to Louis Cazelle.'

'My dear sir,' said Lady Isabelle, even more condescending than usual. 'Need I remind *you* that we have just suffered the loss of our beloved monarch? The whole country is in mourning! As I have already told Philomena, betrothals are quite out of the question.'

There was a strange rushing in Kat's ears and it seemed to her that Lady Isabelle had suddenly sprouted wings on her shoulders and a halo round her head and that heavenly choirs were singing behind that august lady's chair.

'Are you quite well, Miss Revel?' enquired Godstowe anxiously. 'You are very pale. Shall I send for your maid?'

She turned on him a smile so dazzling that it made his heart skip. 'Lord Godstowe, I am quite well, I thank you,' she said with a catch in her voice. 'Better than I have been for months.'

# Chapter Five

In the fields bordering the Wye the swallows were gathering for their yearly migration, swooping and diving to fill themselves with insects for their long journey south. Another summer gone, a cold and hungry winter to come, thought Joshua gloomily. He turned away from the window, settled in the chair and picked up the *Bucks Gazette*.

The news was depressing enough. There had been great excitement in July, when, in the midst of the English borough and county elections, the French had risen once again to overthrow their reactionary king, Charles X. Tories all over the realm of England had held their breath, while English Radicals, waving tricolours, had been sure that their moment had come. In the event the French had simply replaced one king with another and those who had hoped for the upset of an earlier French revolution were disappointed. In England, Wellington and his Tories had been returned to government once more, though with a greatly reduced majority.

'Mister!'

Joshua looked up as Tom erupted into the room. He was barely recognisable as the skeletal waif Kat had found, and good healthy food was slowly returning him to the high spirits natural to a boy of his age.

'What is it, Tom?'

'Ssshh!' warned Tom, putting his finger to his lips. 'We got a thief in the stables!'

'Unlikely, I think, Tom,' said Joshua with a ghost of a smile. 'Why would anyone – '

'I'm telling you, mister! Come over the wall, he did, from Widder Beck's.'

Joshua allowed himself to be drawn out into the kitchen. Standing behind Tom at the window he watched as a man came out of the stables, hands in his shabby jacket, looking furtively about him.

'See, mister, I – ' Tom's voice ended in an indignant squeak as Joshua's hand clamped down over his mouth.

'Not a sound, Tom,' whispered Joshua, drawing back out of sight. 'Understand?'

Tom nodded. His lips stayed obediently clamped together. Joshua gave a rueful smile, for he knew the lad would have obeyed him just as promptly had he bidden him spin cartwheels or stick his hand in the fire.

'We'll let him go, Tom,' he whispered. 'He's – '

His words were drowned by shrieks from the other side of the wall. He hurried out into the yard, but the figure had melted away.

Widow Beck was standing in the middle of her yard next to the pigpen, hands on her hips, looking in bafflement at the wooden bucket at her feet where a few vegetable peelings curled in an inch of murky water.

'What's the world coming to, sir?' she demanded indignantly. 'Not ten minutes since, I set the scraps out for the pig and I turn me back to stop the pot boiling over and they've gone!'

Joshua could see Tom almost bursting to speak and hurried in ahead of him. 'The foxes are very bold this year,' he said sympathetically.

'Why, Mr Joshua, sir, 'tis only September!'

'Probably following the vermin down from the harvest fields.'

There was a crack of gunfire above them in the woods and the shots echoed and re-echoed from one hillside to the other before fading down the valley. The old woman looked up at the wooded slopes above the village. 'Lord Bos'nam'll have game on the table this evening, while the rest of us starve,' she said bitterly, although keeping house for her lumbering son who combined his own trade with the clerkship of the parish guaranteed her a prosperity that the rest of the village would envy.

'If he's let young Tarquin out with a gun, it's scarce surprising the foxes are fleeing the hills,' said Joshua with a twinkle in his eye.

Widow Beck's face cracked into a rare smile. 'Can't think of anythin' worse than young Mr Tarquin out with a gun,' she agreed. 'They say his lordship won't ride to hounds with him no more . . .'

'He was out last week with His Majesty's Staghounds.'

'That's not huntin'!' said the old woman scornfully. 'Shame on them! 'Tis one thing to hunt a wild crittur to put vittals on the table, but that!'

Joshua did not hunt himself, lacking both the time and the inclination, but he too felt that the dealings of His Majesty's Staghounds, who kept a tame stag in the stables at Windsor and let it out periodically to provide them with a good run, defied the description of sport. 'True. But by now his hounds have the scent of the stag so well, there's less risk of him following the wrong trail – '

'Ah! My Robert did say the last time he was let ride with the local hunt, he had half a dozen of 'em in ditches by leadin' 'em athwart. I dessay 'tis his eyes, poor young man. Can't see his hand in front of his face, so Martha said – an' she used t'be nursery maid up at Bos'nam House. To hear her say it, he couldn't tell a bull from a beech tree.'

'But the fox didn't know that, so perhaps we should not be too hard on poor old Reynard.'

Widow Beck looked down at the bucket and shook her head. 'I an't so sure...' She bent a sharp look on poor Tom. 'There's young lads as think it's a lark to torment a poor widow woman...'

'We never saw any boys around, did we, Tom?'

Tom shook his head, red in the face with the effort of keeping quiet.

'Don't fret about the pig,' said Joshua cheerfully. 'Tom will bring our scraps round later for him.'

When the widow had gone grumbling back into her cottage, Joshua latched the yard gate and strolled casually across to the stables. Tom danced at his heels, barely able to contain himself.

'Hello, Samuel,' murmured Joshua, leaning in the stable doorway.

A big bear of a man, too thin for his frame, shambled out of the shadows and doffed a ragged cap. 'Your pardon, Mr Delahaye,' he said courteously. 'It was not my intention to cause you trouble.'

'Step into the kitchen, Samuel, and we'll have a word.'

A look of panic spread over Samuel's face. 'I'd as s-soon s-stay out here, Mr Delahaye, if it's all the s-same to – to you,' he stammered, his face twitching furiously.

Joshua sat down on a bale of straw and gestured for the big man to do the same. 'Tom, will you draw us two tankards from the barrel?' he asked. 'And there's some cold meat and a hunk of bread in the pantry you can fetch out.'

The two men were deep in conversation when Tom brought the food out. Joshua was saying '... and so if you could start in the stables straight away, Samuel, I'd deem it a favour. With the new machinery to set up in the second mill, I've my hands full already.'

Tom's face fell. The stable was *his* territory. It had been all but promised to him by Joshua, who had sworn he need never go on the road again. 'But mister,' he began, 'I don't see as how – '

'Thank you, Tom,' said Joshua without looking round. 'Set it down over here. Then you could look in on my father and see if there's anything he needs.'

Tom opened his mouth to protest, then clamped his lips together, turned on his heel and stalked out of the stables. Joshua listened for the creak of the kitchen door and the ghost of a smile flitted across his face when he didn't hear it.

When Samuel left the yard a few moments later, a new set to his shoulders and his head held a little higher, Joshua dusted the straw off the seat of his britches and crossed to the feedstore. 'You can come out now, Tom,' he called softly.

Tom emerged, dusting spiders' webs from his shoulders. 'Couldn't hear nothin' anyway,' he grumbled, a mutinous expression on his face.

'Just as well. Listeners rarely hear any good of themselves.'

'Why d'you want him, mister?' he demanded plaintively. 'You said I could work in the stables. I done it fine yesterday, didn't I? You never said I weren't no good an' – '

'You worked very hard,' agreed Joshua. 'And then fell asleep when you were sitting with my father.'

Tom flushed painfully. 'I never meant to, mister. It's just that – Look, I'll get stronger, honest I will!'

Joshua squatted down beside the lad. 'Tom,' he said gravely. 'Who needs the stable work most: you with a roof over your head and food on a plate in front of you, or a man so starved he has to steal from the pig's trough?'

Tom couldn't look him in the face, for fear of bursting into tears. He swallowed hard. 'But if you have him, you won't – '

Joshua gripped the boy by the shoulders and turned him back to face him. 'Who needs it most, Tom?' he persisted.

'He does,' said Tom sulkily. 'But you could've give him a shillin', like you usually do.'

'He wouldn't have taken it. He's too proud.' The district was scattered with men like Samuel, offspring of a landowner over Maidenhead way who had peopled the villages around with his bastards, each a faithful replica of the man himself. He'd ensured they were educated above their station and then left them to fend for themselves. Not surprising that the one thing they had in common besides their looks and education was their pride.

'He could've gone on the parish if he's from round here an' – '

'He has no family, Tom. His cottage burned down last year and his wife and children all died.' Samuel had taken to drink then, and disappeared from the village. And then, when he had laid his ghosts, he had returned, homeless and jobless. But it was a poor time to be looking for work. 'And he can't go to the workhouse: he has such a fear still of closed in spaces. That's why he sleeps in the woods – but it will soon be too cold for that. Working here, he might bring himself to sleep in the hayloft when winter comes.'

82

Tom's face puckered up. 'But if you have him, you won't need me,' he said plaintively.

'Of course I need you! I couldn't have found anyone better to look after my father, Tom, not if I'd advertised in every newspaper in the land.' Will Delahaye had taken on a new lease of life since the boy had come into their house. For a few weeks it had been debatable who was nursing whom, but they had settled down into a system of mutual support in which Tom fetched and carried for Will and Will saw to Tom's sadly neglected education. Joshua even had hopes of persuading his father at last to consider a wheeled chair now that his movement was so restricted; he had commissioned William Wingrove to make a special chair and he'd been helping Tom adapt it in the hope that his father wouldn't be so churlish as to reject the boy's handiwork.

'But that's not a proper job, mister. I – '

'Not a proper job? There's not many lads your age who could take on such a responsibility!' He was delighted to see the smile return to the boy's face again. 'Come on,' he said, heading back for the stables. 'I've an hour till the vestry meeting: if we can get those wheels set to rights, you could take my father for a ride today!'

The slopes above the village were eerily silent. The mists of the morning had melted away and a weak sun lit the silent and empty fields, fields that should have been echoing with the cries and shouts of men cutting the crop and stacking the sheaves, and the creak of wheels as they led the carts to the barns. But the sun had come too late: what little there was to harvest had already been cut and carted away. The curate had held a harvest feast for the sake of tradition, with a few raised pies made from the skinny rabbits trapped by the harvesters, but it had been a poor affair: after the second poor harvest in a row and with the prospect of a harsh winter ahead, no one had the heart for dancing and roistering.

An urgent meeting of the vestry had been called to discuss winter relief for out-of-work labourers and papermakers. Even those in work might have to turn to the parish for an extra dole; with so many men clamouring at the gates for work, many mill owners had cut the pay of the labourers yet again. In some mills, men would labour for as little as five shillings a week, though it was not near enough to feed a family.

Joshua would rather by far have been discussing adequate wages than charitable dole, but that was in the hands of the politicians; the rest of the well-meaning could only do their best in the face of the approaching winter. Not that all the vestrymen would be working for the interests of the poor: experience of earlier vestry meetings had taught him that much. The tradesmen would press for allowances to those who owed the shops money, the landlords would want a dole made to those who owed back rent, while the landed interest would, as ever, be pressing for all farmers to be forced to take a fixed number of labourers, whether or not they could use them or, indeed, afford them.

'I disremember when there's been such a bad harvest,' said Beck, the vestry clerk, pushing his battered leather hat back on his head and surveying the muddy fields above the village.

'My old dad, he says there's been nothin' like this since durin' the French wars,' agreed Fowler, his short legs pumping like pistons to keep up with the rest of them as they skirted the muddy village green.

'Ah. If we had to feed an army now, we'd be right hard put to do it!' As they reached the green, a skinny goose hissed and skittered towards Beck, and he sidestepped hurriedly out of its path. 'Talkin' of old soldiers, what news of old Sergeant Hunsford? They do say up on the common as the old feller's proper poorly.'

'I doubt he'll see the month out,' said the curate. 'His son says the bad yield was the last straw.'

'Ah. He has it as bad as the rest of us – I was up there last week and the grain's fair rattlin' round in the barns.'

'There was word goin' round the village – ' Joshua thought, for 'village' read 'alehouse' – 'that his son do intend to bring in the thrashin' machines. It'll be a sorry day for the labourers up top if he do.'

'The vestry must take prompt action,' said the curate. 'Last week they found five labourers dead under a hedge, just the other side of Uxbridge.' He swallowed hard. 'It said in *The Times* that there was nothing in their stomachs.'

'And if that can happen in harvest season, what about winter?' said Joshua, looking away hastily as the curate passed his hands over his eyes. The villagers were openly contemptuous of the man, calling him at the least a dandy-go-russet, for the old shabby coat he wore, and at worst a will-jill. Joshua thought the latter too hard; the curate was a well-meaning man doing his ineffectual best to take the place of an absentee vicar, who, like the squire, had as usual pleaded prior engagements.

'Winter a-gone were bad enough...' began Lunnon.

'And this one's a-goin' to be as bad or worse,' said Witney. 'I been watchin' the critturs, an' all the signs are there.' Witney, like his father and grandfather before him, could tell you things about the weather to come from the way the skeins of wild geese flew over the village in September, or the time of year the drakes on the Wye lost

84

their brighter markings, or even the way the ivy grew up the oaks. In living memory they had never been known to be wrong.

'That's one thing to be said for machines,' said Lowfield with an evil chuckle. 'They en't a charge on the poor rates, an' they're right cheap to keep through the winter.' But nobody else laughed.

'And it can't be disguised,' said the curate, 'that the threshing machines get at least the tenth part more out of the harvest than the men ever did.'

'Well, an't that just right fortunate for you, curate,' sneered Fowler. 'One tenth more. Thass just about enough to pay church tithes!'

'Aye!' exclaimed Kimble, another small farmer struggling to hold onto his land. 'All well and good for the labourers to demand more money, and I'd be a happy man if'n I could give it 'em, but what I says is this: whiles I has to give the tenth of me money to the parson and to the squire – which the neither of 'em even lives in the village no more! – and whiles the poor rates is as high as they are, how am I to find another penny to give 'em, eh?'

'Thass the truth,' agreed Fowler as they crossed Windsor Hill and approached the workhouse. 'We could talk ourselves hoarse about raisin' the men's money – but 'twould only work if the tithes are cut, and that rests with the church. The rest of us'll just have to didge along as best us can.'

'Machine threshed or hand threshed,' said Joshua, 'what corn there is this winter will be too costly for the poor.'

'True as we stand here,' said Witney, leaning against the rag wall that ran alongside the workhouse. As a Nonconformist, out here, before the meeting, was the only way he was going to get his views across. 'Only ones going to benefit from high prices is the landlords – half the villagers can't even afford bread any more. I was visiting old Widow Parslow only yesterday.' He shook his head sadly. 'Poor crittur, she's little enough docity left in her; I doubt she'll see the winter out. Her neighbour came round while I was there and I axed her to keep an eye to the old woman. Well, she took me into her own house, and she'd only a bit reasty bacon and a shiver of bread herself, with two little 'uns to feed, and a man that had been out on the rounds all day.'

'Same with all the day labourers. Where once my men had their bread and cheese and bacon, now they've only potatoes in their field bag. Like the veriest itinerant Irish labour.'

'Thass the problem, that is. If the big estates hadn't brought in the Irish labourers to put our men out of work ... Bloody Irish, workin' for pennies ...'

Joshua shook his head. The problem had been there for years; it was only recently, when poverty began to bite so hard, that scapegoats had been looked for, scapegoats such as the Irish labourer or the Scottish farm steward. No doubt some landowners *had* brought the Irish peasantry over to keep the day labourers in check and remind them that theirs was not the only labour available, but others, with estates in Ireland, had been motivated by thoughts of bettering the lot of the Irish peasants.

'We goin' to loppet out here all day?' Beck made a show of consulting the turnip watch the vestry had presented to him on his appointment as parish clerk. 'Churchwardens should be here by now. Let's get inside and have the business over and done.'

The portrait of the third King George looked benevolently down at them as Kattrin unfolded her letter. For once, thanks to Dickon, *she* was the source of information and excitement and they were all – even Lady Isabelle – eagerly waiting for her to read them the news from Liverpool.

Dickon had been sent away to the Cazelles in London, ostensibly to see how the Stationers' end of the paper market worked, but in reality to prepare for his betrothal to Sarah Cazelle, a colourless pudding of a girl. When Henry Cazelle was invited to attend the opening of the first passenger railway from Liverpool to Manchester, he had naturally included Dickon in the family party.

'You should reflect, Miss Katherine,' said Miss Gibbons, the governess, with a gloating smile, 'that if you had been less obstinate in your behaviour to young Mr Cazelle, you too might have been of the party.'

Much as she envied her brother the chance to be present at such an historic occasion, Kat rather thought the treat would have been outweighed by the necessity to be polite to Louis and his father.

'Never mind that,' said Drusilla. 'Who did Dickon meet?'

'I imagine that young Mr Revel was more interested in the scientific basis of the engine than in the hollowness of social intercourse,' said Miss Gibbons reprovingly.

'Quite possibly,' agreed Lady Isabelle. 'Men never do know what is really important.'

'And we must not forget that the Revels are in trade.' Philomena smothered a yawn behind her hand. 'Did you not say, Miss Katherine, that your father wished to bring the railways to the Wye Valley?'

Kat nodded. Her father had been thinking for some months of following Dickinson of Rickmansworth, who had greatly increased his output of paper since converting Apsley Mills to steam; the new railway could bring coal into the valley to fuel the steam engines, although Kat couldn't imagine why Wooburn needed steam when Clapton Mills had the best head of water in the valley.

'I dare say your brother was at some distance from the really interesting people,' continued Philomena, determined not to be impressed.

'You are quite mistaken, Philomena,' said Kat sweetly. 'The Cazelles rode directly behind the Prime Minister in the directors' carriage.'

Lady Isabelle was impressed. 'And who rode with Wellington?' she demanded.

'Mr Huskisson. He is the Member for Liverpool and a staunch supporter of the railways. Oh, and the chief engineer, Mr Stephenson.' She cleared her throat importantly and began to read.

> In spite of the grey sky there was an air of immense excitement among the hundred or so assembled in Liverpool. I had the pleasure of making my bow to Miss Fanny Kemble, who is *exactly* like Lawrence's portrait of her as Juliet. Imagine, if you will, three stagecoach bodies fused together to make one carriage, with seats placed back to back; the carriages are drawn by a little engine consisting of a boiler, a stove, a small platform, a bench and a barrel containing water enough for fifteen miles. The wheels are moved along two iron bands which form the rail road, by bright steel pistons propelled by steam. The more steam is applied to the pistons, the faster the wheels move; if one wishes to slow the motion, the steam is released through a safety valve. Joshua would have been fascinated.
>
> Huge crowds lined the rail roadway, shouting and waving as we flew past, at about ten miles an hour. So exhilarating, as if I had drunk too much champagne, although Miss Cazelle was in hysterics, for she had read that above a certain speed, humans cannot breathe. Such a waste to have taken her! Dear Kat, you would have loved it!
>
> We suffered an unfortunate accident, about which you may read in the newspapers shortly, when we had to take on more water for the boiler. Lord Wilton, Mr Huskisson and a number of other gentlemen descended from the carriage to observe; indeed, had it not been for Miss Cazelle's continuing hysterics, I would have joined them. An engine on the other line (Stephenson's *Rocket*) was parading up and down to show off its speed (much greater unladen, of course, as much as thirty miles an hour!). The

driver, unaware of the intruders on his line, came down on them like lightning. There were frantic cries of 'Clear the track!' and 'Stop the engine!' Most sprang back into the carriage, but poor deaf old Huskisson became quite bewildered. The oncoming engine struck him a terrible blow, knocking him down and crushing his leg. There was the most deathly silence, apart from the ghastly sounds of the impact and Mrs Huskisson's scream. Wellington was all for returning, but he was persuaded to continue, for fear the disappointment in Manchester might occasion rioting. The rest of the trip passed in considerable gloom.

There is great distress in Manchester, particularly among the weavers, so machinery of any sort is not welcomed. A thin and ragged weaver, together with his loom, had been set up above the crowds as a protest, and Wellington was greeted with hisses and groans – a striking contrast with our departure from Liverpool!

We dine this evening with Lord Wilton and I shall ask him for a frank for this, so that you, my dear Kat, may be the first person in the south to receive the report of the first passenger railway the world has ever known – and the first railway accident!

She paused in her reading, and there were gasps and horrified comments from the others. 'The next is just family business,' she said, 'but there is a postscript.'

PS Even as I was folding this, Lord Wilton called to inform us that Mr Huskisson has died of his injuries.

The news from Liverpool formed the whole topic of discussion over luncheon, with Drusilla and Miss Gibbons exclaiming over the horror of such a happening, while Lady Isabelle asserted that she had always known that no good would come of going against nature in such a way.

Unfortunately the rest of the day did not unfold so smoothly. It all started during the young ladies' afternoon instruction, with a chance remark about the papermakers, which led in turn to a pronouncement from Miss Gibbons about the ingratitude and general feckless attitude of the poor. Kat spoke up for them and Miss Gibbons, who was not accustomed to having her statements questioned, became quite agitated. In spite of Drusilla's attempts to pour oil on troubled waters, a heated argument ensued and Miss Gibbons succumbed to an attack of the vapours.

Lady Isabelle, exceeding displeased, read Kat a stern lecture on the error of her ways and then sent her back home alone in the Bosingham carriage, Miss Gibbons having pronounced herself quite unable to contemplate accompanying Miss Revel to her home; nothing, she said with a shudder, could be worse than a half-hour shut up in the family carriage with that young lady.

'I shall not tell your father that we have had this little contretemps,' said her ladyship gravely, 'as I am aware that he may – ah – react somewhat too severely. But I am appalled that you should set yourself up in defiance of Miss Gibbons in such an unbecoming manner. For a young lady to claim an understanding of politics is . . .' She shuddered. 'Miss Katherine, words fail me.'

'I didn't mean to be impertinent, ma'am, but she says that all the poor are idle and they're *not!*'

'I do not wish to discuss the matter any further!' snapped Lady Isabelle. 'I am aware that someone as unfortunately situated as yourself is in closer contact with the poor than is desirable, but what would Mr Cazelle say if he were to hear you going on in this manner?'

'Louis? He offered to accompany me when I took a basket of food to Margaret!'

'One naturally cares for one's retired retainers. And soup for the deserving poor, of course. I hope I do not need you, Miss Katherine, to teach me my duty in that matter!' she bristled. 'But that is as far as it should go.'

But soup lists were only for the deserving poor – and it was people like Lady Isabelle who decided who was deserving. Kat had had no end of lectures when she had taken soup to poor Rachel, struggling to bring up three sickly children by herself in one room in a miserable hovel round the back of the Pound. They had all been unanimous, even Dickon, who turned rather red about the ears and tried to change the subject, that Rachel was not one of the deserving poor. It seemed so unfair, when the girl had done her best to brighten up the little cottage, dividing the sleeping end off with a pretty dimity curtain and draping the bed in a brightly coloured shawl.

Kat scowled as the Bosingham carriage bumped across the humpbacked bridge by the church. The sun had lasted barely an hour and the heavy sky lay over the village once more, like a grubby featherbed. Peering out of the window she saw the grave-digger raising his hat to her and forced herself to smile back: it wasn't his fault that she was in such a foul temper.

She drew out the letter from her bag and read once more Dickon's enigmatic message.

We return to to London in a few days and Louis and I

89

hope to come to Clapton Revel soon after that. I shall try not to let him vex you too much. As to the question of a betrothal, I believe I may have a solution to offer, but more of that anon.

Meanwhile, I remain as ever affectionately yours,
Dickon.

It was all very well for Dickon to hint at a way out of the betrothal, she thought, but if he couldn't fight for himself, there was little chance that he could fight for her. He wouldn't try to talk her out of anything; he would just stand helplessly by while both their lives were ruined. But she had got her courage up once to run away – she knew she could do it again!

For the moment she was safe: Lady Isabelle took a more rigid view of court mourning than most, which meant that any public engagement was still out of the question. That protection could not last much longer, although Parliament had recently debated a new regency council, since King William was not in much better health than his late brother, and his niece, Alexandrina Victoria, was still so young. The new king seemed an amiable figure and Kat wished him no ill, but she could not help thinking that a second period of court mourning would be very useful.

She had hoped to talk the problem over with Joshua and ask his advice, but she had not seen him for weeks. Her father had recently forbidden her to go near the mill, telling her to her great indignation that Louis considered it undesirable, but it also seemed to her that Joshua was avoiding her: even Dickon's letter had been brought to her by Tom. She shivered as she remembered the day she had run away, the feel of his hands on her body through the velvet britches. As the carriage passed the old fingerpost at the edge of the green she had a sudden inspiration: she would stop the coach here on pretext of visiting old Margaret, and slip away instead to the Delahayes'.

Joshua stopped at the Red Cow on the way back from the vestry meeting. He was passing the time of day with Jem when they heard from a cottage on the far side of the green a wailing cry that turned swiftly to furious screams. Joshua saw Kat dashing towards it out of old Margaret's cottage and the old servant hobbling breathlessly in her wake, lace pillow clutched in her arms and the bobbins clacking about her knees. He was already running across the green with Jem hard on his heels.

The diminutive figure of Tess Branchett dominated the room. She stood in the middle of the floor, waving a cleaver over her head and screeching at her husband Adam, who, for all his bulk, was cowering on the earth floor at the foot of the rickety ladder that led to the sleeping loft. Thankfully there was no sign of their two small children, but Adam's dog leaped from one to the other, barking hysterically. Josh's heart skipped a beat as Kat, who had reached the cottage just ahead of him, stepped out of the shadows and interposed her slender body between the screaming fury and her intended victim.

'Put the cleaver down, Tess,' said Kat quietly, never taking her eyes off the woman's face even when the other villagers pushed in behind Joshua and crowded into the tiny, low-ceilinged room.

'I'll kill 'un!' screeched Tess, tears of fury spilling down her pale cheeks. 'He's left my Jackie in a spring trap! Left 'un to die!'

'No, I an't!' Adam protested weakly.

'If you put that down, Tess, we can talk,' said Kat.

The hand holding the cleaver never wavered. 'Too late for talk!' she cried. 'If he an't died in the spring trap, Lord Bos'nam ull send 'un to rot in Aylesbury gaol!'

'Tess, hearken to me now!' said Kat. 'I was talking to Lord Bosingham not an hour since, and there was naught amiss then.' There was a muttering behind her in the doorway and she gestured impatiently to the others to keep still.

'Put down the blade, Tess,' she repeated softly. 'Tell me what's happened.'

Tess brought her free hand up to dash the tears from her eyes, but when Adam made a tentative move to shuffle away from the bottom of the stair, his wife grasped the cleaver more firmly and waved it threateningly, inches from Kat's nose.

'This won't help Jack!' snapped Kat.

'An' what would you care about Jack – about us?' demanded Tess. 'The fine Miss Kattrin Revel!'

'You've mebbe forgot so soon, Tess, but I an't!' said Kat angrily, slipping into the local speech as if she had never left it, as if she and Tess were still sitting together in Mistress Savage's lace school. 'Time's a-wastin' for Jack while you're arlickin' about here, girl! If you're agreed, us'll go on up to Bos'nam House right now and codgel summat together with Lord Bos'nam. But I'm losin' my patience fast, an' if you don't put down that cleaver this *minute*, then I'm away back to Clapton Revel and Jack'll have to take his chance!'

A great shudder convulsed Tess's slight body and the hand holding the cleaver wavered. In one stride Joshua was between Tess and Kat. He caught the cleaver before it could do any damage, and with the other hand he jerked Kat from where she stood, far too close to the wicked blade, and clamped her to his side. She was trembling and it was all he could do not to take her in his arms and hold her tightly to him. It was only one of the men clearing his throat over by the door that recalled him to the present.

Tess was leaning weakly against the table, her dishevelled hair half hiding her pale, worn face. There was barely a year between her and Kat, but three pregnancies and a hard life had taken their toll on Tess Branchett. Unlike her neighbours, Tess had never been able to support her family when times were hard, for she was very unhandy; no one would pay a farthing for Tess's lace.

'What the devil is all this about?' demanded Joshua, in no mood to be sympathetic.

'Ask him!' cried Tess, tears chasing down her face once more as she pointed an accusing finger at her husband. 'Ask him where young Jackie is!'

'Well?'

Adam, white as a sheet after his second close encounter with danger in an hour, panted out the sorry tale. 'You knows I been out of Hedge Mill now nigh on four months, mister, since Spicer brought the machines in. I been on the tramp everywhere an' the answer's allus the same – no work goin'.' He shrugged. 'No work, no money, no food.'

'You could get help from the vestry.'

'I got me pride, mister,' said Adam, his face set.

'Pride don't feed a family,' muttered Tess.

Adam looked sadly at his wife. 'I knows it, lass.' He looked back at Joshua. 'So me an' Jackie an' the dog, us went up to Widmoor. Had to put meat on the table somehow.'

'Poaching?' Joshua inferred.

Adam's eyes swivelled to two pheasants lying in the shadows, their bright plumage glowing where the dim light of the tallow dip on the table caught them. 'You can call it that, mister. If your little 'uns was cryin' for the pain in their bellies, I do reckon you might call it summat less harsh.'

There was a murmur of agreement from the knot of men by the door.

'On our way home, us were, when the mists come down. An' Jackie slid in the mud and went tiddly-bump down the slope afore I could catch 'im. There were a rusty ol' trap at bottom of the batter and 'e caught fast by the foot in it.' He turned to his wife. 'I couldn't get 'un free,' he said pleadingly. 'God knows I tried.'

'If you tried so hard, how are you here and he an't?'

'Garrowby, the keeper, he come by with two o' Bos'nam's men,' said Branchett helplessly. 'I hid in the bushes.'

'The brave feller, you!' sneered Tess. 'Hid in the bushes, did yer? An' poor Jack in a spring trap! An' him not fourteen year old!'

'They got 'im out soon enough!' he protested. 'I couldn't stay, could I? They'll mebbe let 'im off, account of 'is years, but not me. They been out to get me fer a long time.'

Even in the good times Branchett was suspected of doing a little poaching on the side and it was partly on his account and as a disincentive to poaching that the vestry had recently proposed to adopt the Burnham rules and refuse parish relief to any man with a gun or a dog.

'Just a few birds as no one 'ull notice,' he said angrily. 'God put them critturs on earth to feed us all, not just Bos'nam and the parson!'

'But why on Bosingham's land?' Joshua frowned. 'Why not this side of the valley, where there aren't so many gamekeepers?'

'Frackle men take this side,' said Branchett. 'An' they're starvin' worse nor we are.'

'Besides, he has the right,' said Will Delahaye from the doorway. 'Widmoor was always open land.'

Joshua whirled around, cursing as his head collided with one of the low beams. He'd heard no tap of crutches; in the press of faces around the cottage door he could just make out Tom's face behind the wheeled chair. 'Father, please!'

'You can't blink the fact that that were allus open land,' agreed Jem.

'We're talking about natural justice here, not the grand lord's justice!' snapped Will. 'Adam's grandfather and *his* father before him . . .'

'That's right,' said Adam mulishly. 'Allus was open land. I'm entitled – '

'That was then, this is now!' interrupted Joshua. 'Now it's enclosed and none but Bosingham has rights there any more. And the law says Jack can be prosecuted for going on his land.'

'Where's the justice in that?' Adam turned to the villagers crowding round the doorway. 'I don't take a penny from the vestry – damned if I ever will! An't it better I take the odd rabbit for the pot, or birds for the spit, than take parish relief?'

'Except that parish relief is ordained by the law and poaching is forbidden by it!' said Joshua, struggling to keep his temper under control.

'It an't right,' said a voice from the street. 'Follow the Kent men, we should!'

'Aye. Burn a few ricks!' Adam, agreed. 'Thass what they was doin' in Kent when I was on the tramp round the Kent mills! We should work the labourin' men up to fight for their rights!'

There was a ragged cheer from the knot by the door.

93

'You club-head!' hissed Joshua. 'Men have been transported for less! You have such a longing for Botany Bay?'

'An' would us papermen be any worse off if they did transport us?' Adam came back at him. 'Can't be worse than here. Least there they feeds you!'

'That's right,' said Joshua icily. 'They feed *you*. But your wife and children stay here and starve.'

'You'd throw them on the parish, would you?' said Kat, crossing to stand in front of Adam Branchett, her hands on her hips as she looked up at him. 'Where's your proud boast then? "No, sir, I wouldn't take a penny off the parish – but they're feeding my wife and children back in England."'

'Learn to guard your tongue, man,' said Joshua. 'There's a world of difference between asking for a decent wage and incitement to riot.'

'Several oceans of difference!' said Kat, snatching Tess's shawl from the hook behind the door. 'But enough of grand speeches! Come, Tess! We'll go to Bosingham House to see what we can do for Jack.' Her gaze swept the men crowding the doorway. 'Are you going to stand there all night gawping?' she demanded.

The men drew swiftly aside for her to pass and she sailed through, head held high, every inch Miss Revel of Clapton Revel once more.

Outside in the shadows, waiting for the carriage to be summoned, Joshua drew Kat to one side. 'Go home, my dear,' he murmured. 'Let me deal with this.' His head ached villainously from the collision with the beam, but he knew how furious her father would be if he discovered that she had involved herself with the villagers. His mind, dazed, began to wander, and his thoughts were no longer of Jack, only of Kat and how beautiful she looked. 'Oh, my dear love,' he murmured, 'you know I would do anything for you...' Was it his imagination, or did she move in closer to him?

'Oh, Joshua,' she breathed – and then someone moved in the shadows and they sprang apart.

The coachman seemed to drive through every rut and dip that he could find; by the time they arrived at Bosingham House Joshua's vision was overlaid with a red mist and it was as much as he could do to stand straight. Kat, overriding the butler's protests, drew Tess into the house and summoned Lord Bosingham from his dinner. Watching her stand her ground in front of Bosingham, Godstowe and the gamekeeper, her eyes sparkling and her curls tumbling around her face, Joshua's heart swelled with pride. He determined that, once Tess and her brother had been delivered safe to the green, he would tell Kat of his love for her. He might be only the mill deputy in Revel's

94

mill, but Delahaye was a proud name and on his mother's side he was a Garnett of Shottenham.

Bosingham, a benevolent enough man, did not need much urging to let Jack off, once Joshua had guaranteed his future good behaviour. Only Garrowby, Bosingham's gamekeeper, opposed them, he'd waited a long time to get even with Adam Branchett.

Jack, his ankle dressed and bandaged, hobbled ahead on Tess's arm, but as Joshua and Kat took their leave, Lady Isabelle swept into the hall. She would not hear of Kat travelling without a chaperone and insisted on sending her companion with them, upon which Godstowe decided to join them too, ostensibly so that Miss Selby would not have to travel home alone – as if anyone had ever bothered themselves about the poor woman before! And Joshua had to sit between Tess and Miss Selby, listening to the silver-tongued diplomat laughing with Kat about her recent visit to London with Lady Isabelle, where it was clear that Godstowe had spent a great deal of time in their company, while his head ached and throbbed and the words he had wanted to say died in his throat.

# Part II

# Revolution

Ill fares the land, to hastening ills a prey,
Where wealth accumulates, and men decay...
Goldsmith. The Deserted Village.

# Chapter Six

The mare trotted along the rides, scattering the crisp brown leaves beneath her hooves. Joshua screwed up his eyes against the low November sun flickering through the branches and wished his head would not pound so.

It must have been the ale, he decided: poor stuff Sarney served at the Leathern Bottle and Joshua had drunk more of it than he had intended. Almost every night these past few weeks he had called in at a different alehouse in and around Wooburn to talk to the men and he didn't know how much longer he could keep it up. Though if his words last night had found their mark and he had succeeded in talking the Flackwell paper men out of their wild schemes, a thumping head would be a small price to pay.

A more immediate concern was how Revel would react when he saw his mill manager at Salt Hill.

'You'll leave the new machine for today, mister,' the mill owner had said that morning, to Joshua's great relief. Although they had had a small rag-cutting machine at one of the mills for some time, it did not seem to Joshua the most politic of times to be installing a new rag-grinder to take even more work from the local families. 'Take over here, mister,' said Revel over his shoulder. 'I'm off to Salt Hill.'

'The magistrate's meeting?'

'Haven't you heard? They're to make me a magistrate,' said Revel, preening himself. 'Just let Freeman Spicer try to lord it over me now!'

Revel on the bench, thought Joshua despairingly. God help any poor villager who came up before him!

'I knew about Spicer,' said Joshua. 'He had a great deal to say at the vestry meeting.' And if Revel was to be made magistrate, he should have been there too.

'Vestry meeting?' snorted Revel. 'Waste of time! With all the idlers you're supporting, the vestry will have run out of poor rates before Christmas tide! D'ye hear me, mister? Before Christmas tide! It's the magistrates' meetings where the decisions are made. The Marquis of Chandos himself wrote to invite me to attend,' he crowed.

And he had strutted out of the mill, peacock proud at the prospect of dining with the son and heir of the Duke of Buckingham, who owned more of this county – and of the counties around – than bore thinking of, and sent two Members to Parliament for the county as well as two each for the boroughs of Wycombe and Aylesbury.

Within minutes of Revel's departure in his racing curricle, however, a messenger had arrived from Lord Bosingham, requesting Joshua's attendance at the Salt Hill meeting in terms so strong as to amount to a command.

Not that Joshua was loth to go. As surely as the green leaves of summer had turned to gold and scarlet, so the unrest which had been simmering all summer in Kent, Sussex and Hampshire had turned to violence. By the end of October it had spilled into Oxfordshire and Berkshire and now it was beginning to close in, pincerlike, on Buckinghamshire. In towns as close as Wantage and Little Milton, the summer's threatening letters had given way to armed attacks on barns and threshing machines. The labourers, taking heart from the sight of a once complacent gentry quaking in their elegant shoes, were marching on market towns to voice their anger and resentment against low wages and machines. Sometimes they were led by 'captains' who claimed to have marched there at the head of a mob of Kentish men to spread the fight, but more often it was a local blacksmith or shoemaker, imbued with Radical beliefs, who stood spokesman for them when they confronted the aldermen and justices with complaints about cruel poorhouse overseers and absentee landlords.

Some of those who addressed the meetings demanded reform of the political system that allowed such suffering, often in terms that caused more cautious listeners to shudder and remember the worst excesses of the first French Revolution, but in the face of the appalling harvest and the onset of the winter cold, the most frequent cry of the crowds was: 'Give us bread!' The vote was their right, but it would not feed a starving family.

So far there had been only that one dangerous moment in Wooburn. Joshua shifted restlessly in the saddle and ran his fingers around a cravat which had suddenly grown too tight. He had kept away from Kat for weeks, resolving to put her out of his mind, but once he started thinking about her, he could think of nothing else. And today he needed a clear head.

Yet wasn't he deluding himself that he had anything to contribute? Who was going to listen to him? He was neither master nor man. True, by dint of falling between the two he was more able to see both

100

viewpoints, but standing between the powder and the spark, while it gave a clear view of both sides, was none the less a perilous position. Should the spark ever reach the powder barrel in spite of him, he'd be blown to kingdom come just as surely.

Wellington's ministers, reaping the harvest of years of suppression and neglect, had no idea how to deal with the discontented labourers, beyond alerting the militia and sandbagging the Tower of London, and there was no indication, for all their fine words, that whatever government would shortly replace Wellington's, now that the King had so unexpectedly dismissed his formidable prime minister, could deal with the problems any better. It was years since any government had concerned itself with the labouring classes. A few individuals, like Whitbread in the Commons and Winchilsea in the Lords, had tried again and again to bring in measures to help the poor and the hungry, but for most of the well-fed and prosperous, the sufferings of the poor were of less significance than trying to score points over one's Parliamentary rivals, and influence was worth exerting only to obtain valuable posts for relatives or cronies. The poor had no pressure to bring; it wasn't as though they even had a vote to sell.

During the wars against Napoleon there had been attempts to protect the poor and the powerless by tying wages in with the cost of bread, but those laws had been set aside when prices briefly fell after the advent of peace. In spite of later rises, they had never been renewed, although all office-holders, whose salaries had also been raised to meet the higher prices, had quietly absorbed those rises into their annual stipend. The labourer, forbidden by the Treason and Sedition Acts to speak out against such inequality, could only bite his tongue, tighten his belt yet another notch and, if he had children, pray that the winter would pass without another tragic procession to the churchyard.

Revel's face when Joshua strode into the panelled room at the Windmill Tavern was a sight to behold.

'Delahaye?' he exclaimed, turning abruptly away from one of the Burnham magistrates with whom he had been in deep and earnest conversation. 'What is it, mister?' he demanded, his eyes popping and his skin flushing darkly. 'What the deuce brings you away from your work? I gave you orders to – '

'I was invited to attend the meeting, sir,' said Joshua, uncomfortably conscious that all conversation had died and all heads were turning to the disturbance by the door.

'Invited to attend?' Revel echoed his words with a sneer. 'This is a meeting for magistrates, man!' He became aware that the room had fallen silent and lowered his voice. 'Landowners, clergy and magistrates,' he hissed. 'Why, the Marquis of Chandos himself – '

'Delahaye?' Unnoticed by Revel, Bosingham had come up behind him with a man in a uniform so heavily encrusted with gold braid that Joshua would not have been surprised to find that it was the Duke of Wellington himself. 'I think you know everyone here except the Marquis.'

'Pleased you could come,' said Chandos, favouring Joshua with a nod. He smoothed his luxuriant side whiskers with a well-manicured hand. 'Vital to have all interested parties here. Absolutely vital. Bosingham tells me you have some influence with the working men.'

'I do my best.'

'Excellent. Excellent.'

As Chandos and Bosingham moved on, Joshua could see the veins swelling on Revel's temples and prayed that for once his employer would keep his temper under control.

Everyone from the southern part of the county was there: Joshua knew most of the Beaconsfield and Wycombe men and there were a few from Burnham and Marlow he knew by sight. A surprising number were in military uniform, including a skeletal general, face as white as his hair, who looked far too frail to support the rows of medals that obscured the chest of his scarlet coat.

The Marquis passed from one group to another with a soothing and encouraging word for everyone, gravely assuring his listeners that he was most desirous of hearing the opinions and views of all those in positions of responsibility in the county, but Joshua was taken aback to hear from a Beaconsfield man that, as Lord Lieutenant, Chandos had been given carte blanche by the government to do whatever he felt necessary in the county to maintain peace.

A number of those present had, like Joshua, received letters from the elusive Captain Swing. Some had refused to take them seriously and simply thrown them away, but others were taking great delight in reading them out to anyone who would listen, curdling each other's blood with the threats they contained.

'Should be hanged, the lot of 'em,' said one man.

'We must not be too harsh,' argued a clergyman as they took their seats and the bottles began to pass around the table. 'There is, it must be admitted, a great deal of suffering among the poor – '

'And will be more,' agreed a farmer from Marlow. 'This will be a hard winter and I scarce think that the poor rates will suffice for – '

'Damn it, sir,' said the elderly general, 'what we need is a good war! Breeds independence of spirit, sir! None of this depending on others for handouts! Stap me, their grandfathers would have died before asking for alms the way these fellows do!'

102

'But their grandfathers had their cow, general,' said Joshua, as mildly as he could manage. 'And their rights of common and their own cottage – '

'Damned unhealthy places, most of those old cottages, y'know,' said the General sagely. 'Tumbledown.'

'I grant you, general, they were not ideal, but at least a cottager felt he had some sort of stake, some sort of belonging, and – '

'Why, I recall,' bellowed the General, overriding Joshua's words, 'back in ninety-three, or maybe ninety-four, old Milford's cottage up on the heath fell down one day.' He looked around the table, making sure that he had everyone's attention. 'Not a puff of wind about, just gave a sort of groan and keeled over: nothing but a heap of worm-eaten timber and a pile of thatch. We rode past and there was old Milford and Granny Milford and a gaggle of girls, all standing there looking at it with their mouths hangin' open. "Damn me," says Lord Frederick, "what's that?" And Sir Archibald...' The General could hardly finish the story for chuckling, his face growing quite pink as he was convulsed with mirth. '... Sir Archibald comes straight back with "Must be a cottage, old fellow. No one would build a haystack so untidily."' He slapped his thigh and roared with laughter, along with a number of the less sober at the table.

Joshua had a strong urge to take him by the bony throat and throttle him.

'Many of you will have read in the newspapers reports of outrages in Kent and Sussex,' said Chandos, calling them to order. 'Now you may think it won't happen here, but I assure you, gentlemen, it will come, and we must be prepared.'

There was an outburst of conversation as each man tried to convince the others that he had everything under control in his own village, or suggest that the neighbouring squire was letting matters run slack on his doorstep.

After a while Joshua realised that Chandos, seated impassively at the head of the table, was no longer leading the meeting, but leaving it to Charsley, the Wycombe coroner with whom Joshua had already exchanged sharp words over the burial of Tom's mother and sister, to keep the discussion flowing.

A Marlow farmer was holding forth. 'Of course, where the squire and the minister are there to give an example to the ignorant – '

'Take a place like Wooburn,' said Charsley, darting a sly look at Revel and Spicer. 'No one to give direction to the labouring classes but the mill owners. I heard there was someone in Wooburn spouting rebellion quite recently, but – you will find this hard to believe, gentlemen – I'm told no action was taken!'

'Just a little domestic upset,' drawled Bosingham, shooting a warning look at Joshua. 'Villager falling out with his wife. Mr Delahaye and I soon set all to rights. I can assure you, Charsley, there are no more problems in Wooburn than anywhere else.'

Joshua closed his eyes in relief when he realised that Bosingham had no intention of mentioning Kat's involvement. Time had given him a different perspective on that day and he realised now that Godstowe's presence had been providential. Kat was a rich man's daughter and he a humble wage-earner, however well-born his antecedents. The example of his own parent's ill-matched marriage, which had started in love and ended in tragedy, should have been lesson enough.

He heard Charsley talking about Branchett, and brought himself back to the present with a guilty start.

'I'm sure Miss Revel stands as an example to us all,' said the coroner maliciously. 'I hear that, like Delahaye, she showed a ready sympathy with the villagers. One might almost have confused her with the lady of the manor.'

Revel choked on his brandy. 'What the – '

Bosingham's hand was on the mill owner's arm and he whispered urgently in his ear. After a moment Revel reluctantly subsided, contenting himself with a look of the utmost malevolence directed at his mill manager.

'Come, Delahaye,' said Charsley, who had been watching the interchange with interest. 'We are told you have much influence with the men, so it is only right that we should hear from you.'

Joshua looked at the faces around the table, some concerned, but most smug and arrogant. It would be so easy to say what they all wanted to hear, but he could not let the villagers down. No one else could speak for them today but he.

He painted for them a vivid picture of the life of the paper-mill worker, speaking of the pride they took in their work and the constant struggle to feed a family even before the advent of the machines.

'In the villages I speak of, gentlemen, *our* villages which you will ride through on your way back to your homes, your firesides and your well-fed families, in these villages children will go to bed this night crying in pain for lack of food in their bellies.' His voice grew harsh. 'What must it feel like, gentlemen, to watch your children cry in hunger and know that you cannot feed them?'

He looked slowly round the table at each of them in turn.

'And yet it takes so little to make the difference between poverty and self-sufficiency.' And he told them of John Dafter, who in his leisure hours had built himself a cottage on a piece of waste where once there had been a pool, and how on the patch of garden he had

104

cleared, he had grown sufficient to feed a large family. 'Just land enough for a pig, a few fruit trees and a vegetable garden,' he said. 'And there he has brought up ten children without parochial aid. With a small parcel of land, so many, like Dafter, could take themselves off the parish rates next year. Give our labourers hope, gentlemen, and you will hear no more talk of rebellion.'

'Fine talking, Delahaye,' said one of the Marlow farmers. 'But land now will not give them food tomorrow.'

'It would give them hope,' repeated Joshua. 'But, yes, there would still be the need for charity and benevolence to see them through the coming winter.'

'What?' roared the General. 'Parish rates and more charity besides? Madness!'

'We send money to the victims of the St Petersburg fire and the Aleppo earthquake,' said Joshua, as calmly as he could. 'Gentlemen, that is most praiseworthy. But what of the men – and women and children – who are starving, sometimes on our own doorsteps?'

There was much clearing of throats, and mutterings of 'All very well, but...'

At his side one of the clergy drew out his handkerchief and blew his nose violently.

'We cannot be seen to be giving in to threats, sir!' said one of the Marlow men.

'You would not be giving in!' said Joshua, struggling to control himself. 'Most of our labourers are good men, loyal to their king and country. They just want a decent wage for their day's work: enough to stop their children starving! Surely that is not too much to ask?' He looked entreatingly at Chandos, but the Marquis looked away. 'For this year, I beg of you, spread your charity to your villagers – and the revolutionaries will stand alone.'

'But this talk of a base wage is so much nonsense! The market must fix the wages.'

Joshua turned a look of contempt on the speaker, a comfortable landowner. 'It is easy to talk of the market on eight thousand a year,' he said. 'Not so easy when your family is struggling to survive on sixpence a day!'

'You ought to be ashamed of yourself, Delahaye, stirring up the villagers to stand against their betters,' said Charsley. 'Wouldn't be surprised if you weren't a damned Jacobin yourself!' He turned to the Marquis. 'Only the other day, my lord, he demanded burial certificates for two out-of-parish paupers for whom we held no responsibility! No responsibility whatsoever. Why – '

'Gentlemen,' snapped the Marquis, 'this is not a time for settling old scores!' His whiskers bristled with indignation as he picked up one of the letters on the table. 'In Kent and Sussex there is open insurrection – arson and machine-breaking of the very worst kind, threats to life and property.' He picked up another. 'In Hampshire the rioters are on the point of taking control. We could see the whole of England in the hands of these rebels!'

'But my lord,' said one of the clergymen diffidently, 'could we not simply dismantle the machines for the moment and – '

'Weakness, sir! Fatal weakness!' cried Charsley. 'If the trouble spreads here – '

'Gentlemen, gentlemen!' Chandos shook his head sadly. 'It is no longer a question of *if* these outrages will spread to Buckinghamshire, but *when*. My honoured friend Lord Carrington has already experienced the worst kind of outrage on his Hampshire estates at Mayfield. And in Pit House, the scoundrels laid siege to a gentleman's home, *with his wife and children still within*!'

A collective shudder ran around the table. 'Hanging's too good for 'em!' cried one.

'Send in the army!' demanded another.

'The army is deployed in the cities,' said Chandos smoothly. 'Needless to say I have requested military support, but we cannot count on it.'

'We should never have disbanded our militia!' said one of the borough burgesses who had taken his turn as paymaster in the Southern Regiment of the Bucks Yeomanry and made himself a tidy fortune by it.

Chandos permitted himself a small smile. 'As you know, gentlemen, I have – at my own expense – continued to keep up the Mid-Buckinghamshire Regiment of Yeomanry at Stowe.' Murmurs of appreciation rippled around the table. 'I have today received permission to rebuild the southern and northern regiments,' Chandos continued. 'Windsor has raised a Forest Association, so that should cover our flank. I invite you, gentlemen, to subscribe to a fund for the protection of property, and to raise the regiments necessary to uphold the king's peace. Naturally you will also enrol your servants and tenants as special constables forthwith. I suggest there is no time to waste.'

Charsley glanced around the table at the eager faces. 'We are surely all agreed on the necessity – '

'I don't like it,' said a clergyman. 'I cannot think that matters will come to such a pass.'

'Matters are already come to such a pass in Hampshire that the Duke of Wellington himself is threatened,' said Chandos, producing his trump card.

'Threatened? The victor of Waterloo?'

'The head of His Majesty's Government? Disgraceful!'

Soon to be the head of His Majesty's Opposition, thought Joshua. But his decisions would still have to be carried out until a new leader took over the reins.

'I pass on Wellington's communication for your consideration, gentlemen.' The Marquis picked up the last of the papers in front of him and read it out.

> I advise all landowners and magistrates to put themselves on horseback, each at the head of his own servants and retainers, grooms, huntsmen and gamekeepers, armed with horsewhips, pistols, fowling pieces, whatever you may get, and to attack in concert, or singly, these mobs, disperse them, and take and confine those who cannot escape.

He looked around the table with a steady gaze. 'My father already has this under way in his Hampshire estates,' he said. 'Gentlemen, I put it to you that Buckingham *must* follow Hampshire's example.'

The vote was a foregone conclusion. Joshua had gambled and lost.

The late-November wind whipped the last of the dead leaves from the chestnut trees and laid them in a mourning veil across the village green, turning it as sere and dark as the fields and hills around. The lacemakers had disappeared from their doorways, village housewives no longer lingered to pass the time of day with their neighbour and the life of the community began to fragment as each family turned in on itself.

Few could spare more than a thought for the poor souls passing through who had failed to find work for the winter at the hiring fairs. One night in the workhouse was all that there was for those without Wooburn settlement certificates; the kind-hearted found it harrowing to travel out of the village, whether to Wycombe or Beaconsfield, Marlow or Maidenhead, for at every turn there were emaciated men, women, sometimes whole families, pleading for food.

As a cold and hungry winter stared them in the face, all that mattered to the villagers of Wooburn was to keep wood in the hearth and something in the pot without running up against the squire's gamekeeper or woodman, and finding themselves wintering in Aylesbury gaol.

On St Cattern's Day, 25 November, the Delahayes sent a sack of flour around the village so that even the poorest lacemakers could make Cattern cakes in honour of their patron saint. Although unrest and discontentment simmered beneath the surface in Wooburn, the prentice mill boys still carved lace bobbins for their sweethearts, as village boys had done for centuries, and as the lace girls stuck the cross-shaped bobbin winders with pieces of apple and candle and hung them from beams to bob for blindfold, and set the candles on the high candlestick for the 'Jack be nimble' jumping games, the village seemed a world away from talk of revolution. When St Cattern's Day passed without incident, the danger seemed to all but the most pessimistic to have passed.

The next day, as Joshua was working on a new guard he had devised for the heavy guillotine blade on the paper-cutter, he was struck by a belated recollection: St Cattern's Day was also Kat and Dickon's birthday. And for the first time since he had known them, he had forgotten.

He found it hard to believe that his brain had failed to make the connection. Caught up though he was with concern about the unrest, his every spare waking moment – and much of his sleep – was filled with thoughts of Kat and in particular the recollection of Kat in his arms in the Branchetts' cottage. Even now, lying on his back beneath the machine with the oil and the dust and the acrid smell of wet paper all around him, he had only to close his eyes to recall the feel of her warm body crushed against his, and to breathe once more the fresh scent of her hair.

He rolled out from under the machine and leaped to his feet, cursing as he caught the side of his head on the dandy roll. Snatching up a rag, he called Bedford over and showed him what still needed to be done. 'Test out the guard yourself before you let any of the lads use it,' he warned, wiping the oil from his hands. There had been no injuries to the apprentices in his time as manager, and he had no intention of losing that distinction, a rare one among the surrounding mills where apprentice children all too frequently had fingers and sometimes arms torn off in the machinery. 'I'll be up at the house if anyone needs me.'

As he crossed the sluice he looked up at the house, hoping to catch a glimpse of Kattrin, whom he had not seen for weeks. Like many of his neighbours, Revel had had barred grilles fitted at all the windows. Probably bars on the inside of the inner doors as well, and a hiding place behind the panelling to hide his strongbox. Revel, clearly, did not believe that the trouble had passed. With a frown Joshua straightened his cuffs and cravat and wondered what sort of welcome he would receive at Clapton Revel. Kat would surely excuse his lapse of memory under the circumstances, but whether he got to see her at all would depend on whether her father was at home. Revel had been in a black mood ever since the Burnham meeting; he had waited for years to be accepted by the local gentry, assiduously cultivating Bosingham and his connections, and he must have thought his moment of triumph had come with the invitation from Chandos. With hindsight Joshua could understand how the gilt must have been tarnished when his deputy walked into the room.

To his surprise it was Mary, and not one of the housemaids, who opened the door to him. 'You can't see Miss Kattrin,' she said, before he could announce his errand.

'Miss Thornton?' said Joshua.

Mary shook her head. 'She an't seein' no one,' she said, with a cold smile on her thin lips. 'Nor Miss Kattrin. Master's orders.'

'She's not ill, is she?' he asked in alarm. It was, after all, the first time she had failed to come to the mill to give pennies to the apprentices on her birthday.

'No,' said Mary curtly. 'No. She an't ill.'

Joshua ran his fingers through his hair, wondering whether to risk antagonising Revel by forcing the issue. Why risk it? asked a small voice at the back of his mind. He could not compete with Louis Cazelle and his business dynasty, even less with Lord Godstowe, at present on a diplomatic mission to the new French government. And yet, in spite of his resolution, he still felt a desperate need to see Kat.

Before he could speak, Bedford hailed him from the mill. 'There's a message come for you from Wycombe, mister,' he panted, hurrying across the sluice. 'Lord Bosingham begs your attendance at the Guildhall meeting – there's trouble.'

He had no choice but to go.

The sound of the doors slamming roused her, but it was too painful to move. She lay limp and motionless on the bed. The tears of rage and despair that had washed streaks across her bruised and swollen cheeks and stung her split lips with their salt had long since ceased to fall.

She had lost track of the number of days since her father and Mary had locked her in her room for refusing to sign the marriage contract. Was it yesterday or the day before that she had put the heavy new iron bar across the inside of the door to lock *them* out? She could no longer remember, only that it was the day they had told her that Joshua had been dismissed and had gone up north to the mills.

Barring the door on her side had stopped the beatings and the threats, but it had also put an end to the bread and water. She supposed she would starve to death, but she no longer cared.

The market-day crowds drew hurriedly aside as the foam-flecked horse galloped down the High Street, its rider crouched low over the mare's neck; sharp hooves struck sparks from the cobbles but neither horse nor rider showed any sign of slowing. Housewives with laden baskets, idle loungers chewing on straws and farmers in from the surrounding villages for the market pushed back against each other to evade the plunging hooves.

Outside the Guildhall where the justices of the Desborough Hundred had assembled to appoint a defence committee for the district, a seething mob of men was shouting and waving sticks. Joshua slid reluctantly from the saddle. It took very little to tip a mob into violence and he dared not risk a kick from his horse being the catalyst.

'Are they still in there, Jackman?' he asked the one-eyed crippled pedlar. A foolish question, for the shouting and crashing emanating from the upstairs room resembled no other Guildhall meeting he'd ever experienced.

'Aye, Mr Delahaye,' said the old soldier, scuttling across to his side, his tray of bootlaces and pins clutched precariously under his one arm.

'You best git in there, Mr Joshua,' said a Holtspur farmer, unclamping his stained teeth from the stem of his pipe. 'Someone did ought to knock some sense into them.'

'I'll do my best,' said Joshua grimly. 'You'll mind my horse for me?'

'Ah.' He grasped the reins in a leathery hand. 'It's the papermen as lost their places, I hear. They do say there were three hundred on the Rye this mornin'.'

Damnation! thought Joshua. If only he had gone to Sarney's alehouse last night, as he had intended, he would have heard about it.

A press of men crashed down the stairs from the Guildhall Chamber and were greeted with cries and cheers as the crowd below parted reluctantly to let them through; some on the fringes ebbed towards the churchyard, others backed away into the market, causing booths and stalls to sway dangerously. That part of the crowd hemmed in, like Joshua, beneath the Guildhall, was not so fortunate; only a very few on the edge were able to slide away into the Shambles but most were pressed so tightly against one another that they could not move. The situation was beginning to look hopeless until the farmer's son Dick, hovering at Joshua's elbow, saw a small gap and began to wriggle through, drawing Joshua in his wake and admonishing a burly farmer in his path to 'Let Mr Delahaye through there!'

'I wish I knew what the devil had been happening up there,' said Joshua, as Dick drew him down a back alleyway and through a door he hadn't seen before.

'Prime fun, mister, it were!' said Dick, darting a look up at him. 'Me an' Harry, we heard as how there was goin' t'be a kick-up. Harry Hailey – his uncle's high constable, see. So while old Hailey weren't

110

lookin', we slipped up the back way. Better nor a play, it were!' he said, growing excited with the telling. 'Old Lord Carrin'ton's got hisself voted in at head of Aldermen's Committee, see, and so Dr Scobell, he goes to give 'un the chair. No sooner does Carrin'ton go to sit down than all the papermen comes rushin' up the stairs an' one of the Wycombe men ups and shouts at 'un, "Get outa the chair, you scoundrel! Pay yer election bills!" Harry says he still owes 'em, see, from when 'is son got elected fer the county. Well, that were like a signal, an' some o' the papermen, they picks up the chairs an' starts wavin' 'em round their 'eads. An' the old Abbot, 'e goes paler than 'e were before, an' that were pretty pale! But then Harry's uncle sees us. Belted us fer bein' there,' said Dick glumly as they emerged into the chaos at the foot of the Guildhall stairs, which were creaking ominously under the weight of the men on them. But as he took the first step he was almost knocked off his feet by a burly figure.

'Get outa my way,' snarled the man, shaking his fist. 'Oh, sorry, mister. Didn't see 'twas you.'

'In God's name, what are you doing here, Davey?' demanded Joshua. The labourer had spent three months in Aylesbury gaol the previous winter for stealing firewood; it would go hard against him if he was caught up in more trouble.

'We're only fightin' for our rights, mister,' said Davey angrily.

Joshua shook his head. 'Go home, Davey,' he urged.

'Not till we gets our twelve shillin' a week!'

'Twelve shillin' a week!' shouted the man behind him, and the refrain was taken up by the others pouring down the stairs.

Joshua put his head down and fought his way up the stairs against the stream of labourers coming down.

The chamber was in utter chaos, with broken chairs and tables everywhere he looked. Corralled in one corner were the aldermen and burgesses; dazed and pale-faced with shock they watched the last of the papermen depart. One turned in the doorway and threw a broken chair at a window. Glass tinkled down on the wooden floor. Beside the splintered remnants of the mayoral chair, Scobell intoned the last few paragraphs of the Riot Act to the empty air.

'Delahaye!' Bosingham appeared at his elbow, his face grey and strained. 'Thank God you're here!'

'I wish I had been here sooner,' said Joshua, pushing his hair out of his eyes and looking at the haze of dust that hung over the scene of destruction.

'Try to talk some sense into them, will you? They won't listen to me. I held Scobell off from reading the Riot Act as long as I could.'

'Mr Delahaye. M'lord.' The High Constable picked his way through the wreckage to their side. 'A bad day, gentlemen.'

'Brace up, man! They are dispersing at last.'

'Don't you believe it, m'lord. Off to look for more trouble, they are. Likely a bit of machine-breaking, for some of 'em has hammers and the like. Now, if you'll excuse me, I'll have to be off after 'em.'

'But you haven't enough men,' Bosingham protested. 'You've barely a handful of constables and – '

'And not all o' them sure to stay, for all they swore in voluntary. Thass true. But I shall have to go after 'em all the same, m'lord,' said Hailey doggedly. 'Thass my duty, see.' He straightened the lapels of his uniform and strode to the stairs, and the sound of his highly polished boots crunching on the splinters of wood echoed around the hall.

'Hell and damnation!' swore Bosingham. 'Machine-breaking!' He turned to Joshua with a frown. 'Do you think – '

'I think I had better go with Hailey,' said Joshua.

'What can you do?'

He shrugged. 'Perhaps nothing. But I have to try.'

'Dare say you're right, m'dear fellow.' He patted Joshua on the shoulder. 'Yes. Yes. Better see what you can do.'

Of the magistrates, only Dr Scobell had pulled himself together sufficiently to accompany Hailey and his pitifully small band of constables, although what use the cleric would be, apart from reading the Riot Act yet again, was not clear. Still, one had to admire the man's tenacity.

'See if you can shake your men out of this destruction, Delahaye,' said Bosingham, bidding him an anxious farewell at the top of the stairs, 'or we shall have a blood bath.'

*My* men? thought Joshua, as he hurried down the stairs to find his horse. It would be easier if they were his men, but he had no influence with the Wycombe men.

After a few false scents the band of riders caught up with the crowd at Ash Mill. The men, a number of them carrying heavy stone-breaking hammers from their time on parish piecework, had gathered on the green between the mill and the neighbouring farmyard. There was no sign of John or Joseph Lane, the owners, but on the other side of the millstream, in front of the mill, the foreman and a group of Ash Mill papermen, armed with metal staves, watched grimly as the crowd dragged a wagon out of the farm buildings as a makeshift platform and a diminutive fellow with a patch over one eye began to whip the crowd up to fever pitch. Local farmers and villagers, hearing the shouting, began to drift across to see what was

112

happening, until there were almost as many behind the wagon as there were in front.

'Who the devil is he?' Joshua asked Hailey.

'Itinerant barber, so they say. He's the one as wound 'em up to wreck the Guildhall. Got a voice like a squeaking wheel.' The High Constable's words were lost as the crowd began to howl, 'Down with the tithes!', 'Burn the mill!' and 'Reform! Now!'

'Come, Hailey,' said Scobell, edging his roan alongside them. 'You must call on the mob to disperse.'

'Call on them, sir? Aye, I can do that.' He looked round at the handful of constables. 'But we surely an't got enough men to make 'em, no matter how many heads get broke.'

The minister was persuaded to allow five minutes to see whether the men could be talked out of their proposed violence. If they still failed to disperse, the law would demand that he read the Riot Act. But before Joshua could even begin to make his way through to the platform, one of Hailey's constables whispered that the militia was on its way.

'I never sent for 'em, sir!' Hailey protested. 'Veary reckons they was on their way back from manoeuvres over Hounslow way. Someone in Wycombe must have sent them after us.'

Joshua scanned the crowd in desperation. Most of them were hard-working journeymen who had been thrown out when the machines were installed, although he recognised a handful of troublemakers among them. If he could but speak to them man to man he might be able to stop the destruction, but if the rumour of the militia was true, there was no time for such a leisurely approach.

The trouble with the militia was that they were pretty well independent of any control, civil or military; having been disbanded some years ago, the three Buckinghamshire Yeomanry regiments were no longer on government pay, and the Second had survived only because the men and officers were paid by the Marquis of Chandos. The men were raised from tenants of the large landowners and the few remaining independent farmers, while the fourteen regimental office holders, including the quartermaster, paymaster and adjutants, were the whole Corporation of Buckingham Town, whose fourteen votes formed the entire electorate and regularly gave Chandos's father, the Duke, the Parliamentary member of his choice. The Buckinghamshire Yeomanry Cavalry was effectively the Marquis of Chandos's private army, answerable to no one but Chandos.

There was the briefest of lulls as the speaker paused for breath and Joshua imagined he could hear in the distance the drumming of hoofbeats. Without further thought he leaped out of the saddle, handed his reins to Hailey and plunged into the crowds.

Five minutes. Scarcely time enough to make his way through to the front, let alone talk the men into going home. He was almost halfway to the wagon when Farmer Grimmond caught his arm. 'You an't a-goin' to spoil the fun, are you, Mr Delahaye?' he said with a chuckle. 'Let 'em crack a few heads, say I. We an't had this much fun in Wycombe since I don't know when!'

Over the hubbub of the crowd Joshua could hear the jingle of harness. A whisper ran through the crowd behind him: 'The militia! Damn them! They've sent for the militia!'

Joshua turned on Grimmond with an angry snarl. 'Don't you hear the militia, you fool? Think you *they* will stop at a few cracked heads?'

Grimmond looked over his shoulder and blanched as he saw over the heads behind him the shakos of the soldiers whose arrival at the edge of the green had effectively funnelled papermen and onlookers alike into a trap from which there was no escape. The officer, a slim young man who scarcely looked old enough for his wispy moustaches, formed his soldiers into two ragged lines and gave the order to dismount.

A group of apprentices, most of them no more than fourteen or fifteen, had followed the crowd out from the Guildhall in the hope of a little excitement to brighten their workaday lives, and they greeted the new arrivals with catcalls, calling out, 'Firtht rank dith-*mount*!' to each other in cruel mockery of the lieutenant's lisp. One or two of the troopers smiled broadly at each other, and the young officer flushed angrily.

'It's the bloody Second!' yelled the blacksmith's apprentice, enjoying the officer's discomfiture.

'They stoned 'em at Aylesb'ry!' shouted another lad. 'We an't goin' ter let 'em get away with less than Aylesb'ry give 'em, be we?'

One or two boys began to prise cobbles from the yard, but the officer had no intention of being humiliated as his colonel had been outside the George in Aylesbury the previous week. On his command the rear rank of troopers trained their muskets on the apprentice boys, who abruptly lost interest in the texture of the cobbles and, putting their hands back in their pockets, turned their faces to the sky and whistled nonchalantly. The more thoughtful among them began to melt back into the crowd. Not a moment too soon, for the sergeant barked out another order and the air around the green rippled with the swish of metal on metal as the front ranks, swords drawn, began to close in.

'God help us!' Grimmond gulped. He turned to the men standing between Joshua and the wagon. 'Clear the way for Mr Delahaye!' he bellowed.'You there! Let him pass!'

114

But Grimmond's belated intervention served only to draw attention to Joshua and a burly trooper in the uniform of the Newport Pagnell Cavalry caught him and swung him towards a grizzled sergeant with a levelled musket. The dying sun glinted off the bayonet aimed rock-steady at Joshua's heart.

The militia captain picked his way carefully between the swords and bayonets until he reached his sergeant. 'And where do you imagine you are going, my good man?' he drawled.

Joshua tried to explain his purpose, but as the apprentices, scenting a new entertainment, were at the same time shouting enthusiastically for him to be allowed to pass, it was impossible for the young officer to hear one word in three of what Joshua had to say.

'He'll likely quieten 'em down,' said Grimmond, eager to make amends. 'Send 'em all home with their ears pinned back.'

The officer looked at Grimmond as if he had just been swept out of a stable. 'Get out of my way, man,' he snapped.

'You 'eard what the hofficer said!' barked the sergeant. 'Get out of the hofficer's way! All of yer,' he shouted, turning on the apprentices, 'or yer'll all find yerselves in Aylesbury gaol. And there'll be more than just yer ears pinned back!'

Another soldier placed his bayonet against Grimmond's chest and, baring his teeth in a parody of a smile, prodded gently at his greatcoat, just below the top button. Grimmond turned deathly pale and backed away as rapidly as the crowd would allow, stammering incoherently that he meant no offence, not in the least. Joshua, to his fury, found himself laid hold of by three thickset troopers and unceremoniously thrown to one side.

He swore as he cracked his shoulder against the flint wall and struggled to keep his feet. The apprentices, balked of their opportunity to rile the soldiers, were quick to spot a second chance. Before either Joshua or the soldiers knew what was happening, they'd dragged him into the crowd and, twisting this way and that, thrust him to the front. 'Let's hear Mr Delahaye!' called one of the apprentices as he was whirled swiftly from hand to hand. 'Aye! Way for Mr Delahaye!' The rest of the crowd took up the cry.

He arrived breathlessly at the foot of the wagon; his heart was thumping and, in spite of the cold, he was sweating in every crease of his body. Behind him he could hear Scobell's voice reading the Riot Act, the sonorous tones, redolent of the pulpit, contrasting strangely with the high-pitched squeaking of the speaker on the wagon. How long did it take to read the Riot Act? Five minutes? Ten? He didn't know. The soldiers would have to hold off until Scobell had finished, but no longer.

He took a deep breath and hauled himself up onto one of the

wagon shafts, clamped his hand over the ranter's mouth and dragged him down from the wagon before anyone realised what was happening.

There was a brief moment of shocked silence: even Scobell ceased his reading of the Riot Act.

'It's Mr Delahaye!' cried one of the men, swinging a hammer high above his head.

'Let 'un go, mister,' shouted another, as the two men wrestled on the floor. 'Come to talk to us, he has. Which is more'n anyone else is willin' to.'

'He's had his say,' panted Joshua, rising to his feet with his arm around the speaker's throat and struggling to avoid the kicks and punches that the little man was aiming at him. 'Now someone else is going to take the platform!'

As all eyes swivelled to watch the mêlée around the wagon, on-lookers and hangers-on at the rear took the opportunity to slip away. Daniels, one of the Wooburn men, who had lost his two young children soon after being put out of his work at Snakeley Mill, was the first to find his voice again. 'Let's hear what Mr Delahaye has to say!' he shouted, and a host of voices echoed his call.

But others, still unaware of the arrival of the soldiers, had no intention of abandoning their planned attack on Lane's mill. 'An't we heard enough from the masters?' demanded Dandridge, smashing his fist down on the wagon. 'All they understands is force!'

'We an't here to talk!' shouted another, a stranger to Joshua. 'We're here to smash the machines as has robbed us of our work!'

'I say we give 'un a hearing!' shouted East. 'Allus been a fair man, has Mr Delahaye!' And although one or two of them followed Dandridge's example and returned to hurling insults at the mill workers, the majority clamoured to hear what Joshua had to say.

'Put 'un up on the wagon an' let's hear 'un!' they shouted, and Joshua, reluctantly relinquishing his hold on the rebel barber, found himself hoisted up on the platform.

'You all know me,' he began, 'and you'll know I have your best interests at heart. There's a better way to solve – '

He broke off as the two men who had climbed up on the wagon with him dropped swiftly to the ground. There was a deathly hush, followed by a sharp gasp from the crowd beyond the wagon.

'Ta-ake aim!' came the captain's voice from the back of the crowd. In the silence Joshua heard the sound of a musket hammer being cocked and his heart leaped into his throat and cut off his breath.

'Hold your fire!' bellowed Hailey, and as he spurred his horse towards the soldiers, Joshua breathed again.

'Damn you, sir, will you defy me?' demanded the militia captain, waving his sword at the High Constable. 'I'll have you in Aylesbury gaol!'

Bosingham, who had arrived somewhat belatedly, turned his horse in front of the militiamen. 'In the name of the justices I forbid you to fire!' he cried, his furious tones rising above the crowd and carrying to the far side of the green. 'Sir Thomas – call off your hounds, sir, this instant! You will not lay hands on Mr Delahaye!'

In the face of authority – and one, moreover, who had known him since he was in short coats – Sir Thomas reluctantly ordered his men to halt.

'If you're to arrest anyone for this disgraceful mêlée,' said Bosingham, 'then look to that damned rebellious barber!' But the undersized demagogue, freed of Joshua's restraining hand and realising that he had lost the crowd, had fled.

What he said to the men that day Joshua could never remember, but the arrival of the cavalry had robbed even the boldest of any hope of destroying the Ash Mill machines. To those who had allowed themselves to be swept along by the mob, returning home with a whole skin seemed suddenly a most desirous prospect.

'We could go home, sir, and we would willingly,' said Fisher, 'but that won't change the fact that we're starvin', sir. Us an' our families.' He turned to the magistrates. 'We an't wantin' trouble, masters,' he said pleadingly. 'All we wants is a good day's work, sirs, an' a good day's wage for it.'

'We wants twelve shillin' a week!' shouted another.

'An' us'll 'ave it, too!' went up the cry. 'An' no more machines!'

'Quite! Quite!' said Scobell hastily. 'But this is no way to go about it! Write it down, man, write it down!'

Joshua rolled his eyes in despair. Many in the crowd could not even read, and not one could draw up a petition.

The cries of protest went up. 'Why can't yer talk to us now?' and 'It's *our* livelihood! Are they to settle it?'

'Why won't they promise us a decent wage?' shouted another.

'Why did Scobell go and call in the cavalry?'

'Aye. An' why have they turned the soldiers on us?'

Joshua realised despairingly that he was losing them. 'No one called the soldiers in, I promise you.'

'Ho, yes? Jest a-passin' through, was they?'

'So I believe,' said Joshua mildly. 'But they won't go away while you're threatening the mill. Why don't you go home and we'll talk this out?'

'Who'll talk to us?' sneered Hancock. 'Who cares what we think?'

'Aye. Who cares if we starve?'

117

'I'll talk to you,' said Joshua. 'And represent your case to the masters, if you are willing.'

'We trusts you, sir,' said East.

'Aye. You'll speak fair for us with the masters!' cried another.

Hurrying back and forth between the men and the magistrates, he realised grimly that with his rash promise to represent the men to the masters he'd put himself squarely in the firing line where he could end up pleasing nobody.

For a while the promise that the papermen would disperse if the militia withdrew seemed fated to founder, as neither Hailey nor Scobell was eager to take responsibility, and Bosingham was out of his jurisdiction, but in the event Sir Thomas was only too pleased to be asked to leave. For a brief moment after his arrival he had had visions of himself as the hero of the hour, sending dispatches post-haste to Wellington explaining how he had put down a bloody uprising, but the moment had swiftly passed and in the grey light at the end of the day the rebellious peasantry were revealed to be nothing more than a shambling and ragged crowd of pinch-faced men, half of them scarcely more than boys. And the most rebellious upstart, the one who had made such a fool of him in front of his own men, was now hurrying back and forth between the magistrates and the mob, apparently the man of the hour. Sir Thomas decided to gather the shreds of his dignity around him and leave before he was dismissed.

'My lord, I have no more time to waste,' he said. 'Having diverted my company here in support of the magistrates – '

'Pity you lost that damned agitator,' said Bosingham brutally.

Sir Thomas drew himself up in his saddle. 'With your leave, sir, I will take my men – '

'Yes, yes,' said Bosingham impatiently, peering through the dusk to see how Joshua was faring with the crowd. 'Give you good day, Sir Thomas. My regards to your father.'

'You are making a serious mistake, my lord,' snapped the Captain. 'The whole of Berkshire and Hampshire in the hands of the rebels and – '

'What?' Scobell was appalled.

'The workhouses at Selborne and Headley were levelled to the ground, I hear, and the overseer carried out of the parish in the dung cart. Were you not aware of it, sir?' he said with mock solicitude. 'One can only hope that you have not, by your leniency here today, brought Buckingham to the same state of open rebellion.' He favoured Bosingham with an infinitesimal bow. 'Rest assured, sir, I shall inform Chandos that I withdrew on your orders.'

Once the soldiers had left, the men began to disperse. The rage had gone out of the mob and most were only too willing to return home to anxious wives and families. Hailey waited until most of the mob had moved off before he headed back to Wycombe. 'For I'll need to swear in some more constables, Mr Delahaye, as many as I can lay hands on. God knows I wishes you well in all your dealin's. But I knows the mill owners too. So I'll swear me in two hundred constables, and send for a load of staves, sir, just in case.'

# Chapter Seven

'So you've deigned to show your face, have you, mister?' Revel snarled, as Joshua came through from the salle late on Friday evening. He reached behind him for a leather bag which he set on the desk between them. 'There's your sack,' he said, baring his teeth in an evil smile.

Joshua found his voice again. 'I've only been away half a day! And Lord Bosingham himself asked me to – '

'The devil take Bosingham!' snapped Revel. 'I don't tell him how to run his estates; damned if he'll tell me how to run my mills! Now I'll thank you to take yourself off my premises, mister.'

Shaking with suppressed anger Joshua reached for the leather bag and his dark eyebrows snapped together as it swung loose from his grip. 'But there's not a half of my tools in here!' he said.

'I'm keeping the rest – and this month's wages – to make up for all the time you've been spending running round with those damned rebels.'

'You have no right to keep my tools!' he protested hotly.

'Then take me to court,' said Revel with a sneer. 'Now you may get off my premises, mister, as soon as you like, or I'll have the men see you off.'

Joshua was aware how much that would damage his cause. If he hoped to avert bloodshed, the perception the men had of his standing was far more important than money or tools; much as it went against the grain, he would have to cut his losses and depart with some dignity.

He hesitated a moment by the sluices, then turned towards the house, but before he could reach the little bridge Revel erupted from between the drying houses. 'Where do you think you're going?' he demanded.

'To take my leave of – Miss Thornton.'

'She's in London!' Revel glared at him. 'You have nothing to say to her, nor to any member of my family. So get out! You set foot on my land again and I'll have you arrested for trespass.'

For the next forty-eight hours Joshua barely saw his bed. Every waking hour was spent making the rounds between the employers and the labourers.

'You would have my costly machines lying idle the whole winter?' demanded one millmaster. 'Are you all about in your head, man? Would you have me bankrupt and my mill idle like Snakeley's?'

'If you would consent to it for a few weeks? Just until the present crisis blows over?'

'As it surely already has!' said the mill owner, leaning back in his chair and lacing his fingers complacently across his ample stomach. 'They tell me you and Hailey sorted it all out yesterday, sent that damned agitator out of town with a flea in his ear. Pity you didn't lock the fellow up, though,' he said, helping himself to a generous pinch of snuff. 'We can do without the likes of him, stirring up the men. The villagers were peaceful enough before...'

'But have you not read the papers?' asked Joshua. 'Discontent and rioting all over the south of the country! We must do all we can to stop it happening here.'

'Nonsense, Delahaye! Our fellows are not like that. They know which side their bread is buttered.'

The French aristocrats had probably said something very similar in 1789 just before the sans-culottes marched on Paris. 'Most of our labourers have forgotten what it is like to have butter,' he said, struggling to keep the anger out of his voice. 'Some of them are beginning to forget what it is like to have good wheat bread.'

'Let them eat barley bread then! They grind rye for their coffee, after all! Lord, what a doom-monger you are, Delahaye!'

He had no more success with the farmers. One declared that he'd see the lot of them dead and his house burned down before he would let anyone lay hands on his machines, but others, seeing the suffering of the villagers, expressed their willingness, in view of the bad harvest, to dismantle their threshing machines at least for this winter, and give work to some of the poor. He tried to put a brave face on the situation when he met the papermen at the Leathern Bottle, but with all the rumours of a great uprising sweeping across the southern counties, led by the shadowy Captain Swing, he knew that it would take more than half-hearted promises to turn them from their purpose.

Sunday was no day of rest for him: he spent most of it in the saddle going from church to chapel trying to persuade the ministers to use their influence to calm the situation. At St Paul's he had no success:

121

the curate had shown his private sympathy for the poor, but his curacy depended on Dupré and the landowner had made it quite clear where the curate's duties lay. At the Bethel chapel he learned that three evictions were to happen that Monday, two from Dupré cottages and another from one of Hall Barn's. He could not conceive of a more dangerous spark in the present volatile situation than to see three families, all with young children, put out onto the streets on a cold, raw November day.

He had gone straightway to Beaconsfield, in the hope of talking the landowners into a stay of the evictions, but at Wilton Park he was informed that Dupré was not prepared to discuss estate business on a Sunday. At Hall Barn he met with the same reception. If he cared to call on Monday, said the butler, the land agent would see him then.

He rode his horse back down the turnpike to Marsh Green Mill, one of only two in the valley where the machines had been closed down.

'I was so sorry to hear about your troubles, Delahaye,' said Allnutt. 'Still, there will be any number of mill owners who'll give you a place when this has blown over.'

'News travels fast.'

'I was at Clapton yesterday trying to persuade Revel to close down his machines. He refused, of course. Damned you for a rebel and told me he'd turned you off. Positively gloated about it. You know he's talking of bringing the military from London? I wanted him to send the women to Bosingham House till the troubles are over – the house is so close to the mill – but he wouldn't hear of it.'

'But I understood Miss Revel was in London?'

'One of the ladies was still there. Heard someone weeping upstairs.' With a curse Joshua leaped to his feet and made for the door, the thought that Kat might be in trouble clearing the shreds of weariness from his brain, but Allnutt stopped him. 'You'll only make matters worse, Delahaye. You know that's the real reason he dismissed you? Someone told him you and she were together at the Branchetts' . . .'

'Damn the rat who told him!' said Joshua, remembering with pain that brief moment of intimacy as they waited for the carriage. 'Pray God she *is* in London! Or the least he will do is lock her in her room. To be frank, Allnutt, if he thinks she was encouraging me, he's far more likely to beat her.'

'Lizzie said as much after the Bosinghams' election dinner. Damned great bracelet on the girl's wrist that Lizzie's never seen before or since. She looked close at it when Miss Revel was handing the tea in the drawing room, and sure enough there was a great deal of swelling and bruising beneath.'

'The devil there was!' snarled Joshua. 'If he's laid a finger on her I'll set the law on him!'

'Thought of that myself,' said Allnutt. 'But the law is powerless, Delahaye. A man is master in his own house, after all. I'm off to Hedsor within the hour, to hand the whole thing over to Bosingham. I'd back Lady Isabelle against Revel any day.'

And with that Joshua had to be content.

Dawn crept along the ridge, sweeping the night mists away to the river valleys, leaving behind only wispy shreds which clung like rotted graveclothes to the skeletal outlines of the bare cherry tree that emerged from the half-light, gnarled branches seeming to claw at the half-seen figures in the advancing crowd.

In spite of himself John Sarney, the alehouse keeper, known to everyone as Old Sawney, shivered.

He drew his collar up around his ears and cursed his aching bones.

'Keep up, boy!' growled a voice behind him. 'You fall behind and Tom Chase'll have you!'

Someone in the rear of the crowd gave a muffled sob. Old Sawney suppressed a sigh and fell back.

'Tom Chase an't goin' to come fer me, is he, Mr Sawney?' said a white-faced boy, coming to an abrupt halt.

'No, lad,' said Sawney, putting his arm round the boy's shoulders and drawing him along. How old was Arthur now? Sixteen? Seventeen? He looked about twelve.

'On'y Mr Butler said – '

'Will Butler was having a jest with you,' said Sawney, scowling at his brother-in-law.

Butler laughed callously and strode off to the front of the crowd, blowing vigorously on a horn.

'Why don't you take yerself off home, Arthur?' said Old Sawney, scratching at his grey whiskers. 'You shouldn't be here, boy.'

'Go back? All alone?' cried the lad fearfully. 'Tom Chase 'ud get me for certain!'

Thomas Chase, a religious martyr popularly supposed to have been strangled on the orders of the Bishop of Lincoln in the dungeons of Wooburn Palace, was held to haunt the crossroads at the head of Blind Lane where he had been buried some three hundred years before. It was a tale used to frighten children.

'Mary said as I'd got to come with you, else she wouldn't come to the fair with me, see?' gabbled Arthur. 'She said as I'd to show I was a man. Don't send me back!'

That'd be right, thought Sawney. Just like Mary Smith to torment poor Arthur to do something he wasn't fit for and then go to the fair with someone else anyway. 'An't no one goin' to send you back, Arthur,' he said soothingly. 'On'y try to keep up, there's a good lad.'

His words were drowned by a loud blast from the horn at the head of the column.

It had all seemed so simple when they had planned it. The first indication that all was not going well had been when the men had turned up at the Leathern Bottle, Sawney's alehouse, long before Joshua Delahaye was expected.

Dell and his companions had refused to wait on Joshua. 'We said dawn,' snapped Dell. 'If he ain't here, then we starts without him.' Sawney was beginning to regret his part in leading Joshua such a merry dance, sending him from one to the other, pretending that Dell was a lace buyer instead of – well, instead of whatever Dell actually was. Cobbett's man, he'd said. But Cobbett was a country man and Sawney had never expected Cobbett's man to have a Cockney accent.

'We march now,' insisted Dell. 'Not losing your nerve, are you, Sawney?' He looked around the crowd of excited faces. 'All these young lads who've looked up to you – if you back out now...'

'Who said I'm backing out?' he said truculently.

'Good. Because we tried it your way, John. We tried talking.'

'Aye,' said Butler. 'An' where did it get us?'

'They still an't stopped the machines!' said Dandridge, banging one fist angrily against the other. 'Not even at Lane's, after all their promises! I say we march now!'

And so they had marched, from Wooburn through Northern Woods, Sedgemoor, Flackwell Heath, Heath End. As they passed through each hamlet on the ridge, the crowd swelled until it seemed to take on a life of its own. Sawney was no longer a voice to be reckoned with, now he was no more than one very small part of the whole, and it was Dell with his oaths and his blood-curdling cries who seemed to have taken charge.

'We've unfinished business at Lane's, lads!' he exhorted the new arrivals.

'To Ash Mill!' they cried. 'We'll show Lane who he's dealing with!'

'Aye! Wreck the machines!'

'Wreck the machines!' they echoed.

'And this time we won't be talked out of it by traitors with only the masters' interests at heart!' shouted Dell, grinning scornfully at Sawney.

The full-length portrait of Josias Dupré, resplendent in the robes and regalia of the governor of Madras, looked disapprovingly down on the figure pacing the length of the elegant room.

Joshua drew his watch from his waistcoat once more and checked

124

it against the mantel clock. He should have been back in Wooburn by now, in case Sawney tried to get in touch with him again; instead he was cooling his heels here at Wilton Park and he was beginning to suspect that Caledon Dupré's steward was keeping him waiting deliberately.

With a muffled oath he resumed his pacing up and down the saloon. Only his anxiety over the pending evictions had kept him in Beaconsfield this long; over the past two days the papermen had remained somewhat guarded with him, but if Dupré or his steward would let him pay the outstanding rents, he could go back to Wooburn with the assurance that the rent defaulters would be allowed to stay in their cottages and then the papermen would see that he was in earnest. Stifling a huge yawn, he wondered how Kat was faring in London.

Kat was startled into wakefulness as the door rattled. Eyes wide with terror, she looked across at the door. The bar was still in place and she let her breath out slowly, wincing at the pain in her side.

Which one of them would it be this time, she wondered? Whichever it was, the speeches would be the same – talking to her brightly of Louis's wedding plans, of visits to London to order bride clothes, and then growing increasingly furious and threatening when she still refused to open the door.

Each day she grew a little more tired, a little more weak, but she never quite gave up hope. She watched and waited for an opportunity to escape. Mary was living openly with her father now, and at night she listened to their footsteps echoing down the corridor that led to his rooms, praying that just once they might have forgotten to lock her door on the outside. So far that hope had been in vain.

Her one fear had been that they might bring Dickon back from London to talk her round, but it had never crossed her mind that her father would let the most skilful engineer in the valley go. Because of her obstinacy, her father told her, Joshua had lost his job and gone north to seek work.

With that she had given up hope. It was not that she had really believed that Joshua would ride up to the house on a white charger like young Lochinvar to demand her release – she was not so foolish – but nor had she ever imagined that he would leave the village without a word to her.

In the dark, cold hours that she had been locked up she had had ample time to think. She knew now that if Joshua had asked her she would have given up everything – her home, her family, her good name – to go with him. To the ends of the earth, if need be. But she had never told him – and now it was too late.

125

Hailey leaped from his horse and raced across the millstream; two hastily sworn in special constables, Morton and Veary the butcher, followed him into Ash Mill, their heavy boots ringing on the stone floor.

'Lane! Lane, I say!' He strode through the salle, shouting above the deafening clattering and juddering as a constant stream of pulp spewed out on the shaking wire bed of the Fourdrinier machine. 'Fasten the doors, man!' he gasped, catching sight of Howard in the dusting room. 'Bolt the windows! The mob's not two minutes behind me!'

'The mob? But that was all over with on Friday!' The machine man's face turned grey.

'Don't stand there, man!' said Hailey, mopping his face with a large red kerchief. 'Don't you hear them coming? Shut those machines down!'

The sound of the mob as it came along the turnpike seemed to root Howard even more firmly to the spot. 'But someone should talk to them,' he gabbled. 'It worked last time – '

'Veary! Morton!' shouted Hailey, taking charge. 'Get those bars across the doors! Close up the windows! You there!' he snapped at the workers clustering anxiously in the doorway. 'Shut those machines off – now!'

The mob, with Dell at its head, was already spilling onto the mill green as the last bar fell into the sockets across the main door.

'There's not as many of 'em this time,' said Veary, his voice echoing in the eerie silence as the paper machines and the rag-grinders rattled and chugged to a reluctant halt. 'Doubt if there's a hundred there.'

'Still too many for us,' said Morton.

'Where's the militia?' Howard was hopping from one foot to the other in his agitation. 'They saw 'em off the last time and – '

'We won't have that much good fortune twice,' said Hailey. 'The militia's up north – Aylesbury way.' For all he knew, the whole of the north of the county could be in flames by now and the south about to follow. 'Brace up, men,' he said with a heartiness he did not feel.

'They've come well-armed this time,' said Howard, looking at the array of axes, hammers and crowbars being waved aloft on the other side of the millstream. He wished Mr Lane would hurry back to take charge. This was a responsibility he could do without.

'Who's leading them?' asked Morton. 'Not that barber again, is it?'

Hailey peered out of the window at the crowd forming up in ragged ranks on the far side of the millstream. 'I'm nigh on certain the grey-haired one's Sawney of the Leathern Bottle, and thass most

126

likely Will Butler with him. But the one doing all the shouting – I an't ever seen him afore.'

'What do we want, men?' cried the leader.

'Bread!' the men shouted back, waving their fists in the air.

'An' if they won't give us bread?' called Dell.

'Bread or blood!' they howled.

'Bread or blood! An' no more machines!'

'Smash the machines! Smash the machines!' they yelled, and their cries, bouncing off the mill walls, echoed and re-echoed around the green as the vanguard streamed across the bridge.

Hailey checked the priming on his pistol and tried to put out of his mind the rumours he had heard that London and Windsor were already in flames; whatever the truth, he had sworn to do his duty.

'My God!' said one of the mill workers. 'They're goin' to kill us! An't you goin' to stop them?'

'How?' asked Hailey.

'Shoot them! Kill the ringleaders!'

'If there's any threat to life, I'll give the order to shoot,' said the High Constable as calmly as he could, 'but no one fires except by my order. You, Veary, get up above the machine room. Keep yourself ready.'

Tommy Bowles was the first to appear at the window. 'Is that you, Howard?' he yelled. 'Open the door and let us in!'

'Why?' challenged the machine man. He had regained some control over himself, but was still as pale as death.

'You knows why!' said Bowles, waving a hatchet angrily above his head. 'We're here to smash the machines as are takin' work from honest men!'

'The machines have all been stopped, lads,' said Hailey. 'Let's talk – '

'No more talking!' came the cry.

'Talk?' said Dell with a sneer. 'Haven't we talked long enough?'

There was a ragged chorus of assent.

'Are you goin' to open up?' repeated Bowles.

'No.'

'Then us'll force it open!' cried Bowles.

'Lay on, lads!' cried Walduck, waving his shoemaker's hammer round his head, and before the words were out of his mouth the mob began hammering and chopping at the door.

'Is there any hope that help will arrive before they break through?' asked John Lane, hurrying down the stairs.

'I doubt it, sir,' said Hailey, whereupon Lane nodded his head and walked back into the salle.

The mill gates were stout and had stood for years, but little by little under the concerted attack cracks began to appear in the door, cracks which soon widened to holes, revealing the faces of the attackers, first Bowles, then Blizzard, attacking the hinges with a crowbar, and Bryant.

Suddenly a shot rang out and the attackers recoiled, but the bullet went wide and buried itself in the wood. Hailey whirled round. Behind him, an array of ancient pistols in their hands, were a number of Lane's mill hands. In the shadows he couldn't see which weapon had been fired.

He turned on Lane. 'I told you – no one fires without my orders!' he hissed. Firearms in such untrained hands presented as much danger to the defenders as to the attackers.

Above him, on a ledge overlooking the machine-room door, Veary shifted his primed pistol from one sweaty hand to the other as the attackers, angered by the shot, returned with increased fury to breaking down the doors.

'Damn his eyes, there's Lunnon!' said the mill worker at Veary's side. 'Used to work here. And Weedon too!' he said as the holes in the door widened to reveal more faces. 'Come here to put us out of work, curse 'em! If only I had a gun!'

'First one as comes through that door, I shall fire on 'im, don't you fret,' said Veary grimly. 'I an't waitin' for no *orders*.'

'Good for you, Mr Veary,' said the mill hand with a wolfish grin. 'An' I just might have an idea how I can help you.'

Joshua was riding fast, but not as fast as the rider who passed him in Windsor End halfway between the church and Hall Barn Lodge.

He frowned. What the devil was one of Hailey's men doing in Beaconsfield?

'Hi! Pearce!' Joshua wheeled his horse and rode after the man.

'Mr Delahaye!' exclaimed Pearce when Joshua caught up with him. 'Didn't see you there. Terrible trouble, Mr Delahaye,' he said, the words tumbling off his tongue. 'The mob's out again an' this time there's no turnin' 'em back. Marched through the town this morning, shoutin' an' a-hollerin' that they was goin' to wreck everything.'

Joshua felt as though the grey sky was pressing down on him and suffocating him, until it became a fight to catch every breath.

'Are you sick, Mr Joshua?' asked Pearce anxiously. 'You look right poorly.'

'What's Hailey doing?' gasped Joshua at last.

'Just followin' 'em about. Not enough men, see. Must be nigh on a hundred of 'em went through Wycombe Marsh. And others joinin' 'em all the time. And the militia's all gone up to Aylesbury, bein' as how they thought the trouble in Wycombe was over and done with.

For they do say Stone and Waddesdon has risen, sir. Burnin' down farms and all kinds of outrages up there. They say this Captain Swing, he's in control of all the top o' the county, sir. An' Hampshire. An' Wiltshire, they say, not to mention – '

'We can only deal with here, Pearce,' said Joshua sharply, cutting off the rising note of panic. 'What is Hailey's plan for dealing with the trouble?'

Pearce scratched his head. 'Don't know as he's got one, sir. Can't have a plan without you got some force to plan with. So Mr Hailey, he sent me up here for reinforcements. Mr Bradford has sent to Windsor for the soldiers.'

'Oh, God!'

'There'll be bloodshed for sure, once the soldiers catch up with them,' said Pearce gloomily. 'The mob is – '

'Were they heading back to Lane's again, do you think?'

'No. It's the thrashin' machines they're after, you mark my words, sir. This Captain Swing of theirs, he's sent 'em against the thrashin' machines.'

'I hope you're right,' said Joshua, wheeling his mare around. 'But I think I'll head for Lane's all the same. If I'm wrong, tell Hailey I'll head back into town to find him. But I beg him, if the soldiers come before I do, to hold off using them for as long as he can.'

'I'll tell him, sir, to be sure. But I doubt – '

'Have you warned the mills this end of the river?' said Joshua, reining in his mare with difficulty.

'They're for the farms, sir, I told you. No need to – '

'There's a shilling for you if you warn them at Clapton Revel,' said Joshua. 'They'll pass the word along.' If they should turn on the mills, then Revel, the harshest employer, would certainly be a prime target.

The most direct route to Lane's was across the fields to Wooburn and over Flackwell Heath and One-Handed Cross. He had hoped he might pick up some information in Wooburn or Flackwell about the marchers' intentions, but both villages were all but deserted.

His lips thinned in anger as he rode past Sawney's alehouse, shuttered and empty. They had fairly strung him along, sending him from one place to the other, telling him the strangers he met were lace dealers. It was a bitter reflection that they had taken him for such a fool.

Close by Hard to Find Farm, a group of men cleaning a ditch had seen the mob earlier in the morning.

'Blowin' horns they was,' said an elderly man, 'and took Jed's mattock from 'im.'

'Said they was for Mr Collins's, farm.'

'Aye. To break up his thrashin' machine, sir.'

Joshua hoped that that was all they planned to do. If the rioters had heard of the destruction of the poorhouses in Selborne and Headley, and the mistreatment of the overseers, then the overseer of Wycombe's workhouse could also be in for a rough time.

'Don't look so fretted, sir,' said the ganger. 'They're only doin' the magistrates work for 'em. After all, the magistrates has said all the machines is to come down – '

It was a common misapprehension that would be the undoing of many. 'A few magistrates may have said the machines should be set aside,' said Joshua, 'but that doesn't mean that anyone is justified in smashing them. Machine-breaking is a transportable offence.'

'I 'eard 'em say as they was for Lane's mill,' said the elderly man. 'On account of they an't took down the machine, after they give their word.'

'You only ever hears half a tale, Sol,' said his companion, patting him on the shoulder.

'Took Will and Moses,' grumbled a beardless youth, leaning on his pickaxe and glaring at old Sol. 'If grandfer hadn't been here I'd have gone too.'

'More fool you,' said the ganger. 'Enough trouble about without you goes lookin' for it.'

It took almost three quarters of an hour, a tense three quarters of an hour during which those inside the mill could only pray that by some miracle the militia might once more appear on Ash Mill Green, but the cracks widened to holes, the holes to large gaps, and at last the axes and hammers broke through.

'Stand back!' ordered Hailey, levelling his pistol at the front ranks. 'In the name of the law I order you to withdraw!'

'We don't mean you no harm, Mr Hailey,' said Weedon, standing his ground beyond the door, tossing his pickaxe from one hand to the other.

'Nor even the owners...' agreed Bowles.

'But we means to smash the machines,' said Lunnon cheerfully, 'so you'd best not try to stop us.'

More and more men were piling up behind them, half a hundred determined men flourishing axes and hammers.

Hailey dropped his pistol slowly to his side; if the mob was interested only in wrecking the machinery, he was not going to shed blood, his or anyone else's, to stop them. Reluctantly he gave the order to stand aside and the doors gave way with a groan of splintering wood, spilling in the first wave of attackers.

Above the roar of triumph a voice overhead bellowed, 'This 'ull give you summat to shout about!' There was a rush of sound like

130

water pouring off the mill wheel – but the mill wheel had been stopped.

Old Shrimpton looked up in surprise and the contents of the vat of vitriol caught him full in the face. Screaming and writhing he fell to the floor, his hands pressed to his eyes. Most of the others managed to step back in time to avoid the main torrent, but a handful of them were badly splashed by the burning liquid. Bowles, leaping back as the stream of acid hit the stone floor and splashed up at him, caught his arm on the buckled metal of the torn hinges and screamed as the flesh was torn off.

There was the briefest moment of shocked silence, broken only by the gentle tinkle of glass falling from a smashed window, then Bryant, who had been only slightly spotted with the acid, gave a great roar of fury and charged through the wreckage and into the mill, heading straight for the ladder that led up to Veary's perch.

Veary recoiled in horror at the terrible effect of the acid, but seeing the crowd hot for his blood, he pulled off a shot in panic. Bryant staggered back from the foot of the ladder, clutching his right arm and watching in disbelief as the bright blood welled up through his fingers.

Three or four men grabbed Shrimpton from the floor. 'Clear the way, there!' they yelled, and the others who had been splashed hurried after them, frantically taking up the call as they rushed towards the water.

The crowd parted, watching in horrified silence as their comrades leaped into the mill pond where they ducked themselves and Shrimpton in the water to wash off the worst of the vitriol. Dell, fearful that the shock might lose him the momentum, jumped up onto the mounting block.

'Remember!' he cried. 'Bread or blood!'

The crowd turned back to the mill, as if suddenly remembering why they were there.

'Bread or blood!' shouted Dell once more.

'Bread or blood!' they roared back.

'Smash the machines!'

'Smash the machines!' they echoed, and with renewed enthusiasm followed him into the mill. Hailey and his men found themselves adrift in a sea of men, axes and hammers. Pushing the defenders effortlessly aside, the mob poured into the machine room, striking furiously at the machinery with hammers, mattocks and pickaxes, shouts of triumph mingling with the ring of metal on metal as the framework began to buckle.

But the remaining Loudwater men, many of whom had known Will Shrimpton all their lives and worked alongside him in the paper

131

mills, ignored Dell's urgings; looking grimly at each other, they turned with one accord towards the men overhead. Before Veary could reload they rushed the ladders, pulled him and his companion roughly off the ledge, and manhandled them down to the millpond where, to furious cries of 'Kill them! Kill them!', they ducked the two men under the water and held them there.

Hailey, helpless to stop them and unwilling to aggravate an already volatile situation, trailed after them; he stood on the bridge, the clang of hammers and axes on metal and the eldritch shriek of buckled machinery ringing in his ears. His lips thinned angrily as Shrimpton's comrades hauled the old fellow out of the river and laid him, coughing and spluttering, on the bank alongside Bowles and Bryant, who were having their wounds bound up. As the water streamed off Shrimpton's white hair and whiskers Hailey could clearly see the marks etched on him by the vitriol. Damn Veary and Johnson! he thought angrily. A ducking was the least they deserved.

But when the thrashing of the bodies under the water began to grow weaker, and the mob showed no sign of letting them out, he drew back the hammer on his pistol and called on the Loudwater men to unhand their victims.

His demand was met with a chorus of jeers from the men in the water.

'Let them go!' repeated Hailey steadily.

'They tried to kill us!' cried one of the men.

'An' look what they done to poor old Shrimpton!'

Johnson's head bobbed clear of the water, just below the bridge, and the mill hand whooped desperately for breath.

'It's enough!' said Hailey, more sharply this time. 'He's taken his punishment. Now let him go.'

'He deserves all he gets,' bellowed Carpenter, throwing himself on top of his victim and forcing him back under the water again. 'An' Veary too!'

'Veary's my special constable. Let him go now or I'll fire.'

'We're more than you!' taunted Blizzard.

Hailey remained steadfast. 'However many you are, let them go or I shall have to fire.' Some of the men were wavering, their initial blood lust cooled by the shock of the cold river water, and he pressed his point home. 'If either of them dies, Carpenter,' he said strongly, 'then you'll hang, every last one of you.'

On the bank, old Shrimpton propped himself up on his elbow and caught a wheezing breath. 'Let them go, lads,' he gasped. 'They an't worth the trouble.'

Kattrin closed her eyes once more, deciding that she must have

132

imagined the key turning in the door. Dream and reality were becoming increasingly difficult to separate. She was even imagining that she could smell some of Cook's freshly baked cakes. In spite of herself her mouth watered.

'Plum cakes and spice cake.' Mary's voice oiled its way under the door. 'Cook's made them all special for you.'

Kat sat up unsteadily and rubbed her red-rimmed eyes.

'Smell good, don't they?' the tormenting voice went on. 'I've brought some up on a tray for you. The rest is for when Lady Isabelle gets here. Your father's sending you and your aunt up to Bosingham House while the village is so restless.'

Lady Isabelle would save her! She'd not let them get away with treating her like this! Barely conscious of moving, Kat found herself at the door. She was just about to lift the bar from its socket when she thought she heard whispering in the corridor outside. With her ear to the door she could just make out another whisper, deeper than Mary's, her father was there too. She looked down at her hand on the bar and realised with horror how nearly she had been tricked.

'Drop cakes Cook's made, and honey cake too,' came Mary's voice, softer than she ever remembered it.

Kattrin turned away from the door, hands clapped over her ears to block out that siren voice, but there was no way of blocking out the smell. She had to open the window. She crossed the room, her stomach growling, her knees so weak by the time she got there that she had to cling onto the window bars to keep herself upright.

'Her Ladyship 'ull be here any minute. You wouldn't want her to see you all untidy, would you?' she wheedled. 'Let me in and we'll smarten you up a bit.'

By twisting her arm through the bars Kat succeeded in pushing the sash window up a little way and she gulped in as much of the cold November air as her bruised ribs would allow. She leaned her head against the cold metal. The smell was so heavenly, but she would not give into temptation. If she concentrated on the view...

A pair of ducks rose up from the surface of the lake with a startled cry and she thought back to the morning she had run away and Tom peering at her through the mist. Would Tom have left without a word to her?

Someone was scraping metal on stone and making a dreadful screeching sound that put the teeth on edge. She shook her head sharply and focused on a group of men dragging something along the path from the stables.

It was something long and heavy and so shrouded in sacking that only the wheels beneath were visible. She frowned as she mentally reviewed all the machinery in the mills and knew that no part of them looked like this.

One of the wheels caught on the cobbles and the sacking slid to one side. Kat's knuckles tightened on the bars as her horrified eyes made out the smooth lines of a cannon; behind the gun a cart emerged from the stables, filled with metal shreddings from the mill machinery. She shook her head: what could her father possibly want with a *cannon*?

Revel had given up all hope of tricking the girl out of the room and had crossed to the window at the head of the stairs to watch the gun's progress. 'Just let them march on my mill,' he boasted, 'and they'll have more than they bargained for!'

Mary chuckled and the sound made Kat's blood run cold.

'Best be off to oversee the setting-up, master,' she said. 'Don't want those fools turning coward at the last minute.'

Kat hurried to the side window, craning for a view. The men dragged the heavy gun around the side of the house and into position on the road, midway between the house and the mill; her jaw dropped as they began to pack the cannon's mouth with nails and metal shreddings. She could scarcely believe what she was seeing. How long, she wondered, had her father had this planned?

She stood irresolutely at the window. She *had* to do something – get to the village somehow and warn the men. But how?

She bit her lip as she tried to think of a solution, then jumped in pain as her teeth encountered the half-crusted cuts.

'The fools will get more than they bargained for,' crowed Mary. She raised her voice. 'You watching, Miss Kattrin? Look close. You might see your lover's brains splattered all over the – '

The sound of a blow echoed down the corridor.

'You stupid drab!' hissed Revel. 'Keep your mouth shut!'

At the back of her mind Kat was aware of Mary cursing, and the sound of her father's footsteps as he hurried down the stairs, but she forced herself to concentrate on the immediate problem confronting her. Even if she could get downstairs, her father and the men stood between the door and the stables, so that taking a horse was out of the question. Her eye fell on the punt tied up on the river just upstream of the sluices. She and Dickon had been familiar with boats since their childhood and under normal cirumstances she knew she could easily have managed to pole upstream to Loudwater. But her ribs hurt where her father's fist had pounded them and she was so weak she didn't know if she could even pick up the pole.

But she had to try to warn the men. She couldn't stay here and watch them being cut down. And if she was to warn them, she had first to get out of this room. A plan was beginning to form in her tired mind. She faced the possibility that she might not get down the stairs and past her father, in which case she would be in for an even more severe beating. So be it, she told herself bracingly. If you fail, you fail, and you'll just have to take what comes. At least you will have tried. And what was one more beating against the lives of so many?

Before she could think too deeply about it, she closed and locked the window, crossed the room and lifted the bar.

Mary was standing on the stairs, her hand pressed to the side of her face where the marks of Revel's fingers stood out scarlet against her pale cheek.

'Oh, my God!' she whispered, eyes widening with shock. 'What 'as 'e done to you?'

Kat rolled up her eyes and fell.

She felt herself being half lifted, half dragged back to the bed and forced herself to stay limp, not reacting even when her hem caught on the corner of the bed and tore.

'I never meant 'im to kill you!' Mary panted desperately. 'I swear it!'

A damp cloth was laid on Kat's brow and it felt delightfully soothing. As she sensed Mary turn away again, she opened her bruised eyes a crack. She had a strange sensation that it was not her on the bed at all, that she was actually on top of the bedposts, looking down on the whole scene, totally detached from it all.

She watched herself bend down stealthily and pick up the footstool, watched herself gather the last remnants of her strength, raise the footstool in the air and bring it down with a thud on Mary's head. She watched herself stand for a moment over the prostrate woman, looking down on her handiwork with a look of horror. Then she was running out of the room, turning the key behind her and racing down the stairs.

From the outside, Lane's mill looked at first glance quite normal, save that the wheel was not turning, but as Joshua spurred his horse up to the main doors, it became all too obvious that the mob had been there before him.

He looped the reins around the hitching post and picked his way carefully through the remains of the splintered doors. Joseph Lane stood in the dusting room surveying the wreckage of the Hollander machine. He looked up as he heard Joshua's footsteps crunching on the glass from the broken windows. 'Come to talk the mob round again, Delahaye?' he said savagely. 'Well, I'd say you've left it a little late this time!'

Joshua bit back a sharp retort. 'So I see,' he said.

Lane pressed the palms of his hands to his eyes. 'I'm sorry,

Delahaye. Quite wrong of me to lash out at you. But they have almost certainly ruined us.'

Joshua looked around the dusting room. 'Did they only wreck the one machine?'

'Can't understand it,' Lane murmured, so low that Joshua had to strain to hear him. 'They've completely wrecked my rag-cutting machine – brand new, y'know, hardly had it in operation any time – and yet they hardly touched the papermaking machine.'

'I think it was only the time, Mr Lane,' said Howard. 'They suddenly took it into their heads to go after Collins and – '

'You'd think they'd be pleased to have a machine take over the rag grinding,' said Lane, as if Howard had not spoken. 'Working with the rags is a filthy job.'

But if it was that job or starve, thought Joshua, you would not welcome a machine to do it in your place.

It took him an age to get away and with a grim set to his face he spurred his horse towards Wycombe.

In the High Street, those shopkeepers who had not been swift enough to put their shutters up were out on the pavement, sweeping up broken glass, while those who had paid the mob to pass them by were busy trying to justify to their neighbours why they had given in to extortion.

'Fine pass we've come to, Mr Delahaye,' said Crockford the linen draper, 'when the mob can rampage through the town and extort money.'

'It's a bad day,' agreed Hardy, shaking his head. 'But now they've got beer money, 'twill all fizzle out in drink, I've no doubt.'

'Where were the soldiers?'

'Gone north,' said someone sourly. 'Gone to protect Chandos's property, and left us with Hailey and a handful of night watchmen to look after us.'

'And all Hailey does is tag along behind 'em.'

'What can a handful of men do against sixty?' asked Joshua.

'Sixty?'

'Lane said there were about sixty of them in the mill.'

'Then Lane was fortunate,' said Hardy with a scornful laugh. 'It's nearer five hundred now. I dessay there were many as watched to see which way the wind blew before joining.'

'All power to them, I say,' said his neighbour.

'That's treasonable talk, that is!' cried the baker, who had found himself forced to 'volunteer' the entire morning's bakings of pies and bread as a contribution to the mob. He darted a look of pure venom at Joshua. 'We did ought to have set the militia on 'em when we had

136

'em by, instead of lettin' people as thinks they know better talk us out of it.'

'There an't no call to blame Mr Joshua for the mob,' said Hardy. 'We each does as we thinks best and he an't to be held responsible for what the papermen do. It didn't never ought to have come to this! What for did the town send Dashwood-King and Baring to Parliament? There they sits in a comfortable berth, and spouts against Reform, and votes down any help for the poor, on account of the poor an't got no vote!' He looked round at the other shopkeepers. 'What did they ever do for the poor of Wycombe?' he demanded. 'Eh? And as for Wellington –'

'You cannot blame it all on Wellington,' bleated Crockford.

'An' why not?' demanded Jackman, shuffling awkwardly towards them on his misshapen legs, the empty sleeve of his coat flapping against the strings of the pedlar's tray slung around his neck. 'Duke of Wellington, ho, yes, a great soldier, so he was. I seen 'im many a time on the parade ground. But since he was prime minister, what's he done for you and me?'

'Nothing. Except to stop Reform, so as to keep us in our places!'

'He still has his whole skin too,' said Jackman bitterly. 'Both his arms an' both his eyes and the use o' two good legs. And for that they gives him a pension of sixteen thousand a year and a gurt great mansion paid for by the nation. And what do they give me, as fought in the same battles? Eh?' He pointed to the patch covering the empty eye socket. 'I tell you what they gives me – nothing! So I has to beg, from the townsfolk and from the overseer. An' if old Collins is in a good mood that day, he might give me enough to eat – just. I tells you, if I had two good legs I'd be on the march with 'em!'

Joshua left them to their arguments and set off down the turnpike towards Collins's farm. The corn mills, Pann Mill on the edge of town and Bassetsbury, beyond the Rye, were unscathed; perhaps the attack on Lane's mill had been an isolated incident, he thought, and the mob were now going after the threshing machines.

That hope was dashed when he reached Marsh Green and found Allnutt and his wife standing in the midst of the wreckage, contemplating the destruction.

'This was our life,' said Lizzie tearfully. 'All we've worked for. Everything. Gone.'

'I offered to take the machines down,' said Allnutt, his face white with shock. He dragged his gaze away from the mass of mangled metal that had once been a gleaming new machine and when he looked at Joshua there were tears in his eyes. 'They wrecked it all anyway.'

137

'It's so unfair,' said his wife. 'We were always good to our people...'

But the mob had gone past the stage of distinguishing between good and bad employers. Their leaders selected the targets and, drunk on beer and power, the men followed blindly, determined to put every machine on the river out of use.

The wrecking of John Hay's Marsh Mill had taken a little longer, for the Marsh men opposed the mob; while one of the men outside tried to set a charge of powder to blow the machine-room door, one of the Marsh men snatched up a red-hot poker and thrust it through the lock, nearly putting the attacker's eye out. When the door finally gave way, the man with the poker barely escaped with his life.

'Fifty-three men and boys thrown on the parish,' said Hay when Joshua reached his mill. 'How can that help. Eh?' He shook his head in despair. 'What more could we do, Mr Delahaye? What more could we do?'

Kat lifted the pole again and plunged it into the riverbed, gritting her teeth against the pain in her ribs as she pushed her weight into the poling. She and Dickon had poled upstream many times, but then she had not been hampered by long skirts, nor by a body weak from hunger and bruised from beating.

The punt shot forwards and she forced herself to ignore the flames of pain that licked up her arms as she drew the pole up to start the agonising process once again. She could not hear any sounds of pursuit, but her breathing was so loud in her ears that it was not easy to tell. Once she was around the bend and out of sight, she might feel a little safer.

The Burnham magistrates, meeting at Salt Hill, had been none too pleased to hear the news from Wycombe. Vyse of Stoke Park, the High Sheriff, and a handful of the more active among them turned their back on an excellent dinner, took to their horses and rode over to see what was happening. Meeting up with the mob on the turnpike, they instructed Vincent, the vicar of Hughenden, to read the Riot Act and called on the labourers to disperse. But the mob, which had rested from its labours only long enough to drink dry the cellars of the Red Lion before serving Plaistowe's mill the same as all the others, were in no mood to turn back now. The magistrates were met with a hail of abuse and a volley of stones, a surprising number of which met their mark. Glorying in the sight of the High Sheriff with a gash on his chin from a particularly well-aimed stone from Jacob Knibbs, one of the Little Marlow woodmen, the jeering, howling mob surged away to King's Mead. Vyse, realising that matters were

138

beyond his control, decided to ride to London for reinforcements, leaving his unfortunate colleagues to deal with the situation as best they could.

'Dammit, they've gone beyond the bounds this time,' said Roberts, blinking away the blood that trickled down his forehead and into his eyes. 'Stoning the High Sheriff – they'll hang for this!'

'They were too many for us,' said Swabey to Sullivan of Richings Park who had just ridden in. 'We caught some of them but we could not hold them.'

'They got away this time,' said Roberts, 'but I have their names, and I'll see them hanged, by God!' He caught sight of Joshua. 'Well, man? I hope you're pleased with your handiwork?' he said savagely. 'If you'd let us turn the militia on them on Friday we would have been spared this. Still, it's something that you've seen the error of your ways, I suppose. Come to be sworn in, have you?'

Joshua shook his head.

'We don't need turncoats like Delahaye,' sneered Sullivan. 'We saw Captain Montague of the Guards out from Windsor with His Majesty's Staghounds not ten minutes' ride from here; he swore he would fetch the rest of the hunt to our aid.'

'Let me speak to the men,' begged Joshua. 'Just a few minutes – '

'I'll tolerate no more delays!' said Sullivan.

'But you can't turn the hunt on them!'

'I would remind you, Delahaye, that once the Riot Act has been read, we may do whatever we consider necessary to restore order.'

'Are we to allow a mob of illiterate youths to dictate the peace of this realm?' demanded Swabey.

'I suggest you be sworn in without delay, Delahaye,' said Sullivan. 'Because with or without you, we shall finish this once and for all.'


Revel looked up from the cannon with a frown; he thought he could hear someone shouting. Drat the girl! he thought. Mary should have made sure that all the windows were shut. If any of the men heard her . . .

One of the men he had posted further up the Oxford Road came hurrying towards the mill. 'The Beaconsfield special constables are just come down from Glory Mills, sir. Mr Spicer sent for 'em. They're for Hedge Mill, but they says if you need 'em they – '

'Tell 'em they can go their way,' said Revel, caressing the smooth curve of the cannon. 'I need no help in defending my own!'


Joshua heard the labourers before he saw them, a dull murmur in the

139

distance, like the humming of a swarm of bees on the move, broken by the occasional ragged cry of 'Bread or blood!' or 'Smash the machines!'

They would turn on Hedge Mill next, for Snakeley had been idle for six months, since Davis's last tenant had gone bankrupt. Joshua spurred the tired mare on, only to find as he crossed the river that the mob was advancing on Snakeley. He was on the wrong side of King's Mead, and five hundred men lay between him and Snakeley Mill.

A hand came up and caught at the mare's reins as she picked her way carefully through the seething crowd.

'You come to join us, mister? We're right happy to – '

'What the devil are you doing here, John?' said Joshua, recognising one of the lads who had until recently worked in the wire mill.

'We're here to fight against tyranny. Mr Dell says so.'

'Aye,' chimed in a lad at his side who could not have been more than fifteen years old. 'We're come to stop the machines!'

'You – Will Russell isn't it? – you'd far better go back to your home!' said Joshua strongly. 'The military will be here ere long, and your Mr Dell won't be able to defend you against them.'

'The military won't touch us!' said another in the crowd. 'Look how they turned from us Friday last. They knows we an't doin' nothin' wrong. See, the magistrates 'as said the machines is bad – '

'Said they should come down, they did,' echoed Arthur Wright, his simple face wreathed in smiles. 'So we're doin' it for 'em, see.'

Joshua tried to explain to them the folly of their belief and the danger in which they stood, but they were in no mood to listen.

'If you an't with us, then you're agin us, mister,' said one harshly, grabbing at the reins. Joshua had to push him away with his boot to free the mare, and it was something he had to repeat again and again as with increasing urgency he rode on, trying desperately to reach the crowd before it erupted into the Snakeley Mill buildings. His last hope was to head off at least some of the papermen, for once the military arrived, they would give no quarter after the trail of destruction that the labourers had left behind them from West Wycombe to Loudwater.

The crowd was too dense for him to make much progress and he was no more than half way across King's Mead when, from his vantage point in the saddle, he saw a group of the Beaconsfield special constables, staves in hand, take up position on the edge of Davis's Mead, between mob and mill. Solid and well-fed citizens they looked, in good coats and stout corduroys, a few even in fine beaver hats and tail coats. Sullivan, who seemed to have constituted himself the leader in the High Sheriff's absence, began to read the Riot Act once again, in clear and ringing tones, but his voice was rapidly

140

drowned out by howls of anger from the insurgents who drove on still towards Snakeley Mill.

Joshua caught sight of the Reverend Bradford of Hall Barn in a corner of the field, swearing in a group of men on horseback, who proceeded to spread out across Davis's Mead, reinforcing the entrance to the mill. As well as the local landowners, here in their position as magistrates, he recognised a couple of Excise officers and Huffam, a retired naval man from Wycombe. No more than fourteen horsemen in all, and half a dozen special constables from Beaconsfield on foot. Barely twenty against five hundred. A very thin line with which to hold the gates.

He'd hoped the sight of opposition might check the crowd, if only for a moment, but it served only to incense them. The howls of anger rose to a crescendo that made the hair rise on the back of Joshua's neck; he knew that nothing he could do now would stop the attack.

Many in the crowd were still in their work clothes, leather aprons full of rocks and broken bricks picked up in the course of the day for just such an eventuality. 'Go to it, boys!' cried one of the leaders, and a ragged hail of stones and brickbats rained down on the defenders. Two or three among them took blows on the head that stunned them and one man was removed into the mill buildings with blood pouring from a head wound.

'Bread or blood!' cried one man and the others took it up until the whole wide meadow rang with the cry. As wave after wave of the crowd surged forward, Sullivan's thin line wavered and broke, the horses plunging and rearing as the mounted guard scattered. The special constables fell back on the mill yard where they joined with Davis's men in a hand-to-hand fight with that part of the crowd which had succeeded in following them through the gates.

Sullivan, unable to relieve the mill, withdrew his mounted guard on King's Mead to try a new tactic. Most of the men armed with hammers or other weapons had pressed to the front of the crowd, so the horsemen, swords drawn, moved in on the fringes of the crowd to cut out the stick wavers and stone throwers in ones and twos and pen them in until Bradford's newly sworn-in constables, who seemed to be increasing by the minute, could come up and secure them.

James Barton, finding himself caught between two horsemen and two swords' points, tossed away the stick in his hand and tried to look like a man out for a quiet walk in the country, but it fooled no one; Charsley the coroner held him fast until Thomas Lacey came up on foot and hauled him away by the collar. When the coroner turned away to pick out another target, Barton began to struggle once more and call for help. 'Hello! Here! Here!' he cried. He was out of luck, for the rest of the crowd had their full attention on the mill yard, but

Lacey, thoroughly alarmed by the shouting, struck him on the head with his staff. Barton rolled up his eyes and crumpled in a heap at the foot of the nearby oak tree.

The labourers had split into two, the main force under Weedon holding the approaches to the mill yard, while others followed Fisher and one of the Salter brothers in a great surge to the mill doors where James Davis stood wringing his hands. 'If you will not meddle with the machine it shall never go to work again,' he said. 'I swear it! You know it has not been worked since the last tenant went bankrupt and – '

'No bargaining,' said Fisher, tightening his grip on a large piece of iron that he had earlier wrested from one of the wrecked machines. 'It must come down as well as the rest.'

'Aye. Break the machines!' cried Reynolds, and the cry was taken up by all those around him. 'All for one!' they shouted. 'No more machines!' Davis dropped his head in defeat and stood aside; the doors crashed back on their hinges and the crowd poured in.

Blizzard and Moody began to break the drying-cylinder frame, while Joseph Bryant broke the large wheels; Crutch attacked the copper pipes leading from the stuffing box to the drying cylinders and William Hancock turned his attention to the vat gearwork; Summerfield smashed with a blind fury at the gearwork of the drying cylinders and Arthur Wright, a broad smile on his simple face, hacked at the pressing cylinders until there was nothing left of the machines but a heap of twisted and sheared metal.

Kat caught at an overhanging willow branch and looped the punt ropes around it. Slipping and sliding as she scrambled up the muddy bank, she cursed her flimsy shoes and herself for not thinking to change them for her stout jean and kid boots.

At the sight of the meadow solid with men she came to an abrupt halt, catching her breath in shallow, painful gasps. Biting her lip at the pain in her side, she stood on tiptoe to try to get a view over the heads of the crowd but she could see nothing but a sea of heaving backs. An ill-aimed missile flew past her ear and she ducked; as she straightened up, a wave of dizziness washed over her and it seemed to her once more that she was not on the edge of the crowd at all, but somewhere up in the willow branches, watching herself from a distance. When she saw a group of huntsmen ride into view, attired all in scarlet coats, she could only rub her eyes in disbelief.

Joshua rode from knot to knot, trying to persuade the papermen to disperse, but his efforts were all in vain; they were convinced that they had the magistrates on the run.

The rest of the special constables, arriving at last from Beaconsfield, had been led to expect nothing more than an angry demonstration of a hundred or so papermen and were staggered at the magnitude of the fighting. Another attempt was made to break through, with the horsemen in support, but they were driven back by a hail of brickbats, stacked near the drying house by the previous tenant, before bankruptcy had ended his hopes of expansion.

'Drive the bastards back!' someone cried.

'Into the river with 'em all!' cried Fisher, emerging from the mill waving his hammer.

With a torrent of abuse, they surged forward, attacking anyone who stood in their way with stones and sledgehammers, sticks and fists, but the circumstances that awaited them as they fought their way out of the yard were not the same as when they had first entered the mill.

Joshua pulled his horse up short as about five and twenty horsemen in scarlet coats rode into King's Mead, some with swords drawn, others with pistols and hunting horns, and ranged themselves behind Sullivan. He could see Tollemache, Captain Montague of the Guards, Tarquin Bosingham . . .

The King's Staghounds – in his agitation he'd forgotten all about them!

He rose in the saddle, risking making a target of himself 'Sullivan! Montague!' he shouted across the heads of the crowd. 'You can't do this. You – !' A brick caught him a glancing blow on the side of his head and for a moment it was all he could do to keep in the saddle.

The papermen, tiring fast, were just about holding their own in the gateway between Davis's Mead and King's Mead, but the effects of the hard drinking earlier that day were beginning to show. Dell and the other leaders, blissfully unaware of the recently arrived reinforcements, turned to urge them on.

'To Clapton's next!' cried one of them.

'Aye! To Clapton's!'

As they took up the cry, edging their way forwards, and out of the yard, two shots rang out from the King's Staghounds.

The front ranks of labourers at the mill gate threw themselves down in the dirt in panic. There was a moment of shocked silence, broken briefly by angry voices as one of the clerics remonstrated with the huntsmen who had fired the shots.

Covered by a hail of brickbats from their comrades, the men who had dropped to the ground rose warily, but one of their number stayed on the ground, shot through the breast.

'They've killed him!' said an ashen-faced apprentice. 'They gone and killed Bowrey!'

'They got me too,' gasped Edmund Barton, blood welling from his arm.

Blizzard, rather shamefaced at having thrown himself in the mud, saw the men around him wavering and determined to regain his position. 'Drive 'em into the river!' he screamed in fury as he rose to his feet. 'We an't goin' to let John Bowrey die unavenged, are we?'

'No!' they howled. It was the spur they needed to make them forget their tiredness.

'Then follow me, boys. Vengeance for Bowrey!'

'Vengeance!' they cried.

'To Clapton's!' shouted Blizzard.

'Aye. To Clapton's!' they echoed him.

'We'll burn old Revel out!' called a voice from the back of the crowd, and with renewed vigour the crowd began to fight its way through the mill gates.

'No!' A woman's voice, screaming somewhere over to Joshua's right, brought his head up with a jerk; he had not been aware that there were women on the field. But before he could turn and see who it was, he saw Sullivan and the huntsmen wheeling their horses away.

What the devil were they about? thought Joshua with a deep frown. Despite the brickbats raining down – and supplies of them must surely be exhausted before long – the magistrates were by no means beaten. It seemed most unlike Sullivan to quit the field and leave it to the rebellious papermen.

Blizzard's men, seeing the horsemen's retreat, gave a shout of triumph and came pouring out of the gates, waving their hammers and metal bars aloft.

Joshua wheeled his mare around; standing up in his stirrups he saw over by the hedge a slight figure in muddied dress and no cloak, pale hair plastered to her head, passing agitatedly from one man to the other, catching them by the arm and trying to make them listen. In a brief lull in the shouting he heard a high familiar voice and his heart leaped into his throat.

'Not Clapton's!' she cried. 'He has a cannon. He'll kill you all!'

As the papermen poured out of Snakeley Mill, Joshua turned his horse to ride across to her, but as he was about to give the mare her head, someone behind him shouted the view halloo and he saw with a chill shiver what the papermen, running out of the mill yard in their mad moment of glory, had not realised: that the withdrawal had been but a feint.

'Kat! *Kat*!' he bellowed across the meadow. 'Look out! Get back! It's a trap!'

The huntsmen, far from leaving the field to the insurgents, had fanned out along the edges of the Mead; as the labourers were drawn

144

out into the open, in the pathetic belief that they were in pursuit of their enemies, the huntsmen and magistrates simply turned and rode down on them.

The crowd, realising far too late the danger they had run themselves into, began to disintegrate in panic. As they fled the horses' hooves, isolated fighting broke out around the field, but the bravado which had carried the mob this far swiftly evaporated as small groups found themselves ridden down and cut off at sword point and pistol muzzle. Those who had only sticks to defend themselves simply dropped them and ran. And the huntsmen, horns blowing, went on doing what they were best at: rounding up, cornering and then going in for the kill.

He gave up trying to push the mare through the crowd and set her to run parallel with the line of horsemen, the one thought in his mind now to fetch Kat safely from the Mead. But he was never going to reach her in time!

He rode around a huge oak tree, dimly aware of hooves thundering up behind him, and saw Kat and another woman cowering in each other's arms between the bank and a knot of horsemen. Rumsey, the Burnham surgeon, on his big black stallion, was riding shoulder to shoulder with Charsley, the coroner, and trying to cut Sawney and one of the Salter brothers out from the crowd at sword point. Rumsey reared the stallion up on its hind legs and backed the horse around to get a better line of attack. There was a shrill scream and the two women fell beneath the plunging hooves.

Coming up on the surgeon's blind side, Joshua intended only to take the stallion's reins and draw him away from the women, but Rumsey's face swam up through a red mist and he dragged the man out of the saddle, laughing out loud at Rumsey's cry of panic.

He threw himself from his horse and lifted Kat out of the mud, cradling her still body and frantically calling her name. Through the mud and the blood he thought he saw her eyes flicker, then rough hands pulled them apart.

He turned with a snarl and found himself looking down the barrel of a gun.

The red rage receded, leaving him icy cold and strangely calm. Then he saw Charsley's face behind the pistol and his stomach lurched: if it went off it was as likely to kill Kat as himself for Charsley was not renowned for a steady hand. He let his eyes flicker over Charsley's shoulder and widen in surprise. It was an old trick, but he succeeded in throwing the coroner off guard long enough to allow him to get a grip on the older man's wrist The sweat stood out on his brow and he gritted his teeth as he forced the hand and the pistol away.

Rumsey rose unsteadily to his feet and called up Heyford and another man, who fell upon Joshua and succeeded in breaking his grip on Charsley, though not before the pistol had discharged itself harmlessly in the soft earth of the bank.

'Why, it's Mr Delahaye!' said Heyford, easing his grip. 'Mr Charsley, you din't ought to be fightin' Mr Delahaye. He – '

'He's a damned Jacobin!' cursed Charsley. Taking advantage of the fact that the other special constable still held his opponent fast, Charsley drew his fist back and knocked Joshua to the ground.

Salter, seeing the attention diverted away from him, dropped his hammer and fled. Sawney, thanking heaven for a lucky escape, was on the point of following him, but when he saw Charsley on his knees trying to throttle Delahaye, the tavern keeper retrieved his metal bar and took a swing at Charsley, just to even things up. Another Beaconsfield special came up just in time to push his arm aside; the bar buried itself uselessly in the mud, and the special, seeing that Joshua had succeeded in freeing the coroner's hands from his throat, kicked out at his head. The impact drove Joshua's body towards the hedge and laid him out cold.

Heyford was about to protest at such dirty fighting when he saw Sawney pull the bar out of the mud again. No time for the niceties, he decided, and snatched up the fallen hammer to defend himself.

Sawney, thinking that Heyford too was about to strike a defenceless man, turned on him in a rage that gave him strength far beyond his years. 'Damn your eyes, Heyford, put it down!' snarled the old man, tightening his grip on the bar. 'Put it down! Or I'll knock your brains out!'

It took three men to subdue the tavern keeper and in the fray, Joshua's crumpled body was trodden on, kicked and pushed to the edge of the ditch.

# Chapter Eight

Kat opened her eyes, startled for a moment not to find herself lying on her bed in Clapton Revel. She bit her lip, winced at the pain, and remembered. Clapton Revel was in the past. For her it could never be more than a terrible memory.

She shivered uncontrollably. In the darkness her groping fingers found Joshua, as icy cold to the touch as she. Although he was more warmly dressed, the bitter November night would prove even more dangerous to an unconscious man.

What was taking Emmy so long? She should have gone herself, but with the blow on the head and then the shock of seeing Joshua when she had thought him at the other end of the country, she had not been thinking straight. Perhaps Lizzie Allnutt would refuse to see Emmy. Perhaps the girl, who had come to King's Mead looking for her brother, had gone home: what loyalty would she feel to the daughter of the man who had wanted to mow them all down at the cannon's mouth?

No. Resolutely she refused to let her mind wander down that track. After all, it was scarcely an hour since the last of the Windsor soldiers had left the field to take up their guard duties at the mills and Emmy would have found it difficult to slip past them.

She tried in vain to ease her cramped and frozen muscles, but she dared not risk making a precipitate move. It made her shudder to think how close she had already come to ruining everything. After being knocked down by the horse, she had lain winded behind the tree, for a while quite incapable of speech, close by Emmy but some distance from Joshua, while the constables brought up prisoner after prisoner and shackled or tied them to the oak and to each other. Hearing Tarquin's voice she had opened her mouth to call to him and it had been Emmy who had laid a hand over her mouth and whispered, 'Wait!'

And so she had lain there, obediently silent, and listened in horror as the magistrates and huntsmen gathered on the far side of the copse and laid their plans to remove 'these damned rebels' from King's Mead. She had heard the clatter of harness as the soldiers from Windsor rode up, too late, and agreed to take charge of the prisoners.

'We have one of their leaders,' gloated a voice she didn't recognise. 'The one they called Dell: it was Delahaye all along and the show he put on at Ash Mill last week was just to throw us off the scent. Saw him laid out when he tried to kill the coroner. Two women with him. You'll find him behind that tree – or was it t'other one?'

She could barely make out Emmy's face in the gathering gloom, but with one accord they rolled Joshua's body into the ditch and themselves with it.

'Called himself a gentleman, but I always knew Delahaye was one of those cursed rebels,' said another voice. 'Bosingham's off to Beaconsfield now to lay charges.'

'Are you quite sure?' came Tarquin's fretful voice.

'No doubt about it, old fellow.'

'Tried to kill Charsley, y'know. Saw it myself.'

'And he warned the rebels that it was a trap.'

'But surely he was warning – ' Tarquin's voice faltered and stopped.

'– the rebels, man! He was warning the rebels! Should be a hue and cry against him, eh, major?'

'A gentleman in with the rebels? I should think so!' There was the scrape of a sword being drawn from a scabbard. 'Get up, you scoundrels! Get up, I say, or you'll feel my boot on your idle back-sides! Here, sergeant,' he called, 'keep an eye to the prisoners, there's a good fellow. They're expected in Beaconsfield.' There came the sound of groaning as the papermen staggered to their feet; one of the young boys was weeping as they untied the prisoners from the trees and marched them across the Mead to the road. 'Damn his eyes,' said the Major, turning back to the magistrates, 'hangin's too good for him, sir!'

'Treason,' said another voice. 'That's what it is.'

There was the gurgle of flasks being emptied. Someone belched. Kat held her breath as she heard the clash of spurs a few feet above her head.

'No sign of him here, sir. Nor yet the two women.'

'Try t'other side of the copse.'

'I say hangin's too good for traitors like that,' said another vaguely familiar voice. 'Should hang, draw and quarter him, that's what they did to Arthur what's his name ... led the Cato Street Conspirators...'

'Thistlewood.'

'The very one. Year nineteen, was it, or twenty, when they tried to

148

assassinate the Prime Minister? Hanged, drawn and quartered,' he repeated with relish.

'I think, Sir Godfrey, that they never actually – ah . . .'

'You're right. I remember. Government lost its nerve. Cut off their heads, though, after they'd hanged them. A lesson to all these damned Jacobins!'

One by one, two by two, they had marched them off to the Oxford Road, where carts were waiting to take them into Beaconsfield, to the lock-up. And Tarquin ahead of them, to swear out an affidavit against Joshua – Joshua, who, unless help came soon, might well not survive to be arrested.

She caught her breath sharply at the stabbing pain in her side and eased the arm which was holding Joshua's head clear of the icy mud. She pressed her aching body close to his in an attempt to conserve what meagre warmth they had.


'Miss? Miss Revel?'

She must have drifted asleep again. Slowly she stirred herself, parted the long grass and found herself staring into Emmy's thin and haggard face. Over her shoulder she saw a tall figure huddled in a thick cloak.

'We have the military quartered on us,' said Zachary Allnutt, reaching down a strong arm to pull her out of her muddy hiding place. 'We had to wait until they went on duty at the mills before it was safe to leave.' He wrinkled his nose. 'I must say, I never thought you would still be in the ditch!'

'I couldn't pull him out,' she said tearfully. 'And he was so cold, I couldn't leave him.'

'Damn!' Allnutt corrected himself swiftly. 'I beg your pardon, Miss Kattrin. Hadn't realised he was still unconscious. It makes matters a little more difficult.'

'We ought to have a doctor to him,' said Allnutt, as he and Emmy between them heaved Joshua out of the ditch, as stiff as a log, 'but I daren't take the risk.'

'Tarquin Bosingham is gone to swear evidence against him,' she said. 'But Joshua wasn't part of the mob! I swear it! He was only trying to stop the trouble.'

'I know. I've tried to explain that to the military,' said Allnutt wearily, 'but they are not in the mood to listen tonight.'

'He needs someone to see to him,' said Emmy grimly. 'If he an't goin' to git a doctor, then p'raps the old herb lady bottom o' Treadaway Hill – '

Allnutt shook his head. 'We have to take him right away from the

149

village,' he said curtly. 'There's vengeance in the air. And if he has a price on his head . . .' He didn't need to finish his words.

'I know where I can take him,' said Kat, brushing her hair out of her eyes and leaving a dark smear across her forehead that stood out against her skin, pale in the cold starlight.

'You?' exclaimed Allnutt. 'You'll go nowhere, my girl, except straight back to your father's.'

'I can't go back,' she said. 'He's thrown me out.' If it was not exactly the truth, it was as near as Allnutt could cope with. And whatever happened, she could never go back.

They reached the ferry shortly before dawn. The journey had taken them far longer than it should have, for they had held to the woodland tracks to avoid the armed guards at the mills and on the roads. Travelling over the high ground through Fennels Wood, Northern Woods, down Bunker Hill and up Wash Hill, and across the common to Harvest Hill, the tired horse turned at last into the hollow way that ran between the church and the towers of the folly – built somewhat prematurely by an earlier Bosingham to celebrate George III's recovery from madness – and down to Hedsor Wharf. The night was cold and clear and Bernard knew the tracks well enough not to need a lantern.

Emmy had provided them with the transport, a rough dung cart in which her neighbour carried night soil from the villages to the surrounding fields; in case the stench should not prove sufficient to deter questions, Allnutt had arranged for Bernard the Walker to drive the cart, carrying official papers ordering Burnham, Cookham and Taplow to swear in special constables.

As the sky lightened behind the tall trees lining the riverbank, turning the river a steely grey, Bernard tethered the cart to the railing and his bent figure disappeared round the back of the boatman's cottage. In the stinking depths of the cart Kat stretched her cramped limbs, raised the sacking an inch or two and peered out.

Beyond the cottage loomed a group of mill buildings; almost drowned out by the rush of water and the creaking of the millwheel she could hear the faint murmur of the day workers as they arrived to take over from the night shift. An oblong of yellow light broke the shadows of the mill yard as the door opened to admit them.

Carefully she moved across the cart to look upstream. On the long row of barges tied up at the wharf, below the cluster of buildings that had stood there since Elizabeth had been queen, there were already signs of life as the bargemen removed the hooped canvas awnings that had sheltered them through the night, and began to kindle small stoves to heat water for something hot to drive the night's chill from

150

their bones. On the far bank, from among the piles of spoil where the new cut was being dug through Sashes Island, a heron rose, flapped its wings and glided silently downstream like a pale-grey ghost.

Kat's mouth was dry and her throat full of the acrid stench of the cart; she thought longingly of the kitchen at Clapton Revel with a kettle singing over the fire and Cook unlocking the tea caddy to spoon out the leaves.

Something dripped down her cheek and she brushed it away with the back of her hand, not daring to investigate further. 'Will you take bohea, Lady Isabelle?' she said under her breath. 'Will you have bread and butter? Or a rout cake?'

Another life. Another world.

She caught her breath as she heard the sound of footsteps coming towards the cart – two pairs of footsteps. As she lowered the sacking, Joshua stirred in the bottom of the cart and began to mutter something. Dropping down onto the boards, she edged across to his side and put her hand over his lips. 'Hush, Joshua,' she whispered, her mouth close to his ear. 'Not now.'

'You an't got to trouble yourself,' said Bernard, his voice booming only a few inches from her ear. 'I got to give it 'im in his hand anyways, so I'll take meself over. I give the signal, so the boat an't goin' to be long a-comin'.'

'Right, then.'

One pair of boots moved away down the path to the mill, metal rims tapping on the stone. With a sigh of relief she raised her head. The ferry would be here soon, with Nonie's husband John; it would be a relief to let someone else take the decisions. She felt Joshua's mouth stir against her hand and eased the pressure, only to have it snatched back by Joshua, who pressed his lips to her palm in a kiss that made her shiver.

She made to roll away, to return to the front of the cart to listen for the ferry, but Joshua's arm was still around her waist and it tightened as she moved. 'Not now, Joshua,' she whispered. 'Let me go!'

His hand came up behind her head and pulled her back down. His breath was warm on her cheeks as his questing mouth sought hers. In the darkness the first kiss went awry, but then his lips found hers. She jumped at the gentle pressure on her bruised mouth, but he stifled her whispered protests. For a moment she tried to hold her body stiffly away from his, tried to pull her head up again, but when he persisted she deemed it wiser to acquiesce, in spite of the pain in her lips, than to resist and risk discovery. The long slow kiss seemed to go on for ever, and so stirred her blood and warmed her chilled body that she ceased to care about the pain or the need to keep him quiet. The feel of his mouth moving warmly over hers and her body pressed close to

151

his aroused feelings in her that she had never before experienced and she was in no hurry to bring them to an end. One hand slipped down to move among the dishevelled curls on the nape of her neck and the other ran up her spine in a manner that made her even more breathless than his kisses. And when, after what seemed a lifetime, his hips bucked against hers, it seemed the most natural thing in the world to return the pressure. Joshua gave a deep groan and pulled her urgently to him.

His lips left her mouth reluctantly and moved to a sensitive spot just under her ear. She found herself murmuring his name as the skin on her throat basked in his warm breath.

'What in Hades are you doing in there?' came John's voice in an urgent whisper that acted on them both like a bucket of icy water.

'The old cart's shaking like it's got the ague!' chuckled Bernard.

Joshua released his hold abruptly and Kat rolled away across the filthy boards and lay in the corner, her face hot with embarrassment.

One at a time they hustled them from the cart and onto the ferry where they laid them on the bottom, covered with a sheet of canvas. Within minutes they were in the cottage and Bernard on his way back to the other bank.

'My! Master Joshua, what have you been a-doing?' demanded Nonie as her erstwhile charge staggered in, leaning heavily on John. 'You do look as if you spent the night in the dung heap!' Joshua smiled weakly at her, opened his mouth to answer, gasped, and crumpled into John's arms. Before Kat could speak, Nonie held up her hand.

'Let's see you warm and dry first, child,' she said, bustling about with kettles and a hip bath she had set in front of the fire as soon as Allnutt's message came. 'You look no better than he does. We'll get those filthy rags off you as quick as we can, before you catch your death of cold.' She turned to her husband. 'Do you strip the lad off in the kitchen, John. We'll have the explanations later.'

As the cottage door opened, Nonie looked up with a start from the pancheon where she was knocking back the bread dough after its first rising.

'Look like that when the soldiers come, lass, and they'll know for certain there's something amiss,' said John, crossing the room to give his wife a hearty kiss.

'You gave me a fright, creeping in like that!' she scolded. 'Why aren't you at your work?' she demanded, as he tossed his tally books into the corner and settled into the rocking chair at the fireside. 'I thought we agreed – ' She stopped abruptly and put a hand up to her mouth. 'Have the soldiers been across this side then?'

152

'No. Nor are likely to.' He swung the kettle over the fire, then cocked his head to one side to listen. 'Our visitors still asleep?'

'Aye. All bathed and tucked up under the eaves.'

He raised his eyebrows. 'Not both in the same room?'

'Scarce proper, I know,' said Nonie, flushing. 'But I have to be down here in case we have unwelcome callers. And Master Joshua, he do keep calling out in his sleep. The lass says she *can't* sleep, so I left her to watch over him.'

'You ought to give her one of your sleeping draughts, girl. After the night she had, she'll need sleep almost as much as he does, for all she's not as bad hurt.'

'Not in the fighting, she wasn't,' said Nonie grimly. 'But she's in a terrible bad state for all that.' She pummelled the bread dough viciously 'Got cuts and weals and bruisings on her as bad and worse than anything Master Joshua got at King's Mead. And her face – ' Her voice broke and with floury hands she wiped away the ready tears, leaving two streaks of white on her flushed cheeks.

John swore under his breath. 'Her father?'

'She wouldn't sign the marriage papers,' she said as she divided and shaped the dough. 'Seems the plan was to beat her and starve her till she agreed.'

'So Revel has a betrothal and no bride?'

'Aye.' She shook her head and smiled. 'Always knew she had spirit, that one.'

'A father has a right to chastise his child, lass,' said John with a frown.

'Chastise! Aye. But this – this is cruelty, John.'

'Revel is a hard man, I know it. But if he comes here looking for his daughter, it could endanger Joshua. Better we send her back.'

'I couldn't do it, John. Nor could you, if you'd seen what I've seen. Oh, John, you'd not whip and starve an animal the way he's done to her. Cut her off from everyone. Even told her that Joshua had gone away. And that's another consideration ...'

'What is?'

'It's Master Joshua. I don't think she'd leave him. And I'm none so sure he'd let her go.'

'So that's the way the wind blows, is it?' He leaned forward to light a taper from the fire and touched it to his pipe. 'Well, they'd best get themselves to a preacher.'

Nonie's sleeping draughts were renowned for their swift effect and Kat slept through the rest of that day and all of the following night, waking only when the sun stole its way through a chink in the dimity curtains and fell on the crisp cotton pillow.

153

She looked across at the bed on the other side of the room and saw with relief Joshua's chest rising and falling steadily. His skin had lost the grey hue of the previous day, and there was healthy colour in his cheeks.

She was trying to get out of bed to cross to his side when she heard a sound from the doorway and looked up to see Nonie standing there, hands on her hips.

'Here's a change in a day!' said Nonie, beaming with satisfaction. 'But back into bed with you now!' She crossed to the bed and helped Kat sit up. The girl winced as Nonie plumped the pillows up behind her. 'Aye. It'll pain you a few days yet. That devil of a man's maybe cracked a rib casing, but I doubt there's any bones broken.'

'And Joshua?'

'I've always said he was as tough as whip leather, even as a child. Don't you fret, child. He'll waken shortly and be as fit as fivepence, barring a bit of a headache. You've been luckier than either of you deserves!' she said, shaking her head. 'Walking into the middle of a rebellion! But there's no use crying over spilt milk. And if so be you feel up to it, there's a young man outside wishful to see you.'

Her eyes widened in fear. Who knew that she was here? 'Who is it?' she said, in a voice barely above a whisper.

'It's me, miss!' The door bounced back against the wall and Tom erupted into the room. 'Gawd! Look at your face, miss!' he exclaimed, taking in the bruises, now turned all the hues of the rainbow. 'We all thought you was safe in London, for your maid told Mister Joshua you was gone. And then you turns up in the middle of all that fightin'. Why di'n't you get a message to me, miss? I'd ha' gone in your place, taken messages for yer, straight up I would've. Weren't no need fer you ter – '

'Hush, Tom!' said Nonie. 'You'll wear Miss Kat out with all your chatter!'

But Tom was too wound up to bide his time. It all came pouring out, how Bernard the Walker had told Mister Will where Joshua was, and how, when they had heard of the warrant out for him, they had fretted about how best to get him to safety. 'An' Mister Will says best get Mister Joshua to his uncle,' he concluded. 'So I got a lift on the carrier's cart into Bone End and made me shift along here. But don't worry. No one saw me come over 'cos I hid on one of the carts as was waiting for the ferry.'

'His uncle! Of course!' said Nonie approvingly. 'I dare say with time I'd have thought of that, but with a warrant out, maybe we wouldn't have had that time.'

'A warrant?' whispered Kat and her stomach lurched. 'How could

154

they?' she said with growing indignation. 'They know that all he wanted to do was help!'

'Until we can persuade them of that, we'll help him best by getting him out of here to safety,' said Nonie.

That opinion was strengthened by John, who returned from taking Tom back over the river with the grim news that the soldiers had been at Hedsor Wharf and on Sashes Island questioning the boatmen about strangers seen around the area.

'They've sent reinforcements from the barracks at Windsor,' he said. 'Searching the woods all around, they are. Caught two of the papermen yesterday. They do say one or two has turned king's evidence to save their own skin.'

'That settles it,' said Nonie. 'You'll take him to his uncle tomorrow.'

Kat, who she had thought was sleeping by the fireside, tucked up in a blanket, opened her eyes. 'I thought Joshua and his father had no other family,' she said with a puzzled frown.

'It's a sad story,' said Nonie, looking to John for guidance.

Her husband puffed steadily on his pipe. 'Reckon you'd best tell the lass,' he said at last.

Kat, warm and snug in her blanket, felt as if she were a small child and Nonie her own nurse, telling her a bedtime story in her soft country voice.

Will Delahaye and his brother Saul were the sons of a Leicestershire lawyer, himself the younger son of a worthy squire. The lawyer was a good man who had all but bankrupted himself opposing the enclosures of the common land on behalf of the villagers. After their father's death both sons had, through their grandfather's connections, found positions on the estates of local landowners. Will had fallen in love with the daughter of a prominent and wealthy man whose estate adjoined the property he managed. There had been a great deal of opposition from the young lady's family to an alliance with one they regarded as no more than a farm bailiff, but when she came of age they had married and for a year or two been very happy.

'It was a love match, no doubt about it,' said Nonie, 'although being cast off by her family did set the poor lady back. She so hoped that they would relent after the birth of young Joshua, but they never did. Little by little it came between them and things began to go awry. And in the end she left him.' Nonie compressed her lips and Kat knew there were some things she would never tell.

Joshua's father had tried everything he could to bring her back, but in vain. At last, unable to stay in the house where once they had been so happy, he had accepted a post with Lord Bosingham and moved, with his son and Nonie, the boy's nurse, to one of the estate houses in Hedsor.

Only once had Will Delahaye travelled back to Leicestershire, to settle some business from his grandfather's estate, and had fallen into a violent argument about the use of traps against poachers. Will had stormed out of his brother's house, intending to take the first stage-coach south.

'There was never any talking to him, then as now,' said Nonie sadly 'Will Delahaye in a rage could have walked through Bona-parte's retreat from Moscow and not noticed anything.'

He had gone through the woods in a blind fury and, not watching his step, had himself been caught in one of the mantraps. It had been a poacher who found him in the end, but not till hours later. They had called a surgeon who had done what he could, but Will was a stubborn man.

'Swore he wouldn't stay under the same roof as a man who spoke in favour of mantraps, no matter what Saul said. Sent for a carriage, the obstinate man!' said Nonie. 'His leg broke out bleeding, it did, and got infected. Never was right after that. In the end they had to take the leg off to save his life. And that was the end of his work.'

'And Saul?'

'He blamed himself, of course. He left his work and his home and came down to nurse Will. Swore he would be a bailiff no more.'

'Is he in Wooburn?'

'No. When Will recovered, Saul went off to live with the bodgers in the woods.'

'So he'll be back in Wycombe now?' The bodgers, wood turners who set up their huts and pole lathes in the Chiltern beechwoods every spring, were always back in town come October to sell their bundles of chair legs and stretchers to the workshops and small chair factories.

'Not him,' said John. 'Proper hermit is Saul now. Couple of times a year I go up to the woods to fetch his work and see if there's anything he needs for the winter.'

'So that's where Joshua will go tomorrow, if he's fit to be moved.'

'Take me across the river first, if you please,' said Kat, pushing the blanket off her lap and standing up with a look of determination on her face. 'It isn't right that Joshua should be a fugitive for something he didn't do,' she said. 'And I'm the only one who can do anything about it.'

They swooped down from the woods and were upon her before she well knew what was happening. The old horse, taken unawares, stumbled, almost unseating her from the improvised side-saddle.

There were about a dozen men in scarlet uniforms – mounted guards, not the local militia. The watery sun raised a feeble glint on their epaulettes and scabbards as they surrounded her. She cursed herself. She should have had her mind on her surroundings, instead of wondering whether Joshua was yet safe away from Cookham.

'Goodness, how you startled me!' she exclaimed, struggling to bring the horse under control. 'I swear I thought you were highwaymen!'

'Ho, yes!' said one of the soldiers, looking her up and down mockingly, as if to say, What would a highwayman want with you?

She blushed, reminding herself that she must cut rather an unimpressive figure on the old horse and in Nonie's shapeless old cloak. But when one of the young officers reached out to take her reins, she drew herself up in the saddle and fixed him with a haughty stare.

'Pray unhand my horse, sir,' she said stiffly, as like to Lady Isabelle as she could manage. 'I am in some haste.'

The officer looked round his men with a knowing smile. 'We'd have expected any *proper* young lady to be safely at her fireside, with all the other law-abiding citizens, wouldn't we, lads? We'd expect her to leave His Majesty's highway free for the brave soldier lads hunting out all those nasty rebels!'

A snigger ran along the lines and she coloured angrily. It would be the easiest thing in the world to put back the hood of her cloak and tell them who she was. Their attitude would change, no doubt, but there was no certainty that they would not send her straight back home. Once back at Clapton, she would never get away again. And where would that leave Joshua?

She would have to try another cast. 'I am on my way to see Lord Bosingham,' she said.

'Have a long wait. His lordship's not in residence.'

'Of course.' She corrected herself swiftly. 'The family has gone to Ireland, to Lord Dunster's family. Then I must go to Beaconsfield. Lord Bosingham would wish me to pass on my information to the authorities.'

'Information?' For a moment she thought she had convinced him, then a scruffily dressed man who sat his horse like a plough boy pushed his mount alongside and muttered something to the officer. The officer's brows snapped together in a hard line beneath his shako. 'This would be information about the rebel leader, would it?'

'I know nothing about any rebel leader,' she said through frozen lips.

The officer stroked the ends of his moustache thoughtfully. 'Don't know Delahaye? Why, I thought everyone hereabouts knew Delahaye. I dare say there's a queue of 'em in Beaconsfield even now, looking to collect the reward.'

'Reward? But he wasn't with the rebels!' she exclaimed angrily. 'Ask anyone! We all know he was there to stop the fighting!'

'Ah! You were there, were you?'

'Haven't I just said so?'

'Right. Sergeant! Take her in charge. Put her in the cart with the rest.'

She opened and closed her mouth like a stunned trout caught up in the millwheel, but no sound would come. At last she found her voice once more. 'On what grounds?' she protested.

He shrugged. 'Conspiracy, riot, destruction of property . . . Plenty to choose from.' The soldiers closed in around her, leaving the old horse no choice but to proceed along the road between them. Kattrin's hands were shaking and her legs seemed no longer to do her bidding; it was only by a great effort of will that she held her seat.

Around the curve of the road they found a cart full of men, some of them from the village, chained to one another like common felons.

Rough hands pulled her down from the horse and pushed her to the cart. 'Wrists!' commanded the guard.

She looked blindly at him. 'Wrists!' he snarled again and she jumped at the feel of the cold metal as he placed a shackle over one wrist and chained it to the other.

She stumbled as they dragged her to the back of the cart and rough hands caught her and pushed her in. Most of the men had their heads bowed, absorbed in their own misery, and hardly looked up as the soldiers pushed her down onto the bench.

'Don't fret,' said a voice in her ear and she looked up warily to see young Jack Aycott grinning at her. 'They brung us a message in the woods,' he said in an excited whisper. 'Aye. Stormed Aylesbury gaol yesterday, they did, an' freed all the men as was took at King's Mead. Broke up the treadmill too. I said as how they wouldn't abandon us, di'n't I, Dan? I said Captain Swing would – '

'Hush yer row, Jack!' hissed his neighbour. 'Or you'll talk a noose round yer neck.'

Jack's lip quivered and he fell silent.


Kattrin sat in a corner of the cage, her arms clasped round her knees and her head buried in the hood of her cloak. She fought to hold back the tears, fearing that if she once gave way she would never stop.

On the other side of the cramped space some of her fellow prisoners were discussing her in low tones.

'I tell you 'tis her!' said one. 'I was behind 'un in the workhouse when they read 'un the charge. Pulled the hood back, they did, an' I knowed 'un straight off. An't many round here got that colourin'.'

'Is it likely they'd put someone like her in the cage?' said another scornfully. 'That knock on the head have addled your brains, Thomas!'

'They'd ha' put her in the women's cage!' agreed a third man.

'They wouldn't ha' put her in the lock-up at all, you simpleton. Anyways, this *is* the women's cage!' The speaker laughed, but there was little mirth in it. 'Men's side is full to burstin' since day afore yesterday. Never 'ad so many in 'ere, gaoler said, not even on fair days with all the drunks!'

The fair. How many years was it since Joshua had brought her and Dickon to the fair? Oh, such a day that had been! They had been thirteen or fourteen and it had been the most exciting day in her life. The May sun had shone brightly out of a clear blue sky and the three of them had passed among the crowds, she with her face and hair hidden beneath an old-fashioned cottage bonnet, Dickon with a hat pulled down over his ears to hide the distinctive colouring, talking to one another in the local dialect, not a difficult feat for two children who had for too long been left to their own devices around the mills. They had bought fairings and sticky toffee and watched wide-eyed the travelling theatre, the sword-swallowers and the fire-eaters. But Joshua would not let them go into the booths with the bearded lady, the dwarfs and the two-headed man.

'It's their misfortune they were made that way, but we don't have to take entertainment from it,' he said firmly, and carried them off to the local inn to dine.

He had taken them home in the early evening, when the town began to grow rowdy, and neither Dickon nor Kat had ever forgotten that splendid day of freedom. Whenever she drove through Beaconsfield – and it was usually only to go to church – she would see, not the silk pelisses and braided parasols of the gentry in their carriages in Windsor End, but the rough shawls and the garish bonnets, the fustian and the best corduroy breeches and the sound of rough boots clattering across the cobbles as the villagers came from miles around for a day's freedom at the Charter Fair.

She looked up as the metal door rattled and a constable appeared in the doorway. She half rose to her feet, convinced they had realised their mistake. But now they knew who she was, her father might even now be waiting to take her back to Clapton Revel.

'Bates!' growled the constable and a young man sitting by himself at the back of the cage rose unsteadily to his feet. 'Out!'

'Traitor!' hissed a thickset man, turning his back on the youth.

Young Bates, son of the man who had been leading the soldiers on

159

their sweep through the woods, began to protest, but one by one the other men turned their backs on him. His shoulders slumped and he stumbled through the door, which the constable locked behind him.

'They'll likely come for Holt soon,' said one of the older men, trying to inject a more cheerful note. 'I told 'em, Moses,' he said, patting the arm of the little man beside him, 'I said as how you was forced to come wi' us.'

'Aye. And Joseph Priest with 'un.'

'It's not fair to hold 'em, bein' as how they was pressed.'

The little man with the round head looked up and tried to smile at his companions. 'They won't let me go, boys,' he said, and the smile went awry. 'What with me bein' from Kent. Anyways, I've no wish to put myself apart. I won't turn from you. All for one an' all that . . . you know.'

A fair-haired lad, scarcely more than a boy, began to weep in the corner.

'Come, William lad, bear up,' said the thickset man, crossing to his side and putting a comforting hand on the heaving shoulders.

'I'll be better soon, Aaron,' sobbed William. 'I an't givin' way, boys, really I an't . . .' His voice trailed away. 'It's just, I'm that fretted about mother – how she'll manage without me.'

'Your father's no better, then?'

The boy shook his head.

'Death's the only cure for old Russell in this world,' whispered Holt. 'The cankers has got a hold on his mouth and gullet, see. Boy's mother'll be a widow afore many days.'

'It weren't right to bring the lad along,' said another man. 'It weren't right to force nobody.'

'I an't blamin' no one but meself,' said William fiercely, dragging his sleeve across his eyes. 'Mr Delahaye told me to go home and I should ha' listened to him the first time.'

'You spoke to Mr Delahaye?' Kat sat up so abruptly that the hood fell back. A rustle of excited whispers ran round the room.

'Why, yes, miss. Spoke to him twice,' said Russell with a puzzled frown. 'Well, rightly, 'twas he spoke to me. Told me to go home. Wished I'd ha' listened.'

'Don't speak to her n'more, Will,' said Moses Holt urgently. 'A trap, it is. Aye, you can look down your nose at me, missie, but why else would they put you in here?' He turned to the others in great agitation. 'Her father, he's one of the worst against the papermen. Why, they d'say he even set up a great gun to mow us all down!'

'But she an't her father!' An elderly man who, like Kat, had been slumped with his head in his hands, taking no part in the talk, raised his head and looked angrily around the room. 'She come to the field to warn us about the gun. She di'n't have to come, but she did. Told me – aye, an' Jamie Miller too.'

'Why else would they put her in here, Jem?'

'For being on the field at King's Mead,' she snapped. 'That's why they put me in here.'

'You an't got to speak to her, Will,' urged Lunnon, the shoemaker from Flackwell Heath. 'I've heard tell they do sometimes put traps in the cells, agents like, to swear they heard you confess.'

'Is it likely Revel 'ud put his own daughter in the lock-up?' Jem asked scornfully. 'Use your head.'

'Then why an't he come to git her out?'

'My father doesn't know I'm here,' she said, hoping against hope that it was the truth. 'I came to Beaconsfield only to clear Mr Delahaye's name, but they will have it he's the rebel leader.'

'But he stopped the Wycombe men on Friday at Ash Mill!'

'I reminded them of that fact. They won't listen. But if William could tell them – '

'That he told me to go home? I already told 'em, miss,' said the boy, looking at her with great sad eyes. 'Tried to, any rate. But one of the gentlemen as was with the hunt have swored out powerful evidence against him. I an't thinkin' my word's goin' to count anythin' against that.'

Long before dawn the cage was already so full that the men could no longer leave her and the other woman their own corner.

In the course of the night, some of them had perforce to avail themselves of the bucket in the corner of the cage; showing as much courtesy as was possible under the circumstances the others arranged themselves between that corner and the women. It struck Kat that they were behaving with considerably more propriety than some of Lord Bosingham's guests at a recent hunt dinner, who, far on in drink, had thought nothing of relieving themselves behind the screens within earshot of the ladies, nor of belching openly in their presence.

Kat racked her brain to think what she should do next. She had a few passing acquaintances in Beaconsfield from the brief few months when Revel had brought his family to worship there. Although brought up a Nonconformist, for years Revel had not attended either church or chapel, but his ambitions to be made a magistrate had brought about a change of heart; considering Wooburn's own church of St Paul's in its present state of ruin quite unsuitable, with the coffins breaking through the floor between the high box pews, he had begun to attend Beaconsfield's parish church, although now the Revels worshipped with the Bosinghams at Hedsor.

161

Any of her Beaconsfield acquaintances would arrange her release most speedily. What was equally certain was that every one of them would consider it his duty to return her promptly to the bosom of her family. At the moment, that prospect terrified her far more than another night in the Beaconsfield lock-up.

She became aware of Martha shifting uncomfortably next to her and saw in the grey light the livid marks that the chains were gouging in the woman's pallid flesh.

'Those chains are too tight,' she said angrily. 'We must call for the constable and have them taken off!'

'I wouldn't do that, missie, if I were you,' said Martha with a watery chuckle. 'Not unless you wants 'em to put us all in chains.'

'Why should you be chained when the rest of us are not?'

''Cos the rest of us got more sense than to fight with the soldiers!' said Martha's neighbour, who had been thrown into the cage at the same time as her.

'Laid one out wi' an iron skillet,' said Martha with grim satisfaction.

Kat tore a strip from Nonie's best shawl and threaded the soft silk between the chains and the skin as the flame in the lantern overhead flickered and died.

It seemed to her that she had only just closed her eyes when the order came to turn out. The prisoners were marched between two rows of soldiers with fixed bayonets towards two large, old-fashioned travelling coaches. In the flickering light of the lanterns she saw a man slumped against the back of the nearest carriage Her breath caught in her throat as he straightened up.

'Joshua, no!' she gasped, and their eyes met and held. To her horror she saw that he was held to the carriage by a length of chain.

'Keep moving, there!' came a shout from the rear and someone gave her a hefty shove between the shoulder blades, almost pitching her onto her face.

'Keep your hands off her!' snarled Joshua. 'Don't touch her, you – '

'An't no one goin' to touch her if'n she gets herself into that there coach,' said the sergeant.

'Damn you, let her go!' said Joshua, his voice hoarse with concern.

'Let her go?' said the soldier who was checking the prisoners against a list. 'Your brains gone a-beggin', man? She's for the courts, same as the rest of you.'

'But the constable said he'd let her go when I surrendered to the warrant!' he exploded.

'Joshua! No!' After all she had done to keep him free!

'Constable of Wooburn – Nash – he said she could go! He agreed that it was all a misunderstanding and – '

'But Nash an't here, is he?' said the soldier, spitting contemptuously at Kat's feet. Joshua growled deep in his throat and jerked impotently at his chain; the soldier raised his musket threateningly above his head.

'Don't! Don't, Joshua!' she begged, picking up her skirts and climbing obediently into the *fourgon*. A part of her mind detached from her immediate troubles noted that it bore the coat of arms of Lord Carrington. 'If we must go to Wycombe to sort out this folly, then by all means let us go to Wycombe.'

The soldier laughed and spat again.

The seats had all been taken out to allow greater numbers to be carried, and the first prisoners ranged themselves around the walls, sitting or squatting; those who followed filled up the centre, leaning against each other. As the *fourgon* set out down Wycombe End there was a silence you could have cut. Until now all the villagers had expected that the misery of the night would end with a brief appearance before the Beaconsfield magistrates, agreeing to be bound over and sent home with a flea in their ear. But the courts in Wycombe were a different matter.

The coach had just passed the old inn at Holtspur and was starting down the steep hill through Cut-Throat Woods when they were all catapulted forward and thrown in a heap on top of each other as the coach slewed across the road, the iron bands on the wheels screeching on the road surface.

'What's amiss?' asked the guard, disentangling himself from the cursing mass of bodies and sliding back the communicating hatch.

'Fool of a woodman's spilled his logs across the road!' shouted the driver, cursing as he fought to bring his horses under control.

There was a pounding of feet and the coach door was jerked open from outside; bodies shot out and rolled all over the road. The guard was scrambling to his feet, struggling to cock the hammer on his pistol when he found an old-fashioned pike inches from his nose.

'Wouldn't make no move if I was 'ee,' observed the masked man at the other end of the pike handle. He looked round impatiently at the prisoners, picking themselves up and dusting themselves down.

'Well, boys, what be you waitin' fer?' demanded the squat man at his side, waving his hand at the woods. 'Be on your way afore the soldiers – '

His words were drowned out by the thunder of hooves as a small body of the Windsor troops topped the hill.

'Run, boys! Miss Revel, run!' shouted the man with the pike. 'Get out o' here!'

163

But the prisoners never stood a chance. Cold, tired and hungry after a cramped night in the cage, they were in no state to outrun armed and mounted men. The would-be rescuers, accepting the inevitable, melted back into the woods, all but one, who caught his foot in a tree root and was brought down as he scrambled up the slope. After a brief fight, he was captured, unmasked and brought to stand with the rest of the prisoners.

'Thass Tommy Hughes!' said a voice behind Kattrin.

'We'll take no more chances,' said the officer. 'Chain them up.'

'Not the women!' said Joshua angrily, as one of the soldiers grabbed ungently at Kat's wrists. He turned to the officer. 'There's no need to chain the women!' He moved protectively towards her and a second young trooper, misreading his move, swung his musket at him. Still fuddled from the blows he had received at King's Mead, Joshua was in no state to dodge the blow. The musket end caught him in the stomach and he fell at the officer's feet. Doubled up in pain, he vomited over the shiny leather boots. The officer looked down in disbelief and with a snarl of fury drew back his boot. The first kick narrowly missed Joshua's head and struck his shoulder; as the sickening crack rebounded from the trees and echoed over the hills, the officer kicked him again and this time the soiled leather found its target.

The troopers pushed the wagon and the logs aside and the chained prisoners shuffled despondently back into the *fourgon*. In spite of the chafing of their chains they cradled Joshua's unconscious body against the jolting all the way to Wycombe, and when there was no room to take them in there, they cradled him all the long and weary way to Aylesbury gaol.

# Chapter Nine

The hoarse cry of pain and the sound of bone crunching on bone echoed off the dripping walls. The surgeon straightened up from Joshua's pallet with a sigh and mopped the sweat from his forehead.

'There. I dare swear that shoulder will be good as new in a few months.' He fished a pot of salve out of his bag. 'Put this on your wrists,' he said to Martha. 'They won't put the chains back on, if you give no more trouble.'

'I don't hold with violence,' said Martha, a birdlike woman in her middle years, so tiny she barely came up to the surgeon's chest. 'But when I saw four on 'em layin' into my Amos, as weren't even at the fightin' . . . seemed to me the skillet evened things up.' She squinted at the spidery writing on the little pot. 'Will I put it on the lass's back?'

'Aye.' He glanced across the cell at Kat, who was wiping Joshua's face with aromatic vinegar and water. 'Though if she's any sense she'll send for her family without delay. This is no place for a young lady.'

'You saw her back!' exclaimed Martha. 'She an't got them stripes in no riot! Would you have her go home to that?'

The surgeon shrugged. 'There must be friends who could intervene . . . Look at the alternative!' he said, with a sweeping gesture that encompassed the stained walls, the metal-studded prison door and the small barred window. 'Going home must surely be the lesser of the two evils!'

'I'll talk to her,' said Martha, unconvinced.

'Aye. And soon.' He shook his head. 'She can do more good outside than in here.' He turned back to Joshua and Amos, both lying unconscious and deathly pale but for the livid marks of the beatings they had each suffered. 'There are fevers in the hospital ward and to keep them away from there will take money.'

'But they can stay here for now?' said Martha anxiously.

'One night is all I can promise,' he said. 'After that you'll have to bribe the turnkey. Mind you' – he jerked his head towards Kat – 'one night in a common cell should convince her to go home.'

'He's right, y'know, missie,' said Martha, looking down at Kat. 'This place an't fit for the likes of you.'

Kat looked up at them, her eyes blurred with tears. 'I have already sent to Wooburn,' she said. 'I thought Joshua was going to die, you see.'

She'd been so convinced that once they reached Aylesbury gaol – its solid stone walls mocking rumours of its destruction – the truth would come out and both she and Joshua would be released. But when she saw that no argument of hers would sway the authorities, she had been left with no choice but to send messages to the Allnutts and to Clapton Revel.

She bit her lower lip. 'It is possible, of course, that my father may not come.'

'Surely any father – '

'Mr Emberton, you have not met my father. But come!' she said, as Martha's face fell. 'The case is not as desperate as we first thought.'

'Aye.' Martha forced a smile. 'God be thanked, neither of 'em's goin' to die.'

'We must trust to justice,' said Kattrin confidently. 'The courts will soon find that there is no evidence against any of us.'

Mr Emberton cleared his throat. 'I fear not. As I told the Wooburn men earlier, if it can be shown that you were present at the riot, then you may be held guilty of any crimes committed by any of the mob. It is the law.'

'But that is unjust!' said Kat. 'How may we be held responsible for the actions of others?'

'Once the Riot Act has been read, those who do not disperse are deemed as guilty as the original rioters. It is the law.'

'Then *damn* the law!' she exclaimed, rounding on him.

'Oh, missie, don't!' cried Martha.

Kat ran her fingers through her hair. 'But it is quite unfair of me to rail at you, Mr Emberton.' She forced a smile. 'I dare swear you hear tales of woe and cries of "unfair" every day.'

The surgeon busied himself with the leather ties on his bag. It would be too easy to smile back, to lose himself in those huge golden eyes. 'I long ago concluded that I should not meddle where I cannot mend,' he said gruffly. 'I confine myself to dealing with the bodily hurts.'

But he had done something more for them: the arrival of the prisoners from Wycombe, following so quickly on the heels of the farm-machine breakers from Stone and Waddesdon, had stretched the town gaol well beyond its limits. Heeding the doctor's warning that the typhoid fever prevalent in the Aylesbury area might spread through the overcrowded prison, the governor had transferred the debtors into the juvenile ward, and put the papermen in their place; the men with the worst injuries were in smaller cells nearby, normally reserved for debtors with influential friends who could afford to grease the gaoler's palm.

Kat spent the day in dread and fear, shaking every time she heard the clanging of a gaol door above the rumble of the treadmill, convinced that it heralded her father's imminent arrival, but when by nightfall not even a message had been received from Wooburn, she felt paradoxically rather hurt. Scarce surprising if her father had turned her off, but what of Dickon and Aunt Lucy? And the Allnutts, who had so often professed themselves her friends?

The arrival of the mean prison fare of grey bread, oozing cheese and water that looked as though it had recently been dipped from some stagnant pond, was the signal for an outbreak of screeching and fighting in the common cells just along the corridor; the small cell, which earlier that day had seemed to close in on her, was now, in spite of its squalor and cramped condition, a safe haven. When the deputy chaplain, an elderly man whose head and hands constantly twitched with the palsy, came on his rounds urging them to pray for God's mercy upon their evil-doing, she begged him to intercede with the gaoler to permit her to stay with Martha and the men.

'Stay here?' he exclaimed 'An unmarried young maiden in a room apart, with two men? Out of the question!'

'She'd be safer in here under my eye than in the common cell!' snapped Martha. But all entreaties were in vain, and when Martha began to show alarming signs of losing her temper once more, with dire consequences not only for herself but also for the two men she was nursing, Kat knew she had to give in. Before she was escorted from the cell she contrived to slip her gold and coral bracelet, which amazingly had survived the previous days, to Martha. It might buy Joshua and Amos a few days' grace.

She was held back for some time in the dank stone corridor while the turnkeys finished their task of returning men and women to their own separate sections of the gaol for the night, after the free movement allowed during the day. On the other side of the corridor the Wooburn and Wycombe men needed no bidding; they were already in the debtors' cages, some trying to make beds out of the grubby rushes and straw, others crouched on the floor, heads sunk in hands as they contemplated their fate.

The women's cage was lit by the flickering light of the turnkeys' lanterns, hung on hooks above the barred entrance, and to Kattrin it seemed like a scene from hell. In one corner two women were

167

fighting, rolling over and over on the filthy floor, cheered and jeered by a circle of howling spectators as they slashed at each other's faces with their nails; by the door squatted an old woman, rocking back and forth as she howled an obscene song. At the back of the cell, close to the bars that divided them from the adjacent men's cage, a woman moaned and tossed on a pallet in a high fever, while two emaciated women stripped the body of the dead child alongside her; everywhere underfoot, paying no regard to the actions of their elders, little children in rags played or slept in the foul and stinking straw.

At first no one took any notice of her; heart pounding, she crept to the back of the cell and tried to lose herself in the shadows. She might have succeeded had not the two fighting women rolled so far across the cell that they knocked against her. Hurriedly she rose to her feet, pressing herself against the damp and slimy walls, trying to avoid the fitful rays of the lanterns in the corridor.

But in vain.

'Hey, Moll!' cried a raucous voice. 'We got a new mort come in. Come over 'ere, wench. Let's take a glim at yer!'

Kat froze against the wall, but rough hands pulled her away from its meagre protection and a shove between her shoulder blades propelled her to the front of the cage.

A tall, plump woman with red hair piled up on top of her head caught her wrist with a grip of iron and pulled her into the shaft of light at the front of the cage.

'We got a swell mort here, Moll!' she said to the dark-haired harpy who had hurried to her side. 'Lookee here at this lace.' And before Kat could utter a protest, she had torn the lace trim from the neck of Kat's robe; someone behind the girl ripped the remaining earring from her ear, tearing the flesh.

The feel of the blood dripping down her neck galvanised Kat into action, kicking and punching at her two tormentors, but she was vastly overwhelmed in numbers and with a skill born of long practice they stripped the dress from her, leaving her in nothing but her under-petticoats.

'Mind yerselves, girls,' said the red-haired woman, contemplating a bleeding hand with a grim smile, 'she bites! Us'll have to teach her a lesson.' At a nod from her, someone pinioned Kat's arms behind her back.

'It's a wicious bit, Sal, to be sure,' said Moll, the darker of the two, prancing around the cage with Kat's dress held up to her.

'Handsome dress, Moll,' said Sal. 'I'll give it yer.'

'What d'yer mean, yer'll give it me?' screeched Moll. 'I already got it, an't I? 'Sides, there an't no stays an' 'twouldn't fit you wi'out stays.'

Kat tried to wriggle free of the restraining hands and had her arm twisted painfully for her trouble. 'Why must you torment me?' she gasped. 'I mean you no harm!'

'An' we means you no 'arm,' said Sal, catching her kicking feet and drawing the tattered satin slippers from them. Again she gave a signal and Kat's arms were released as swiftly as they had been caught up. She stumbled and caught wildly at one of the bars. Gasping as she felt the shoulders of her flimsy petticoats slipping, she folded her arms across her bosom in a vain attempt to retrieve a little modesty.

'Yer could 'ave the petticoats too, Sal!' guffawed Moll. 'Too loose on the wench, an't they?'

The two women began to walk, hypnotically slowly, towards Kat; caught like a rabbit with a stoat, she found herself giving way before them. But the cage was not long and within a very few paces she found herself backed up against the bars that separated this cage from the next.

She recoiled at the feel of the cold bars on her back, only to be caught by a steely arm insinuated through the bars from the adjoining cage. She felt hot breath on her bare shoulder and, in spite of herself, cried out in fear. There was a light of enjoyment in the eyes of the women before her; this was a game they had often played before.

'Don't go 'way, sweetheart,' said a gruff voice in her ear. 'We's on'y just beginnin' to get acquainted.' For a brief second the grip eased on her waist, but before she could move, an arm locked itself painfully around her throat. Wide-eyed with terror she felt a hand grope at her waist, then creep up to her bosom, cruelly exposed by the loss of her dress.

'A good pair o' bubbies she got on her, the swell mort,' said Sal with a cackle of laughter. 'Long time since you had such a fine perfumed handful, eh, Bill?'

'What's yer name, swell mort? Eh?' Moll, dancing around with Kat's dress as if at a ball, came to a halt in front of her. 'I said, what's yer name?'

A rough hand squeezed her breast and she cried out in pain. 'Kattrin!' she gasped. 'Kattrin Revel.'

There was a flurry of whispers from the other side of the corridor and a rattling of the bars.

'Hey, you!' The voice from the debtors cage echoed and re-echoed down the corridor.

The man holding Kat gave a throaty laugh. 'Wait yer turn, hayseeds! Yer can get at the women termorrer.'

'Aye. Plenty o'whores in 'ere t'give yer a roll in the straw fer a penny.'

'But this un's quality. Not fer the likes of you!'

169

'You!' The voice was sharper now. 'Darkie! Carroty!'

Sal and Moll turned indignantly. 'Hey! Who you callin' names on?'

'You got any sense, you'll let her go right now!' said another voice, hoarser than the first.

'An' who's goin' ter make us?' asked Bill scornfully.

'How many would you like?' said the first voice, softer now, but with a chill to it that raised the hair on the back of Kat's neck. 'Her and Delahaye di'n't ought ter be here, 'cept they risked 'emselves to save us. That we an't lyin' in bloody shreds at a cannon's mouth we owes to her.'

She had thought her intervention a wasted effort: it made her feel less wretched to know that someone had noticed. She only hoped that no one would mention that the cannon in the case had been her father's.

'What's that to us?' growled the voice in her ear, still full of bravado, though the hands ceased in their torment and the grip on her throat eased a little.

'Thass right! Who d'yer think y'are?' sneered Moll.

The measured tones from the other side of the corridor cut across Moll's words. 'We're Wooburn men. We all feels, as you might say, responsible for her. If any harm come to her, like . . .' He let the threat hang unspoken in the air.

'All the papermen feels that way,' said his companion, and there was a low rumble of assent. 'How many d'you reckon we are, John?'

'Nigh on two hundred of us,' said the soft voice. 'Thass not countin' the Waddesdon men . . .'

The hands behind released her so abruptly that she stumbled and almost fell. Moll caught her and stood her on her feet again.

'Look!' she said, dragging the girl to the front of the cage and showing her to the men opposite. 'Look!' she said, anxious to please. 'Ain't no harm come to her.'

In the flickering light Kat could make out the faces of John Dandridge, the brother of the Wooburn shoemaker, and one of the Bryant sons, whose wife had died in childbirth, leaving him to bring up his little child alone; his father was in the debtors' cell next to Joshua with a bullet hole in his arm. The other man she didn't recognise, but his heavily tattooed hands gripped the bars as if he would rend them like Samson in the temple.

'Give her back her dress, an' anythin' else you've took from her,' commanded Dandridge.

The women scurried round to do his bidding; they helped her into her dress, drew a pile of mouldering straw together for her and after that gave her a wide berth.

170

When Joshua opened his eyes, he could not at first remember where he was, but the grey light of early dawn filtering through the barred window soon brought it back to him.

Sweat broke out on his forehead. 'Kat!' he cried hoarsely. 'Kat! It's a trap!' He fought to sit up, but gentle hands pushed him back on the pallet.

'Nonie?'

Someone murmured in his ear, but the words kept floating away. He tried to lift his head, but the effort proved too great. He closed his eyes and drifted back into sleep.

The moment the cages were unlocked the next morning Kat hurried back down the corridor to Joshua's cell. 'How is he?' she asked, sinking to her knees at Joshua's side.

'Holdin' his own, girl,' said Martha. 'Woke up in the night an' seemed to know what was what. Called out your name, he did.'

Kat could feel herself blushing under Martha's scrutiny. 'And Amos?'

'See for yourself.'

Kat looked across the room to see Martha's husband propped up on one elbow and watching her with bright brown button eyes. 'Good night's sleep was all I needed, missie,' he said. 'Only time I stirred was when there was all that row in the night.'

'Aye. We was that worried for you, girl,' said Martha, and Kat found herself blurting out what had happened.

'Thank God the village men was there to stand up for you,' said Martha, much distressed. 'But I'll have you under my eye tonight if I has to see the governor hisself!'

'Acourse it's only an unwed lass that they makes a to-do about,' said Amos, stroking his stubbly chin. 'If she was wed to the lad, that 'ud settle it all wi'out any problems.'

'Never spoke a truer word, Amos,' said Martha, crossing to her husband's pallet and giving him a resounding kiss. 'We've on'y to tell him what happened an' – '

'No! Oh, please, no!' said Kat in distress. 'You mustn't say anything about this! He needs all his strength for – '

She jumped as a knock fell on the door, then chided herself for her folly. When had Ezekiel Revel ever felt the need to knock? Opening the door, she found Dandridge and another man in the corridor. She startled them by shaking them by the hand while she thanked them gravely for their help.

'We all got to help each other where we can, miss,' said Dandridge, shifting from one leg to another.

'Bad places, prisons, missie,' said his companion. 'The strongest

171

allus picks on the weakest. An' the turnkeys just an't wantin' to know aught about it.'

'Knibbs has been in here afore,' said Dandridge.

'For stealin' turnip greens,' explained Knibbs. 'Winter afore last.'

They were the first of a constant stream of callers, each knocking diffidently on the door to enquire about the progress of the invalids. For the papermen, to have their hand shaken by the daughter of the least amenable of the mill owners was just one more bizarre occurrence in a world gone mad. Each of them was dealing with the shock of incarceration in a different way but most were simply dazed – even the ones who had been the most ferocious in the riot. One of them burst into tears whenever anyone spoke to him. 'I shall never see my dear ones more!' he wept. Poor Benjamin Francis, who was already struggling to bring up seven children on the parish when his wife died in childbed, sat apart from the others, head in his hands, and would take no comfort from anyone.

Some, like John Dafter, had simply found themselves in the wrong place at the wrong time. 'Oh, I threw a stone all right,' he said stoutly. 'It were the same stone some fool had just lobbed at me when I come out me cottage to see what all the trouble were about.'

In the early afternoon, the surgeon came back to see his charges and brought with him the long-awaited message from Allnutt.

'Well, girl?' said Martha impatiently. 'Is yer pa comin' to take you away?'

'Martha!' scolded Amos. 'Don't be so forward!'

Kat looked up from the letter with tragedy written across her face. Her father's conditions were brutal. Only if she cleared her name by implicating Joshua would Louis Cazelle be induced to cast his respectability over her tarnished person. How her father must have enjoyed planning such a perfect revenge on them both.

'Why ever has he taken against your Joshua so?' Martha wanted to know.

'It's a long story,' said Kat, and ripped the letter from top to bottom.

'What now?' said Martha, breaking the shocked silence which had descended.

'Now I am disinherited,' said Kat calmly.

'Oh, missie!' gasped Amos. 'Do you consider what you are about!'

'I will not help put him in the dock. He has done nothing wrong!'

'Can you take another night in the common cell?' Emberton found his tongue at last.

'If I must. But you could ask the turnkeys to let me sleep in here.'

'I cannot! Miss Revel, it is not possible! Your reputation!'

A bitter smile twisted her lips as she held up the two halves of the

172

letter. 'I no longer have a name or a reputation.' She crossed to Joshua's side and plumped herself down on the straw. 'So here I am and here I stay,' she said calmly. 'If they want me moved, they will have to carry me out.'

When Joshua woke again he was puzzled to find Kat bending over him.

'What in Hades are you doing here?' he demanded angrily.

'Hush, Joshua,' she said, wiping his forehead gently with a cloth. 'Lie back. Don't fret.'

He sat up with a jerk and pushed her hand aside.

'Joshua!'

'You should not be in here!'

One of the turnkeys looked in at the open door to see what the noise was about.

'Take her out of here, man, and tell Hailey I want to see him.'

The turnkey scratched his head. 'Hailey?' he said. 'An't no one here name o' Hailey.'

'Hailey's in Wycombe, Joshua, and we're – '

Before she could finish explaining, Martha came bustling in from the next cell, where she had been helping Emberton change the dressings on the gunshot wounds.

'Do you wait outside while we see to 'un,' she said. 'No point agitatin' the man.'

And to her disgust, Kat found herself hustled out. In the corridor a group of prisoners – none that she recognised – were gaffing, playing toss the ha'penny and gambling on the outcome, to the accompaniment of many oaths and profanities.

In the women's cage two bodies writhed and bucked in a corner, panting and groaning, while the rest of the occupants went on singing, gossiping and gambling around them. She pressed her hand to her mouth and hurried out into the yard.

'I'm right sorry to see you in this place, missie,' said a man by the wall. He looked vaguely familiar, but he was better dressed than most of the inmates.

'I'm sorry to see any of us here,' she said, huddling herself into her shawl against the bitterly cold air. 'Are you one of the papermen?'

'Not me. Thomas Hughes is a Beaconsfield man. Born and bred.' It was the man who had tried to free them all on Cut-Throat Hill.

'Then how did you get caught up in all this?'

'I tried to stand bail for young John Watts. Well, his father's been my friend these many years. But they wouldn't take my money.'

'But you called my name on Cut-Throat Hill.'

'Ah! That wasn't me. That was – well, we won't name names. But a

173

certain person who isn't here, thank the Lord...' He lowered his voice so no one else could hear. 'A certain person whose family you helped? He heard Nash bring your man in. Made him right mad when they broke their word and wouldn't let you go.'

'Adam?'

'I'm not sayin' you're wrong. But hush on that, missie! See, we'd already planned to hold up the coach and set young John free. We'd have done it too, if it hadn't been for the soldiers.'

Kat had not the heart to tell him that by calling her name so openly, Adam could only have added to the suspicion against her.

Joshua was staring fixedly at the wall when Kat came back in some time later. He didn't look at her when she came to sit at his side.

'Why did you not tell me?' he asked.

'Tell you what?'

'About the cells and – '

'Martha shouldn't have told you!' she said, angry colour flooding her face. 'You were unconscious, Joshua. There was nothing you could do.'

'I can't bear to think that you had to deal with it alone,' he muttered, grinding the words out between his teeth. 'That those animals – '

She laid her hand over his. 'It's over now.' She didn't want to think about it. That way lay despair and panic.

'I should have been there,' he said grimly. 'I should have protected you.'

'I'm here now, Joshua. I'll be safe with you.'

He turned his face away. 'You can't stay here,' he said. 'That would be most improper.'

'You sound just like the chaplain,' she said, trying to make light of it. 'Believe me, given the choice, here I stay.'

They talked over every possibility, again and again, until at last Joshua sank back on his pallett, grey and exhausted.

'Go to sleep, Joshua,' she said softly, brushing his hair out of his eyes. 'We'll talk about it when you're stronger.'

'I cannot believe that you are taking all this so calmly!' he exclaimed.

'If I make myself ill with fretting, what will that change?' she said. 'We'll still be in prison. I'll still be disinherited.'

'Aye,' said Martha, coming back into the cell. 'One step at a time.' She put her hands on her hips and looked at the small fire and the two flickering candle ends. 'This may not seem like much to you, sir, but we've become mortal attached to it. If the chaplain 'as 'is way, the gel 'ull be out of 'ere an' back in the cage with no one to look out for her.'

'If we an't come up with a goblin by this evenin', we'll all be out,' said Amos. 'No more fire to warm us, no more glims to light us...'

'A goblin?' said Kat with a frown. 'What – ?'

'A touch o' gold to grease the gaoler's palm. Without that, yer man an' me an' them next door are for the prison hospital, with the typhoid and the cholera, an' you an' Martha for the cage.'

As if to echo his words, the turnkey appeared in the doorway and slopped down a pail of grey, scummy gruel. 'Surgeon says you'm fit to be moved now. So unless ye can make it worth my while,' he said, rubbing his fingers together, 'I'll be showin' yer to yer new quarters.' He lifted his lip in a parody of a laugh, revealing a mouthful of blackened stumps. 'They just brought the condemned men down: there'll be riot an' rumpus this evenin' afore the hangin' termorrer.'

Joshua sat up carefully. 'I need to see the chaplain,' he said.

'Think I've the time to run errands for you?' sneered the turnkey.

'I dare say the chaplain will make it worth your while. So fetch him!' said Joshua in steely tones. As the turnkey departed, he pulled himself painfully to his knees, ignoring Martha's protests, reached awkwardly for his boots, lying at the bottom of the bed, and handed them to Kat.

'Money under the linings,' he said with an effort. 'Don't let the turnkey see it – best to pay him through the chaplain. If... if anything happens to me – '

'Joshua, don't!'

He squeezed her hand. 'If anything happens to me, you must use it as you think fit. Let Martha do the bargaining, she's more accustomed. She'll make it go further.'

Joshua was alone in his cell when the turnkey brought the deputy chaplain in.

'Best act fast, sir,' said the turnkey, his attitude changing dramatically at the sight of the gold coin. 'I'm a-comin' soon to take the wench back to the cage for the night.' As if to lend weight to his words, a mournful shrieking and howling echoed down the corridor at the arrival of the condemned men. Quickly Joshua explained what he wanted from the cleric, who flung his palsied hands up in horror. Such a thing, he explained, with much trembling of the head, could not be decided overnight. The bishop must be consulted, perhaps even the archbishop.

'Have you no discretion for emergencies?' Joshua pleaded. 'This is a gaol, sir!'

The man bleated something more about the governor and the bishop, but Martha, entering from the adjacent cell with Amos and Kat, cut him off angrily. 'Whiles you ducks your duties, she gets thrown into the cage, when she could be here with her man! Call yerself a man of God? Y'are a weak, spineless, grovelling excuse for a man!' she called as he hurried away.

The turnkey watched him go, scratching his stubbly chin with a grimy fingernail. 'Got any more o' them coins?' he asked.

'None to waste on useless bodies like that one!' snapped Martha.

The turnkey looked from Joshua's grey face to Kat's anxious one and gave a knowing leer. 'Wait on,' he said, and stumped out into the corridor. In a moment he was back, dragging with him a bemused elderly man in rusty black coat and knee breeches with white linen bands at his throat.

Joshua and Kat looked at him with astonishment on their faces, but Martha smiled and clapped her hands. 'No need to fret ourselves over bishops now,' she crowed. 'You've no quarrel with the Quakers, have ye, sir?' she asked when they still looked puzzled.

'None whatsoever. But I don't understand . . .'

'Samuel Hallstead of the Society of Friends,' said the elderly man, shaking hands with the four prisoners. 'I was praying with the poor souls in the condemned cells when I was informed that thee wished to see me. How may I be of service to thee, Friend Delahaye?'

Joshua reached out and caught Kat's hand in his. 'I want you to marry us tonight,' he said in a firm voice.

Kat looked down at his grim face, her mouth opening and closing while she tried to find words to say.

'It's the only way to keep you safe here with me, Kat,' he said.

'If the young lady is not willing – ' said the Quaker.

She blinked back the tears that pricked at the back of her eyes. 'I am most willing, sir,' she said, smiling down at Joshua. She knew with an absolute certainty that this was what she wanted, to join their lives together, to face the world side by side. If they spent the rest of their days fighting the injustice which had brought them to their present pass, they would do it together.

When Friend Hallstead returned to the little cell that evening, they were ready for him. Joshua stood unsteadily between Amos and Martha, his cravat tied roughly around his neck, beads of sweat standing out on his forehead.

'In the fear of the Lord and before my friends here assembled,' he declared, 'I take this my friend Kattrin to be my wife, promising through Divine Assistance to be unto her an affectionate and faithful husband until it shall please the Lord by death to separate us.'

Joshua had to sit on the little three-legged stool while Kattrin made her declaration, then with trembling hands he took from Hallstead the thin worn ring for which he had traded another of his precious coins, and slid it onto Kat's slender finger. There, in the filth and the squalor, with Martha and Amos as their witnesses, Kattrin Revel became Mrs Joshua Delahaye.

She woke in the middle of the night to find that she had rolled to the edge of her straw mattress and was lying so close to Joshua that she could feel his breath warm on her hand. She could just make out his features in the last dying embers of the fire. My husband, she thought, with a strange, rather dizzy feeling. Joshua is my husband. I'm here safe with him, not in the cage.

She shivered and shifted restlessly as she remembered the crawling terror she had felt when the man had pawed at her through the bars. She blinked rapidly to drive the images from her mind, only to find them replaced by the scene she had witnessed that afternoon. *That* was what men and women did, she thought. *That* was what husbands and wives did. And now she was a wife.

She waited for the terror to return, but there was only a warm flush that radiated up from her toes and set her face afire, and a stirring, trembling feeling deep in her stomach that took her breath away. She knew with a heartfelt certainty that what she and Joshua would do in each other's arms would be a world apart from those nightmarish visions.

She edged across towards Joshua until her legs were burrowing under his blanket, her breath coming in short gasps as her body brushed against his.

Joshua stirred and lay a moment wondering dazedly what she was doing there. Then, abruptly, he came full awake and his hand reached out and pushed her sharply away.

'Joshua!'

'Hush!' He sat up, wrapping himself in his blanket so that no scrap of it touched her. 'You'll wake Amos.'

'Why are you so cross?'

'It's a cold night,' he said. 'Cover yourself up.' The sight of her shoulders rising out of her chemise and her hair in a dishevelled veil over her creamy skin was having its effect on him, despite the injury and the laudanum. He gritted his teeth and reminded himself that he had entered into this sham of a marriage to protect her, intending it to be annulled as soon as she was out of here.

'Joshua, don't turn away from me.'

He fixed his eyes on the far wall. Even with his injuries it would be the simplest thing in the world to reach out and take her. He curled his fingers into his palms, digging his nails into the barely healed flesh. 'Go to sleep, Kat,' he said harshly.

'Lie down with me, Joshua.'

177

'I've slept too much.' He drew his knees up under his chin, still not looking at her. 'Now let me be. I've a great deal to think about.'

She must be dreaming again, one of the dark and terrible dreams that had haunted her sleep these last weeks, but when she blinked, the thin figure with the halo of silver-gilt hair was still there in the doorway, looking at her with infinite sadness.

Kat flew across the cell and held her tightly for a moment. 'You shouldn't have come, Aunt,' she said in distress. 'Papa will be furious that you have defied him – and you know how you hate that.'

'How could I not come?' cried Lucy. 'My own daughter in prison...' Her face crumpled and she began to cry softly.

Kat froze to the spot, quite incapable of moving or speaking as she struggled to take in what Lucy had said.

After a moment Martha left her patient and crossed to Lucy's side. 'Come, m'dearie,' she said softly, pushing her down on the stool by the rough pallet bed where Joshua lay sleeping. 'Sit you down and calm yourself. The Lord above knows there's been enough tears shed over this to last us all a lifetime.'

'Aunt?' Kat moved across the tiny cell as if in a dream. She knelt in front of Lucy and took her cold hands in hers. 'You said – your own daughter in jail?'

Lucy looked up at her, mouth agape. 'I said that?'

'You surely did,' said Kat in a whisper.

'I never meant to tell you,' she said piteously. 'I thought, I haven't let it slip in all these years. Why should I burden her with that now? I'm so sorry, child...'

'Aunt Lucy! I mean...' She forced herself to take a deep breath. 'You can't just leave it there. You must see ... you must tell me...' She shook her head in confusion. 'I can't believe it. My mother ... Dickon's mother!' She looked up sharply. 'Does he know?'

Lucy looked at her for a long moment. 'Dickon is Cattern's son,' she said at last.

'But it's not possible! Dickon and I – we're twins!'

'No. You were born within months of each other. But you are not twins. He was born on St Cattern's day. Only then was I permitted to give you a name.'

'But I was called for my mother! Oh, I know it was written differently...'

'I never wanted you to have her name,' she said viciously. 'But what choice? When Dickon was born on St Cattern's Day ... We had to call you twins, you see. So you had to be named for the saint. In a village of lacemakers a girl born on St Cattern's day is thought doubly blessed. For all she already bore the name, we couldn't have

178

called you anything else. Naturally, being younger than you, when you were babes he was the smaller, but it is sometimes so with twins that one grows in the womb at the expense of the other...'

Kat knelt down in the dust-laden shaft of sunlight that slanted across the cell, edging the dripping walls with light before extinguishing itself in the filthy straw that covered the floor. She looked up at the woman she had always known as aunt and took her thin hands in hers. 'I don't wish to give you more pain,' she said softly. 'But my father ...?'

Lucy looked up with a smile that illuminated her face, showing traces of the pretty young girl she had once been. 'Your father used to lodge with us, you know,' she said, almost conversationally. 'When Cattern and I were young girls. Seventeen I was and Cattern barely sixteen.'

'My real father lodged with you too? I know that Mr Revel – '

Lucy looked at the girl as if she were simple. 'Child, Ezekiel Revel *is* your father.'

'But he can't be. He – You said that he – '

There was a stirring from the bed and Kat looked down to see Joshua's eyes wide open.

'Kat,' he said weakly, 'if you keep interrupting, we'll never hear Miss Thornton's story.'

The story was soon told. Lucy had been the older and prettier of the two Thornton girls, much courted by the village lads. The Thorntons scraped a living on the little farm on which they were tenants. Like all small farmers they raised a bit of everything and grew a bit of everything: cattle, pigs, poultry, wheat, barley, rye, oats and cabbages. Like all farmers' daughters, the young girls helped around the house and in the poultry yard, but they differed from the other village girls in two respects. Cattern and Lucy, with their mother, were the finest lacemakers in the village, and it was to them that the lace man brought any special commissions. 'Even made some of the lace for one o' the royal princesses' wedding dress, we did,' said Lucy proudly.

More important still was that Lucy was known to have expectations from her godfather Jem Dawson, a childless distant cousin of her mother's who farmed his own land the other side of Burnham Beeches. With such prospects – and it would all come to Lucy, for Dawson didn't believe in breaking up land – she could have looked higher than the local lads, even if she had been plain as a post.

But prospects will not put food on the table, and one year when Thornton had borrowed more money than he should have on the strength of his daughter's expectations, and prices on the corn exchange were going through one of their frequent slumps, Lucy's

179

father was reduced, like so many others, to taking in lodgers to make ends meet. Ezekiel Revel, assistant to a Burnham corn dealer, was one of the Thorntons' lodgers, sleeping across the yard, above the barn.

'Ezekiel were nothin', from nowhere,' said Lucy, slipping into the dialect in her agitation. 'Heard someone say once he were son of a chapman, a travelling tinker from out Aylesbury way.' She shrugged. 'Maybe he were. But you wouldn't think it to look at him, no, nor to hear him talk. And if he were – well, credit where 'tis due, even then he'd worked hisself up to be Drysdale's assistant. Ah, he was a big man. Big in everythin' he did, everythin' he said. Big ideas too. But not hard like now. Oh, he could sweet-talk a girl somethin' shockin'.'

'And he sweet-talked you?' said Joshua.

He'd sweet-talked his way into her family's confidence to the extent that he was trusted to take Lucy on her weekly drives to Burnham to call on the ailing Uncle Dawson, sometimes with her mother, but often without. And on one of those drives, on an evening when Uncle Dawson had sent her away early, they'd come back by way of Burnham fair.

'Autumn hiring fair it was,' said Lucy reminiscently. 'Never been to a fair before, see, Father bein' a bit of a Methodist. Got dark early, bein' November. I can still remember the smell of them pitch torches . . .'

There had been all kinds of travelling booths: peepshows and waxworks, stands selling patent medicines, thimble riggers and fortune-tellers, beer and ale tents and stalls selling fairings. Ezekiel had bought a couple of savoury pies and small beer to wash it down with, and all manner of foolish things for her from the stallholders. And then there had been the soldiers, the Volunteer Riflemen in their bonny green jackets, out for a spree before they marched off to the coast and the war in the Peninsula. Most of them finished the day fighting drunk and of course Ezekiel had to put his arm round her to protect her.

'I went with him to his workplace. He said there were some pretty little kittens out back in the barn and I should have my pick of them. All cream they were. Never seen anythin' like 'em before or since. Some kind of foreign cat, he said, as old Drysdale's nephew had brought back from abroad. I knowed it was wrong,' she said, her voice shaking, 'but mebbe 'twas the drink, or the moon, or jest . . . the way he flattered me, told me he loved me. And there was no one there, see. So we – I – ' She buried her face in her hands at the shame of the memory. 'I lay with him,' she said in a whisper.

Martha put her arm round Lucy's shoulders. 'You wasn't the first

180

to be fooled by fine words,' she said softly. 'Nor you won't be the last.'

Lucy took a deep breath. 'I cried all the way home. I was afeart I'd have a babe, and what would I tell my parents? Ezekiel said we'd have to marry.' She looked up from her contemplation of the floor. 'I thought then that was the worst time of my life. Part of me was so happy that Ezekiel wanted to marry me; he was such a big, handsome fellow. I thought what a life we'd have, with him always there to protect me. Yet part of me was terrified of what my father would say. I was in such a state I raised a bit o' fever and my mother thought I should not go to Cousin Dawson's the next Sunday. But I persuaded her I was better. I knew I had to. Mother was all for coming with me, but her head were terrible bad and I persuaded her she should rest. I remember thinking what luck that she had the headache.' She looked up at the tiny barred window, seeming to see something, or someone, that no one else could. 'How I despised myself for that afterwards!

'Ezekiel drove me to Cousin Dawson's, as always. And we came back by a roundabout way. Stopped off in this tiny village, we did: never seen it before nor since. The minister was waiting in the church, all done up in his bands, and two people for the witnesses, men I didn't know. But they knowed Ezekiel.' She shivered. 'Afterwards, I couldn't even remember the minister's name. All I remember is how cold it was in that church. I couldn't stop shaking and shivering. And so I married your father. Special licence.'

Kat had been sitting, head bowed, but at that she jerked her head up. She started to speak, but at the pressure from Joshua's hand she stopped.

'Ezekiel said he'd best go back to Burnham that night, give father time to come to terms with it all. He'd wait in Burnham for me to send for him.' She sighed. 'But it didn't work out that way. When I got home mother and Cattern were both abed, very ill, and father soon followed them. It was the smallpox.

'Strange to say, I almost forgot about Ezekiel.' Her mouth twisted in bitterness. 'And he certainly was in no hurry to remember me. I had to nurse 'em all: there weren't no sweathouse up the common like now. And none of the neighbours would come near, not even old Mother Hedgerley, the old woman as usually come to nurse. There was only the cowman from down the road; being as he'd already had the cowpox, like me, and wasn't likely to catch from them, he come in to feed the beasts and left us food and the old woman's potions outside the door. Ma and Pa died early on. The cowman took 'em up to Hedsor to bury. Cattern had quite a mild catching, though she ended with worse scars than anyone.'

181

She shifted on the stool and Kat craned forward, anxious not to miss anything.

'Soon as she were able to sit up and feed herself, I went down sick. Not with the pox. I never caught that, bein' as I'd always done the milkin', maybe. Just – like as if the strain of it all got to me, I suppose: the worry and the nursin' and all that time with no sleep. And when I finally *could* stop and close my eyes, I went into a sleep that no one could rouse me from. So they tell me, for I was that bad, I remember nothing of it,' said Lucy. 'As it weren't a catchin' sickness, old Mother Hedgerley had me carried to her cottage. They say I lay there weeks as if I were already dead.' Lucy gazed into space, and Kat wondered whether she was seeing the old farmhouse and her dead parents. She held her breath, fearful of interrupting in case Lucy didn't finish the story.

'Good as blind, were old Mother Hedgerley,' said Lucy at last. 'An' one day she thought I was dead and gone. Told the cowman when he came past on his way to Burnham Market. Turned out he was passin' our news on to Ezekiel, neighbourly like, and to old Dawson too. Next thing anyone knows, the old man's changed his will. For fear of his land goin' out of the family, old Uncle Dawson willed everythin' to Cattern. Within the day he was dead.

'Word must have got around Burnham that old Dawson had changed his will, but no one in Wooburn knew. Certainly Cattern didn't.'

'And Ezekiel came back?' prompted Kat.

'Came back all right. Acourse I only heard the rest of it afterwards, bein' as I was still up at Mother Hedgerley's, half dead an' half alive. Ezekiel, he pitches up at the farm, not a word about what had happened. Been travellin' on business for his master, he says. If only he'd known, he'd have come over like a shot to help poor brave Cattern.' A look of fury, quite alien to the old Lucy she'd always known, came over her face. 'Cattern was exhausted and weak, scarred bad, all her looks gone. She'd just lost her parents, for all she knew her sister too. She never was that strong a character anyway and now she was like clay in his hands.' Her mouth twisted. 'He told her he'd always loved her, told her she needn't be alone any more: if she'd marry him, he would look after her. He carried her down to the church there and then, afore she could change her mind. And straight after the service, for all she was so weak, he...' Her eyes filled with tears and she pressed her hand to her mouth as if the memory had the power to sicken her even after all these years. 'He bedded her. Just to be sure that no one could have the marriage set aside.'

'But you survived?'

'Yes. We both survived. Both of us with child by the same man.'

'Oh, God! You with me and – '

'– and Cattern with Dickon!' said Joshua.

'But you were married to him first,' said Kat with a frown.

'Who would believe me? By the time I was well enough to think straight, it was all done. I didn't know then that I was with child and he said he'd destroyed the records. I didn't even know where he had taken me for the wedding. I could prove nothing.' She took a deep breath that rattled in her throat. 'With Dawson's new will and his marriage to Cattern, he'd got everything. I was dependent on him even for the roof over my head and the food in my mouth. I . . . I just gave up. I hadn't the strength to fight.'

'But when you knew about the child? Why didn't you tell your sister then?'

'To what purpose? By then the whole village knew he had married Cattern. Whatever I did it would mean disgrace for all of us. If I could have proved it, not only he would have gone to jail, but Cattern too. To lie with your sister's husband – they'd call that incest.'

Ezekiel had made it clear that Lucy had to follow his plan or he would turn her out onto the street. He informed Cattern that she was to cover her sister's shame by pretending the child was hers, and poor scarred Cattern, unaware of the true nature of her sister's misfortune, but pathetically eager not to cross her husband, agreed to do all she could to protect the family name.

Revel had sold the two farms to Lord Bosingham to increase his hunting land, and the unlikely threesome had moved to a new house in Wooburn, where Lucy, with the excuse of her recent illness, was kept out of sight. Locked away in the attic, her only connection with the outside world the occasional glimpse of the villagers crossing the small corner of the village green visible through the crack in the shutters, she bore her weak and undersized babe unattended.

She stayed confined to the attics until November, when Cattern was at last delivered of her child. For the plan to work she too had to be delivered without assistance, even though with the money from the farms Ezekiel Revel could easily have paid for a midwife and day nurses. The newborn boy was only a little smaller than the mewling ten-week girl, and they were immediately placed end to end in the crib of plaited straw. But as ill fortune would have it, a woman from Cookham, who often acted as midwife in her own village, was visiting in Wooburn; even Ezekiel had found it impossible to prevent her looking in on the mother of twins without arousing suspicions. She was known to be fond of the bottle, so he plied her with drink before sending her on her way.

'And she suspected nothing?' asked Kat.

'We'll never know. She never reached the ferry. They found her body in Blessings Ditch a few days later.' She shivered. 'When we heard that, we knew we had to do as Ezekiel told us. I gave you over to Cattern and from that day I was the spinster aunt and she the blessed mother of twins.

'We settled down. What choice did we have? To all outward appearances we were a contented family. For a while I even thought I could forgive her. Then one day I looked at her, sweet, placid Cattern with "her" twins at her feet, and I knew I still hated her.'

'But it was him! He was the one who – !'

Lucy raised her eyes as if the effort were almost too much for her. 'Do you think I don't know that?' she said tiredly. 'God knows I tried to hate him too, but I hated her most of all. He spent most of his time in London, buying and selling, I suppose, working up to his next move. For a few years more he seemed content to live in the village. You and Dickon went to the village school. We went on like any other family.

'And then Cattern fell pregnant again. She was so sickly. Oh, how I gloated over that! A judgement on her, I thought. And when he turned away from her ugly fat body and her bloated, scarred face, I saw it as a chance to revenge myself on her for taking my husband.'

Kat could not prevent the shock from showing in her face. 'He lured you back?' she said.

'Lured? No. I went happily to his bed.'

'How could you?'

'I thought, At last, I am revenged. But God sees all – and He had his own revenge for my wickedness.'

'Cattern found out?'

Lucy looked up, eyes huge in her shadowed face. 'I fell for a child again. And Cattern knew. I wonder if she'd always suspected. She never asked who had fathered you, and you'd have thought . . .' She blinked hard. 'She confronted me with it and I never was good at lies.'

'What then?'

Lucy looked her daughter in the eye. 'You know what happened then. She took the sporting curricle and killed herself.'

'But that was an accident! The horse was too fresh for her and –'

'She knew what she was doing. She killed herself And her baby.'

'And *your* child?'

'This time there was no Cattern to cover my shame. He was going to throw us out, but then who would have looked after you and Dickon?' Her face seemed to collapse and suddenly she looked very old. 'He took my baby away,' she said and they had to strain to make out the words. 'Told everyone I'd been suffering from dropsy. I couldn't fight him without bringing shame on all of us. I wanted to kill myself. Like Cattern. But someone had to look after you. God had no mercy – He took that choice away from me too.'

Silence fell on the little group in the cell, a silence disturbed only by the rustling of unseen creatures in the filthy straw. Kattrin sought desperately for something to say, something that would bring comfort. But there were no easy words.

'It was around then that Ezekiel seemed to get a second wind,' said Lucy after a while. 'It was something to do with Lord Bosingham, but it was more than just the farms. Before that, Bosingham had favoured us when it suited, but now everything turned the other way. Bosingham arranged for Dickon to go to Eton and suddenly there was money, more money than Ezekiel had ever had before. Much more than Uncle Dawson's inheritance. Within months of Cattern's death Ezekiel bought Clapton Revel and after that he never looked back.'

'But why did he not marry you?' asked Kat in a small voice. 'When Mama – I m-mean, when Cattern died, he could have married you and put right all the wrongs – '

'Deceased wife's sister,' came a voice from the doorway. 'Don't you read your prayer book, Kat?'

'Oh, God!' Lucy shrank away from the grim expression on Dickon's normally placid face. 'I never intended you to know!' she sobbed.


Matters moved on apace after that. Dickon, bereft for the first time in his life of Kat's support, was forced to act alone. The Bosinghams were in Ireland and Godstowe in France but he was pleasantly surprised to find he was perfectly capable of setting things in motion. The first priority was to engage a lawyer for Kat and Joshua and within a day of Dickon's visit, Mr Stimpson of the Inner Temple presented himself at the gaol.

He sent Martha and Amos out of the cell to consult with his clerk, leafing through his papers and clearing his throat until the door had shut behind them. Fingers steepled against each other, he looked over the top of his gold-rimmed spectacles at the little group assembled before him, Joshua propped up on his straw mattress flexing the fingers of his injured arm, and Kat and Dickon on two rickety stools.

Stimpson addressed himself to Dickon. 'I regret to say, Mr Revel, that matters do not proceed as smoothly as I had at first hoped. The charges for the affray on – ahem – Cut-Throat Hill . . .' He permitted himself a twitch of the lips, as near a smile as was the shining brass plate on a coffin lid. '. . . those charges have now been dropped. But I

185

regret to say that the charges concerning the riot on King's Mead still stand. And until Lord Bosingham returns from Ireland – '

'It isn't right!' protested Kat. 'Joshua was only trying to disperse the men.'

He swivelled his pale-grey gaze across the room at her, as if aware for the first time of her presence. 'As I believe has already been explained to you, Miss Revel, to remain at the scene of riot is to be regarded in the eyes of the law as a part of that riot; indeed, it is to be equally culpable of riot with those who set out expressly to do damage and cause alarm. You, dear lady, have the rare distinction of being the only female in gaol in Buckinghamshire on these charges – Mistress Beckford being here for assault.'

'But they will not proceed against my sister, surely?'

Stimpson put his head on one side and considered the matter. 'I am inclined to think not,' he said at last. 'Though the charges are anyway less serious in your sister's case. For Mr Delahaye, I am less sanguine. In Wooburn we have charges of breaking machinery used in *manufacture*, which is considered a capital crime.' He paused while his words sank in. 'If they charge you with a misdemeanour, then your counsel may speak for you,' he said, 'but if they persist in charging you with a felony, then you must speak for yourself.'

Joshua's jaw dropped in shock. 'I have some confidence in my own eloquence,' he said at last, 'but what of the rest of the Wooburn men? To force them to plead on their own behalf would be a travesty of justice!'

'For a felony, be they rich or poor, young or old, educated or the veriest dullard – a foreigner, even, – they must speak for themselves,' explained Stimpson. 'I share your indignation, Delahaye, but it is the law. Of course, if they were charged with treason or arraigned before the House of Lords, then counsel could speak for them.'

'But for trying to save their livelihood, in the only way they know, they are forbidden any help!' said Kat bitterly.

'My clerk will do what he can for them,' said Stimpson soothingly. 'But I am more concerned for your case, sir, than theirs.'

'But I was told they had found Dell,' said Joshua.

'He was here in the gaol all the time,' growled Dickon. 'Hiding under another man's name!'

'Surely now that they have him – '

'They must set you free? I had hoped so. Unfortunately, I have so far failed to prevail on the authorities to grant bail for you.'

'But – '

'Miss Revel, however, has been offered bail.'

'Good,' said Joshua. 'I want her out of here as soon as may be.' Kat was indignant at being discussed as if she were not there; not

186

trusting herself to speak, she rose from Joshua's side and crossed to stand in the weak ray of winter sunshine filtering through the window.

'But they will only release Kat if she lives at home,' said Dickon, carefully avoiding his sister's eye.

'And father will only take me in if I give evidence against Joshua,' said Kat impatiently. 'I already know that.'

'You never told me,' said Joshua sharply.

'What point was there?'

'Every point,' growled Joshua. 'You could have been out of here and – '

'Any of the Wooburn men could have been out of here if they'd agreed to give evidence against their friends.' She glared across the cell at him. 'They will not do it. How *dare* you think that I would?'

For two days she could hardly bring herself to speak to him, so angry was she that he should have doubted her. He could have made his peace with her, but life in the prison cell was a little easier when she spent most of her time with Martha and as little as possible alone in the cell with him.

He sat at the table in the cell with the papers Stimpson had brought in to him, writing out his statement in the flickering light of the candles, racking his brains to find a chink in the prosecution and worrying what to do about Kat.

If only he'd known that Dickon would come to the gaol, he need never have taken the desperate step of the marriage; if only he had not been so befuddled with pain, exhaustion and laudanum, surely he could have found another solution? But it was done now, and she was safer with him than out in the common gaol, at the mercy of every villain and scoundrel in the county.

The following day, the turnkey brought news that the special constable was willing to drop the charges against Martha 'for a consideration'. When Joshua produced the sovereigns, Martha and Amos were bound over to keep the peace and released.

Now there were just the two of them in the cell.

On Christmas Eve, with the snow lying heavy on the windowsill, blocking out what little light remained, and the papermen singing their carols in the debtors' cage, they had an unexpected visit from Lord Bosingham's agent. His lordship had been appalled to hear that it was Tarquin's deposition which had delivered Joshua into the law's hungry and vengeful maw, and he had sent to assure Joshua that he would use all his influence to force the system to deliver him up again, as soon as he returned from Ireland.

'Don't you fret, dear fellow,' read the hastily scrawled note. 'I'll persuade m'sister to take Miss Katherine in and then we'll have you out of there in no time, you mark my words. And I'll send a bottle or two for Christmas cheer.'

The hamper that the agent set down on the filthy straw contained all sorts of delicacies and they dined well that night, and drank deeply, trying to bring themselves a little comfort against the cold, hoping against hope that the end was in sight. When the fire fell away during the night, Kat snuggled up against Joshua for warmth; fuddled with drink, he had not the presence of mind to push her away as he always had before. In the still, small hours of the morning he stirred in his sleep to find her warm breath on his cheek and not even the cloak she slept in between them.

He nuzzled his face in the soft curls below her ear and when she sighed contentedly, he tightened his arms around her and drew her close to him, to kiss her soft lips and caress her face, to let his hands roam over her throat, her breasts, her body. Her arms slid around his neck and her breasts brushed against him through the shift. Her body moved enticingly against his and then the shift was no longer between them. Warmed by the heat of their mutual passion and only half conscious of what they were doing, their bodies pressed urgently against each other until there was no way that they could cease. Alone together in the stinking little cell they found comfort at last in each other's arms.

Waking with a pounding head on Christmas morning, he did not at first remember what had passed between them. He watched her for a moment moving around the little cell, setting it to rights, singing softly under her breath. He wondered blearily why she was walking so stiffly and when the full realisation of what they had done came crashing in on his mind, he turned his face to the wall and cursed himself for a villain.

# Chapter Ten

'What the devil are you doing in here?' Joshua asked angrily, elbowing his way through the women's cage to Kattrin's side. He had woken from a brief nap to find Kat missing; with Martha no longer there to keep an eye on her he had panicked, and his anxiety for her safety made him speak more roughly than he had intended.

'Hush, Joshua!' she said softly, handing him a small bundle. Without thought he took it from her. 'We don't want to waken the baby. Look, isn't she beautiful?' She stroked the corner of exposed pink skin with a gentle forefinger.

'Baby?' He almost dropped the bundle. 'Whose baby?'

'Dora's. She was born last night and – '

He handed the baby hurriedly to a woman nearby, took Kattrin firmly by the arm and dragged her out into the corridor.

'What possessed you to go back in there?' he demanded.

'I wanted to see the baby. I heard her crying and – '

'I told you to keep away from them,' he said through gritted teeth. 'They are not fit company. Most of them are prostitutes.'

'Most of them have no choice,' she said. 'Besides, there are some good women among them.'

'And some bad ones.'

'They are in here for making a living the only way they can. Why should they be criminals and not the men who – who . . .'

'Yes, yes. I dare say you are right,' he said hastily, urging her along the corridor.

She came to an abrupt halt. '*That*'s why no one wanted me to take soup to Rachel, wasn't it?' she demanded. 'Because she was a prostitute. *Not one of the deserving poor*,' she said, in a cutting imitation of Lady Isabelle. 'But what of the men who went to Rachel? No one said rude things about them, did they?

'No, but – '

'And I saw Tarquin coming out of there once.'

'I dare say, but – '

189

'Did you, Joshua?' she demanded, turning to look him in the face. 'Did you ever – visit Rachel?'

'No, I did not!' he said, feeling rather harassed. 'At least, not the way you mean. I used to give her money for the children, but not for ... not for anything else.'

'Dora says that all men – '

'I dare say we may accept Dora as expert in that field,' he said acidly, 'but I'm damned if I'm going to discuss it with you!'

'But I'm your wife, Joshua. Don't wives want to know who their husbands – ?'

'Kat, listen to me!' He gripped her arms, but when she smiled trustingly up at him he dropped his grip as swiftly as if he'd been scalded. 'You mustn't tell people you're my wife. When you get out of here – '

She looked at him in confusion. 'But you married me,' she said, her hand feeling for the string around her neck with the ring, too loose for her finger, suspended on it, cold between her breasts. 'And the other night we – '

'Put it out of your mind!' he said harshly, struggling in vain to put it out of his. 'It should never have happened! If we are to have an annulment – '

She took an involuntary step away from him. 'Is that why you pushed me away last night?' she said in a small voice.

'And shall do every night.' He heard her grinding her teeth. 'Kat, listen. I only went through the ceremony to keep you safe. If I'd known that Lucy and Dickon were coming for you I would never ...' He bit his lip. 'When you get out of here – and I pray God it's soon – Dickon can take care of you better than I can. The marriage will be annulled and you will be able to start your life over again.'

'But I don't want an annulment,' she said, sticking her lip out mutinously. 'Maria said if I had a baby I could plead my belly. She said Aylesbury judges don't like to send mothers and babies on the convict transports.'

'Kat, there's no prospect of you being transported!' he said, nothing loth to change the subject.

'Of course not. We'll both be out of here in days. Lord Bosingham said so.'

'In the meantime just take care.'

'You need not worry about me, Joshua,' she said. 'No man in here would lay a finger on me again, for fear of the papermen.'

He winced at the unintended reminder of his earlier feebleness, then frowned as she shivered. 'Let's get you back to the cell before you freeze. Where's your shawl?'

'I gave it to Dora. She had nothing to wrap the baby in.'

'Kat, it's folly! She'll sell it tomorrow to buy drink!'

'Not Dora,' she insisted. 'Dora's no sot. If it had not been for the man she was to marry running off and leaving her – '

'Oh, Kat!' he said, shaking his head at her. 'My kind-hearted Kat! There isn't a woman in here – nor probably a man either – who couldn't spin you a heart-rending tale and you'd swallow every word of it!'

'And are we so different?' she asked with spirit. 'Or might their heart-rending tales be every bit as true as ours?'

He returned to the cell the next morning, his face damp from the pump, to find Stimpson and Dickon waiting for them, with release papers for Kat.

'I'll call her,' he said. 'She's probably gone to see the baby again.'

'Stimpson has some fresh information,' said Dickon, putting out a hand to stop him. 'Best you hear it first.'

What Joshua saw in his friend's face made his heart sink. 'You have not persuaded the court to drop the charges?' he asked.

'The court have dropped charges against only one man,' said Dickon. 'And that man is Dell.'

'The leader?'

'Dell is a government agent,' said Dickon, 'an *agent provocateur*.' His mouth trembled and it was all he could do to look Joshua in the eye.

'He was undoubtedly put into the district to draw out all those with ideas of rebellion,' said Stimpson.

'And did his dirty job well!' said Joshua savagely.

'Indeed.'

'But what about Bosingham?' Joshua was struggling against the panic that threatened to overcome him. 'He was so sure he would have me out of here!'

But Bosingham's intervention had only compounded the difficulties. Until he wrote from Ireland to persuade Sir Thomas to give evidence on Joshua's behalf of the earlier troubles at Ash Mill, that gentleman had been unaware of Joshua's incarceration. Then he had hastened to Aylesbury to inform the authorities that in his opinion, Joshua had been all along the prime mover in the rebellion. Still smarting over his humiliation outside Ash Mill, the young militia officer made it his business to round up the gentlemen of the hunt to back him. Bosingham alone was prepared to speak for him, but Bosingham had not been on King's Mead.

'They are left to cast around for a ringleader,' said Dickon miserably, 'and they have settled on you.'

191

After a silence that seemed endless, Joshua turned to look at Stimpson. 'Is there any hope?'

'The judges in Wiltshire and Hampshire have handed out much harsher sentences to those educated or more prosperous men caught up in the troubles,' explained the lawyer, looking very grave. 'Particularly if there is any connection with Cobbett, for they would dearly like to see that gentleman in the dock with his supporters, and charge him with conspiracy.'

'They will not need to look far in my case,' said Joshua, his mouth twisting in a mockery of a smile as he remembered the occasions when he had taken his father in his fitter days to the Rotunda to hear Cobbett and his Radical friends speak. The orator had even stayed under their roof when he came to Wycombe to speak.

'Two papermen have already given evidence of the connection,' said Dickon bleakly. 'In the hope of more lenient treatment. It's despicable!'

'I can't blame them,' said Joshua. 'To a man with a noose around his neck no doubt it seems a sensible course of action.' He looked from one to the other and gave a grim smile. 'The evidence is piling up,' he said, 'and not in my favour.'

Dickon sought for comforting words, but could find none.

'I had hoped to persuade some of the men from the earlier Ash Mill gathering to testify on your behalf,' said Stimpson, wiping his spectacles on a large silk handkerchief, 'but it is becoming increasingly difficult to find witnesses. Men have spoken out on behalf of prisoners only to find themselves sent into the dock alongside them; others are released on the understanding that they will turn king's evidence.'

Joshua sank his head into his hands. He knew what it could mean if he were found guilty, for Bosingham's bottles, which had already caused so much mischief, had been packed in crumpled newspaper with reports of the trials. In Hampshire, where no one had even been wounded, one hundred and one men and boys had already been sentenced to death.

Joshua swallowed hard. 'It's looking rather black,' he said at last.

'I never give up hope.'

'If they believe me to be the leader of the riots, they could hang me.'

'I consider hanging most unlikely.'

'But not impossible?'

'It's far more likely to be imprisonment – transportation at worst.'

Joshua covered his eyes with his hands for a brief moment and when he looked up again, his brown eyes were hard. 'Get Kat out of here,' he said coldly. 'Do it now. Don't bring her back in.'

'You can't do that!' Dickon protested. 'You'll break her heart!' He

192

gripped the table until his knuckles turned as white as his face. 'At least say goodbye.'

'No.'

'What am I to tell her?'

'Tell her it's over. Finished. Dead.' He turned his face away, struggling to keep control of himself. 'Prepare the papers for an annulment,' he said, pushing away the memory of Kat in his arms. 'Bring them to me; I will sign them.'

For two days after they brought her from the gaol, Kat lay in the bed in the lodgings that Dickon had taken for her in Aylesbury, and spoke to no one. Dickon wanted her to go to Lady Isabelle, or even to Drusilla in Ireland, but she refused. She, who had always been his strength, collapsed completely and he could do nothing.

On the third day Stimpson arrived to discuss annulment of her marriage.

'There was no difficulty arranging the annulment, Mr Revel,' he said, holding out a little travelling desk with papers, pen, inkwell and sand. 'If your sister would just sign here, and you in lieu of her guardian there,' he went on, pointing with a finger as dry and yellow as the parchment, 'then the papers will be sent to – '

Before he could finish Kattrin bounced up in the bed, causing Stimpson to avert his gaze hastily at the sight of the beribboned nightdress and the veil of golden hair tumbling down over her shoulders; with one wide gesture she knocked everything out of his hand.

'Have you arranged Joshua's release yet?' she demanded.

'As I explained to your brother, Miss Revel, that has not proved as – '

'Then why are you wasting your time here?' she snapped. 'Get Joshua out of prison instead of vexing me with all this! And don't ever mention annulment to me again!' she shrieked, pulling the covers back over her head as Stimpson scuttled away.

'How could you?' she sobbed, as her brother returned to pick up the papers and wipe the spilled ink from the boards. 'To arrange an annulment without even consulting me ...?'

'Oh, Kat! It wasn't me.'

The covers stirred and two dark-ringed golden eyes peeped over the edge of the counterpane.

'Not Father, surely! He has washed his hands of me.' Dickon said nothing. 'Not Lady Isabelle?'

'No. It was – ' His voice choked; his lips would not shape the words.

But this time words were not needed. She knew him too well. 'Not

Joshua?' she said brokenly. 'Oh, Dickon, not Joshua?' She felt a sharp pain deep inside, as if a part of her had been torn away, leaving her with a gaping wound which would never heal.

He crossed to her side to comfort her, but she turned from him. This time his comfort would not be enough. 'If you make any more mess you must ring for the maid to clear it,' he said at last. 'I have an appointment in London.'

'London? Oh, Dickon, no!' She looked at him piteously. 'Don't leave me! Please! I – '

Dickon stood up and brushed the dust from his trousers. 'If it agitates you so, Kat, then of course I shall cancel my appointment and stay here with you. You are after all my sister and must be my prime concern.' It went to the heart to speak to her so harshly when she had already suffered so much, but if she was to survive, he had to put a little fight back into her. 'I *had* thought Joshua's need far greater, but perhaps you feel that under the circumstances...'

She peeped over the edge of the counterpane. 'Joshua?' she said with a frown. 'But – '

'I shall send the stable lad to London to tell Godstowe that I cannot keep our appointment,' he said, reaching for the bell. Before he could pull it she was out of bed, assuring him that she was better and demanding why he was not already on his way.

Without Dickon she would never have survived the next few weeks. The ordeal in prison seemed to have sapped her of more than just her physical strength, but as her determination faltered, so he began to find hidden depths within himself that he had never known he had. As she had been his pillar, so he would now be hers.

The Marquis of Chandos paced from window to window, looking up from the letter in his hand to gaze out across the gardens to the Octagon Lake. The view, one of many at Stowe in a landscape liberally endowed with vistas and embellished with Greek temples and triumphal arches, was held to be one of the best in England and the Marquis always found it soothing in times of trouble.

'What d'ye think I should do about this Revel girl and her brother?' he demanded, turning back into the ornately decorated room. 'Time to fit them in before we see Strutt, eh?'

'Most difficult to advise you, my lord,' said his secretary. 'Although Miss Revel is at present lodging in Aylesbury – having just been released herself from the gaol – she is from the other end of the county. Wooburn. Not one of our people.'

'But she comes recommended by Bosingham.' He creased his brow in an effort to remember. 'Father's a magistrate, isn't he?'

'A most recent creation. And if I might venture to observe, my lord, we have limited influence in Wycombe, whereas the election for the county – '

'Is imminent. And it wouldn't do to upset the electors of Aylesbury.'

'Quite. Then again, my lord, the young lady has been turned off by her family for her – ahem – association with the rebel in question.'

'Wild ideas, Delahaye, but he never struck me as a rebel.'

'And while Bosingham, who wishes us to see her, has the standing, her father, who has no cause to love Delahaye, has the money. Influence in the City.'

Chandos's gaze lifted from the pile of papers on the richly inlaid desk and wandered out across the park. Position the Grenvilles had aplenty, but ready money was the more pressing need. His father, the duke, had plunged the family deeply into debt, and Chandos spent too much of his time meeting creditors and struggling to preserve the vast estates in all their splendour for his son. Disregarding the fact that his titles were of recent creation, he liked to think of himself as the latest in a long line of Buckinghams, custodian of the tradition of centuries; although the great estate had been laid out not by the Grenvilles but by the Temples, he could not bear to contemplate the possibility of losing Stowe, for with the estate would go the family's paramount position at the head of the county.

His secretary cleared his throat. 'There is – ahem – also the consideration that his Grace your father is to be one of the commissioners at the trial. The jury will consist of the landed interest and you, sir, would be the natural choice as their leader. It might prove a little awkward for you and your father if – '

'If I were seen to be in any other way involved? Yes, I do see that. And yet...'

He was resuming his contemplation of the vista when a footman brought him a letter from Wycombe Abbey and word that his man of business was waiting on him.

The Marquis slit open Lord Carrington's missive and read it swiftly; his eyes almost started from his head. 'Damned upstart!' he exclaimed wrathfully. 'Offers to take the Yeomanry off my hands! And all for a miserable two thousand pounds!' He turned anxiously to his secretary. 'You don't think Carrington has had wind of our problems?'

The young man gave an elegant shrug. 'It is possible, sir. I can only advise that we see Strutt straight away and set matters in hand before our difficulties become generally known.'

'Say all that's polite to the young lady, Giles,' said Chandos, 'but I regret I cannot be of assistance. Now – what to tell Bosingham?' He rasped an elegant nail up and down his luxuriant side whiskers.

'If I might suggest, my lord, we might inform Lord Bosingham that, sadly, matters had already gone beyond the point where you could bring any influence to bear.'

'Excellent, Giles. See that it is done, will you? And tell Strutt to bring the papers through.'

It was the same everywhere Kat and Dickon went: from the local gentry to the paper-mill owners, no one seemed willing to stand up for Joshua. Zachary Allnutt promised to speak for him at the trial, but he and his wife were spending all their time in London, for the insurance companies were proving reluctant to pay the costs of reopening the damaged mills. Damage by riot, they insisted, was the government's responsibility.

'Dickon?' Kat's soft voice was barely audible above the lashing of the rain against the windows.

'Mmm?'

'Dickon, how are we paying for Stimpson's services?'

'Don't worry about that,' said Dickon, not looking up from his newspaper. 'It's all taken care of.'

Kat turned back to her contemplation of the raindrops running down the windowpane. For a brief moment Dickon thought the subject had been dropped.

'Then there are these rooms,' she went on. 'Mrs Clegg told me only this morning that she could have let them twice over for the trials, so I know they do not come cheap.' She swung her legs from beneath her and turned to look at her brother. 'For sure Papa won't stand the cost, not now he's disowned me. And you have not enough money to pay for them.' Even when Revel was sending his son up to London on business, he had always kept him short of money.

Dickon looked harassed. 'I tell you, there is no need for you to fret about it.'

'Dickon, is Lord Bosingham paying?'

'No.'

She bounced out of the window seat, crossed the room and snatched his paper from him. 'You surely didn't ask William?' she demanded, her eyes huge in her pale face.

'Godstowe? Of course not!' He pursed his lips primly. 'That would have been most improper.' He saw Kat's lips twitch at his attempts to lecture her on the proprieties of the situation. 'Not that he was averse to playing the knight in shining armour when he heard of our difficulties,' he said, seizing on the diversion. 'Since he's come back from France, there's little he would not do for the sake of a smile from your *beaux yeux*!'

'For me, perhaps, but not for Joshua.'

'He would not see a man suffer injustice merely because he is a rival for your affections,' said Dickon, more sternly than he was wont to speak. 'He is not so petty.'

'I know.' She was ashamed that the thought had even crossed her mind.

'He has no influence himself with the courts, but has promised me the introduction to a friend in the Home Office.'

'I am indebted to him. But you still have not told me who is paying for Stimpson.'

Dickon was beginning to look hunted. 'No, really, Kat,' he protested. 'I can't tell you.' He drew out his watch. 'Well, it's time I was setting off for Wooburn...'

'Don't change the subject.' She tossed the paper aside and advanced on him. 'I warn you, Dickon,' she said, 'I'll wear you down. I always have.'

The two mirror images gazed at each other. Dickon was the first to look away. 'I don't know how to tell you,' he said at last, and they both knew that he had surrendered.

She snuggled down on the sofa alongside him. 'Try,' she said.

'You remember when I was last in London, before...'

'Before all this?' She wrinkled her nose. 'When you were staying with the Cazelles.'

'I was with the lawyers, drawing up the terms for our marriage settlements.'

'Dickon! How could you! I told you I would never marry Louis!' How long ago that all seemed.

'Don't mind all that now,' he said impatiently. 'It's what I found out about Mama's – Cattern's – dowry that's really interesting. You see, everything that old Dawson left in his will – first to Lucy, then to Cattern – was *dowered*. Whoever inherited from him had the use of the farms, but they couldn't be sold. They were in trust for her children – for you and me.'

'Yes, but I'm not – '

'In the eyes of the law, it was in trust for us.' he said firmly. Then, unexpectedly, he chuckled. 'Father must have been furious! After all his scheming, even after abandoning poor Lucy for Cattern, it was all still beyond his grasp. There was no way in law he could get his hands on either the Burnham or the Wooburn farms; the land was tied up for us!'

'I still don't see – '

'As far as I can tell, Bosingham was prepared to pay handsomely for both farms; he needed them to complete his enclosures. Between them, he and father found a lawyer who would get round it, but selling the dower lands was illegal. We could have taken him to court

197

when we were of age, but that would have dragged on for ever. It seemed to me much more sensible just to take it back.'

'But he'd never let you – '

'I didn't ask his permission.' His lips twitched. 'I've learned a few crooked ways and means while I've been working for him in London. My instructions were to set up a separate account for the marriage-settlement funds; all Papa had to do was to sign the authorisations along with some others I put in front of him. What he didn't know, though, was that the new account is in my name only.'

'Dickon, no! How did you dare to do it?'

'Anger, I suppose, that he had tricked us of our inheritance. To this day I don't know.' His voice shook. 'I thought my nerve would fail me. To the last moment I was not sure I could go through with it. But he was too busy to bother with the details; so long as we were wed before we came of age and found out he'd stolen our inheritance from us, what did he care?' The ghost of a smile crossed his face. 'He thought I was doing his bidding – haven't I always?'

'But you were not of age.'

'If he ever finds out – and I do not intend to tell him! – he can't get the money back without taking me to court. And he can't do that without exposing his own misuse of the dowry!'

He couldn't tell her the other things that he had found out during his time in London. It had taken time, and a fair sum of money, but he had at last managed to find the baby farm, one of the many in the East End of London, to which his father had taken the second baby girl born to Lucy. The old woman who had run it was dead, but plying her daughter with gin had given Dickon a view of the books, which had been written up with a view to future blackmail. Against each name given by the person bringing in the baby 'to be cared for' was a scrawled note of their real name and residence: the old woman had had them followed. The trail to Lucy's baby had ended at an unmarked grave, but the entry of Bosingham's name a few lines before Revel's had at least explained the hold his father had had over their influential neighbour.

'But all this must have happened long before he disowned me.'

Dickon grinned. 'You remember when I wrote to you from Manchester that I might have an answer to your problems? It just took a little longer to set up than I had thought. But all the time I was watching you and Joshua; while I didn't care enough to refuse to marry Sarah, I thought it cruel to force you to marry Louis when you loved Joshua. If I could nerve myself to take back our money, I would be able to give you a choice. I never realised how much *I* would enjoy feeling free of his tyranny! Then, before I could get back home and tell you what I'd done, you were caught up in the riots, and I thanked God that I had the means to look after you. Don't you see, Kat, we need be dependent on his whims no more. With our inheritance I can set you up in Bath or Cheltenham, or Ireland – anywhere you like!'

Every day she went to the gatehouse at Aylesbury gaol and every day she was turned away. The prisoner Delahaye, she was told, refused to see her. It went to her heart that he could so turn his back on her after all they had been through together.

He could not stop her going to court, however, and she was there, heavily veiled, on a grey and bitter day in January when Justice Park of the Court of Common Pleas, Baron Bolland of the Court of Exchequer and Justice Patterson of the Court of King's Bench, direct from the trials in Reading and Abingdon, opened proceedings for the Deliverance of Aylesbury Gaol.

'There are so many who know him,' whispered Kat to her brother, scanning the grand jury with its seeding of landowners: Smith of Wycombe Abbey, Dupré of Beaconsfield, Verney of Clayton and Drake of Amersham, with Chandos as their foreman, while his father the duke sat as one of the commissioners. 'They must know he wanted only to stop the trouble!'

'We must hope so,' said Dickon. But to him it was clear from the start, from the moment Sir James Park began to speak on the state of the country and the ingratitude of the labourers, that the authorities were more interested in making an example of those who had dared to demand a living wage than in any investigation of the true causes of the discontent.

'As we have abstained from speaking on the doctrine of machinery,' Justice Park continued, 'so also have we abstained from considering the causes of the rioting; I do not think that necessary.' His voice rose. 'But some wicked and malicious instigators to mischief, placed beyond need themselves, have, in speeches and pamphlets published to excite the deluded and the turbulent, stated that it is the oppression of the rich over the poor which caused these riots.' He fixed the jury with a stern eye. 'This is a foul and false calumny! Though there *may* be some niggardly examples to the contrary, there is no country on earth where noblemen and gentlemen are more open to the fair complaints of the poor, and more disposed to relieve their wants.' There was a rumble of discontent from the packed benches at the rear of the court.

The jury, said Justice Park, would hear a number of cases of destruction of threshing machines from the north of the county; contrary to popular opinion, such destruction did not carry the death penalty, but was punishable by seven years' transportation, or two

199

years' imprisonment, with the option of a private whipping in addition. In Chepping Wycombe, however, property used in manufactories had been damaged, and that was a capital crime; it grieved him to see such a vast number of men in the dock on trial for their lives, so many from the one village.

Another groan went up from the rear benches as all eyes turned on the men in the dock: there were nigh on a hundred and thirty men on trial, most of them young men and boys from Wooburn and Flackwell Heath, with barely a handful above forty years of age.

Justice Park pointed out that while one offence could lead to transportation for seven years, conviction of a second similar offence could lead to fourteen years, and a third to transportation for the term of a man's natural life. Moreover, an accessory before the fact would be liable to the same punishment, whether that punishment be imprisonment, transportation or even death.

'Clearly the wicked instigators of these disturbances, who misled these ignorant wretches into crime with their seditious papers, writings and speeches, deserve even greater punishment than those they misled! I would remind you, gentlemen, that accomplices may also be credible witnesses against those who drew them into such folly; if the evidence of an accomplice is confirmed in some particulars, then it may be assumed to be correct in others. Likewise, if it be accepted against one individual, then it may be accepted against another, against whom no evidence was previously known.' He looked down the list of indictments. 'Finally, gentlemen, we come to the charge of refusing to be sworn in as a special constable. It is the law of the land that it is an indictable offence to refuse to be sworn in, or, having been sworn, to refuse to act. I am glad to say that there is only one such charge.'

Kat, knowing that he could only be talking about Joshua, shivered.

They sat through three days of evidence and cross-examination by Mr Gurney and Mr Stork for the prosecution and Mr Bodkin for the defence. Some were acquitted of the charges at one mill, only to be indicted on the same charges at another mill; some of those who had been most active in the destruction were not in the dock at all, while others who had simply been bystanders were held guilty of riot.

Joshua was brought in on Thursday afternoon with the last batch of men. To Kat he looked a different person from the man who had held her in his arms and loved her on Christmas Night. He had shaved himself and wore clean linen, brought in for him by Stimpson, but the light had gone out of his eyes and his face was drawn and

200

haggard. She wished that Dickon were there with her, but Dickon had been summoned to London.

Joshua's eyes raked the courtroom. He prayed that Kat was not there – and yet, perversely, some small corner of his heart hoped that she had not forgotten him entirely. There were a number of labourer's women at the back of the court – wives, sisters, mothers – some burdened with babes in arms; some wore bonnets, but most had only shawls around their heads against the raw January day. There were few enough for a hundred and thirty prisoners, but how many would have time or money enough to take the cart twenty-five miles to Aylesbury? His eyes scanned the gallery and the benches nearer the front where those ladies sufficiently bold to attend the trials were indistinguishable behind their heavy veils.

He had not known how long the trial would last, but he had not expected everything to happen so fast. Bosingham was still delayed in Ireland and the few witnesses who had agreed to appear on his behalf were forced, under cross examination, to admit that he had often spoken to them of the injustice done to the labourers and of his great desire to see a reform of the parish system, and to concede that they knew his father to be a supporter of Cobbett. It was enough: he could see the condemnation in the eyes of the jury even before Charsley was called into the witness stand to horrify them with the tale of the vicious attack launched against his person by Sarney and Delahaye.

It did not bode well for Joshua that he was followed into the dock by the last group of papermen to be charged with the capital offence. He listened in astonishment as one after another they all pleaded guilty, even Ben Francis, who had been on the fringes of the mob and who with an unblemished past would have had a good chance of acquittal, and Joseph Priest, who had been caught up by the mob while working on the road gang, and was so deaf it was doubtful he understood half of what was going on, and John Dafter, who had not even been of the mob, but had merely returned the stone that had hit him. All pleaded guilty, with Will Bryant even pleading guilty to destroying machinery at mills which had been attacked after he had been shot in the arm at Ash Mill and removed from the field.

'What the devil are you thinking of?' he demanded when the men were removed from the dock to allow the judges to deal with the men from Stone and Waddesdon. 'Dafter, you were not even in the mob! Did you not heed a word Stimpson said to you?'

'It were the justices' clerk, Mr Joshua,' said Dafter. ''E said their lordships was tired out with the trial going on so long, and likely to look kindlier on us if we spared 'em any more an' pleaded guilty. So us did.'

'What matter to them whether we plead guilty or no?' growled

Miles, the young apprentice shoemaker from Flackwell Heath. 'There's no justice for the likes of us.'

'Fools, the lot of you,' grumbled Stone, the Kentish papermaker who had been on the tramp from Dartford to take up a job in Leicester, when he had been caught up in the riots. 'You heard the judge. Said such pleas proved you to be really guilty; with my luck I'll get tarred with the same brush.' He looked angrily at the other men. 'I think ye must all be perfect fools, not to take your chances at least.'

Joshua sank his head in his hands. By pleading guilty they had, in their ignorance, robbed themselves of the chance to bring witnesses to speak for their character. Those among the men who had pleaded not guilty, even if they were known to have been at the head and forefront of the attacks, would be able to call on men of standing, such as a minister or a former employer, to speak on their behalf and give them a good character in the hope of a lesser sentence, while those who had been less active in the violence but had been persuaded to enter guilty pleas were left, unrecommended by any, with none to speak for them.

The rest of the afternoon proceeded relentlessly; at the end they were brought back into the dock to hear verdict pronounced. Joshua was standing at the back of the dock and even over the prison stench, a miasma that filled the nostrils and that the most diligent toilette could not scrub away, he could smell the fear in the press of men around him.

'Remove James Stone from the bar,' intoned Judge Park, and the Kent man was with difficulty removed from the tightly packed ranks and bound over to keep the peace. Joshua held his breath, hoping for a lesser sentence at least for Dafter, East, Francis, Holt, maybe for himself – but no order came.

There was little doubt of the eventual verdict: the gentry were both judge and jury and after the fright that they had had at the hands of the Captain Swing rioters throughout the southern counties, their intention was to visit such terror on the poor and starving that never again in this generation would they dare to speak, much less act, against the landowners.

It was difficult for him, with all his education, to follow the judge's homily with its long-winded references to his learned brothers, its endless sentences and subclauses littered with witty Latin tags to raise a smile among the lawyers; the other men in the dock were perfectly bewildered by it. He heard a sighing and a moaning in the body of the court as judgement of death was pronounced against forty-five of the papermen and a buzzing in his head as he heard his own name among them.

'I don't understand, Mr Delahaye,' said little John Crutch, a lost

202

and bewildered look in his hazel eyes as they were hustled away through the trap door.

Joshua, who had once worked with the boy's father at the Overshot Mills, looked down on him with pity.

'Mister?' It was young Will Russell, the boy with the dying father whom he had sent home from Allnutt's mill; he scarce looked old enough to be at work, let alone on trial for his life. 'Be they a-goin' to hang us or n-not?' he stammered. 'On'y, I don't rightly see what they m-means and, well, I'd rather kn-now, see.'

How to explain to a simple country boy this last gruesome refinement of the judicial system? 'What judgement of death means, Will, is that they *could* hang every one of us, but they probably won't hang more than four or five.'

'How will we know?' asked John, close to tears.

'When will we know?' said another.

'When it suits them to tell us,' Joshua answered with a shrug. 'But they've little enough left to do in Aylesbury, so it may not be too long.'

That night he was surprised to receive a summons to the governor's office where he was received, in the governor's absence, by the prison chaplain and two strangers, dressed plainly but with elegance; they had, he was told, come expressly from London to see him. His heart leaped: perhaps Godstowe and Bosingham had had some success on his behalf after all.

He was seated in a comfortable chair, a glass of wine was poured for him and one of the strangers offered him a pipe, which he declined.

The two men had come from London, but not at Godstowe's request. They came bluntly to the point: Joshua was known to have frequented the local alehouses where sedition was preached; his father was known to be a supporter of Cobbett; witnesses had stated that Will Delahaye had attended Radical meetings at the Rotunda and spoken in praise of the Great Perturbator. It would not be surprising, therefore, if Will's son had been led astray by Cobbett's seditious words.

'If you would agree to give evidence that Cobbett was the prime instigator of these troubles, Mr Delahaye,' said the older of the two, 'we are empowered to offer you a pardon.'

'Just cast your eyes over this document,' said the other, pushing a pen and ink pot across the table. 'Append your signature and you can walk out of here tonight.'

'Safe home by the marital hearth with your new wife,' said the chaplain ingratiatingly.

203

Two visions struggled for supremacy in his mind, of Kat, her eyes dark with passion, holding her arms wide to welcome him home; of Cobbett, irascible, self-important, a man he had never taken to, stumping around the country and writing bitterly against society's wrongs.

He passed his hand wearily over his eyes to drive the visions away. Looking at the lawyers, he realised that they were holding their breath until he signed. 'Gentlemen,' he said at last, pushing the document away, 'I am not the man you seek.'

'It is not an easy decision. You should take time to consider – '

Joshua shook his head. 'I cannot put words into another man's mouth. I never heard Cobbett preach revolution.'

'But your wife – ' squeaked the chaplain.

'My wife married an honourable man, sir,' said Joshua, rising to his feet and drawing himself up straight. 'I have vowed not to disappoint her.'

She read and reread the letter from Tarquin, trying to make up her mind what to do. If only Dickon had not gone to London! But he had business to do for their father, and until they could decide their future plans, Dickon could not afford to arouse his suspicions.

At last she decided that she must accept Tarquin's invitation. Time was short and it had, after all, been Tarquin's deposition that had put Joshua in prison. If there was a chance that she could appeal to their old friendship and persuade him to withdraw it, she could not afford to turn her back on it.

The militia, brought to Aylesbury to keep the peace during the trials, had been quartered on the George Inn, so, with the veil on her bonnet drawn well down over her face, she crossed the square and slipped around to the back door, where the landlord, well accustomed to veiled ladies visiting gentlemen's rooms, showed her up the back stairs as arranged.

Tarquin opened the door with a glass in his hand and a foolish grin on his lips. For a moment it was all she could do not to turn tail and run back down the stairs.

With a wink at the landlord, Tarquin drew her into the room and handed her to the sofa. 'Will you join me in a glass?' he said, crossing to the decanter.

'No, thank you,' she said, perching primly on the edge of the sofa, watching him refill his glass, drain it and then refill it once more. She reminded herself that she was doing this to help Joshua. 'In your note you said you'd thought of a way to help Joshua.' She looked up at him with tragic eyes. 'He wouldn't be in trouble if he hadn't tried to protect me and – '

He gave a low whistle. 'So it was you on King's Mead! Someone said they were sure they'd seen you!'

She nodded her head. 'If he hadn't called out to warn me...' Her voice faltered and she bit her lip. 'I'll do *anything* to save him,' she said.

'I don't want to see Joshua hang,' he said, crossing to sit beside her. 'Lieutenant Walton has seen dozens of hangings, you know. He says the eyes bulge out and the mouth turns blue and the hanged men lose all control of their bodily functions. Sometimes the bodies twitch for hours afterwards. Dancing the Newgate hornpipe, that's what the soldiers call it.'

Kat's hand slipped up to her throat as she willed herself not to faint.

'I could withdraw my deposition,' said Tarquin, slipping his arm round her waist. 'If you make it worth my while...'

It took a moment for the full import of his meaning to penetrate her clouded mind. Unabashed, he clamped his arm more tightly around her shrinking body and drew her to him, breathing brandy fumes into her face.

'Only fair, sweetheart,' he said, his eyes greedily devouring her. The terror on her face, the panting breath and the rapid rise and fall of her bosom only made his pulses race the more. 'You want me to tell them all that I was wrong, so that your dear Joshua is released from prison.' His eyes narrowed. 'You love him, don't you?'

'Yes, but – '

'So that's why you wouldn't marry me. You get Joshua. Joshua gets the girl I love.' His tongue darted over his lips. 'Only right that I should have my share first.'

She opened and closed her mouth, trying desperately to think of a way to appeal to his better nature, but she was not sure that he had one where Joshua was concerned. 'You don't love me, Tarquin!' she said at last, struggling to control her panic.

He shrugged. 'Love, desire, where's the difference? You want me to bring you and Delahaye together? Damned if I won't have some benefit first!'

She shuddered as she felt his lips brush her hair. In all the novels she and Drusilla had ever read, the heroine, whether nobleman's daughter or simple village maiden, would always leap up at this point and speak movingly of death rather than dishonour, but Kat's lips could not shape the words. A slow decline into death, such as the fictional Clarissa had chosen, might prove a welcome escape if she were to lose Joshua, but to know that she had by her cowardice condemned the man she loved to imprisonment or, worse, a painful and undignified death as a common felon, was a prospect more dreadful to contemplate than anything Tarquin could do to her.

What had happened in Joshua's arms in that stinking cell in Aylesbury gaol would never be erased from her memory; whatever Tarquin did to her body, he would not touch her soul as Joshua had done. Deny Tarquin now and she might deny Joshua the right to freedom, perhaps even to life. It wasn't as if she had a reputation to lose: in the eyes of the world she was ruined anyway, even before anyone knew of the prison marriage.

She lifted her head and looked him directly in the eye. 'You wish me to undress?' she said, surprised at how calm her voice sounded.

'That privilege I claim for myself,' he said hoarsely and in one stride he was at her side, ripping the shawl from her shoulders, his bright-blue eyes hot with lust. She thought she would faint when she felt his hands fumbling at the lacings of her dress, his breath on her shoulder, but she bit her lip and stood still, willing herself to feel nothing, to show nothing. Once more, just as in those last terrible days in Clapton Revel, she seemed to stand outside her own body, on another plane, watching in frozen detachment as this stranger stripped the clothes from a body from which all feeling had departed.

Tarquin had stripped her to her shift when he stopped abruptly, took her by the shoulders and shook her furiously. 'Damn you, are you made of ice?' he shouted 'Say something! Do something!' He wanted her to shout, weep, beg, anything but stand there with that blind look in her eyes.

She blinked at him, a look of puzzlement on her face. 'Do what you wish,' she said tiredly. 'I have said I will not stop you.'

He turned away from her with a muffled groan and slammed his clenched fist against the panelled wall. When at last he turned back to her, beads of sweat stood out on his brow and upper lip; he clutched at her hands and looked at her pitifully, almost pleadingly, but she didn't seem to see him at all. After a moment he swore angrily and pushed her away so abruptly that she stumbled. 'Get out of here!' he said through clenched teeth.

She opened her mouth but no sound came out.

With an angry curse he picked her clothes up and thrust them into her arms. Then, before she fully realised what was happening, he opened the door and pushed her out on the landing. For a brief moment he looked like the Tarquin she remembered, but the moment passed as quickly as it had come. 'Go back to Delahaye!' he snarled, his face contorted with rage. 'Unman him as you have me!'

Scarlet with mortification she scrambled into her clothes as best she could, praying that no one would cross the landing and find her

206

there. With trembling hands she drew down her veil and hurried back to her lodgings in Walton Street.

It was Saturday before it pleased their lordships to call the prisoners into court to hear the final verdict, and two days had never seemed longer to those men with 'Judgement of Death' recorded against their names. The Quaker who had married him to Kat and had organised the Society of Friends to help the most destitute of the fatherless families in Flackwell Heath and Wooburn, came in to pray with them on the Friday night. Joshua found himself praying with them, for the memory of the comfort that it had once brought him, rather than any belief in the power to which they were praying: that had long since left him.

Their lordships dealt first with the men from the north of the county, and contrary to expectation their judgements were on the lenient side, prison sentences mostly, although the three men who had taken guns with them when they had gone about to destroy the threshing machines and demand of the vicar that he reduce his tithes, were each sentenced to seven years' transportation.

'Should be better for us,' said one of the Wooburn men when they heard of it. 'Not any of us had a gun, did us, lads?'

But the hopes raised in the breasts of the Wooburn men were shortlived. One by one the men's names were called over. Of the forty-six against whom judgement of death had been given, forty-three were recommended to the King's mercy; fourteen of them were sent to hard labour in the house of correction – but the other twenty-nine, including all three of the Bryant men – father, son and nephew – young Will Russell and little John Crutch, were condemned to transportation.

'Shall I ever see you more?' wailed one woman, children clutching at her skirts and her belly swollen with child. She tried to reach a hand to her man beyond the rail, until she and the other women were dragged away by the court attendants.

'What about my babe?' said one man from the front of the dock. Dazed with shock, he turned beseeching eyes to the judges on the bench above him. 'My lords, may I not take my babe with me beyond the seas?' he pleaded. 'Her mother's dead and we have only each other.'

'You should have thought of that before,' said one of the lawyer's clerks with a callousness that shocked all within hearing.

'Take them away!' came the order, and the dazed father was taken through the trap door and back to the cells with the rest. At last only Joshua, John Sarney and Thomas Blizzard were left standing at the bar.

'Stand forward, Joshua Delahaye,' intoned the clerk.

Joshua stepped forward, his eyes fixed on the coat of arms above the judges' heads. He caught at the brass rail and clutched it, his knuckles showing white.

'We have studied most anxiously to prevent the extreme punishment of the law,' said Mr Justice Park, fixing him with an icy glare, 'but my own inclination is most certainly that this punishment should be invoked in your case.' Terror scoured his gut and twisted his marrow, unmanning him totally and rendering him as helpless and feeble as a child. He curled his fingers around the edge of the dock and willed his knees to stiffen and his legs to hold him. 'You, sir,' Park continued, 'are a man who could allude to no suffering, claim no poverty as an excuse for your behaviour. Worse, you were responsible for leading many ignorant and less favoured souls into their peril and exciting them to act against their betters, to destroy the property of those who would give them work.'

'No!'

'You will be silent, sir!' He looked down at his papers. 'You are fortunate that so many – although, I note, *not* your employer – have spoken out on your behalf, believing you to have had a genuine if misguided desire to help the poor and a young man's overweening conviction that you knew better than your elders. They believe you also to have been drawn into folly by the pernicious and inflammatory writings of one who will shortly, we understand, himself answer to charges of sedition in the highest court in the land.' He paused to see what effect this would have, but Joshua was unsurprised; the authorities were determined to draw Cobbett into this and he would not have been the only man to have been offered his freedom in exchange for incriminating a bigger fish.

'For myself I would consider you deserving of the ultimate penalty for no other cause than your brutal attack on the coroner in the course of his duties, but my fellow judges, mindful of Mr Heyford's assertion that you were bent only on preventing further bloodshed in that case, and heeding Mr Hailey's strong defence of your conduct, have in the event prevailed over me. You are therefore commended to His Majesty's mercy, with the recommendation that you be cut off from all communion with friends and family and transported beyond the seas for the rest of your natural life.' He nodded to the warder. 'Take him away.'

They had to pry his fingers from the bar before they could drag him from the dock. In the gallery a lone figure rose to her feet with a loud sob and everyone turned to look. Even with the heavy veil on her bonnet he knew it was Kat and turned his head sharply away, unable to bear the pain of seeing her again.

The judges had already reached for the squares of black cloth to drape over their wigs as they turned their attention to Sarney and Blizzard. With a last heart-rending cry of 'Joshua!' ringing in his ears above the sobbing of old Sarney, he was led away to the cells.

# Chapter Eleven

Lifting the hem of her skirts, she followed in the wake of the under-sized crossing sweeper brushing a path clear for her through the ice-crusted filth of the street. Reaching the safety of the swept pavement, she gave the boy a handful of small coins; his bony fingers closed like claws around them and his eyes, sunk in pallid and begrimed skin, almost started from his head as he saw how much she had given him.

Kat went on her way with his blessings ringing in her ears. After years without a penny to call her own, she found it strangely liberating to give to others so much worse off, from what seemed an endless supply.

Accustomed to comparative freedom around Wooburn, she was somewhat embarrassed to find herself the focus of all eyes as she walked down Whitehall, through knots of clerks gossiping in doorways; it was fortunate that Dickon had insisted on her engaging the daughter of their Aylesbury landlady as maid, although the girl had not a word to say for herself. Lord Godstowe was waiting for them outside the building in Whitehall and took them up several flights of stairs to an anteroom where two young men and an army of porters were trying to bring some order to a room where every surface appeared to be lost under a sea of papers.

A clerk hurried forward with profuse apologies for the state of the room. Some of those who had been awarded office under Earl Grey's new government had not yet taken up their positions, he explained to Godstowe, and as undersecretaries and other minions were appointed by them, until the principals deigned to return from travel on the continent or from their distant estates, no one could be appointed to deal with the business of state which was piling up.

'And all because Wellington hurt King Billy's feelings!' said Godstowe, as the young man, wringing his hands, turned back to the papers.

'Did he?' Kat looked at him wide-eyed.

'When the present troubles started,' said Godstowe, moving a pile of papers to enable her to sit down, 'the King was due to dine with the Lord Mayor and aldermen, to mark his accession. Alderman Key demanded a strong military escort to the Mansion House, in case of demonstrations. Wellington advised the King not to go, but William's no coward – he was in a number of naval engagements in the late wars – and he refused to listen. Wellington, being unused to having his advice ignored, promptly cancelled the dinner anyway, whereupon William dismissed Wellington.'

'He might have held his temper and spared us all this confusion,' grumbled the young man behind them. 'I always thought he was such a genial old buffer.'

Godstowe's lips twitched. 'I'll wager Wellington thought so too,' he said.

The wait seemed endless, and Kat had to suppress an urge to sneeze every time someone disturbed another pile of paper. At last they were shown into the office of one of Melbourne's assistants, a friend of Godstowe's, but he had no good tidings for them.

'I fear there will be no pardons,' he said, when the introductions had been made and the usual courtesies exchanged. 'I have pursued the matter as far as I may, but Lord Melbourne is as determined as Wellington to crack down on civil unrest.'

'But the trial was a mockery!' Godstowe protested. 'And the main accuser has since withdrawn his deposition.'

'Tarquin?' Her face was mantled with blushes as she recalled the humiliation of the scene in the George.

'Yes.' He looked at her with narrowed eyes, then turned back to his Home Office colleague. 'And Lord Bosingham, who was a witness when Delahaye dispersed the rioters at Ash Mill, will speak at a retrial.'

'The deposition was made on oath. Withdrawing it does not change the evidence against the accused. There will be no retrial. I have it on the highest authority that no appeals will be allowed.' There was a flash of sympathy on his face, quickly suppressed. 'Criticisms that the new government cannot be as firm against law-breakers as the Tories must be shown to be false. Lord Melbourne is determined to make examples of all those involved in the recent riots and Mr Delahaye will be treated exactly like all the others.'

The blood drained from her face as her last chance of saving Joshua faded away. 'Then what will happen to him?' she whispered.

'He will shortly be transferred to the prison hulks and then to one of the penal colonies. New South Wales or Van Diemen's Land are the likely destinations.'

'Is there nothing you can do, Davenies?' asked Godstowe. 'The man does not deserve this.'

'Your only hope of saving him from the convict hold is for one of the voyagers to request him as a servant. You will need to act speedily: such places are eagerly sought by the gentlemen convicts.'

'And at journey's end?' enquired Godstowe.

'Find a decent landowner in Australia to take him on and I will try to ensure that he is assigned to him. I can do no more.' He cleared his throat. 'Between ourselves, Godstowe, take care what ship you set him on. The administration of the two colonies is quite separate and the regime in Van Diemen's Land is much harsher than in New South Wales, especially for political prisoners.'

'I can tell you now who to assign him to,' said Kattrin. 'Me.'

Godstowe looked at her aghast. 'My dear lady,' he said hoarsely, 'you don't know what you are saying!'

She looked at him with a steady gaze, the knowledge that there was something she could do to help already beginning to take away some of the agony she had felt since the trial and the separation from Joshua. 'I was never more serious in my life,' she said.

They were lit up the steps of the elegant town house by liveried footmen with flaring links, and shown into the house with great ceremony. As the butler relieved her of her cloak, William Godstowe emerged from the shadows and drew Dickon aside. 'You found Miss Thornton, I hear?' he said.

'I am just returned from escorting her to Leicestershire,' said Dickon. 'She will be staying there for the moment – it is no longer possible for her to remain at Clapton Revel.'

'That must be a great relief for you both.' He dropped his voice. 'Can you not persuade your sister to join her aunt? Talk her out of this mad scheme...'

'I can't do it, Godstowe. It's the only thing that keeps Kat sane, stops her from thinking about what's happening to Joshua on the hulks...' It was the rock to which she clung in a sea of misery and he could not prise her loose from it.

'What are you two talking about so seriously?' asked Kattrin.

Godstowe shifted uncomfortably from one foot to the other. 'I wonder, Revel, if you would permit me a moment alone with your sister?' he asked. 'We shall join you presently.'

Kattrin went sunnily into the anteroom with him, wondering what it was that William had to say to her that could not be said in front of her brother. 'It was good of you to arrange this meeting with Sir Anthony Cawfield,' she said. 'I understand he has a great deal of influence in Australia?'

'Indeed. You will also meet Sir Richard Bourke tonight. If Cawfield has his way, he will be the next governor.'

'I hope he is a kinder man than Governor Darling,' said Kat anxiously. 'I understand Darling is very harsh with the convicts.'

'Bourke did much for the inhabitants of Cape Colony,' said Godstowe, pacing up and down the room. 'I hope he may go to Australia, but there is talk of him returning to Leinster – he was much loved by the Irish – or to Barbados. He dreams of warmth, his daughter tells us, for he is much pained by his wounds. His jaw was shattered by a ball in the Helder campaign in ninety-nine.' He stopped his pacing and came to a halt in front of her.

'But I didn't bring you in here to talk about Bourke,' he said with a forced laugh. 'Kattrin – may I call you Kattrin?' He didn't wait for an answer. 'Will you reconsider this mad idea?' He caught her hands in his. 'Stay in England and marry me.'

She snatched her hands away with a gasp. 'But I am already married!' she exclaimed. 'I'm married to Joshua.'

'But that was a prison marriage and you were underage. It could easily be annulled.'

The echo of Joshua's words cut her to the soul. She turned away sharply. 'My lord, I am flattered by your proposal, but my station is well beneath yours. Your family would scarce approve of a connection with the disinherited and outcast daughter of a mill owner!'

'I care nothing for their approval!' he said sharply. 'I know my father would come round if you marry me – and Lord Bosingham would add his voice to mine. He is very fond of you.'

Kat turned back to him and put her hand on his arm. 'William, if I loved you, I wouldn't care either.'

'I feared that was the case,' he said with a sigh. 'So it wasn't just a marriage of convenience to protect you?'

'Partly. But I love him, you see. And I think he loves me.'

'You *think* so? It's not a very firm foundation on which to sail to the other side of world!'

She said nothing.

'Kattrin, I think you do not understand the difficulty of what you are undertaking. If you will not marry me, then I beg of you, at least go to Drusilla in Ireland and give yourself time to think it through.'

'I cannot do that either, William,' she said. 'With your help or without it, I shall go to Australia.'

'Then I must accept defeat.' He raised her hand to his lips and kissed it. 'Never forget, my dear, if anything happens to Joshua, there will always be a home for you with me.'

'Thank you.' She pressed his hand. 'But if anything happens to Joshua, life would mean nothing to me.'

He gave a wry smile. 'Then we must make sure that nothing does.'

The dinner was an intimate one, with Sir Anthony Cawfield and his secretary, Godstowe and a couple of military gentlemen in civilian clothes. She was the only female present. She was seated next to Sir Richard Bourke at dinner but her head reeled so with Lucy's flight from Clapton Revel, and Lord Godstowe's unexpected proposal, that he had addressed several remarks to her before she gathered her wits sufficiently to answer him. His rather severe appearance, however, hid a warmer nature and while she recovered herself he began to talk to her of Marlow and High Wycombe.

'My wife and I spent several happy years there until the year four,' he said, running his fingers lightly over the knotted flesh of his jaw. 'After Helder I was invalided out and sent to the Duke of York's Royal Military College which had just then commenced in High Wycombe. I went on to serve as superintendent of the junior military department in Great Marlow. Those were happy days. Who would ever have imagined that those pretty little villages around Wooburn would have known such trouble?'

He was a sympathetic listener, drawing her out to speak of the villagers and the trials. Although he was still in two minds whether to take up the Australian appointment, he took an active interest when the discussion around the table turned to the antipodean colonies.

'I wish you could dissuade Miss Kattrin from going, Cawfield,' said Godstowe. 'I've told her it's folly . . .'

'I believe we can smooth the way,' said Sir Anthony, folding his hands across his ample stomach as the desserts were set on the table, 'if the young lady is willing to be of assistance to us. Howick, the new minister for the Colonies – who is, we must not forget, the Prime Minister's son – is considering proposals to relieve some of our worst slums by offering free passage to Australia, where there is, it appears, a great shortage of artisans.'

'Won't work under Darling's regime,' said a man further down the table. 'The man's a military martinet.'

'Quite so. We are inundated with complaints from the colonists who have irreconcilable differences with Governor Darling. And we have been frustrated in our attempts to get a clear picture of the situation, as everyone we have sent out there is suborned to one faction or the other within days of arrival. Howick has set me to look for someone who owes allegiance neither to the landowners nor the Emancipists – they are the smaller landowners, mostly convicts who have earned their freedom.'

'Someone to serve as your eyes and ears in the colony,' said Sir Richard.

'Just until the new governor can be sent out.' Cawfield turned to

214

Kattrin. 'Someone such as yourself, ma'am, with – ahem – wider interests, would be able to report on all aspects.'

'Yes, but a lady!' protested Sir Anthony's secretary.

'Godstowe assures me that the young lady has all the necessary qualities,' observed Sir Anthony. 'You understand, dear lady, that Howick is not able to interfere with the due course of the law – we have no influence with the Home Office – but in return for your reports we shall do all we can to assist you with finding a property and assigning to you any, er, *particular* convict you might care to name.'

'He will be eternally grateful to you,' said Dickon.

'He will know nothing of it!' snapped Sir Anthony. 'Nothing. You will tell no one.'

'But surely the man deserves to know – '

'If word of this ever got out . . . !' protested his secretary. 'Don't you see, sir, it is what our political enemies are waiting for, a sign of weakness.'

'You must agree to speak of this to no one,' insisted Sir Anthony, 'or I fear I must withdraw our assistance.'

Hastily Godstowe intervened, agreeing that neither he nor the Revels would speak of it again.

'But how will she report?' asked his secretary. 'All mail is sent on government ships.'

Sir Anthony tapped his teeth. 'She must write to her dear friend Godstowe,' he said with a smile. 'No one will bother with a personal correspondence.' He raised his glass to her. 'To you, ma'am,' he said. 'Bon voyage.'

As they raised their glasses to her, she was struck by the magnitude of what she was planning to do: she, who had never set foot more than twenty-five miles from Wooburn in her life, was now committed to travel to the other side of the world. To the ends of the earth. The delicate syllabub turned to sawdust in her mouth.

# Part III

# Australia

From distant climes o'er widespread seas we come,
Tho' not with much eclat or beat of drum,
True patriots we, for be it understood,
We left our country for our country's good.

# Chapter Twelve

She stood at the rail until Dickon was nothing but a dot in the distance, then the *Maria* tacked around the broad bend in the river and the quayside was gone from view. Blinking back the tears, she drew up the hood of her boat cloak against the cold February wind, declining all exhortations to go below, sure that someone would realise, even at this eleventh hour, what a terrible miscarriage of justice there had been. She could not desert her post as long as a single yard of England could still be seen; while they were still in sight of land, anything must be possible.

The weeks since the trial had passed in a blur, leaving her little time for contemplation. Each day she rose and obediently played her part in whatever plan Dickon had made for her, going from the lawyers to the Colonial Office, from Manton's shooting gallery to lectures on farming in Australia, but nothing had made much impact on her, for she had left her heart in Aylesbury, with Joshua.

She stayed on deck until the last sight of land had disappeared. Turning away from the rail she looked around her: nothing but sea and sky. Cast adrift from anything and anyone she had ever known, lost in a sea of an immensity she had never imagined, she staggered below, overwhelmed with panic.

'This is but the Channel, my dear,' said Mrs Proctor condescendingly as she waved the smelling salts under Kat's nose. The wife of the colony's deputy mineral surveyor, Mrs Proctor was one of the two ladies whom Godstowe and Dickon had, unbeknown to Kat, engaged to keep an eye on her during the voyage. 'A small expanse of water – nothing to the ocean, I assure you.'

'I dare say it must all seem strange to a young girl like you,' agreed her companion, a comfortable middle-aged woman travelling out to join her husband who, on quitting his regiment, had set up as a merchant in Sydney. 'Especially living so far from the sea – Widburn, was it?'

'Wooburn.'

'Quite. But this is the fifth voyage I have made, and we are most fortunate in our company on the *Maria*. A voyage will always pass well in superior company.'

The next day, while they took a morning constitutional around the deck, Mrs Hambleden enumerated in greater detail the company on the ship, with the precise degrees of any titled connections she had been able to glean. Kat's mind began to wander and her eyes fell on the deck below, where the crop-headed male convicts were being brought up from the hold and mustered for roll call, before being allotted various shipboard duties in assistance to the sailors. She looked at them blindly, seeing not their faces, but the faces of the men of Wooburn who would soon be following them into exile. Lost in her memories of Wooburn, it was not until she heard the shrill cries that she realised that the men had returned below and that the ship's surgeon was bringing the female convicts up. Shuddering as she recalled how close she had come to being among their number, it was a moment before she realised what was happening on the deck below. As the women emerged from the blackness of the hold, blinking against the light, the ship's officers picked out the youngest and cleanest, poking and prodding them in the most indecent manner, sliding hands up skirts and down bodices, mauling them about like beasts at a cattle fair. Those women drawn out of the file had their irons struck off before being taken below, some less reluctant than others, to spend the voyage in the cabins of their new protectors. The remainder, struggling, shrieking and kicking, had their locks shorn until they were as crop-headed as the men.

Mrs Proctor saw the look of appalled shock on Kat's face and hurried her below to the day cabin, begging her not to speak her mind to anyone else; if the captain thought she was interfering in his right to run the ship entirely as he wished, he had the power to make all their lives most uncomfortable for the duration of the voyage.

'But how can you stand by and let this happen?' protested Kat.

'Pray tell me what alternative you propose for these women,' said Mrs Proctor. 'They are products of the worst London slums; they were fallen women even before they were shipped on board the convict transports.'

'One ought not to speak of such things to an unmarried girl like yourself,' said Mrs Hambleden, 'but such women will not forgo their base appetites, my dear, and will most certainly enter into relationships on the voyage, if not with the officers, then with the convicts. Would you deny them the chance to better themselves?'

'Officers have even been known to make honest women of the better sort,' agreed Mrs Proctor.

'One is scarcely surprised,' said Mrs Hambleden with a knowing smile, 'for a sea voyage is often the sweetener to a romance, as Miss Revel must know.'

'I?' said Kat in some surprise, her attention temporarily diverted from the convicts.

'We have eyes and ears, my dear. And why so coy when there is that nice young Lieutenant Standish and the Reverend Dr Purcell both *desperate* for a sign of favour from you?'

She should have altered the register when she found Dickon had yielded to Godstowe's persuasion and booked her passage as Miss Revel, but at the time it had scarcely seemed worth the trouble. She had talked to both Standish and Purcell at dinner the previous evening because one reminded her of Dickon and the other had already spent several tours of duty in New Holland, or Australia, as the country was now being called, and she wanted to find out as much as she could about her new home.

She soon discovered that, as one of the few young women, it was not such a simple matter to avoid the attentions of the large number of single men on board. She spent a great deal of time in her cabin, finding that sleep, which had for so long eluded her, came easy on a sea voyage, and fulfilling her promise to Cawfield by keeping a journal. When she was forced to emerge, she deliberately dressed in her dowdiest muslin robes, ignoring the trunks of fashionable ensembles which she and Dickon had shopped for, and made a point of talking to everyone, deciding that there was safety in numbers. She spent more time working on her lace and playing cards with the old ladies than the gentlemen thought acceptable, but she refused to fret about anyone else's feelings; for her the voyage was a welcome abdication of responsibility. The last few weeks in England had demanded so many decisions and so much heartache, but on board the *Maria*, sails were set and struck, courses navigated, stores opened and meals prepared, all without reference to her. And she was content to have it so. She had been making decisions for what seemed like a lifetime. If no one asked her to decide anything ever again, she would be happy.

She was shocked to find that she was even able to forget about Lucy for days at a time. She had hoped at first that Lucy would come with her, but in her heart she had always known she was too frail; instead she had set her up in her own little cottage in Leicestershire, next door to Saul and Will and Tom. Now it was as if, once out of sight of land, Kattrin had finally accepted that there was nothing more she could do for any of them.

The weak April sun was sparkling on the broad waters of Portsmouth Harbour as the burial detail rolled Robert Carey into the last of the waterlogged holes they'd dug out of the mud flats they called Rat's Castle. Chains dragging at his wrists and ankles, Joshua set the rough carved cross at the head of the mound and said a short prayer. The poor fellow deserved a little dignity.

'Back to the boat, damn your eyes!' shouted the gaoler, hefting his cat o'nine tails aloft, and the file of chained men shuffled back to the water's edge. As he stepped, muscles protesting, into the boat and took up his oar, Joshua said a last farewell to the lad they had just buried, a fever-wracked shadow of the fresh-faced Wooburn boy, and prayed that someone would take care of Carey's widow and two small children. It was an irony, he thought, that some of the most active leaders of the Wooburn riots, like Fisher and Barton, were still in Aylesbury gaol, while the most inoffensive – young John Crutch and poor deaf Moses Priest – had already left for Van Diemen's Land on the convict ships *Eliza* and *Proteus*, leaving behind only the sick and dying. Beyond the ranks of dismasted prison hulks that filled this part of Portsmouth harbour, other convict transports were loading their human cargo for the other side of the world. It could not be much longer now before he and the rest of the miserable wretches on the *York* were shipped across too.

The spring sunshine dazzled them as they rowed back across the glassy waters to the stinking rotting dismasted ship which had been their home in the weeks since they had been removed from Aylesbury gaol. His shoulder ached from the unaccustomed exercise and as they marched across the deck of the *York* and down to their galley, he forced himself to ignore the man behind him, who was deliberately jerking on the chain that connected them in the hope of provoking a reaction. He'd seen all too many prisoners rise to the baiting of such bullies, and earn themselves a beating or a night in the waterlogged, rat-infested scuppers for a brief moment of sweet revenge, so he bit his lip and let his mind wander once more to Wooburn. He'd only had the one letter from his father and he wondered how he and Tom were coping with their new life with Saul in Leicestershire. He hoped that this time they would all rub along together. What he couldn't understand was why Will had written that he was inviting Lucy Thornton to stay with them a while. Lucy's place was surely with Kat, and what would Kat want with Leicestershire?

In spite of all his resolutions he let his thoughts dwell for a moment on Kat, and so caught up in his memories was he that he didn't hear his name being called. Only when the bo'sun sang out 'Delahaye!' again, this time accompanying it with the whip's end across his shoulders, did he snap out of his daydream.

He was unshackled from the line and led below to the captain's cabin where he and several other 'gentlemen' prisoners were paraded before a half-pay captain, one of those who from time to time came on board to pick out a servant for a forthcoming voyage. Until today, Joshua had always been dismissed out of hand as being too unfit, for his shoulder had healed stiff and continued to give him a great deal of pain, but Captain Hurvine had no such qualms. Handkerchief over his face against the stench, Hurvine asked them all about their education and their previous work and before Joshua rightly knew what was happening, he found himself engaged and carried off the *York*.

Once they had crossed the equator, it was no longer safe for any of the ladies or the more sober gentlemen to stroll the decks, for the large variety of birds circling around the *Maria* tempted would-be marksmen to stagger about the rolling decks, loaded guns on full cock, determined to bring down one of the Cape pigeons, rather inaptly known as the 'passenger's friend'. Seemingly unable to allow for the motion of the vessel, most of the hunters were as likely to hit a sail or a passenger as their intended target, but the sailors laughed and encouraged them, considering even the oiliest and most disgusting bird fair game to supplement their diet.

They did make exceptions, however. 'All we needs is one o' they fools to bring down an albatross!' said one old seaman as a huge white-winged bird, fully fifteen feet from wingtip to wingtip, wheeled overhead like a spectre. 'You gets good money for the crittur stuffed, but 'tis bad luck to shoot albatross. They can bring down all the boobies they likes, though,' he chuckled, pointing out to Kat the cloud of darker birds circling the topsail. 'The feathered sort 'ud be fine company for the boobies on deck!'

Unlike some of the smaller ships, the *Maria* did not have to cross the Atlantic to Rio de Janeiro in order to pick up the currents that would take them south to the Cape of Good Hope; after almost a week becalmed close to the equator, with Mrs Proctor prostrated with the heat and almost deafened by the ceaseless piping of the sailors as they tried to 'whistle up a storm', they at last made their first landfall at Cape Colony, on the southern tip of Africa, where they picked up fresh stores and water.

Kat, dressed in one of the old muslin robes that Mrs Proctor and Mrs Hambleden had so sneered at, looked on at the bustle on the quayside and at the great mountain that loomed over it all. How pleasant it would be to stroll through those colourful crowds, she thought, and sniff the spicy air. But Mrs Proctor was still lying stranded like a beached whale in her cabin, unable to fit into her fashionable robes without stays and quite unable to bear her corsets in all the heat, and Mrs Hambleden felt obliged to dance attendance on her.

The Reverend Dr Purcell was confined to his cabin with the colic, and Lieutenant Standish, despairing of making any headway with Kat, was laying siege to a plump widow. While she was debating which of the other gentlemen might be prevailed on to escort her ashore, a messenger arrived from the Governor of Cape Colony with instructions to carry her reports onto the warship anchored in Table Bay. Realising with a guilty start that she had neglected her part of the bargain with the Colonial Office, Kat hurried to her cabin to fetch her journal up to date. By the time she handed it over to the officer, it was too late to go ashore.

Unfortunately the visitor from the Governor's Office only served to intrigue her admirers even more, and she was hard put to avoid their attentions.

They had barely left the Cape when vast flocks of petrels came into view; some were dark, like those they had seen in the Channel, others, a much prettier blue, kept further away and were only visible through the glass. Storm birds, the sailors called them, harbingers of bad weather, and the *Maria* held a course as far away from them as was practicable.

They made good time across the Indian Ocean, coming within sight of Australia barely three months after leaving England, and the weather was sufficiently calm for them to pass through the Bass Strait north of Van Diemen's Land, rather than take the longer passage to the south. As they began to sail up the coast towards Sydney, Reverend Purcell, the most persistent of her admirers, emerged from his cabin and Kat's freedom was at an end. She went below once more to her cabin and finished the log of the voyage which she was to hand over to the pilot when he came to navigate them into Sydney Harbour.

She had dearly wanted to be up on deck when they entered the harbour, with all the passengers in their best London clothes, but she knew that Purcell was waiting for an opportunity to be alone with her in order to make her a formal declaration of intent, so she cravenly stayed in her cabin, pleading a headache until all the formalities were over and the *Maria* was tied up at the quay. On shore she clung to Mrs Proctor and Mrs Hambleden only long enough to shake off her gentlemen admirers, then she made her adieus to the two women, declining their husbands' pressing offers of a carriage ride into town.

The sensation of firm earth beneath her feet after three months of heaving decks was overwhelming, and the array of eager faces that lined the docks was an exciting challenge after the unchanging and

224

limited shipboard company. On rising ground before her she could see windmills, some sort of church and rows of mean buildings, few of them more than one storey in height, but in the other direction, behind Fort Macquarie, a neat stone building flanked with cannon, there was green land, larger buildings and a veritable hubbub of activity. Dickon had said a Mr Garvey would meet her on the dockside; clutching a small wicker basket she looked anxiously around her, nervous lest arrangements made on the other side of the world might have gone amiss on this.

If the people around her on the dockside had been speaking a foreign language, or wearing outlandish clothes like the people in William's sketchbooks, it might have been easier to deal with, but the setting and the people were so like England that it was even more bizarre. Her mind was dizzy with the sheer otherness of this new land: the raucous voices of Sydney town, with their echo of shrill Cockney accents, the dark faces of the tribal blacks with the gins, their downtrodden women, trailing in their wake, the ubiquitous scarlet coats and gleaming bayonets of the military, the dust, the sound of different birds, the odour of new plants and trees and above all the brightness and clarity of the light in this new country, which far transcended even the most brilliant summer day in England. There was a quality to the light in Australia, the sailors said, that existed nowhere else. And yet this was not spring, according to the sailors, but autumn!

After a while, the brightness, the loudness, the heat and the dust, all began to be too much to one accustomed for so long to the unrelieved expanse of the sea, and she was glad when a stocky, sandy-haired Irishman approached her and introduced himself as her bailiff.

'Bailiff?' she stammered, fearing that the heat had addled her brain. 'But I – I have no bailiff.' She frowned and rubbed her eyes. 'I'm to meet a Mr Garvey.'

'That's me, right enough. Engaged by Mr Revel,' said Garvey.

'Indeed?' said Kat. Perhaps, she thought, the words they use out here are different.

'To look after your land.'

'But I have no land,' stammered Kat. 'Only a small house.'

Garvey pushed his hat to the back of his head. 'Oh, missus,' he said. 'You're in for a wee bit of a surprise, I'm thinkin'.'

'I'll call you Joe,' said Captain Hurvine as he carried him off in the bumboat that brought supplies out to the vessels riding at anchor. 'More suitable for a servant.' And Joshua, looking back across the harbour to Rat's Castle, thought answering to another name a small

225

price to pay to escape the hell of the convict hold. Nor did he argue when Hurvine told him he had too many airs and graces for a servant: 'Joe' took the hint and slipped easily into the country speech of the papermen.

He asked if, as a favour, he might shave off the heavy growth of beard he'd acquired in the hulks, but 'No razors for convicts,' said Hurvine firmly. 'Quite out of the question.' He looked at his new servant from under bushy eyebrows. 'No place for vanity in your situation, Joe, you mark my words. That's one piece of advice I have for you. T'other is, when we set sail, don't look down at the sea, or it'll make you sick. That's because you don't know which way is up. Your eyes tell you one thing, your stomach contradicts them. Take my word – as a man who has crossed these seas and many others too – always look at the horizon. When your stomach knows where it is, it won't feel the need to rebel so often.'

It was strange how invisible you became, especially to the ladies, when you were dressed in shabby working clothes with your features almost obliterated by a heavy growth of beard. Even Mrs Hurvine's maid, a Shropshire country girl who would have been thought most forward to have obtruded herself on the notice of Mr Delahaye, mill manager, looked down on Joe the convict servant; on the few occasions when she deigned to address him at all, while they waited in the dockside inn to embark on the *Perseus*, she called him fellow; the sailors called him mate, the Hurvines called him Joe. Before long he found himself slipping into the new character of humble servant as easily as an actor on a stage. Soon Joshua Delahaye was nothing but a distant memory. Only Mrs Davey, a lady some years younger than her elderly husband, smiled on him, but he swiftly realised that she was not looking for polite conversation and decided to give her a wide berth.

When the rest of the convicts arrived in the lags' van and boarded the *Perseus*, their clothes were stripped from them by the quartermaster and sold to an old-clothes merchant; after a cold bath their faces were shaved and their hair cropped, then they were issued with coarse grey uniforms before being thrust double-ironed into the hold. It crossed Joshua's mind that Hurvine had good reason to want him to keep his whiskers: while many of those on board might suspect that the Hurvine's servant was a convict, the beard at least separated him from those less fortunate.

From the moment he stepped on board ship he determined that he would not let his mind dwell on the future. Deal with life one day at a time: Kat had said that to him once in Aylesbury gaol. He dared not dwell too long on her memory, though, for that way lay madness.

As he passed back and forth to the Hurvines' quarters with a variety of boxes, small trunks and coils of rope, weaving his way across the deck between the pigpens, the hen coops and the deck cage above the convicts' hold, trying to ignore the pain in his shoulder, he listened to the shackled convicts talking about Australia as they loaded the main cargo into the hold. 'It ain't so bad,' said one. 'My cousin Aaron knowed someone in New South Wales. 'E writ 'is parents as life aht there were better nor it ever were in England.'

'They makes it sound like a paradise,' grumbled a raw young ensign assigned to guard duty.

'Don't you believe it, son,' said his sergeant, leaning against his musket. 'It's true that New South Wales ain't so bad as Van Diemen's Land, and the odd convict may get a tidy berth and the chance to work on the land, but the rest . . . Nah. An' it's the cocky ones with the loud mouths like 'im as fares the worst – one word out of turn and he'll be on a road gang. Them road gangs ain't paradise, lad, they're hell. I've seen 'em. One *look* out of turn there and he'll be flogged to within an inch of his life. Half of 'em drops dead anyway with the work. The iron gangs is boilin', burnin', bloody hell.' He shook his head. 'Why they do believe all those lies is beyond me.'

Because that was what they wanted so desperately to believe, thought Joshua. Even if it was as unlikely as the rumour that the magistrates had ordered the threshing and papermaking machines to be destroyed, they would believe it. By the sound of it, Aaron's cousin was in for a rude awakening. And what of himself? He shook his head to halt his wayward thoughts and reminded himself fiercely: one day at a time.

'It only takes one convict to get his ticket of leave and fall on his feet and suddenly they are all going to be men of fortune,' said Henry Hurvine when Joshua ventured to bring the question up. 'But for most of them – yes, the odds on a life of misery and pain and degradation in the iron gangs are much higher.' He caught his wife's eye and cleared his throat hastily. 'Not for you, of course, Joe. Someone has put in a word for you. That's why you are here with us.'

Bosingham, thought Joshua. It had to be Bosingham, assuaging his guilt at the failure to free him.

Later that evening Captain Hurvine returned to the question of prospects in Australia, or New Holland, as he still persisted in calling it. 'There's always hope for those with talents,' he said. 'Look at Greenway: transported for forgery, but now he's the colony's chief architect – Soane and Beau Nash rolled into one! Even plain fellows like Terry and Simeon Lord have to some extent retrieved their name and made their fortunes. And we must not forget that someone has already put in a word for you. After that you'd have to be very foolish or very unlucky to go adrift.'

227

'Misfortune cannot be discounted,' said Joshua sombrely. 'It is, after all, what brought me to this pass.'

'Serves no purpose to brood on the past, lad,' said the Captain, clapping him heartily on his back. 'Nor the future – worry about that when you get to Sydney. Time a-plenty until then.'

'Four months at the least,' sighed Mrs Hurvine.

'A long voyage,' her husband agreed. 'I'd advise you, Joe, to keep your distance from the convicts. There's bound to be sickness when we've been at sea awhile and I'll not have you bringing it to Mrs Hurvine and the children. You'll not be short of occupation: we have two new telescopes to work on, then we've to check Halley's southern charts and tidy up some of Governor Brisbane's uncompleted work. If you've any spare time after that, the captain will demand your attendance to entertain his guests...' He opened a drawer in his wife's desk and drew out a familiar leather case.

Joshua's eyes widened and he almost snatched the case from Hurvine and opened it. He ran his hand lovingly over the smooth surface of the flute, nestled in its velvet bed.

Mrs Hurvine smiled indulgently. 'A friend of yours begged me to carry it for you, knowing you would not be permitted to bring anything of your own on board.'

'Dickon!' he said brokenly, and at the name, all the other unbidden memories floated into his mind. The Hurvines looked tactfully away as his eyes glinted with tears.

The Captain and his family occupied the stern cabins, each about nine feet square, each having half a skylight and two stern windows, which meant they gained more air and light and fewer unpleasant odours than the rest of the ship.

'Papa, are you going to tie up the sails?' asked Maria, intrigued by all the ropes their father had brought on board.

'Of course not,' said Edward with all the scorn of a nine-year-old for a sister two years younger. 'Look! The sails already have ropes in place.'

'These are for the cabins, my dears,' said their father and proceeded to make sure that everything was tied down or lashed to the sides of the cabin, with deep cleats of wood nailed around the heavier chests. Only when they were several days out and met contrary winds did they understand why.

The supercilious maid took to her bunk within hours of leaving the Thames estuary and insisted on being put off again at Plymouth when the *Perseus* called for the last of her passengers. When the sea freshened in the Bay of Biscay the children, being so small, frequently found themselves tossed out of bed, so desks and cupboards had to be moved, and nailed or lashed to the side of the bunks to hold them in.

It was usually late before Joshua found his bed, a cubbyhole between the two cabins, for Captain Hurvine had commissions from the Royal Observatory to bring the star charts of the southern oceans up to date and test two powerful new telescopes against each other. They would sit up half the night making observations and measurements, but Joshua, his eyes opened to a whole new world, was never bored.

'We have had star catalogues since the sixteenth century at least,' Hurvine explained. 'Each new one is thought of for years as the final word, but then the next generation discovers something new and we start the whole process again. And of course, as the telescopes improve, so does our knowledge.'

Each night Hurvine checked the elevation of the telescope and called it over to Joshua, who noted it carefully in the log. 'Tycho Brahe's is the earliest star chart I know of,' he went on as he searched the first quarter of the sky, interspersing measurements and comments in a staccato delivery. 'Fellow made all his observations before telescopes were even invented – note down that reference, Joe – missed telescopes by less than a decade. Now there's an interesting fellow: kidnapped at birth, lost part of his nose in a duel and stuck it back together with gold, silver and wax! Devoted his life to observation of the skies. – 'Pon my soul, that doesn't tie in with this chart! We'll check that again tomorrow. – Had a star named after him, Tycho's star. New star in Cassiopeia, so bright you could see it in daylight. Observed and plotted it. Mind you, they do insist now that it wasn't one star at all, but a collision of stars.'

'And you?'

'I?' Hurvine shook his head. 'I put forward no opinions or theories. I merely observe. Halley went to St Helena for his astronomical chart and it will be interesting to see if our measurements as we approach New Holland are in agreement with his.'

Hurvine was delighted to have found such an eager apprentice; he told Joshua all about Bayer's lettering system: 'not perfect by any means, but we still use it after two hundred years' and Messier's system of numbering the starry nebulae that they were to observe. 'Louis the Fifteenth called Messier the "ferret of comets" but he's most appreciated for cataloguing the nebulae – those misty patches in the sky – so he wouldn't keep mistaking them for comets.'

One blustery evening when there was not much to observe, Hurvine told him about the new and more powerful telescopes. 'The old refractors with the single-lens object glasses produced a deal of false colour,' he explained. 'That could only be dealt with by increasing the focal length. Hevelius had one over one hundred and fifty feet long and Huygens – he was the first to take clocks to sea in an attempt to solve the longitude navigation problem – had one that was more than two hundred feet!'

'How could they possibly move that?' asked Joshua.

'Heaven alone knows, Joe!' said Hurvine with a chuckle. 'Heaven alone knows! Fortunately Newton came along with his reflector telescope and solved the problem. Now we're moving in the other direction, of course, trying to make ever larger lenses to increase the power.' He ran his hands lovingly over the brass casing of the telescope. 'Fraunhofer has made one with a lens of nigh on ten inches, and Oxmantown – Earl of Rosse's son, y'know, sits in Parliament for Oxford – believes it possible to make them even larger. Glass discs are impossible at that size, of course, but metal mirrors are proving most satisfactory.'

Once the boredom of the passage had set in, they were often joined on deck by restless fellow passengers, who annoyed Hurvine intensely with their ignorant questioning, their desire to look through his telescope at the moon and their constant resort to him as an arbiter of the ridiculous wagers that occupied the time of those with too much of it on their hands.

'Settle an argument, would you, m'dear sir?' said one. 'Humphreys here will have it that Newton invented the telescope, and I'm just as sure that it was that Italian chap, Galileo.'

'The wager falls,' said Hurvine with a smirk, 'for you are both half right and both completely wrong. Galileo was the first to make much use of the telescope and Newton invented a better version, but neither claimed credit for the invention.'

'Then who?'

'No one knows for certain,' said Hurvine. 'Many believe it was Thomas Harriott – Walter Raleigh's tutor. For myself, however, I rather favour Sir William Lower, who was one of the first to describe the face of the moon.'

'A sublime experience,' said a gentleman standing close by, puffing, in spite of Hurvine's protests, on a Spanish cigarillo.

'Most sublime,' agreed Hurvine with a twitching lip. 'He said it much resembled a tart his cook had just made: "Here some bright stuff there some dark, and so confusedly all over!"'

But the gentlemen were not to be put off by mockery and each night there were at least half a dozen of them in attendance for at any rate the first part of the night watch.

'It's surprising how many take an interest in stars who on land never look above their heads,' grumbled Hurvine, after explaining for the fifth time why the stars had changed their positions, what was the significance of the Magellanic clouds and why, once over the equator, the night sky would change so dramatically.

'We take it all for granted,' said Joshua. The North Star and the Great Bear, the constellation that country men called the Plough, had seemed to him in England such a fixed part of the universe, and in the early days of the voyage he had often stood on deck and thought that Kat, in England, might be standing at her window gazing on those selfsame stars; in the last weeks he had watched them sink ever lower in the sky until they had at last disappeared over the horizon, taking away his last contact with his home and his love and leaving him curiously bereft. 'On land we have so much to fill the eye, but here there is only sea and sky.'

Only sea and sky, he thought again, as he stood at the ship's rail in the still hour just before the dawn. And beneath that indigo canopy, bejewelled with a myriad silver stars, the *Perseus*, trailing its phosphorescent wake across the vast wastes of moon-sparkled sea, was but the most minute of dots upon a tiny point in the vast universe of stars. And upon that minute dot, he was but one insignificant soul, barely a speck of dust in the wide canopy of the heavens.

Garvey, the bailiff, had gone to a great deal of trouble to polish up the carriage for the homecoming journey, but he couldn't flatter himself that his mistress noticed it at all. He drove carefully through the mean streets and alleys of the Rocks, past the knots of sailors lounging outside the low drinking dens and cheap brothels that spilled down to the water's edge, guiding the horses around the potholes and picking his way through the goats and pigs and chickens that roamed the streets, rooting and pecking in the gutters. The pair of finely matched horses picked up the pace as they left the Rocks behind them, drove past the military barracks and up George Street, a handsome thoroughfare lined with elegant shops and houses. Garvey looked sideways at her, wondering whether to stop, but somehow he didn't think she would be able to cope with Sydney at the moment. The sooner he got her out to the Creek and handed her over to the women to deal with, the better. He didn't like the look of those wide, staring eyes.

'Better put your veil down while we drive past the Brickfields, ma'am,' he said. But the veil was more decorative than useful and Kat choked and sneezed and rubbed her watering eyes as a swirling ochre-coloured cloud of dust and grit blew towards them on the stiff breeze.

Her eyes were still watering when they ascended Perroquet Hill, running through land that was partly cleared and partly bush, but Kat, listening with half an ear to Garvey's commentary on the

231

inhabitants of the houses they passed, set back from the road down dusty tracks, knew that the dust was not the cause. What was she doing here in this strange country, so far from those who cared for her? She wanted to bow her head and weep, and pride alone kept her upright in her seat.

There seemed to be an inordinate number of public houses lining the road; unattended drays and carts clustered around them, the horses and oxen tormented by clouds of flies. There were none of the pretty hedgerows of England to break up the uniform landscape, for many settlers in clearing the bush had totally destroyed the native trees and shrubs. Unlike England, where new residences were planted round with groves and woods to give the illusion of age, the Australian settler on the whole considered trees to be part of the wild and uncivilised bush and preferred to see an expanse of bare land all around his house.

'A bad mistake,' said Garvey, following her gaze. 'Takes away shade for the stock and dries up the land. Then when the rains come, it all washes into the river. They do reckon Governor Phillip settled at Sydney Cove on account of it having better soil and water than Botany Bay, but in forty years of clearance, they've just about destroyed what brought 'em here to start with!'

As they approached Parramatta the landscape grew a little softer and the bush, though still mantled in a thick layer of dust, grew thicker and greener along the roadside. From the top of the toll-hill the whole town of Parramatta was spread out before them, scattered loosely in a hollow. Garvey pointed out the main features to her: St John's Church in the centre, with its angular double-topped steeple, surrounded by open land which the inhabitants fondly thought of as a town square, the handsome brick house of the Reverend Marsden crowning rising ground to the left, surrounded by handsome stands of trees. The soldiers' barracks and the Parramatta factory where the female prisoners were housed stood out against the cottages and villas and the whole was dominated by an elegant Government House, set in the extensive parkland of the Domain running down to the river.

Owing to its low situation, Parramatta was even warmer than Sydney, and though sited on the shores of the Parramatta River, whose waters were effectively no more than a continuation of Port Jackson, it received little benefit from the sea breezes which in Sydney gave such relief from the worst of the heat. Many of the houses boasted pretty gardens gay with luxuriant shrubs and flowers and Garvey pointed out the orange groves, fig trees and vineyards that had been planted forty years before, when the Government Farm at Rose Hill had saved the infant Sydney from starvation.

232

Some of the older houses were covered with vines, their verandahs tapestried with jasmine, woodbine, roses and climbing plants of all sorts. It was a welcome vision of greenness after the ochre dust of Sydney and she would dearly have loved to stop and rest, but Garvey was eager to get her to the house before dusk.

They followed the river out of town for a while, then turned off onto a cart track that meandered up a narrow valley, between pleached hedges of ungrafted peach and quince. 'Just through this paddock and over the next hill and you'll see the homestead,' Garvey smiled.

The first sight that met Kat's eyes as they breasted the hill was a tall chimney stack, surrounded by skeletal timbers, pointing up to the sky.

'Has there been a fire?' she asked anxiously. Had she come halfway across the world only to find the house she'd bought a burnt-out wreck? Was that the surprise Garvey had spoken of?

'No, no, missus,' chuckled Garvey. 'That's the new homestead – half-started, not half-ruined! You'll see the old one in a moment.'

As the road flattened out to follow the valley, a low, whitewashed building came into view, half rough-cut stone and half hewn clapboard, situated just above the river that meandered through the valley bottom. The house was surrounded by a haphazard collection of shacks, some of hewn timber, others more ramshackle, all – even the main house – roofed with a fibrous covering that looked suspiciously like tree bark, held down with stones and shingles.

The carriage swept along a broad driveway, scattering chickens and goats as it went. Garvey handed her down onto a rickety verandah which ran across the front of the main house, and she turned and caught her breath at the stunning view across the river and open countryside beyond, to a range of mountains shimmering blue in the bright light. A door opened behind her and a crowd of roughly dressed, bearded men and a few slovenly women spilled out and stumbled to a halt, looking her over from head to toe.

A plump woman with a face like cold bread dough shuffled out of one of the shacks, from which savoury smells were emerging.

'Welcome to Lacey's Creek, mistress,' she said, dropping a respectful curtsy. The others, recalled to their senses, bowed and curtsied with varying degrees of enthusiasm, not abating their critical glances one whit.

The sound of convicts holystoning the deck over his head and the singing of sea shanties as the sailors heaved at the ropes to shift the sails was the signal for Joshua to rise. Each morning he made his way past the urine barrels where the convicts' coarse blankets were put to

233

soak to kill off the lice and fleas, to fetch a cup of muddy tea or coffee – the two were often indistinguishable – from the galley. Mrs Hurvine would then get up to see to the children, leaving Joshua free to help her husband write up his research.

'How would we have managed without you, Joe?' said Mrs Hurvine one afternoon when he was teaching Edward and Maria to play deck shovel-board. 'To find a scientific man to help the Captain was fortunate enough, but to find one who likes children too . . .'

'The fortune is all on my side, ma'am,' said Joshua gravely. 'When I think of the alternative . . .' He looked speakingly at the deck cage, empty of convicts at the hour when the other passengers were taking the air.

His mistress shuddered. 'I quite despaired when we had to put Sarah ashore, for experience has taught me that few young men can cope with children.'

'I have had some practice, ma'am,' he said, thinking back to the times when he had rescued Dickon and Kattrin from some folly. And Mrs Hurvine, seeing the sadness upon his face, patted his arm but wisely said no more.

He did all he could for the family, and for their sake endured the slights from the pettier members among the passengers, which inevitably came his way. It was always worst on those evenings when he was summoned to the captain's cabin to entertain his guests, for the trials of the voyage conspired with the limitations of the company to strip away the pretended refinements and assumed courtesies of a larger society and expose the true characters of the passengers, whether for good or ill. He always spoke as befitted his station and bit his tongue when provoked, but his resolve was put to its sternest test when he emerged from the cabin one morning to find a flogging taking place on deck.

One of the convicts was triced to the grating, blood dripping down his back from a morass of cuts and weals and welling in a pool around his ankles. As Joshua stood in the hatchway, frozen by the horror of what he saw before him, the soldier drew back his arm again and brought the cat-o'nine-tails down with a crack on the man's back. The man screamed and a gobbet of flesh flew through the air past Joshua's face.

Sickness drove up from the depth of his stomach; a red mist formed before his eyes and he opened his mouth to bellow a protest, only to have the breath catch and gurgle in his throat as an arm locked around it and dragged him back into the shadows of the hatchway. As the pressure eased he whirled around, fists balled, to find himself face to face with Hurvine.

234

'Go below, Joe.' Hurvine spoke softly, but there was no mistaking the note of command in his voice.

'It is inhuman! It should be stopped!'

Hurvine set his stocky figure between Joshua and the hatchway. 'Not another word, mister! You will go below!'

Out of the corner of his eye Joshua could see one of the lieutenants approaching and he had too much pride, both for himself and his master, to continue the quarrel in front of a junior officer. His shoulders slumped and he went below.

Hurvine, following behind, shoved him into the empty cabin and slammed the door. He pushed Joshua onto the bench and stumped across to the cupboard, where he drew the brandy bottle from the tantalus and poured two large measures.

He stood over Joshua while he drained the glass, coughing as the fiery liquid caught the back of his throat. 'It is a hard punishment,' said Hurvine at last. 'But I do not run this ship. And neither do you.' He poured them each another measure and drained his. After a moment he said, 'Captain Bunnett is considered a most humane captain.'

'Humane!'

'Compared to some I have sailed with, yes. He will not have the women convicts mistreated by his officers – and that, I assure you, is uncommon in itself – and he never allows more than a Botany Bay dozen for a flogging.'

'*Twelve?*' Joshua, appalled, started out of his seat.

'You have a great deal to learn, I fear,' said Hurvine, pushing him back into his chair. 'But best you learn it here. A Botany Bay dozen, Joe, is twenty-five.'

'My God!'

'That is considered a mild punishment, man!' said Hurvine harshly. 'On some vessels there may be three or four floggings a day, a hundred or even two hundred strokes, and the men clapped in irons when 'tis done. There are some vicious and violent men among the prisoners, Joe, and they have to be taught a lesson.'

'Who on this earth would not have learned his lesson after the first cut?'

'Don't interfere, Joe! That's an order!' Overhead the sound of the whip and the screaming of the victim finally ceased. There was a shuffling above them as something – someone? – was dragged away, then the sound of water as the decks were sluiced down and scrubbed clean of their bloody evidence. 'You are a convict servant and there are some on this ship who would be only too happy to teach you a lesson. Lieutenant Marsfield, for instance.' Joshua, being one of the earliest risers, had several times seen the lieutenant emerging from

235

Mrs Davey's cabin. 'I doubt he's fooled by your rough accent and there's nothing he would like better than the chance to reduce a well-bred convict to the level of the rest.'

# Chapter Thirteen

Kat spent much of her first month on shore in a state of shock, neglecting even her journal and the promised correspondence with William Godstowe. The months on board the *Maria* had been a suspension of normal life; setting foot on land once more, she was overwhelmed by the audacity of what she had done. She had left behind all family and friends and committed a large part of her inheritance to buy an estate she had never seen, in a country of which she was almost totally ignorant.

She had spent the journey to Lacey's Creek in a daze from which, much to Garvey's alarm, she showed no sign of emerging on arrival at the estate. She took the introduction of the convict servants, nodding dully as he read off each name, stopping him only when he proposed to read out the crimes for which they had been transported. Lord Cawfield at the Colonial Office had told Dickon that some of the servants at Lacey's Creek had barely escaped the gallows. One had been sent out for beating his wife so badly that she had almost died; she decided she would rather not know which. As Garvey moved on from the few women to drone through the list of men, her bemused glance passed along the ranks, but eye and brain quite failed to make any differentiation between one tanned and bearded convict servant and the next. The shock of finding she was the sole arbiter of the fate of so many was as bad as the discovery that she was mistress of an entire and vast estate. She had thought to buy a small property, a yeoman's-size holding, such as they had had in Wooburn before the enclosures – half a dozen fields at most and a neat farmhouse.

'Land is cheap out here,' said Garvey, seeing the shock on her face as he handed her the deeds. 'Government men – what you'd call convicts – they're not allowed to hold land, see, so it's mostly the retired army or navy men who've grabbed the biggest chunks. Like old Macarthur. Biggest landholder hereabouts – one of the few to come near the size of Lacey's Creek, I guess. And the others followed his lead, built around his Elizabeth Farm at Parramatta and then followed him out to the Cowpastures – Camden they call it now. Though whether the ould feller's estates will survive now he's losing his grip, I have me doubts.'

She had heard a great deal about Macarthur on the voyage out, about his attempts to make himself the prime citizen of the colony; how he had led the Rum Rebellion against Governor Bligh and his endless feuds with subsequent governors. 'Is he ill?' she enquired tiredly.

'Ill he is for certain, missus, tho' whether it's senile or insane he is, that's an open question; either way he's out of his senses four days out of the six. So the other big landowners are jostling to take his place – and as mistress of Lacey's Creek, you're as much a leader of society as the rest of them.'

On the rare occasions on the voyage out when she had allowed herself to think about the future, she had visualised herself in a little house, planting vegetables, sewing and working on her lace, sending her reports back to the Colonial Office while she waited for Joshua to arrive. Mere doll's-house playing! How was she to come to terms with the fact that she found herself mistress of more land than Waller of Hall Barn, Dupré of Wilton Park and Bosingham of Bosingham House, all rolled together? Not to mention the elegant house in Sydney which she had not yet seen, or the bonded servants. Whatever had Dickon and William Godstowe been thinking of?

For weeks she drifted about the house, sleeping the day away, refusing all invitations and declining even to admit the many callers eager for a glimpse of the new owner of Lacey's Creek. She sent the servants to Garvey or Will, the young farm foreman, for decisions, and picked at the meals that slovenly Molly put in front of her three times a day, Betsey the cook having fallen sick in Sydney, where she'd gone with the butler to put the George Street house into some order. The bailiff was close to tearing his hair out, for he knew the unsupervised servants were robbing her left and right. But what was to be expected with a mistress who made such a poor show? He could not be everywhere.

He was at the far side of the estates when one of the women, with a tirade of abuse and oaths, refused to do Kat's bidding. It was Molly's misfortune that Will overheard her insolence and decided to take a stand where the mistress would not. He proposed putting the miscreant to the triangle for a light flogging.

'Flogging?' Shock made Kat's voice tremble.

'The triangle, mistress,' explained Will. 'In the yard behind the kitchens, so you won't have to watch 'less you wants to.'

She went perfectly white and demanded to be taken to it.

'It's easy enough, mistress,' said Will, resting his hand casually

238

against the iron triangle and speaking with a nonchalance that chilled her blood. 'You trices 'em up to that and – '

She turned on him white-faced. 'You have *done* this?' she demanded.

'Not often, mistress. Only when we has to make an example. And only a few strokes to bring 'em to their senses. Murray, now, across the river, he whips his servants reg'lar, just to remind 'em who's master. Not as much as Grantham, though. They reckon Grantham never thinks it's worth it for under a hundred lashes. An' old Sam Marsden, the floggin' parson, well, he – '

'Take it down!' she panted, her father's image floating in front of her eyes in place of Will's homely features.

'But mistress!' He saw her sway and hurried to give her his arm. 'What would Mr Garvey say if – '

'*I* am the mistress!' she snapped, in tones he had never before heard her use. 'Take it down!'

It went against the grain for Will to do it, for although Lacey and Garvey had hardly ever ordered a flogging, the foreman had every confidence in its value as a deterrent and its absence could only make their work harder.

The night the triangle came down, the servants lit a huge bonfire and brought out their illicit stores of alcohol to celebrate. Will sent Samuel to fetch Garvey back, then locked himself in his cabin, watching glumly as the night went on and the carousers fell where they sat, overcome by the potent liquor. He didn't see one of them, bolder than the others, creep into the house and into her mistress's bedroom.

Kat woke to see a bulky figure, silhouetted by the moonlight through the half-open shutters, bending over the chest not six feet away from her, rifling through her jewel case. Her heart beating in her throat, she reached under the pillow until her hand closed on cool metal.

'Don't move an inch, or I'll shoot,' she said, swinging her legs over the side of the bed and levelling the cocked pistol at the intruder.

The servant froze, her eyes riveted on the long, slim barrel, stark in the moonlight and pointing straight at her heart.

Kat was surprised to find that her hand and her voice were perfectly steady as she pushed the shutters wide and called for Will.

It was as if the shock had brought her back to life again. By the time Garvey rode back in, she was up and dressed. She sat up talking with the bailiff for the rest of the night and the next morning he assembled the servants in the yard.

She emerged from the house, heart pounding, to find a shuffling, shambling, chattering group of servants. As she raised her hands clear of her skirts, revealing a slim percussion pistol in each hand, a deathly hush fell on them.

They moved rapidly to her command, withdrawing to the side of the yard opposite the chicken coop while Will set up two cockleshells across the top rail of the fence. Narrowing her eyes against the brightness of the sun, Kat calmly extended her arm and shattered the shells one after the other with a single shot from each weapon. As the chickens flapped and squawked and a ripple of surprise ran through the onlookers, she sent up a prayer of thanks to Dickon, who had flatly refused to book her passage until she took lessons; he'd even taken her to Manton's and chosen the set of pistols for her.

She laid aside the smoking guns and turned to the servants.

'Next time I find a servant where she has no right to be, I may not ask questions.' Her eyes moved on and settled on the farm workers. 'You must not think because I took down the triangle that I am a weak mistress,' she went on in a deceptively soft voice. 'I will not tolerate inhuman punishment on my property – but nor will I tolerate anyone else taking the decisions around Lacey's Creek. Anyone stepping out of line will be taken back to the Barracks. With a bad record, who knows where you will end up? Your next master – maybe Murray or Grantham? – may not have the same scruples as I.' She saw from their grave faces that she had struck home. 'Most of you are here because you made one mistake. Go on making mistakes and you will find yourselves ever deeper in the mire.

'I propose to each of you a contract,' she said, calmly cleaning the pistols and reloading them as she spoke. 'Give me good service and you could end your time here with your own cottage and a truck garden; there may even be a ticket of leave before that. The new governor will be out here in a few months and I have some influence with him.'

A ripple of interest ran around the crowd but she took no notice. 'Turn your misfortune to the good and you'll be better off than many at home in England,' she said crisply. 'Those willing to try it my way can make their mark on the contract Mr Garvey and I have drawn up. The rest of you will go back to Sydney with Molly to be reassigned.'

Once they reached blue water, the convicts had their chains struck off and were allowed to take their exercise on deck, with only a few guards on the quarterdeck in case of trouble. Captain Bunnett, a strict Presbyterian, would allow none of the women to live in the officers' quarters, but the ship's surgeon was apt to turn a blind eye to those female convicts who went there, or into the men's hold, in the recreation hours.

Joshua found it hard to accept the number of young convicts, some barely more than children, among the prisoners. On grounds of Christian compassion, Bunnett had excused the younger prisoners the usual convict dress and the cropped hair, but this had, perversely, made them appear more feminine than the mature women with their convict slops and cropped heads.

Joshua made every endeavour to avoid the deck during the convicts' exercise period, but one day, emptying a bucket over the rail, he found his eye drawn to two girls huddled together at one end of the deck, weaving old rope ends into plaits. The younger was about twelve, her sister no more than fourteen, though bidding fair to be a woman, with lustrous dark curls and grey eyes.

Like a little grey kitten.

At the unwonted reminder of Kat he wrenched his eyes away and gazed out across the waves, struggling to close his mind to any thoughts of Wooburn, but as he stared blindly out at the sea, the bright sun turned the silvery blue of the flying fish to the turquoise flash of the kingfishers darting up and down the banks of the Wye.

He turned away from the rail, his eyes misty with unshed tears. As he passed across the quarterdeck, he saw a burly, bullet-headed convict standing in front of the older girl, jerking his head towards the hold. The man's meaning was as unmistakable as the girl's terror.

'Don't forget, Calderson!' called another convict. 'Share and share alike!' Calderson's gang guffawed with laughter and the air was filled with lewd comments.

The younger girl, gangly and awkward, leaped to her feet and stood protectively in front of her sister, fists clenched; in spite of her skirts, something in her stance reminded Joshua painfully of young Tom. Angry words were exchanged and as the man lunged at the older girl, her younger sister stamped on his instep. With a bellow of rage that caused the guards to raise their muskets, the convict drew back his arm and knocked the younger child aside. As she rolled towards the scuppers, the mob cap slipped off to reveal hair that curled only to the collar.

Realisation that the girl was indeed a rather pretty young boy brought hoots of laughter and mockery from the convicts and the sailors.

A slow smile spread across the face of the bully as the girl hurried to her brother's aid. He ran his hand over his stubbled chin. 'Can't have a *boy* in the *women's* hold,' he said with a leer. He passed his tongue over his lips. 'Have to come in the men's hold, he will. An' there's more than one way to skin a cat.'

Joshua had not asked the Hurvines for anything, for he had been only too grateful for what they had done for him, but now he went straightway to Captain Hurvine and asked him to help.

'Interfere with the convicts?' He shook his head. 'That would be a sure way to make enemies on board.'

'But you could request extra servants – '

'My wife deals with all domestic matters,' grunted Hurvine, turning back to his charts.

'You would scarcely wish me to speak of such matters to the lady!' The bile rose in his throat as he thought back to his schooldays, remembering how the slight and pretty young boys had always been a prey for the toughs. 'What chance will the lad stand in a hold full of men who – '

'I can't save every convict,' said Hurvine curtly. 'With you we have all the servants we need. Besides, we have no room for them.'

Joshua bit his lip. 'Then take them in my place,' he said at last. 'The boy seems bright enough. He can fetch and carry for you and the girl can help Mrs Hurvine.'

'And you?' said Hurvine with a frown.

Joshua's head sank down on his chest, weighed down by the knowledge of what he was about to do. 'You must put me down in the hold.'

'I would be sorry to lose you, Joe.'

'Sir, the boy looks scarcely older than young Edward, and if you had seen the look on that fellow's face … it made me sick to my stomach.'

'Yes, yes,' he said impatiently. 'I know the kind of thing that happens on a ship like this. Why do you think Mrs Hurvine and I stay below decks when the convicts are about?'

Joshua passed a wretched hour, hoping that the Captain would intervene, and yet dreading the summons that would put him in the stinking hold with the rest of the convicts. At last Mrs Hurvine put an end to his misery. She would not hear of parting with him, she said firmly. The Captain needed him.

He sank his head in his hands, telling himself he must accept defeat. Then the door opened and the two children stood there in their ragged and stained clothes.

'Only see that they are both well scrubbed,' said Mrs Hurvine as the ragged orphans burst out in thanks for their unexpected salvation.

She cavilled at the sleeping arrangements later that evening, as the two newcomers bedded down alongside Joshua's bunk, but her husband dismissed her protests. 'Don't fuss, m'dear,' he said. 'This is not nearly as improper as in the hold!'

Ben and Lizzie were of little assistance on the voyage, being not much older than the children they were supposed to look after, and unused to life in service. All Joshua had achieved was to double the number he had to look after.

As they approached Table Bay, the convicts were chained up once more and confined to the hold. In sight of the shore, Joshua could only gaze out across the Bay at the great mountain that loomed over it all, and envy the Hurvines their brief time on land; he was on his honour to confine himself to the cabin with Lizzie and Ben.

They had barely left the Cape when vast flocks of blue petrels came into view. Storm birds, the sailors called them, harbingers of bad weather, and soon after sighting them the vessel ran head on into a tempest far worse than anything they had yet experienced. Captain Hurvine was summoned to work shift and shift about with Captain Bunnett as the *Perseus* ploughed through the heavy seas. Banished to the cabins, with the deadlights securely stopping the stern windows and the skylight closely shut, the children slept away the day, while Joshua and Mrs Hurvine shivered in their cloaks, for no stove was possible in such bad weather.

Once the storm struck, Ben and Lizzie were as frightened as Edward and Maria and all four children retched and vomited until they could be sick no more. Those were weary days, with tremendous gales blowing and huge waves being shipped; the bull's eye, the light let into the deck, leaked and leaked and on the third day finally burst, pouring sea water into the stern cabin. It took the joint efforts of Hurvine and Joshua to replace the bull's eye, but the cabin was beyond them. For days there was no hot food and no hope of drying sea-soaked or vomit-covered bedding and the ship rolled and pitched so violently that they felt each plunge would be its last.

Overhead the wind howled and screamed and the roaring and dashing of water, the creaking and groaning of the ship's timbers, sounded so loud and so close in the ears that no one could sleep. It was, said Mrs Hurvine tearfully, worse than all the fiends of hell.

'If it's bad for us, my dear,' said Hurvine, on one of his brief visits from the quarterdeck, 'how much worse must it be for the poor lost souls chained in the hold?'

Joshua told Nonie's tales a hundred times over, huddled in the second cabin with Mrs Hurvine in the pitch dark. In the brief lulls between the violence of the storms they were able to light the lamp; he would draw out his flute and play them all to sleep, until the next howling, shrieking nightmare was on them again.

At last the worst of the tempest died away. The passengers kept to their quarters only long enough for the ship's carpenter and the surgeon to slip over the side the bodies of those convicts too weak to survive the storm, then one by one they ventured unsteadily out of the imprisonment of their cabins. All the cups and wine glasses had been smashed, drawing curses from the steward, for which strong language he begged the ladies' pardons. They were reduced to drinking from old powder canisters and preserve jars; fortunately the damage to the stores proved to be as slight as that to the vessel, and the relief was so universal that even the stiffest could crack a joke about drinking out of an old white marmalade jar.

The house at Lacey's Creek was a long, low building of only one storey, with rooms opening off a long corridor that ran across the back of the house. On the rear wall, extra skilling rooms had been built on over the years like house martin's nests, to provide bedroom space, and as in most Australian houses, a kitchen shack, detached for fear of fire, stood by itself at right angles to the main building. Kat discovered that housekeeping in this new land demanded skills that would have been beyond even a Lady Isabelle. It was fortunate for her that Betsey, the cook and housekeeper, presented herself back at Lacey's Creek the day after Kat's confrontation with the rebellious servants, and took her new mistress swiftly in hand.

There was so much to learn and, like Lady Isabelle, Betsey held to the view that any mistress worth her salt should know what she was asking the servants to do. There were ways to be learned of cooking and preserving meats, some familiar, others quite alien. Walls and shelves had to be wiped with pungent eucalyptus oil to deter cockroaches, which were larger and even more disgusting than in England; great termites would attack any wood not soaked with the proper oil and could bring down a new building in the bush before the locals had well become accustomed to seeing it. Huge spiders, some extremely poisonous, would suddenly appear on the pale wash-painted walls; there were black ants with red heads and blue and purple ants an inch long with a bite as painful as a hornet's sting; others with a black body and yellow pincers would, when disturbed, spring up to sting or bite. Such creatures haunted the pantries, burying themselves in the sugar or drowning in the preserves, the custards, the tarts. The odour and taste they transmitted to the food was nauseous. All food had to be set in vessels of water, just like the legs of the bed, but if the kitchen maids were not closely supervised, they would forget to change the water and the wretched insects would cross to the food on particles of dust!

Kat devoted herself to setting the homestead to rights and learning from Garvey as much as she could about the land. She had never shirked hard work and there was a joy in knowing that soon Joshua would be there to share it with her. Little by little the gaping wound within that had been caused by Joshua's rejection closed up and she began to believe that one day she might be whole again. She even began to receive callers; she could hardly refuse to see Mrs Proctor and Mrs Hambleden, and the two women rarely turned up without one or two young and hopeful men in tow. Word had spread swiftly that there was an unattached young lady in possession of Lacey's vast acres and bachelor officers and younger sons came hurrying to call with invitations to balls, picnics and parties.

But nothing was allowed to interfere with her main purpose. After a month in which no convict ships had reached Sydney, several arrived on successive days and, alerted by a message from the Parramatta signal station, she hurried into Sydney with Garvey to meet them. Only then did she realise how sickeningly false Mrs Proctor's view of the convict women's plight had been. Groups of discarded young women stood bemused on the dockside, chained together for the walk up to the Barracks or the auction rooms where officers, settlers and corrupt clerks connived to circumvent the system of assignment. Those unfortunate enough to have fallen pregnant on the voyage were put in the open skiffs with the sick, the mad and those with babes in arms to be rowed upriver to the Parramatta Factory. Piteously they begged their erstwhile protectors to keep their word and not send them away, but the appeals fell on deaf ears. Most officers made a point of being away from the dockside at the critical moment; others, harder-hearted, even scorned them to their faces. 'Why would I marry a drab like you?' jeered one ship's surgeon. 'I can get another like you any voyage.' A few, like the late surgeon-general Wentworth d'Arcy, had acknowledged their bastards and supported the mothers, but since the turn of the century only one officer, according to Garvey, had ever married his shipboard convict mistress, and that had been such a rare occurrence that they were still speaking of it in the colony twenty years on.

The sights they saw on the quayside were sufficiently distressing, but the horrors that assaulted their eyes and ears in the Hyde Park Barracks, where they went to check the convict manifests, sickened her to her stomach. It was here that Garvey heard about the secret auctions, which threatened to wreck Cawfield's plans for Joshua's assignment, and he urged her to leave the matter to him. It didn't do, he explained, for someone of her social eminence to be seen in the Barracks, still less in the auction rooms. But she didn't care a fig for social position: it was Joshua's plight that had brought her here, and it was his wellbeing alone that mattered to her. Until Joshua was safe, she would continue to meet every convict ship that sailed into Sydney Harbour.

As the months went by without any sign of Joshua, dark fears began to crowd in on her. The history of the colony abounded in tales of shipwreck – perhaps his ship had been lost at sea? Or perhaps someone had submitted new evidence against him and he was facing an even worse danger! She hurried back to Lacey's Creek in panic and wrote up her journal to send to the Colonial Office: if she could keep her side of the bargain, then surely they must keep theirs?

September came, and with it the first of the spring weather, warmer than all but the hottest English summer days, but still there was no news of Joshua. With October came the recall of Governor Darling, who had contrived to make himself unpopular with just about everyone, from convict to free settler. None of the Emancipists, the freed convicts, were invited to the farewell banquet for the departing governor, so Wentworth and Hall, the editors of the two leading anti-Darling newspapers in the colony, the *Australian* and the *Monitor*, promised to celebrate Darling's departure in their own way on the day; Wentworth with a public banquet at his estate at Vaucluse, on a headland overlooking the Harbour; Hall with a firework illumination, bidding good riddance to the tyrant, above the *Monitor's* offices.

Edward Deas Thomson, one of Kat's admirers, arranged for her to be invited to the Governor's banquet in the Proctors' party and although she was in no mood for celebration she allowed herself to be persuaded to attend. She had heard conflicting rumours about who was to succeed Governor Darling and she needed to know that it would be Sir Richard Bourke. So much depended on that.

She found herself seated between one of the younger Macarthurs and Dr Redfern. Mrs Proctor was none too happy with a seating plan that set her protégée between an elderly man of uncertain temper and one of the insufferably proud Macarthurs, when she could have been furthering her acquaintance with Deas Thomson, a rising man in the colony's affairs, but as Dr Redfern pointed out the personalities to her, giving her a swift acerbic commentary on each one, Kat found no cause for complaint.

'Take no notice of him,' said Redfern with a twinkle in his eye as Macarthur, having established that her family had neither connection nor influence with Earl Grey and his new government, swiftly lost interest in her and turned away. 'Old Macarthur brought his tribe up to think they're the most important people in the colony, but when they get too high and mighty I always remind them of two things: the old man was naught but a corsetmaker before he made his fortune in the rum monopoly – his enemies still call him Jack Bodice – and twice came within a whisker of returning to the colony in chains.'

Kat looked up at him in wide-eyed astonishment. No one on board the *Maria* had told her that.

'The Great Perturbator, they call him, and with good reason,' continued Redfern. 'Shot his senior officer in a duel. Could have gone hard with him, but when he was back in England awaiting his trial, the old king – mad Farmer George – heard about his cross-breeding experiments with sheep and sent for him to talk about it. Next thing anyone knew, he'd been let off the charges and sent back here with even more land and some prime rams from the King's own flock at Windsor! Not that he learned his lesson – still couldn't resist meddling. Eight years' exile he got for leading the Rum Rebellion against Bligh. Eight peaceful years they were for the colony!' He drank deeply from his glass and signalled to the footman to replenish it. 'All the Macarthurs will tell you that the money Australia makes off the sheep's back is all thanks to them, but there are those of us who remember that Riley and Isaac Nichols – aye, and old Sam Marsden – were cross-breeding sheep long before John Macarthur!'

Australia certainly seemed to be a land of seesawing fortunes, thought Kat, listening with half an ear as Redfern pointed out some of the other personalities to her. There was Sir Maurice O'Connell, commander of the colony's military forces; his wife was daughter to the unfortunate Governor Bligh who, barely recovered from the fiasco of the *Bounty* mutiny, had been so ignominiously overthrown in the colony's Rum Rebellion some twenty years before. Once an attractive young woman who had scandalised the earlier settlers with her daring dresses, Lady Mary had become embittered by her constant fruitless efforts to redeem her father's reputation. Beyond them, close to Governor Darling at the head of the table, was Sir Patrick Lindesay, colonel of the Thirtieth, who was rumoured to have been chosen as acting governor over the head of Sir Maurice. Further down the table were the churchmen: the Reverend Marsden, known as 'Flogging Sam', the unpopular Archdeacon Scott, who had engineered a monopoly in education for the Anglicans; and John Dunmore Lang of the Nonconformist Church.

'Hypocrites, the lot of 'em,' snorted Redfern. 'Scott was a wine-trader – only took holy orders because his family had the say on who should head the church out here. Marsden thinks we should be like Georgia and Alabama, with him and his like the plantation owners, and England sending them a constant supply of white slaves on the convict transports...'

'And Lang?'

'I do him an injustice to lump him in with the others,' admitted the doctor. 'He may be a bigot, but he's not in it for the power and the glory. He may think the convicts are destined for hell and damnation, but he'll do all he can to wrestle with a repentant soul.'

Driving her home in the carriage, Mrs Proctor was most apolo-

247

getic that Kat had had no one to talk to all evening but an irascible old man.

'Don't trouble yourself ma'am,' said Kat. 'I found Dr Redfern most entertaining.'

'I cannot understand why he was invited at all!' complained another lady whom they had taken up in their carriage. 'They tell me he tends to convicts!'

Kat decided that she would be interested to know more of the much-maligned doctor.

The *Perseus* met no more tempests as it skirted the southern shores of the great land mass which was marked on Captain Hurvine's maps as Terra Australis. The bare, barren islands of Bass's Strait were almost as welcome a sight as green fields would have been, for they were land after months of only sea and sky.

Great flocks of birds darkened the sky above the islands. 'Mutton birds,' said Hurvine, handing Joshua the telescope. 'The sealers live on them. I am told that when cured they taste much like red herring.'

The passengers leaned over the side, sniffing at the land, for the fine earthy fragrance was quite clearly distinguishable above the salt breezes that had filled their nostrils for the past five months. Even the prisoners seemed to become more cheerful at the thought of land; at least it would mean release from the stinking hold. Beneath a clear blue sky the inexorable breeze sped them ever onwards to that mysterious destination: the unknown bourne, thought Joshua grimly, from which no convict traveller e'er returned.

After two days beating up the coast in cloudy weather the lookout called 'Land ho!' as he sighted the cliffs which were the headlands of Botany Bay, where Captain Cook had made landfall. The next break in the coast would be Sydney Cove!

Passengers rushed down to their cabins. During the worst of the storms they had lost interest in what they wore, but now salt-stained clothes and sun-bronzed straw bonnets were put aside and they emerged in the latest London fashion, faces as bright and eager as children scrubbed and readied for a birthday treat.

As the *Perseus* veered towards land, it seemed to Joshua's eye to be driving straight at a vast wall of rock at least six hundred feet high, but just as the more nervous of the passengers began to panic, a chink opened up and showed itself as a narrow channel between two towering and majestic headlands, on the most southerly of which they could see a lighthouse and signal station. Passing between the massive precipices was like entering a colossal gateway – to heaven or to hell? Joshua asked himself. But all such morbid thoughts soon disappeared at the sight of the vast bay sheltered behind the headlands and running off into numberless smaller bays and inlets, all sprinkled with islands. If this was indeed an estuary, as Hurvine insisted, it was as unlike the grey and misty Thames as could be, and immeasurably broader and longer too – a good seven miles, the sailors said. It could have swallowed up the whole English fleet and still had room to spare.

A light shower of rain fell amid the bright sunshine as the *Perseus* took the pilot on board, and a pretty rainbow formed over one of the little bays, much to the children's delight.

'A good omen for a bright future,' said Mrs Hurvine.

Joshua gave a wry smile. The voyage, for all its darker moments, would, he felt, seem to him after a few weeks like a holiday interlude. No such thought appeared to trouble Ben and Lizzie, who chattered excitedly to one another, pointing at the coves where the peculiarly bright light reflected dazzlingly off the pure white sand. Everything seemed to have a clear, crisp outline, quite unlike the English landscape where each feature blended into the next. Here the white villas on the headlands seemed to stand apart from their surroundings, and in the deep olive green foliage you could pick out each tree and shrub growing thickly among the rocks, right down to the water's edge.

'Oh, 'tis all so green, Henry!' observed Mrs Hurvine delightedly. 'Not at all what you led me to expect.'

'You are seeing it at its best, my dear,' said the Captain. 'It is after all spring.'

'Oh, Papa!' protested Edward. 'Spring in October?' But before his father could explain it to him, the pinnace carrying the harbour master and the physician drew alongside, manned by a crew of New Zealanders, their copper-skinned faces and bodies heavily tattooed; Edward shot away from his father's side to a better vantage point.

'Do you keep an eye to him, Joe,' said his fond father with an indulgent smile, 'or the next thing we know he'll be back with a Maori tattoo!'

Hurvine named the little bays and inlets for them: Watson's Bay – where they took on the pilot – named after one of the first pilots, harbour master until he was sacked for theft; Neutral Bay, where foreign merchantmen were obliged to drop anchor while the authorities tried to ascertain whether their flag was friendly or hostile, not an easy task when news from Europe took four months; the naval harbour in Woolloomooloo Cove; the shipyard in Sirius Cove, far enough away from Sydney to keep seamen out of trouble while their ships were overhauled; Mosman Bay, where whale carcasses were hauled up the slipways to be gutted and hacked and melted down in cauldrons – far enough from the town not to offend by the stench; and the little inlet which served as quarantine point, with its attendant tombstones standing bleached and white on the crest of the promontory.

Although a number of the convicts had died during the voyage, there had been no recent infectious sickness, so the *Perseus* was able to avoid quarantine. Those who had come on board with the harbour master and physician passed eagerly among the passengers, demanding the latest news, for the only other vessel to pass the Heads that day had been nearly six months at sea.

'Pity you didn't arrive two days earlier,' said a wiry little man to Hurvine as the pilot brought the *Perseus* about to approach its mooring. 'Missed the illuminations. They say Wentworth had four thousand Emancipists up at Vaucluse for the open-air ox-roast. Look, you can still see the smoke up on the headland.'

'Aye,' said his companion. 'And Hall of the *Monitor*, why, he had such a firework display! DOWN WITH THE TYRANT, it said, all across the night sky, just as Governor Darling was being rowed out across the harbour to take ship for England.'

The pilot brought the *Perseus* up alongside the vessel that had preceded them through the Heads, and they cast anchor opposite Fort Macquarie. The other ship was more advanced in its unloading and its decks seethed with passengers.

'Another shipload of Lang's free emigrants, God damn them!' said the wiry little man, spitting over the side.

'Why?' asked Joshua curiously.

'Damn all Jemmy Grants!' came the gruff answer. 'They take land from the Emancipists. And they lower the wages.'

'Emancipists?' Joshua had only heard the word used in connection with William Wilberforce and the West Indian slave trade. 'But there are no slaves here, surely?'

'Not unless you count that lot,' said the wiry man, wrinkling his nose against the stench of the convicts being mustered in chains in the deck cage. 'Emancipists is what they hopes to become – when their time's up.' Before Joshua could pursue the question, half a dozen bagpipers began to puff and squeeze away on the neighbouring ship, all, to Joshua's ear, seeming to be playing quite different airs.

There was no time for thought after that. The noise and bustle of the harbour was almost painful after so long on board ship. To the right of Fort Macquarie was a long low building with a spacious verandah and green lawns that ran down to the quayside; under the trees, among which he thought he recognised an English oak, red-coated soldiers were forming up. When he emerged on deck with the last of the Hurvines' possessions, the soldiers were already marching the convicts down the gangplanks in chains to start unloading the hold. Joshua knew with a heavy heart that he would not be long following them.

'Captain Hurvine will put in a good word for you, Joe,' said Mrs Hurvine with tears in her eyes. 'I wish there were more we could do for you.'

'Joe has been earmarked already,' said the Captain brusquely, 'so he must sleep tonight in Hyde Park Barracks.'

Hyde Park, where on his last visit to London he had escorted Drusilla and Lady Isabelle sedately down Rotten Row, and watched society coquetting, flirting and making assignations – could they have chosen a more improbable name for the convict barracks?

'Well, Joe,' said Hurvine, taking his hand, 'bite your tongue, man, and I dare swear you will prosper here.'

Joshua saw Mrs Hurvine into the slung chair, ready to be landed on the quayside, but she seemed strangely unwilling to give the signal. 'The Captain has told the authorities that you are a family group,' she said, patting his arm rather awkwardly.

'Yes, yes, my dear. Come, come.' Joshua was taken aback to find Hurvine so short; he seemed only too eager to be rid of them. Mrs Hurvine caught his hand again. 'I shall look after your flute,' she said. 'I will keep it for you until – '

'Until I am a free man. God knows when that will be.' He knew a sudden moment of panic. 'But how will I know where to find you?'

'Sydney society is not that extensive,' said Hurvine impatiently.

'Just ask. Or call at the Observatory,' said his wife. 'They will always know where Captain Hurvine is to be found. Pray God it will not be too long.' She turned away with tears in her eyes and the officer gave the order for the sling chair to be hauled on shore.


As Garvey settled terms for the machine-breaker with the auctioneer's assistant, Samson began to take bidding on the women convicts. No heavy selling would be needed here, for all but the most worn-out hags were greatly in demand in a nation with nigh on ten men to every woman. Most of them would go for domestic servants; some would stay with the same family until they had served their sentence, even beyond, but many of them would end up back in Sydney once they had their ticket of leave, most of them in the brothels that lined the dark alleyways on the Rocks, the young ones usually with a babe in their arms.

One young girl with dark curls and wide grey eyes was being eyed in a not very pleasant manner by most of the colonists gathered in the auction room: the bidding on her would surely be high. If she had not just taken on two girls, Kat would have stayed and bid for her, but, as

251

Garvey had pointed out, many more and Lacey's Creek would be more like a nunnery than a farm.

As she shook her skirts out and reached for her parasol, a piercing shriek rent the air and she turned back to peer through the screen. Her view was partially blocked by Garvey's solid figure and two of the redcoats, but it seemed the two files of convicts had been thrown into disorder by one of the men trying to reach one of the women as they were led onto the auction stand.

The air vibrated as the officer gave a warning crack of the whip, and the sergeant and a private doubled across from the doorway and set themselves firmly between the two groups.

Garvey had someone's jacket in his fist and was speaking urgently to him, and as the redcoats crowded to the front of the auction stand, rifle butts ready to swing down on unsuspecting heads, she saw, with a lurch of her heart, the dark-haired convict for whom she had just bid lying on the floor, tangled in the chains.

Oh, God, she thought. Not now. Not *him*! Don't let it all go to ashes now!

But order was soon restored and the male and female chains removed to opposite ends of the stand. Garvey elbowed his way through to her side as the rest of the bidders, robbed of their spectacle, resumed their seats. At the rear of the platform a young boy was sobbing bitterly.

'You'd best sit down, missus,' said Garvey, setting his bulk between her and the rest of the bidders and pushing her gently back into the wicker chair. 'It's like this, missus,' he said. 'The one we just bought, he – '

'Yes?'

'He was promised, see, by Captain Hurvine, that – ' He swallowed hard. 'Hurvine promised that they wouldn't be sold apart.'

She looked up at him, wide-eyed in her bewilderment. 'I don't understand,' she said. 'Apart? What do you mean? *Who* do you mean?'

'It's a family group, y'see. Him and – ' He mopped his forehead. 'The boy, y'see, he's his brother.'

'But – '

'Brother-in-law, I *should* say. Y'see, missus, the dark-haired wench – well, she's his wife.'

# Chapter Fourteen

As they left behind the swirling dust of the Brickfields and picked up the Parramatta Road, Kat shifted her seat and half lifted the curtain on the rear window of the carriage, enabling her to observe the passengers in the cart behind without them being aware of any scrutiny. The sight of Joshua, clad in a new shirt somewhat too small for him, his handsome features revealed by the removal of the unfamiliar whiskers, made her heart lurch. She bit her lip and tore her gaze away, moving on to the other two, sitting in the back of the cart among the barrels and sacks Will had collected from the dockside warehouses. Looking at the dazed expressions on their faces, their eyes creased up against the brightness of the light, she reminded herself how disoriented they must all be feeling after leaving the vessel which had been their home for so long. It had been bad enough for her, and she hadn't had the indignity of the auction to contend with.

The journey from Sydney to Parramatta was only fourteen miles; normally they would have completed it in an afternoon, but Garvey's orders today were to take it gently, as a consideration to the new arrivals.

'A bit different to what you've been used to,' he said as Joshua turned his head to watch a wallaby bounding across the cleared bushland ahead of them. Close by, a small bearlike animal chittered in panic up a nearby eucalyptus, where it hung from a branch to look down at them, the fur round its eyes making it look for all the world like a bespectacled schoolmaster.

'Such strange animals, and the landscape so bare...'

'Aye. Though there are some places where it's a bit more like the ould country,' Garvey said, as they drove past a homestead planted around with fruit trees and with a few oaks and a huge Norfolk pine towering over the house. 'Some, like Macarthur – aye, and Lacey too – saw the sense of planting to keep the moisture in the ground.'

'Lacey? He is the master of Lacey's Creek?'

253

'Was the master,' said Garvey. 'Wasn't a pie he hadn't a finger in, be it Customs, the mails or the grog trade. Made himself a fortune. But then the government wanted their share of the Customs dues, an' he couldn't explain where their share was. He'll be back in England now. Probably already in prison.'

'And he left you in charge?'

'Me? God bless the man, I'm just the land manager. Government took Lacey's lands to pay his debts and a new buyer bought the estates. Fresh out from the ould country.'

'When will I meet – '

'Oh, you'll meet the new owner when the new owner's good an' ready.' And wouldn't he like to be a fly on the wall when that happened, thought Garvey. Still, it was luck for the new feller that he hadn't come out under the old master. Asked far too many questions for a convict servant, and no other settler would have put up with that. But he'd been instructed to tell him everything he wanted to know – well, almost everything.

'This green enough for you?' he asked as they looked down on the town from the top of the toll-hill. 'Parramatta, this is. Rose Hill as was. Grew all manner of stuff for the first settlers. They'd have starved without their harvest. Still supplies 'em with fruit. All kinds of oranges they grow; I'm particularly partial to the mandarin. 'Tis a pretty little fruit you'll not have come across; fine perfume about it, and Betsey out at the creek makes a fine preserve from it.' Handing Joshua the reins, he reached back into one of the sacks. 'Good lemons they grow too,' he said, passing one across to him. 'Always carry some to squeeze if you're any way unsure of the water.'

'A strange shape,' said Joshua, looking at something more like an ill-formed Seville orange.

'Strange to our eyes, to be sure, but juicy and well-flavoured for all that. We're trying some at the farm.' He looked sideways at his passenger. 'Farming man yourself, are you?' he asked.

'I know more about machines than crops,' said Joshua with a wry smile.

'Ah. In the industrial line.' Garvey pushed his hat back on his head. 'An' there's me thinkin' you were a farming man.'

Joshua shrugged. 'I believe your master knows my history. I was told on board ship that I had been allocated.' 'Earmarked' was the word Hurvine had used, which had made Joshua feel even more like a beast in a cattle market.

The Captain had given him very clear instructions, ordering him not to acknowledge his ability to read and write either on the quayside or at the Barracks, should he have the misfortune to be taken there. 'It means you'll have to take your turn with the unload-

254

ing, and that will do your shoulder no good, but if you once get into the hands of the government men, they'll take you for clerical work. You'd make a pleasant change to the usual forgers and counterfeiters they have to take.'

Joshua turned to look at Garvey. 'No one said anything about auctions,' he said, reliving that terrible scene where, chained like an animal, he had been displayed to the prospective purchasers, haggled over and finally sold. 'And they'd promised I would not be sent apart from the children.'

'The children?' said Garvey, and the surprise in his voice brought Joshua back to the present with a start.

'Th-the boy.' He jerked his head at the two in the back of the cart. 'I meant the boy. And my w-wife.'

Garvey looked at him from under lowered brows, but, remembering his orders, he forbore to question the newcomer any further. After a few more minutes they drew up outside a long, low house with a particularly pretty garden and a spacious piazza in front.

'This Lacey's Creek?' asked the young boy, springing down from the back of the cart at Garvey's command to go to the horse's head.

'A very handsome dwelling,' said Joshua, looking around the garden at the luxuriant and exotic shrubs and flowers, among which he recognised only the pink and crimson china roses.

'Lacey's Creek?' said Garvey. 'Bless the lad, this is no more than an inn.' He pointed to the roof of the house. 'See? Sign of the Red Cow.'

Joshua turned sharply away at the unexpected reminder of Wooburn, and Kattrin, who had been observing them all from behind the curtained window, saw, as the carriage passed into the yard, that his eyes were full of tears.


She paced anxiously up and down the verandah, drawing her gloves through her hands and for once paying no heed to the colourful parrots squawking and chattering to each other in their cages nearby. 'Well?' she demanded, as Garvey came up the steps.

'Aye, missus, all well, although the wench is somewhat overtired. The landlady was all for sending her to lie down, but I thought you might want to speak to her first.'

'And the others?'

'Cleaning themselves up in the back wing. I did think to send the lad out back with Will, but I left him with the other feller instead.' He looked at her curiously. 'The landlady wanted to know about rooms. I said I'd be letting her know.'

She caught at the tip of one gloved finger with her teeth while she tried to think. 'I don't know what I should do!' she said at last, perilously close to tears. 'I had it all so carefully worked out and now it's all ruined!'

He heard the maid in the room behind them setting the table. 'We'll take a turn about the garden, missus,' he said soothingly, drawing her down the steps to walk among the pomegranate bushes and the oleanders. 'Talk is more private there.' He looked at her sideways. ''Tis clear he's a gentleman, for all he tries so hard to sound like a peasant,' he said at last, when she showed no sign of starting the conversation. 'So I wonder, now, what a gentleman is doing among the convicts.'

'I had it all worked out,' she repeated. 'Once I saw that they weren't going to listen, that they cared more about making an example than hearing the truth. He thinks I'm in England still, you see. But all this – ' She bit her lip, unable to go on.

'You planned all this for him?'

She nodded. 'I was going to surprise him,' she said in a small voice. 'And I thought that was best done here, with no one to listen and . . .' She swallowed a sob. 'But I never thought he'd have a *wife*!'

There was such heartache and yearning in her voice that it brought a lump to Garvey's throat. 'You've no thought of sending him back to Sydney to be reassigned?'

'How could I do such a thing?' she said indignantly. 'He's still my dear friend . . .'

'Wife or no wife,' he finished for her. 'Aye. That's what I imagined. Then, as I see it, missus, you've two choices,' he said bluntly. 'You can find someone else, a good master, who'll take them all off your hands, or you're stuck with 'em. And if you're stuck with 'em, you might just as well go ahead with your plan anyway. Speak to them here. Before we get back to Lacey's Creek. Only I should leave *him* till tomorrow, if I were you. Till you're calmer.'

'Sleep on it?'

'Aye. I've business to do in Parramatta. I could take him with me . . . only I couldn't take him into the Agricultural Club.'

'I'd already planned for that. I have a ticket of leave for him.'

Garvey gave a low whistle. These days a ticket of leave was not normally given to even the best-behaved of convicts until most of his sentence had been served; it was a highly coveted paper giving the convict leave to live independently in society and, if he had a skill, to work on his own behalf. The only way a new convict could get a ticket of leave was if he was given into the custody of a free wife, as that had the advantage for the government of taking him off the government stores. Had she really been planning to marry a convict? That would set the whole colony back by their ears!

'They'll take it back, of course. If he's already got a wife . . .'

He shook his head and wished he was back on the farm. He wasn't cut out for this sort of thing. 'If I were you,' he said at last, 'I'd talk to those children before you make any hasty decisions.'

She took Garvey's advice and the minute that he and Joshua left the Red Cow, she sent for the girl to walk in the garden with her. But if she had hoped to gain any information from her, she was to be disappointed. After all she had gone through, the girl was physically and mentally exhausted, failing to be animated even by the activities of the two cranelike birds, the so-called native companions, who followed them round the garden, or the pair of colourful parrots on the verandah. Kat managed to extract from her the information, delivered in a strong country accent, that she and her brother were orphans who had been transported for stealing, but to every other question she returned the same answer: 'Can't rightly remember, mistress. Best you ask my husband.'

The boy was no more forthcoming and under her questioning showed every sign of bursting into tears. Kat had not the heart to pursue the matter any further. If she was going to find out anything, she was going to have to ask Joshua.

Garvey was woken from a deep sleep by a hoarse cry. In the half-light he could see Joshua sitting bolt upright in his bed while Ben slept on in the trestle bed alongside, the sleeping arrangements having been altered by the arrival of a late party from Bathurst.

'Go to sleep, man!' muttered Garvey, dragging the sheet over his head. 'You've been tossing and turning half the night.'

Joshua lay back, shivering in spite of the heat, knowing he dared not close his eyes and relive once more that moment of terror, worse than anything that had happened on the hulks, when he had stood in the dock and watched the judge scanning the list, not knowing where the eye would stop and the hand reach out for the black cap.

In the event it had been Blizzard and Sarney who had been taken down to the condemned cell, but in his nightmares throughout those stormy nights on the *Perseus* his name was always on the condemned list and he would wake up in a sweat just as the hangman came for him.

As dawn broke he lay sweating and wakeful, watching the light creep under the blinds and listening to the alien sounds of the new day awakening. He must have slept a little for Garvey appeared to have risen and gone, but on the far side of the room, Benjamin Trump – son and heir to the late Jedediah Trump, grocer, who,

257

having lost everything in the collapse of the local county bank, had shot himself in a moment of despair, leaving his orphaned children to steal or starve – slept quietly on a truckle bed.

Joshua felt a rare surge of self-pity: life as a convict in this strange country would be difficult enough; he could have done without two millstones around his neck.

The moment passed as quickly as it had come. He could never have turned his back on them, and he knew that only too well.

In the next wing, Kattrin lay between cool sheets fighting the waves of tiredness that washed over her, for she knew that the moment she closed her eyes she would dream, as she had almost every night since their parting, of Joshua taking her in his arms and loving her. And she could not do that tonight, for he was no longer hers to dream of.

From behind the curtained window of the carriage she had watched them, achingly waiting for the knife she knew would cut into her heart the minute Joshua took the girl's hand or smiled down into her face the way he had once smiled into her own. But that moment had not come. Indeed, throughout the journey they had not acted like any married couple she had ever observed. But then, what experience did she really have? She could barely remember Cattern and her father together; Lady Isabelle was a widow and Bosingham a widower. By the time Drusilla had wed, Kat had been in Aylesbury gaol and unable to be the bridesmaid to her friend. She could only remember how Zachary Allnutt had looked on his Lizzie and how Joshua had once smiled on her – but then her relations with Joshua had scarcely been of the traditional sort. In spite of the declarations they had made before the Quaker, she had married him for love and he had married her to protect her. She had been a fool to think that he felt the same.

When she did fall asleep just before the dawn, it was to dream, perversely, of Tarquin and she woke sweating and wild-eyed from the horror of the memory. She had never told anyone of the humiliation of that night, not even Dickon. She felt a longing to talk to her brother once more, but Dickon was on the high seas and would not reach Australia until well into the New Year.

She winced as someone in the kitchen of the Red Cow crashed two pans together, bringing her sharply back to the present. She shifted uncomfortably in her bed; her head ached most wretchedly and she knew she had more urgent concerns than Dickon. Over in the corner on a truckle bed the girl slept on, dark curls tousled, seemingly without a care in the world.

Joshua's wife.

She tried to feel hatred for her, but there was nothing. With a

258

grimace she rose, stretched and crossed to the closet. There was no need to disturb the girl; Kat could manage the fastenings of most of her robes herself and she wore no stays, which had shocked Mrs Proctor to the core.

She picked out one of the old muslins that she was accustomed to wearing at Lacey's Creek, but after a brief hesitation she thrust it back into the trunk and drew out instead one of the fashionable English dresses she had worn in Sydney, when she had been At Home to visitors in George Street. She needed all the confidence she could find. She wanted to run away from all her problems – but where could she run? Back to Sydney and the next boat home? She shook her head at her own folly. She no longer had a home in England – there was only Lacey's Creek.

As she drew on the modish apricot and blue plaid silk taffeta and straightened out the lace pelerine, she felt her confidence slowly returning. Chin up once more, head held high, she left the room, closing the door quietly behind her.

Early though she was, Garvey and Joshua were earlier still. She wondered what it was they were discussing so earnestly out on the verandah and edged forward in the shadows to listen; she gave a wry smile when she found they were discussing nothing more weighty than the parrots.

'They're not at all like the ones I've seen in England. I knew an old woman once had a green parrot...' Margaret, thought Kat with a stab of pain. Her nephew, who had died at Trafalgar before Kat was born, had brought it back to Wooburn years ago from one of his many voyages.

'Ah, we've grey and green ones aplenty, but they're nothing to these pretty things: lavender and yellow, and that bright crimson on the side of the head, sure you'd never think those colours would do so well, all together on the same creature. Bathurst parrots, these are, but "painted ladies" the mistress calls them, for their sly eyes and the bright-red cheeks that look as though they've been rouged.'

'The mistress?' Joshua's face was turned to the cage, but his attention was all on Garvey.

'Vicious things they can be, though, so I'd not put me fingers on the bars like that. Not if I wanted to take all ten through life with me, I wouldn't.'

Joshua hastily dropped his hand from the cage. 'What is she like, the mistress? Is she – '

'I'd best be off and give Will his orders,' said Garvey, catching the slightest movement out of the corner of his eye. 'You wait here.'

Kat glided across to the window, her soft kid shoes making no sound on the boards, and watched Joshua drift around the garden, pausing to admire the oleander and breathe deeply of its heady fragrance. She ought to go out and speak to him while there was no one else about. But how to begin? What to say? Her tongue cleaved to the roof of her mouth and although her brain bade them go, her feet refused to move any further.

How did you open a conversation with your husband – the man who thought to have left you on the other side of the world – while his new wife slept sound above your head? Even Lady Isabelle, that famed arbiter of the awkward social situation, might, she felt, have some difficulty opening *this* conversation!

They might have stayed like that for ever, but Joshua stopped before the huge prickly pear that soared twenty feet above his head and, catching sight of the dark-red, ripe fruit, reached out to touch it.

The memory of the intense pain the spines on the fruit could inflict even through gloves stung her into action and she flew out onto the verandah, but Annie, the little kitchen maid, who had been picking herbs in the kitchen garden, was there before her.

'Don't, sir!' cried Annie, peeping over the fruit bushes. Joshua dropped his hand and turned in the direction of the voice and when Annie saw his handsome face, framed by the dark, somewhat over-long hair, she sent him a coy and dimpling smile. Then she looked back at the verandah and said, 'Beggin' yer pardon, mistress. On'y him bein' from the old country, he'll not be knowin' about them prickles. They'd be in his hands this sennight, and right painful they'd hurt him too!' The maid bobbed a curtsy and hurried back into the kitchen garden, but when Joshua turned to the verandah it was deserted.

They set off for Lacey's Creek immediately they had breakfasted.

'We'll want to be home before the noon heat,' said Will as he backed the horse into the shafts of the cart.

'Hard to believe it can get any hotter,' said Joshua, mopping his brow.

Will chuckled. 'It's barely turned from spring as yet. Wait till you see December. Where's the missus?' he asked as Garvey came up.

'Already in the carriage. Ostler's hitched up the team.'

'She couldn't hardly pass the time o' day with me,' grumbled Will. 'Near bit me head off. 'Tis to be hoped she's not gone strange again like when she first come out. Why, she – '

'Stop your chattering and fetch the carriage!' snapped Garvey, interrupting him without ceremony as he caught sight of Joshua.

Will blinked. Everyone seemed to be in a bad temper today. With a shrug he turned back to the stable yard and the little procession set off along the Penrith road, the sound of the wheels the only noise to be heard above the incessant chirruping, croaking and whirring of the invisible armies of grasshoppers.

Kattrin, inside the carriage, was grateful to Garvey for cutting off Will's loose talk, but in all justice she had to admit that the man had had cause for concern. But there had been no more trouble with the servants once she had taken control. She'd told herself that all she had to do was wait as patiently as she could until Joshua arrived, and then all would be well. She raised the curtain and looked back at the cart. Well, Joshua had arrived now, she thought wryly.

They heard the clanking of the chains and the crack of the over-seer's whip before they saw the chain gang and she dropped the curtain hastily. On the last bend before they turned off up the valley road they saw them, a collection of miserable wretches in chains, their shaven heads scorched and blistered by the harsh sun, carrying rocks to the head of a new bridge over the river for another group to break up. As the cart passed, most of the gang turned away, covering their faces against the clouds of dust thrown up by the wheels. A few of them, however, disregarded the overseer and the sentries with their levelled muskets and stood as close as they could to dart malevolent looks at the passengers.

Garvey heard the sharp intake of breath from Ben and Lizzie in the back of the cart. 'Take no notice,' he advised as the cart turned up a track away from the river.

'But they looked so – so – '

'You'll see many such sights in this country,' said Garvey. 'And worse. Even in the best part of town.' Even outside the fashionable shops in George Street there would still be passing chain gangs and the cries of anguish as another unfortunate met his retribution lashed to the triangle in Hyde Park Barracks only a few hundred yards away. 'This place is part town and part gaol.' He looked sideways at Joshua, who had gone very pale under his shipboard tan. 'You have to learn to look the other way.' Which was something he'd constantly tried to impress on the mistress, but so far in vain. It was fortunate that none of the men in this gang were working double-chained, or with the log on their toes for real or imagined wrongdoing, otherwise she'd have insisted on stopping and there would have been another of those scenes, with the constable – himself no more than a licensed convict – trying to justify his action while the mistress harangued him and threatened to report him to the authorities for his inhuman punishment.

'It's a sobering thought,' said Joshua, becoming aware of the steward's scrutiny. 'God's lottery, that puts me up here and them down there.'

'Not as much of a lottery as you might think,' said Garvey. 'Few enough go straight from the transports on to the road gangs, unless they've been in trouble on the voyage out. Most of them – ' he jerked his thumb over his shoulder – 'are there for repeated convictions.'

'The bottom of the pit,' said Joshua.

'Lord bless the man,' said Garvey, 'there's a long way from being a government man in irons, to the bottom of the pit! There's Port Macquarie, or Moreton Bay. Or even Norfolk Island.'

'Where are they?' asked Lizzie, picking up on the change in Garvey's voice.

'You don't want to hear about them, child,' said Garvey, suppressing a shudder. 'You don't even want to think about them.'

They all fell silent until Garvey made a conscious effort to change the subject. 'Just through this paddock and over the next hill and you'll see the homestead,' he said.

'This is Lacey's land?' asked Joshua.

'Lacey's land as far as you can see. The entire valley, from where we turned off the Penrith road.'

'So much!'

'I told you, only Macarthur and a handful of others like Macleay and Riley have more land than Lacey's Creek. Good land it is too.'

'Has there been a fire?' asked Joshua as they came over the hill and caught their first sight of the homestead.

'That's the selfsame question the mistress...' Garvey's voice trailed away. 'Everyone thinks it's ruins,' he said briskly, 'but it's just the startings of a new building.'

'I can see that now,' said Joshua as they drew closer. 'You said that Lacey's Creek had good land – and a good mistress too?' It was an impertinent question for a convict servant, but he felt instinctively that the open-faced Irishman, who had treated him almost like an equal when he'd taken him round Parramatta, wouldn't hold it against him. Listening to Ben and Lizzie whispering to each other as they took in the sight of the homestead, the shacks, the river and the distant mountains, he'd all but made up his mind to make a clean breast of everything to his employer the moment he met her.

'Well,' said Garvey, weighing his words carefully as the carriage drew up at the front of the house, 'she's not been here that long, but if I'm any judge, she's fair and honourable. Likes everyone else to be the same.'

He looked enquiringly at Joshua, but before he could speak, the cart swerved off round the back of the main house, scattering chickens and goats in its path, and drew up in the yard. Plump Betsey shuffled out of her kitchen door.

Her pale, broad face wreathed in smiles as she caught sight of Garvey. 'These the new ones?' she said, not unsympathetically, dark button eyes looking the three of them over with interest. 'Shall I take 'em into the kitchen?'

'The mistress wants to speak to them first, Betsey. Here, you young 'uns can set down awhile in my place,' said Garvey, pointing to one of the sturdier shacks. 'There's some water to clean up, and you shall have some vittals. Ah, don't fret now,' he said, as Lizzie looked anxiously across at Joshua. 'He's goin' nowhere but to make his bow to the mistress.'

'Do as you're bid, Lizzie,' said Joshua curtly, uncomfortably aware that they were the focus for half a dozen pairs of eyes as more of the hands came out into the yard to stare at the new arrivals.

As he hurried in Garvey's wake to the front of the house, he wiped his hands and face with his kerchief and ran his fingers through his hair. A small grey cat, not much more than a kitten, was sunning itself on the verandah. As Garvey passed by it uncurled itself and began to stretch lazily; mid-stretch it tensed, hesitated, then shot across the sun-bleached boards and began to rub itself vigorously against Joshua's legs.

'Would y'ever look at that now?' said Garvey, turning round to see the cause of the frantic purring. 'That cat never goes to anyone but the mistress!'

Feeling as though the bottom had fallen out of his stomach, Joshua bent to pick up the little cat. 'My God!' he muttered 'It isn't ... surely it cannot be...'

Garvey opened the door and Joshua's voice trailed away as he saw the slim silhouette of a woman against the far windows.

'At last!' she said.

The cat, dropped unceremoniously to the floor from hands suddenly nerveless, stalked off to the kangaroo-skin mat to resume its interrupted sleep; a firm hand pushed Joshua from the verandah into a room where holland blinds were pulled down behind muslin drapes to keep out the heat of the sun. He peered at the slim figure silhouetted against the white muslin drapes, her face in shadow, and told himself he was – he *must* be – mistaken. A muscle twitched in his cheek. That the gods might annihilate time and space, he thought, and make two lovers happy. The woman crossed the room and raised the blinds and when she turned her face back to him he knew his instinct had not betrayed him.

Kat had gone over the scene in her mind a hundred times since the shock of the auction and had had every intention of remaining calm, dignified and, above all, distant, but her resolution faltered as Joshua's dark eyes devoured her, drinking in the details of her face as though he could never see enough of it. When he at last threw wide

263

his arms and muttered a strangled 'Kat!' she flew to him, heart singing as his arms folded tightly around her, pressing her face into his shoulder.

His breath was hot on her neck and her knees seemed to melt beneath her; without his firm grip she would surely have fallen. Could she have thought of anything to say, her dry throat could not have given voice to it. After an eternity his grasp relaxed slightly and she felt a hand on her chin, turning her face up to his. She didn't want to look for fear of what she might see there, but the pressure of his hand could not be resisted and when she did bring herself to meet his gaze the longing she saw in his glowing eyes made her heart leap. When his mouth lowered, mesmerisingly slowly, to hers, she no longer had it in her to refuse him. As his mouth covered her trembling lips it was as if time had run backward and they were once again in Aylesbury, with the snow lying thick on the sill of the high prison window and the haunting sound of the papermen singing their carols.

It was a kiss that seemed to last for ever and the feel of his arms around her was a poignant reminder of all the long, lonely nights since then, when her body had cried out for his.

At last he raised his head, drew a shuddering breath and ran his hand unsteadily down the side of her face. 'But Kat, what are you doing here?' he said at last. 'I can't believe you're here! You're supposed to be in Wooburn.' He clamped his jaw shut against the inane questions tumbling out of his mouth. 'It really is you,' he whispered in wonder. 'My dearest Kat.'

And then the image of the dark-haired girl rushed as swiftly into Kat's mind as mill waters when the sluices are opened, and she recoiled from his embrace. It was a brutal reaction and it brought them both back to their senses.

'Kat, *why* are you here?' said Joshua huskily. 'Surely Dickon did not bring you to Australia?'

'I came out by myself. On the *Maria*.' She clenched her fists at her side. It was all she could do not to rush across the room and shake him.

'The *Maria*? But that's a convict ship!' he protested. 'You –' He bit off the words and struggled to gather his wits: his brain was like treacle from the heat, the journey, above all from the shock. 'Oh, God help us!' he said after a moment, and his eyes widened. 'You're not a convict too?' he said. 'I'd have given anything for you not to be! Damn Bosingham! He gave his word!'

She found her tongue again. 'Joshua, you don't understand – '

'She's bought you too, has she?' he said despairingly. 'This mistress – did she buy your soul along with Lacey's Creek? And yet – you're not dressed like the other convict servants...'

'Because I am not a servant. No one has bought me.' Her voice hovered on the edge of tears. This was to have been her moment of glory and it was turning to ashes. 'Joshua, I am the mistress of Lacey's Creek.'

'You?' He looked at her in disbelief. 'But your father disowned you! You have not two ha'pennies to rub together!'

'It's a long story.'

'Oh, God, Kat.' His voice cracked. 'You married Godstowe.'

'No. Though he asked me often enough.' She ought not to have said that; she ought to have spared him his pride. And yet, had he not ground hers into the dust? 'But I never could have married Godstowe. You see, I thought the vows we made in Aylesbury were for life.'

'I married you to protect you,' he said stiffly. 'I promised Dickon that I would give you an annulment when the troubles had passed.'

'I didn't *want* an annulment! Damn you, Joshua, don't you see, I –' She bit her lip on the words, turning away that he might not see in her eyes the love she still felt for him, even though he was wed to another. 'Though I quite see that you must have an annulment, under the circumstances.'

'Of course. I am a convict.'

'That's the least of it!' she exploded, turning angrily away.

'The *least* of it?' He looked at her, quite bemused. 'How can that be the *least* of it?'

'You are tired, of course. It is a common reaction, after the shock of the voyage. We will talk again later.' She rang the little handbell that stood on an ornately carved table. 'Garvey will show you to your quarters.' Her hand went to the heavy chain that hung around her neck and dipped between her breasts. 'Your wife will be wondering what has kept you.'

'My wife?' A furrow appeared between his brows. 'What do you mean, my wife? You surely don't mean Lizzie!' Distracted a moment by Garvey's entrance, he didn't at first realise that Kat had crossed to the door. Hurrying after her he banged his head on the Argand lamp that hung from a hook in the ceiling.

He reeled back, cursing as stars flashed before his eyes. When his head cleared, Kat had already gone, the door closing behind her with a snap.

'Of course she means Lizzie,' said Garvey testily. 'How many wives have you got?'

Joshua whirled on the steward. 'I've got to make her listen!'

'You poor fool! You could have had it all and you threw it away.'

'She can't think Lizzie's my wife,' he said, carrying on to the door. 'She *can't*!'

'Leave that,' said Garvey, catching his arm with a surprisingly strong grip. 'You don't go through there without the mistress invites you first.'

'Let me go! I've got to explain to her!'

'Don't be forgetting that I'm the steward,' warned Garvey, tightening his grip. 'It wouldn't be a right good start to lay violent hands on me.'

'Kat!' he cried brokenly.

The door half opened and Kat stopped uncertainly in the entrance.

'Not now, Joshua,' she pleaded, struggling desperately to hold back the tears. 'We will talk later. When we're calmer.'

'Lizzie is not my wife,' he said, fixing her gaze with his and speaking to her as though only they were in the room. 'I had planned to make a clean breast of it – '

'As soon as you realised what a good berth you'd let go?' jeered Garvey.

'Damn you, no!' he shouted. 'It wasn't like that!' He saw Kat wince and forced himself to speak more calmly. 'I swear that I had planned to tell my new master – or mistress – the truth. But then the shock of seeing you – '

'That's enough, now,' said Garvey, more forcefully.

'I will go,' said Joshua fiercely, 'but you must believe me, Kat – I never wed the girl.'

He should never have gone along with the deception. He had been playing the flute one evening in the captain's cabin when Colonel Davey had asked after his wife. He had been about to correct him when he caught Hurvine's stern eye; remembering Captain Bunnett's puritanical views, he had gone along with the white lie, even used it himself at the auction, to keep the girl safe with him. He knew Hurvine – or Lizzie herself – could confirm what he said, but for him it was vital that Kat should trust his word.

Garvey, aware of the tension crackling between them, loosened his grip on Joshua's arm and took a hesitant step back.

'She was merely under my protection – ah, not that way, Kat,' said Joshua as he saw the pain cross her face. 'Not that way. I protected her and her brother the way I tried to protect you and Dickon in Wooburn, that was all.'

'Oh, Joshua!' said Kat, running into his arms with a little sob. 'How could I have doubted you?'

Joshua lay for a moment blinking in the half-light, struggling to remember where he was. After a moment the memories came flooding back, followed rapidly by a conviction that he had dreamed it all and would wake in a moment to find himself in his cubbyhole on the

*Perseus* or, worse still, in the cells below the auction rooms where he had been chained up for a nightmare few hours. He rubbed his tired eyes and looked around him: no, it was all true. There were his clothes on the chair by the cheval mirror and his watch – the watch that he had given Dickon for safekeeping when they took him off to the hulks – on the watch stand on the night table, just as he had found it when he came to bed. And all around him were the green gauze drapes that Garvey had insisted on tenting above the bed.

It had been Garvey, hovering discreetly in the doorway, who had taken one look at Joshua's haggard and exhausted face and suggested that he should lie down before he fell down – 'for I don't give much of me chances of catchin' a big feller like yerself without bein' flattened.'

Joshua yawned, reached out under the drapes for his watch and realised with a start that he had slept most of the afternoon away. He poured water into the bowl on the ornate washstand to make himself more presentable and dressed himself in a daze. A clean shirt and cravat had been laid out for him and the coat bought for him in Sydney had been sponged and pressed while he slept. As he reached for his boots, Ben came in.

'I'm right surprised to see you already dressed, master,' said the boy, taking his boot from him and shaking it upside down.

'What the devil – '

'They says we has to do that, sir, before we puts aught on our feet, case there's snakes or scorpions or spiders or summat like in 'em. Seems the spiders out here is a wicious lot, not like them back home.' He handed him back his boot. 'Still, spiders or no spiders, seems we've fallen on our feet here,' he said, looking admiringly about him at the fine, highly polished furniture. 'Oh, and the mistress will see you in the dining room,' he said, recalling his errand. Then he corrected himself. 'She'll see you in the dining room, *sir*. When convenient.'

'Where's Lizzie?'

'With the mistress. She says as how we don't 'ave to pretend she's your wife no more. I'll tell 'em as you're on your way, sir, shall I?'

'Thank you, Ben, yes.' He picked a brush from the dressing table and tried to smooth down his hair, watching in the mirror as the boy disappeared. He seemed to be taking his new circumstances in his stride, but then it was, for Ben and Lizzie, a blessed relief compared to what they had feared awaited them. For him too, said the inner voice, but then darker thoughts came rushing in: what he had to do now might be almost as bad. He'd been a fool to behave as he had; now he had to make Kattrin see that everything had changed. He was a convict, the wretched dregs of society. They could not simply go on

267

as though nothing had happened. Of course he was grateful to her for rescuing him – and the children – from that dreadful auction, but the sooner she moved him elsewhere to serve out his sentence, the better it would be for both of them.

When he presented himself in the dining room, found after opening several doors off the corridor, only the maid was there, a sharp-faced girl with cropped hair sticking out from her head. She started, wild-eyed, as she caught sight of him, and gave a little bob in his direction, neither bow nor curtsy. Picking up a cane implement, something in the style of a small carpet beater, she launched herself across the room to annihilate a fly against the peach-distempered wall.

'Gotta flatten 'em all afore they brings the food in,' she said, flashing him a gap-toothed smile, 'else they falls in the wine and the sauces somethin' dreadful.' She shot sideways and the cane beater swished past his ear, but on this occasion she missed her prey, which fastened itself on Joshua's neck with a furious whine.

'Damnation!' he muttered, wincing as he brushed the insect off.

'Allus the way, sir,' said the maid, not ceasing from her labours. 'Just like men, they are: likes the new flesh the best. Allus goes for the newcomers. After a few weeks they tires of you and moves on to another. Why, when the mistress first come out here, she was a heap o' bites for weeks, but now – '

'That will be all, Jenny,' said Kat, coming up behind the girl and relieving her of the fly swatter.

'Gotta flatten 'em all, missus,' said the maid, giving a manic laugh.

Kat stroked the girl's brow. 'Pray calm yourself, Jenny,' she said soothingly. Jenny gave a little shudder and seemed to come back from a long way away. 'Better now? Then you may tell cook to serve,' said Kat, noticing with a frown that the table had been set as if for a formal dinner, with the two places laid at opposite ends of the table. She could hardly make a fuss now, but she wished she had thought to tell them to lay less formally.

'She has had a fever?' said Joshua, watching the girl scurry out of the room.

'No. Her hair was cropped in the Female Factory – that's where women go if they are too sick to assign.' Sent to Norfolk Island when the women there were prisoners of soldiers and convicts alike, Jenny had been so badly treated that she had been driven almost out of her wits. Betsey the cook had taken her under her wing; little by little she was returning to normality but her self-control was always liable to lapse in the presence of strange men.

A stout, red-faced man in his fifties came bustling into the room, attired in a tight scarlet coat heavily frogged with gold braid and with a bottle under each arm. 'Your pardon, ma'am,' he said, wheezing slightly as he set the bottles down and hurried to hold out the chair at the head of the table for her. 'I should have been here sooner, but was held up by Mr Garvey.'

'He will have told you of our new arrival,' said Kat with a smile 'Mr Delahaye, new out from England. Joshua, this is Jenkins, Mr Lacey's butler – '

'And yours, ma'am, I hope?' said the man, bowing somewhere between her and Joshua before moving in stately manner across the China matting to receive the first course and oversee its serving by the maid.

Joshua addressed himself to his first course, making polite responses to her rather stilted enquiries about his room and confirming that, yes, everything had been to his satisfaction. Neither the presence of the servants nor the vast expanse of white linen between them was conducive to more intimate discussion.

He watched her covertly, searching for some sign of the cowed young girl he had once known, but the mill owner's downtrodden daughter was gone as if she had never been. 'It's hard to believe you're sitting at the head of your own table, waited on by butler and maids,' he said when Jenkins was briefly out of the room. 'And so perfectly at your ease.'

'I have had time to become accustomed to it,' she said with a smile. 'Even before Lady Isabelle took me under her wing, I'd been practising in my mind for years; I'd often thought how much better I could do it than poor Lucy. And if father had bought Hall Barn, as he planned, she would never have coped.'

'Miss Thornton would have been terrified by someone like Jenkins,' he agreed, as the butler withdrew to fetch a bottle of something more suited, in his opinion, to the celebratory nature of the occasion. 'I'm rather in awe of him myself. He'd be greatly in demand in England – quite stately enough even for Bosingham House!'

'He's only being so lofty because he cannot decide who to place at the head of the table,' she said. Normally Jenkins would not have hesitated to put the husband at the head of the table, but in this case the wife was still the owner of Lacey's Creek, for a convict – even a ticket-of-leave man – could not hold property. She saw Joshua's face darken and wished she had not spoken. 'I'm in two minds as to whether I need a butler at all,' she hurried on. 'I may send him to Sydney.'

'He's quite a contrast to the other servants,' he said absently.

'Mmm.' She pulled a wry face. 'They're certainly more familiar than in England. One of the drawbacks, Garvey says, of treating them kindly. They think they're part of the family and entitled to comment on all that you do. And it's worse for me, of course.'

He raised his eyebrow.

'It's so rare for a woman – especially a young woman – to own land.'

Hard on the heels of Jenkins with the specially chosen bottle from Lacey's well-stocked cellar came Betsey the cook, who made it her business to tell Joshua which of the main-course dishes he should try and which might be too strong for a stomach fresh off the ships.

He froze at her words and heard her out in silence. 'Do they know?' he asked Kat, under cover of the clatter of dishes from the sideboard. 'About me being – '

'Transported? Almost certainly. And you were sure anyway to be the prime topic of conversation from here to Sydney!'

He raised an eyebrow.

'Dickon boarded me on the *Maria* as Miss Revel! They'll all be rather surprised to find I've suddenly acquired a husband!' She seemed to expect him to find that amusing, but he didn't. 'You can't stop them talking, Joshua,' she said, looking at him a little anxiously. 'That's all that most of society out here has to do all day. Just don't tell them – society or servants – more of your business than you have to.'

'The sooner I move on – ' he began, but his words were drowned in the clatter as Jenny set one of the removes in the centre of the table.

Kat misread the frustration in his face and smiled encouragingly down the table at him. 'Don't fret, Joshua,' she said as Jenny moved away. 'We'll face them out. Together.'

He shook his head in despair.

The service was a remarkable mixture of palace and cottage. The centrepiece of the main course was a roasted fish, something like a large perch, served on a magnificent silver platter along with a variety of side dishes, but it was dissected with a knife which could have belonged to any of the crew of the *Perseus*, and served up on wooden platters.

'I am greatly envied,' she said when Joshua commented on the delicious food. 'Betsey is skilled in the kitchen and an excellent housekeeper; she's sober and a good influence on the other female servants. There are many who would pay handsomely for just one of those attributes in a cook.'

'As I recall, Lady Isabelle often praised your housekeeping skills.'

She shook her head. 'It's so different out here and I am but a raw beginner. We have insects out here that Dickon would give his eyeteeth to study and they can poison off a family or bring down a

270

wooden building if care is not taken. A good housekeeper is worth her weight in gold.'

Kat did not do justice to any of the dishes. It vexed her that they could not discuss all that lay between them because of the presence of the servants, and so when the dishes were cleared away and the desserts set on the table, she told Jenkins they would serve themselves.

When the butler had left the room, injured dignity in every bone of his body, she patted the table beside her. 'Will you not fetch your glass up here, Joshua?' she said.

He looked at her for a long moment and she found herself holding her breath. At last he picked up his glass and walked slowly up the length of the table. 'May I help you to some dessert?' she asked as he sat beside her. 'We have no jellies, I fear; in this heat it's difficult to hold the set and the cook-maids have not the skill.'

He cut into her chatter about the difficulties of holding cream sound in such heat. 'We can talk about housekeeping another time, Kat,' he said, understanding her desire to put off more intimate discussion. 'You seem to be aware of everything that has happened to me since they took me from the courtroom, but I have not the smallest notion how you come to be here in Australia before me. The last I heard, your prospects were far from glowing – your father had disowned you! How did you become a landowner? How did you come to be here in the colony at all?'

It was surprisingly difficult to talk to him; never before had her conversation with him been so stilted. She didn't want to talk to him about the whys and wherefores of their arrival in Lacey's Creek: she wanted him to snatch her up in his arms and hold her and tell her that everything would be all right now that they were together again. Instead he sat beside her, as distant as if he had still been in Wooburn, twisting his glass in his hands and staring across the table with a frozen look in his eyes.

She explained as best she could how Dickon had reclaimed their inheritance after discovering their father's misappropriation of the Thornton dowry. 'He wanted me to take it all, for I was the eldest and, as he said, the only legitimate child. Of course I refused to take more than half; morally, if not in the eyes of the law, we were both equally entitled. Dickon said he could set me up anywhere – Bath or Cheltenham or Ireland. But what use was Bath to me? Once Stimpson said that transportation was likely, I knew that here was where I wanted to be and nothing he or William could say would change my mind.' It was strange to think that almost nine months had passed since then. She decided for the moment against telling him about the

271

detailed reports that she was sending back to Howick: time enough later.

'Sooner or later your father will find out he was tricked,' said Joshua, suppressing a yawn, 'and then I would not wish to be in Dickon's shoes.'

'Dickon will not be there. He took his share of the money and shipped on board a scientific expedition – just as he always wanted. Isn't that famous?'

'I cannot believe that he let you travel here alone,' he said heavily.

'He wanted to travel with me, but I wouldn't let him. He'd done so much for me, and I hated to part from him, but he had to follow his own dreams.' And she blinked away the tears as she remembered the emotional parting from her beloved brother on the dockside, while sailors whistled and sails flapped in the stiff salt breeze and heavy packing cases were carried onto the *Maria*...

'They are all well in Leicestershire,' she said bracingly. 'Lucy is a new woman away from my father and enjoys helping Saul keep house for your father. I thought, now they are all settled, we could send for Tom. I am sure he would like Australia.'

She had expected some reaction from Joshua, but none came. His eyes, which had been growing heavier by the minute, were almost closed.

'But we can talk about that another day.' she said, eager to turn the conversation to more personal matters. As the longcase clock in the corridor chimed she told herself with a secret smile that it would be easier to tell him about the ticket of leave later, when they were lying in each other's arms. She shivered as she remembered the feel of his arms around her, his body against hers in the chill of the cell in Aylesbury. 'I sent Ben to bed early,' she said, her cheeks mantled in a blush as they rose from the table.

'Good. The boy is as exhausted as I am.' He took up a pair of candlesticks and followed her down the corridor. 'And I believe I am able to put myself to bed.' His voice was curt, bearing no resemblance to the warm tones he had used to her earlier.

'Everyone is tired for the first few weeks,' she said as he struggled to hold himself upright. She crossed her chamber to turn up the lamp that Meggie always left burning on the night table when she had driven the mosquitoes out and lowered the nets around the bed. 'Come in and close the door, Joshua,' she said over her shoulder, 'or the insects will come back in.'

He stepped back from the doorway and bowed. 'I will bid you goodnight,' he said.

She looked at him in surprise. 'But Joshua, you're not – '

'Mine is the next room, is it not?' he asked, and the question came out more harshly than he had intended. 'Unless you wish to give me other orders.' He quirked an eyebrow, but there was no humour in his face. 'I am at your command, ma'am,' he said heavily. 'You are, after all, the mistress.'

'You much mistake the matter, sir,' she protested, tears prickling the back of her eyes.

'Then I will bid you, once more, goodnight,' he said stiffly.

She stood there for a long time after he had gone, willing herself not to cry. She couldn't face the maid, with the inevitable smirks; with difficulty she unlaced herself and divested herself of her clothing. She lay under the satin embroidered netting listening anxiously for Joshua's footsteps, but at last she extinguished the lamp, knowing in her heart of hearts that he would not appear.

As she lay dry-eyed and sleepless, she became aware of a sliver of light gleaming under the doorway of the dressing room that connected their rooms. Joshua, ignorant of the ways of the new country, would not know that fire was one of the greatest hazards, even this early in the hot season. She rose and groped her way across to the door and through the dressing room, guided by the spill of the light.

Joshua had fallen asleep on the bed, half undressed, undisturbed by the insects which had bitten all down his back. The candle, unprotected, was flickering dangerously close to the muslin bed drapes; she carried it across to the mantel and placed it behind the hurricane glass. He stirred briefly, just long enough for Kat to push him under the nets. She stood for a moment watching him sleeping and became aware that she was grinding her teeth, the habit her father had tried so hard to beat out of her. Her hand covering her mouth she returned to her own room, stifling the sobs that were forcing their way out, and crawled back between the smooth sheets of her empty bed.

Kattrin was surprised to be confronted next morning at the breakfast table. 'I heard as how you're alterin' the musters, missus,' said Betsey, more in statement than in question.

'Those, like you and Mr Garvey, who are overseers of other servants will report directly, rather than turn out to morning and evening muster with all the others.'

'I wanted you to know as I never considered meself nor Mr Garvey a criminal,' stated Betsey.

'I see,' said Kat inadequately.

'Mr Garvey's a political, see. Irish thought don't match with English. An' why should it, when all's said and done?'

'Quite so. But there really is no need – '

'An' me, all I ever done was to help nature.'

273

'You did?' Kat gave in to the inevitable and waved Betsey to a seat.

'Stands to reason, don't it?' said the cook, subsiding thankfully into the Windsor chair. 'I mean, when there's no food, like no grass to graze an' that, the animals in the wild, they just don't breed, see. But nature ain't got it right with us. So a poor wench what ain't able to feed herself, she falls for a babe what'll take half the food what she ain't got. Poor harvest or good, we breeds whatever. The blacks 'as it as bad as us, but they leaves the babes they can't feed for the dingoes to take – "yahoo devil" they calls it. Me, I can't see what the missionaries gets so worked up about – it ain't no worse to my mind than leavin' mother and babe to starve in the streets. But my way – well, my way's better yet.'

'Your way?' In spite of herself Kat was intrigued.

'Give 'em a draught – special herbs, see. Nip it in the bud, so to speak, so the poor wench can get on with her own fight to survive. It's a skilled task, just like a pharmacist, really. Me ma passed on the secrets to me when I were a girl, same as her ma passed them on to her, and *her* ma afore her. On'y mistake I made was not bein' careful enough who I helped. Some silly wench went an' bleated to her father an' next thing I know I'm on a slow boat to Terra Australis, as Mr Garvey puts it.'

'And so you gave up these – er – treatments?'

'Bless you, no, missus! Mind you, it weren't no easy task changin' to these Australian herbs. Trial and error, that was. Still, I soon got the hang of it. Ain't killed anyone yet, and I cured a fair few – not just troubles under the apron neither.' She set a small pot on the table. 'Salve I've made up,' she said with a smile. 'For your – um – for the new man. He carries that shoulder badly. Old wound, is it?'

'Yes.' Kattrin didn't want to discuss Joshua now.

'Ned will watch out for him,' said Betsey with a coy smile that sat oddly on her heavy face. 'He's a good man, Ned Garvey. None better.' She surged up from her chair and nodded her head. 'Right good of you, it was, to take us off the muster, missus, even though you took Will off it too, what was a confessed coin-shaver!' She turned in the doorway. 'So if there's anythin' I can do for you, missus, outside of my kitchen work, just you let me know. For men will be men, and women will let them!' She laughed wheezily, ample cheeks quivering. 'An' I've herbs to help a woman breed, as well as herbs to stop it!' With a knowing smile at Kat she stumped back to her kitchens.

If only she knew, thought Kat, pushing aside the bread and butter she had been toying with. She turned the pages of the book at her side while she sipped at her tea, but her mind was not on either task and the heavy footfalls in the corridor were a welcome diversion.

'I've come for me orders, miss.' The farm foreman pulled a mis-shapen hat from his head and smiled broadly, revealing more gaps than teeth.

'Mr Delahaye and Mr Garvey will ride out today, Will. Have the horses saddled. I believe Jenkins has asked Betsey to make up provisions for them.'

'Right. And you, miss? You'll be wantin' the carriage?'

'Not today, Will. I have guests: Mrs Thomas and her sister are coming out from Parramatta.'

'Right. I'll set one o' the men to look out for them; he can see to their horses.' He paused and scratched his head. 'Mr Garvey's sent the farm hands to work on the clearance, but if you're not wanting the carriage out, it's in me mind to set some of the others to clear around the new site – see what we got and what we still needs to get on with the building.'

She tapped her teeth with a dainty finger. 'Mmm. By all means start clearing, but we won't proceed with the building for the moment. I'm not persuaded we can't improve the design.'

'But Mr Lacey sent for them plans all the way to England!'

'I think that may be the problem.'

Will frowned as he tried to make out her meaning, then he was struck by another thought. 'What will I do with the girl, miss?'

Kat sighed. Relieved though she had been to find that Lizzie was not married to Joshua, the girl and her brother were two extra pairs of hands and what to do with them would be yet another decision she hadn't expected to have to make.

'Let her and her brother wander around and see what's going on: the kitchen, the laundry, the dairy. If they talk to Cook and Meggie and the housemaids, maybe they'll come up with their own answer.'

'I thought the boy was to valet the new man?'

'Mr Delahaye has no more need of a full-time valet than I have of a twenty-four hour lady's maid,' she said crisply. She looked at Will, standing in the doorway with his mouth at half cock. 'Was there anything else, Will?'

'I just – um, no. Er – no, Miss Revel.'

'Mrs Delahaye, Will,' she said, opening the book at her side.

'Right. Sorry, missus. I'll try to remember.'

She turned her attention back to the book and did not hear Joshua enter the room until he spoke. 'Don't you think you're making a mistake?' he asked.

'Joshua!' At the sight of him her stomach lurched and to her vexation she felt the colour rush into her face. 'I didn't hear you come in. Did – did you sleep well?'

'I thank you, yes.' He crossed to the table and gripped the back of

275

the chair, looking broodingly down at Kattrin. 'You didn't answer my question.'

'Question?' She furrowed her brow.

'Don't you think you're making a mistake telling them to call you Mrs Delahaye?'

'But you are my husband, Joshua!' She heard the pleading note in her voice and hated herself for it.

He turned away, unable to meet that hurt gaze. 'It would be best if we forget what happened in Aylesbury,' he said deliberately. 'You are a woman of substance now, a woman of position.' He stopped in front of a hand-tinted engraving of *The Town of Sydney in New Holland, anno domini 1821* that hung above the fireplace, and pretended to study it. 'The offer of an annulment still stands.' His voice was harsh. 'You would be unwise to dismiss it out of hand. Once you have an annulment I can be reassigned – '

'No!' She snapped the book shut and a detached corner of his mind noticed that it was inscribed, in Kat's spiky copperplate, RECIPES. 'We can't have an annulment,' she blurted out. 'You can only get your ticket of leave if you're married to me. You were released into my custody . . .' Her voice tailed away at the look on his face. 'It's how the system works, Joshua,' she faltered.

His face went white and he turned on his heel and stalked out.

'We grow maize – Indian corn, they call it, or sometimes Kaffir corn,' said Garvey, pulling his horse in at the edge of a field full of dark-green plants, tall-stalked, each with spires of blossoms crowning a sheaf of broad leaves.

Joshua had to concentrate to hear the steward above the constant squeaking and whirring and chirruping of the myriad insects in the corn field.

'I'd only ever seen it as an ornamental plant at home, but it does very well here. It's less susceptible to blight or the weevils that attack other crops out here. When ye heard them talk of corn at the agricultural meeting t'other night in Parramatta, this was what they meant; anything else is called grain.' He reined in his mount at the end of the field. 'We hope to increase our acreage next year,' he went on, pointing to the land beyond, 'but as you see, there's a deal of hard work to be done before then.'

Joshua turned his horse to look where Garvey was pointing and a depressing sight met his gaze: the native trees had been cut down to within a yard of the ground and the blackened and burnt stumps, seen from a distance, gave the area the appearance of an extensive graveyard. Men were working with bullock teams to dislodge the stumps, but progress was slow and they had cleared no more than a

276

small strip beyond the corn field. 'Grubbing out stumps and roots requires a deal of manpower,' explained Garvey, 'so many of the smaller farmers were unable to clear it properly.'

'It gives a most desolate impression,' said Joshua.

'Aye. But wait till you see the next paddock, just over that rise. The trees were larger there, so they just ringbarked them. That kills 'em, y'see, within the year, but leaves 'em still standing. Great leafless skeletons to dominate the land – 'tis a haunting sight.'

After a while they struck off into the forest – the bush, as Garvey called it. The air was scented with a pungent fragrance that reminded Joshua of one of Nonie's potions against colds and fevers, and the sound of the whirring insects was joined by the raucous calls of a multitude of birds. All around them parrots shrieked, clouds of smaller blue and yellow parakeets chirped as they wheeled above their heads and in the distance unseen, unknown birds cackled, howled and cried, their voices often unnervingly human.

The trees too appeared alien to one accustomed to the massive oaks and elms and slender beeches of England, although an occasional planting reminded him of churchyard yew trees and there were one or two towering pines. From many of the trees strips of dusty bark peeled off and hung in streamers, reminding him of nothing so much as a gathering of mourners with crepe ribbons hanging from their clothes. 'Are these trees dying too?' he asked Garvey, pointing to the strips of bark.

Garvey shook his head. 'Most Australian trees keep their leaves all year round. They shed their bark instead.'

They reined in their horses as a pair of wallabies bounced across the clearing barely fifty yards ahead of them. It was a country that deceived you with its familiarity, thought Joshua, and then confronted you with life so alien that it might as well be the far side of the moon.

About two hours ride from the house they came across a huge sign post standing in the middle of the bush. The letters RUTLAND were still distinguishable on the circle, and the fingers pointed to Main Street, Courthouse Square, Church Street and Lacey's Square.

'This is what finally finished off Lacey,' said Garvey, pointing to the lines marked and pegged in the dusty soil, gradually being overgrown by the encroaching scrub. 'He was a devil for making his mark; never satisfied with what he'd got. Took all the money he had for building the new house and put it into this.' He pushed his hat to the back of his head and mopped his brow. 'Speculating in town allotments has been the end of more than one of the smaller land-owners, but this time it got him too.' He pulled a wry face. 'Mind you, it didn't help that the government chose that moment to ask him to pay up the port revenues he'd been collecting for them!'

An outcrop of rock, clothed in lush green foliage, ran down to the edge of the intended town site; on one face, someone had drawn in black and ochre pictures of wallabies and other animals. True to the topsy-turvy nature of the land, however, they had been drawn as if from the inside out, with every bone and sinew carefully delineated. In the shade of the rock, beside a little spring, they tethered the horses and sat to eat the provisions that Betsey had packed into two saddlebags.

'Does this spring run into Lacey's Creek?' asked Joshua through a mouthful of cured mutton and corn bread.

Garvey shook his head. 'Feeds a waterhole behind the rocks. The black men use it.'

'The natives? Hurvine said there weren't many of them left around here.'

Garvey gave a crack of laughter. 'Lord bless you, Mr Delahaye, you'll not get far on in society if you think the natives are the same as the black fellers!'

'Then who are – '

'The natives? Well, they're anyone – apart from the blacks – who was born here.' He leaned back and lit an evil-smelling pipe. 'Although truth to tell I don't think you'll hear Macarthur's sons, or their like, giving themselves the title, for all that they were born in the colony. They prefer to call themselves Merinos – pure born and pure bred like the sheep. The natives, now, they'd be mostly sons and daughters of the freed convicts, that's to say, children of the Currency, though to be sure, some natives are Sterling.' He saw the look of confusion on Joshua's face and laughed. 'You look puzzled, lad, as well you might. See, this colony has always been strong in the convict taint, so those who want to make the point that they aren't freed convicts, they call themselves Sterling – that means they're good anywhere in the world. The Currency, being freed convicts, are only good in the colony, see?'

'I was told that New South Wales was just like England removed across the seas,' said Joshua, 'but I can see it's nothing of the sort! Everything seems to be entirely miscalled. The blacks aren't natives...'

'That's true. Whatever tribe they come from, the blacks are – well, they're blacks. The older settlers sometimes call them Indians,' he added helpfully.

'... and what you call the Parramatta River is nothing but a sea creek, while the river that runs by the house is called, not Lacey's River but – '

'Lacey's Creek. Aye. There's a deal of things seem topsy-turvy when you first come out here – like high summer at Christmas and winter in June. They do say it's because of being on the bottom of the world, see. But, oh, you've not seen the half of it yet: pull the bung out of a barrel or the plug out of a basin and the water empties t'other way; the barometer rises before bad weather and falls before good; north is the hot wind, south the cold; the humblest house may be fitted up with cedar, fields are fenced with mahogany, and myrtle bushes are burned for fuel, although a carpenter back home would pay handsomely for all three.' He sucked on his pipe. 'Oh, and swans are black, eagles are white, and the mole lays eggs and has a bill like a duck.'

Joshua shook his head in disbelief 'Suddenly it doesn't seem so strange that a woman should sit at the head of the table!'

'Quiet!' said Garvey suddenly. 'There's someone behind you – no! Don't turn!'

Joshua felt the hairs rise on the back of his neck and knew he was being watched. He expected Garvey to reach for his gun, which lay conveniently close to hand, but instead the steward slowly laid his pipe aside and held his hands out in front of him, palms up.

From behind them came the harsh shriek of a bird, so loud it seemed to fill the bush and echo around the clearing. Moving very deliberately, Garvey cupped his hands around his mouth and made the same sound. After a moment more came a call of 'Coo-ee!' and Garvey returned the call.

'Is that you, Jackie?' he called softly, turning his head slowly.

Joshua sensed, rather than saw, a figure emerge from the thick undergrowth behind him, and stand in the shadows; it was hard to tell where shadow ended and figure began. Garvey rose in leisurely manner to his feet, gesturing to Joshua to stay where he was.

Joshua could hear behind him the low-voiced discussion and feel himself under scrutiny, an unnerving experience when you could not see the person scrutinising you. 'Feller Lacey's lady', he heard Garvey say at one point, and he turned and smiled rather inanely towards the shadows. When the conversation ended, he saw a brief flicker of movement and Garvey emerged from the bush.

'Time we were on our way,' he said, picking up his hat.

Joshua was curious to know what had just passed, but his companion had fallen silent; mindful of his lowly situation as an assigned convict, and knowing how dependent he was on the land steward to show him the ropes in this strange country, he forebore to interrupt his blue study.

'Water's more important than anything in this country,' said Garvey after they had ridden some way in silence. 'Fortunately

Lacey appreciated that. The bulk of our land forms a wedge between two watersheds. Lacey's Creek runs down into the Parramatta, but up in the hills behind us we have a small lake, more of a catchment really, and a creek that runs from it into the George River and on to Botany Bay. We have more land holdings there, but it's mainly swamp. And there are further holdings beyond the Nepean, around Bathurst, but there's no telling if that'll ever be useful land again since the great drought burned it out.'

'The Nepean?'

'River. Folk around here always speak of it as a separate watercourse, but it's only the upper reaches of the Hawkesbury.' He snapped off a dead branch and sketched out a rough design in the dry earth. 'D'ye remember, now, where we turned off the Penrith road?'

'Where the road gang was working?'

'Aye. That was the Nepean and on the other bank is Emu Plains – they'll have to be calling it something else soon, I guess, for Emu Plains is all sheep now and you've to go to the Botanical Gardens these days to see an emu! Anyways, Lacey's Creek has large holdings on Emu Plains too.' He looked at Joshua's tired face. 'It's a lot to take in,' he said, with a more friendly smile, 'but I'll show you it all on a proper map tonight.'

Joshua straightened himself up in the saddle, easing his stiff shoulder. 'The land seems very scattered,' he said.

'Aye. Lacey didn't buy it all in one go. Come to that, he generally didn't buy it at all.'

'Then how did he come to it?'

'Oh, a crafty man, was Lacey,' said Garvey with a grin. 'Hadn't the clout at first to buy up all the big chunks like the major landowners. So he went about it a different way and lent money to the dungaree farmers and the Emancipists. Back then they could get a little land grant when they'd served out their term. When the small farmer's crops failed in the dry or in the floods, Lacey moved in and took the land for the debt.

'Nobody saw what he was up to, building his own little empire out of bits and pieces, and before long Lacey held more land than anyone but Macarthur and one or two besides.' He pulled out a red pocket handkerchief and wiped the sweat from his face. 'The more water you can get out here, the better. Green enough now, being our spring, but before you say knife it can dry out and turn brown and the crops all die. But Lacey planned well; we've better-watered land than anywhere this side of the Hawkesbury – and I wouldn't farm on the Hawkesbury or the Hunter, not for all the tea in China! Flourish for four years and get drowned out the fifth.'

He saw Joshua shift uncomfortably in the saddle. 'Best be getting you home,' he said. 'Long time since you've been in the saddle and the mistress will have my hide if I bring you home saddle-sore and fit for nothing!'

Joshua coloured angrily and Garvey, remembering the separate bedrooms, regretted his little joke and fell silent. 'Anything else I can tell you before we get back to the settlement?' he asked after a while. 'Anything you want to know, ask me or the mistress. Doesn't do to ask the servants.'

Joshua found himself flushing again, but he was determined not to pass up on the opportunity. 'Explain to me, please,' he said, his voice grating with dryness, 'about the ticket of leave.'

'It's a kind of probation,' said Garvey. He paused a moment, chewing his lip as he mulled over the best way to put the matter. 'See, fifty years ago when convicts were transported to the American colonies, life meant life. Because they were being sent to a land that was already settled and not short of supplies. But out here it had to be different.'

The first governors, with so many mouths to feed and all supplies to be brought in from India, the Cape Colony or even England, eight months away, had looked for ways to get mouths off the government stores. If a man had been a cobbler or a brickmaker, there was little benefit to the community in sending him to break rocks or haul timber. If he behaved himself, better to give him a ticket of leave to ply his trade and keep himself on the proceeds.

'In the early days it was farmers they needed. James Ruse, the Cornishman, was the first: he was given his ticket of leave for planting out the first government farm. Then it was the women. If they'd had experience as a seamstress or a milliner, better to let them follow that trade than turn to prostitution, as so many did, the colony being so short of women.' He puffed reflectively at his pipe. 'The governors and the ministers of religion, they hold prostitution to be the main cause of crime; meself, I think it's more the drink. Anyway, it got to be that almost any woman with a trade, she'd get a ticket of leave and not have to do government service at all. And once she was earning, then maybe her husband would be released into her custody so she could keep him too. If either of 'em turned to crime again, of course, they'd be taken back into the system to serve out the original sentence.

'For the first twenty years or so, in New South Wales at least, almost any man or woman who wasn't a fool or a deep-dyed, hardened criminal – or plain unlucky – might get a chance to make a fresh start. Governor Macquarie was strong on fresh starts, but the Macarthurs and Reverend Marsden, they hated him for it. Pretty well hounded him out of office. Darling was much more their style of governor and under him tickets of leave have been few and far between, and then only after a fair part of the sentence has been served first.'

'Then how – ?'

Garvey shook his head. 'Oh, to be sure I don't know how your wife did it, but I'm full of admiration for her. She's a plucky little fighter.' He looked sideways at Joshua. 'Strikes me,' he said, 'that when she's set on something she won't stop till she's got it.'


Joshua stopped in the doorway, brought up short by the sight of two middle-aged women sitting either side of the Calcutta needlework rug before the empty fireplace, poker-straight on the silk-covered sofas.

'Joshua! Mr Garvey! You have come to pay your respects to the ladies?'

Joshua took an instinctive step back, but before he could make his escape, a rough hand in the small of his back pushed him into the drawing room.

'You remember Mr Garvey, my steward?' said Kat in what Joshua recognised as her best Lady Isabelle manner. 'Joshua, this is Mrs Thomas – the Thomas land runs alongside ours on Prospect Creek – and her sister Mrs Lassiter from Cabramatta.'

He bowed stiffly over each lady's hand and muttered something that might have been 'delighted'.

'Well, well!' exclaimed Mrs Thomas. 'Now we have it at last! You could have saved us all a great deal of perplexity, my dear Mrs Delahaye, if you had worn your ring in the first place and told us all about your delightful husband.'

Joshua's eyes flew to Kat's left hand, where the cheap ring that the Quaker had bought for them shone out on her slender ring finger.

'It was not my intention to cause anyone perplexity,' said Kat.

'But of course you did!' said Mrs Lassiter, rather more arch than her sister. 'Why, Lieutenant Standish all but called young Mr Murray out Thursday last, at Mrs Huntingdon's soirée – '

'– for Murray would insist your name was Delahaye,' interrupted Mrs Thomas, 'and young Standish swore he had sailed out with you as Miss Revel. When he suggested there might be a mystery, Murray was all for calling him out!'

'To defend your honour.'

Kattrin fixed Mrs Thomas with a stern gaze. 'I thank Mr Murray for his concern, but I need no one but my husband to defend my honour. Not that I believe it was at all necessary on this occasion.'

'But you'll allow, my dear ma'am, that the mystery – '

'There is no mystery,' said Kat coolly. 'The voyage was booked by my brother, before I was wed.'

'At last we know what precious keepsake was on that chain tucked so carefully in your bosom,' said Mrs Lassiter.

'The ring was loose on my finger,' said Kat with a smile, 'and there was no time to have it tightened before we sailed.'

'I do not recall seeing the notice of your wedding,' persisted Mrs Thomas, unwilling to be robbed of her mystery.

'And we have all the papers sent out,' said her sister, acting as chorus.

'There was no notice,' said Kat. 'The marriage took place privately, following a family bereavement.'

There was a little more small talk and arrangements made to meet again at the Government House soirée, then the ladies, smiling archly on Joshua and twitting him on putting all the young men's noses out of joint, took their leave, escorted to the door by Garvey.

As they left in Jenkins's wake, Joshua turned angrily on Kat, a muscle twitching in his cheek. 'How could you throw me into such a situation?'

'It would have caused gossip if I had not,' she said in some surprise. 'Besides, you will see them anyway when we dine with Sir Patrick Lindesay. He's running the colony until the new governor arrives.'

'Convicts do not dine out with the head of government.'

'Well, this one does!' she snapped, rising to face him. 'Sir Patrick has commanded your attendance. I don't know whether he realises you're a ticket-of-leave man, but it appears Mr Brymer is having difficulties with his steam manufactory and is eager to make your acquaintance.'

Joshua cursed under his breath and gave her to understand that Mr Brymer and his manufactory could go their way, severally and collectively, to hell.

She forced herself with difficulty to remain calm. 'It is unusual, I'll allow, to enter society quite so soon, and more than I ever dared to hope, but a command is a command.' She fiddled with the bunch of keys at her waist. 'I beg you not to refuse, Joshua, for your own sake.'

'I am at your command,' he said through gritted teeth.

Garvey reappeared in the doorway. 'I was coming to give you me report,' he said, feeling the tension in the air, 'but I could come back.'

She motioned impatiently for him to come in.

'Am I now dismissed?' demanded Joshua, tight-lipped.

'Assume you are at liberty to come and go at any time, unless I tell you otherwise,' she said, grinding her teeth.

As he left the room she turned swiftly away towards the window, but not before Garvey had seen the tears in her eyes. 'Ah now, don't

'There is no mystery,' said Kat coolly. 'The voyage was booked by my brother, before I was wed.'

'At last we know what precious keepsake was on that chain tucked so carefully in your bosom,' said Mrs Lassiter.

'The ring was loose on my finger,' said Kat with a smile, 'and there was no time to have it tightened before we sailed.'

'I do not recall seeing the notice of your wedding,' persisted Mrs Thomas, unwilling to be robbed of her mystery.

'And we have all the papers sent out,' said her sister, acting as chorus.

'There was no notice,' said Kat. 'The marriage took place privately, following a family bereavement.'

There was a little more small talk and arrangements made to meet again at the Government House soirée, then the ladies, smiling archly on Joshua and twitting him on putting all the young men's noses out of joint, took their leave, escorted to the door by Garvey.

As they left in Jenkins's wake, Joshua turned angrily on Kat, a muscle twitching in his cheek. 'How could you throw me into such a situation?'

'It would have caused gossip if I had not,' she said in some surprise. 'Besides, you will see them anyway when we dine with Sir Patrick Lindesay. He's running the colony until the new governor arrives.'

'Convicts do not dine out with the head of government.'

'Well, this one does!' she snapped, rising to face him. 'Sir Patrick has commanded your attendance. I don't know whether he realises you're a ticket-of-leave man, but it appears Mr Brymer is having difficulties with his steam manufactory and is eager to make your acquaintance.'

Joshua cursed under his breath and gave her to understand that Mr Brymer and his manufactory could go their way, severally and collectively, to hell.

She forced herself with difficulty to remain calm. 'It is unusual, I'll allow, to enter society quite so soon, and more than I ever dared to hope, but a command is a command.' She fiddled with the bunch of keys at her waist. 'I beg you not to refuse, Joshua, for your own sake.'

'I am at your command,' he said through gritted teeth.

Garvey reappeared in the doorway. 'I was coming to give you me report,' he said, feeling the tension in the air, 'but I could come back.'

She motioned impatiently for him to come in.

'Am I now dismissed?' demanded Joshua, tight-lipped.

'Assume you are at liberty to come and go at any time, unless I tell you otherwise,' she said, grinding her teeth.

As he left the room she turned swiftly away towards the window, but not before Garvey had seen the tears in her eyes. 'Ah now, don't

283

# Chapter Fifteen

The door of the town house in Sydney's most fashionable thorough-fare was opened by a slender young footman in knee breeches who ushered them across highly polished ironbark floors into the drawing room; he took Kat's wrap and served them each with a glass of sherry before bowing himself out.

Kat crossed to the ornate gilt-framed mirror above the fireplace to untie the ribbons of her fashionable Clarence-blue capote and tidy away a few stray golden tendrils that had been whipped from under the bonnet by the stiff sea breezes. In the reflection she caught sight of Joshua, handsome in his coat of blue cloth, scowling down into his glass. Garvey had finally persuaded him to set aside his stiff-necked pride by reminding him that Sir Patrick, should he take offence at Joshua's absence, had it in his power to recall his ticket of leave.

'It's a good sherry, Joshua,' she said tersely, turning back into the room. 'I doubt it will poison you.'

He had been unaware of her scrutiny. 'I felt the fellow's eyes boring into me,' he said lamely. 'No doubt wondering what a felon like me is doing in his master's drawing room.'

'You *are* his master,' said Garvey with a chuckle.

Joshua's brows snapped together as he turned to Kat. 'You mean . . . this is your property too?'

'Our property, Joshua,' said Kat. She struggled to suppress the anger in her voice, and wondered how much longer she could go on like this.

'I have no property,' he growled. 'I am a convict.'

'You could write that out on a broadsheet and give it to the town crier,' said Garvey, putting his glass down on the carved and inlaid sideboard with such force that the crystal rang. 'It would save you the monotony of repeating it forty times a day!'

An embarrassed silence followed the steward's unexpected out-burst. 'You're right to suppose that the footman's eyes were boring into you,' said Kat after a moment. 'He'd be trying to work out where you keep your wallet and your watch. It's a habit he can't break, though I understand it's some time since he actually took anything.'

'Sure, an' he always owns up to it,' said Garvey, regaining his customary cheerfulness in a moment. 'And hands it back too.'

'You have a thief for a footman?' asked Joshua, momentarily diverted.

'Timothy was one of the best dips in London before he became a cracksman,' said Kat. 'A real boman prig with rum daddles, so he tells me.'

'Rum *what*?'

'What a sheltered life we led in Wooburn!' she said, laughter dancing in her green-gold eyes. 'I'm told it means he had a skilful pair of hands for the job. He says he ought to have stuck to picking pockets, for the safe-breaking was his undoing.'

'How can you talk about it so calmly?'

'I am much envied for having London forgers and pickpockets for my house servants. They are considered vastly preferable to what they call the "barn-door gentlemen": country bumpkins who fall over the furniture and don't know how to serve at table. Even at Government House you may well be waited on by thieves, horse-stealers and pickpockets.'

'Hardly the same as convicts in the drawing room, however.'

She shrugged. 'There are some Emancipists with whom the stiffer society ladies will have nothing to do, but to expect the Merinos to mix with men like Simeon Lord and Samuel Terry would be like expecting Lady Isabelle to socialise with the blacksmith!' She ran her finger round the rim of her sherry glass. 'But others are widely received. Francis Greenway for one.'

'Architect.' He remembered the name.

'Designed the convict barracks at Hyde Park,' said Garvey. 'And St James's Church – the one we just passed. He was Macquarie's architect, for all he was sent out here as a convict, just like you.'

'Forgery,' said Kat, suppressing a smile at the surprise on Joshua's face. 'I want to ask his advice on some alterations to the plans for the new house. I know you worked on the new mill at Clapton Revel and I'd welcome your assistance.'

'I'll fetch the plans along and we can take a look at them,' said Garvey. 'Then you'll know what we're talking about.'

'But an architect would be an exceptional case,' said Joshua, refusing to be convinced.

'They have so few practical men of any kind out here; the colony lacks engineers, bridge builders – '

'And we've no one at all who understands machinery,' said Garvey from the doorway. 'That's why it took so long to get that damned steamship on the river an' why the steam mill is out of use more often than it's in. Sure, and no one cares any more that Greenway was transported for forgery; likewise, anyone who can get the steam mill working again will be excused a great deal.'

Before they had a chance to study the plans, there was a knock on the street door and Timothy announced the first of a stream of visitors. Half of Sydney, it seemed, had decided to take a stroll down George Street and drop in to see if the Delahayes were at home. Word of her new status had travelled fast – news confirmed to the eagle-eyed by the gilt-edged invitation tucked into the frame of the mantel mirror, requesting the presence of Mr and Mrs Joshua Delahaye at Government House on the morrow. The less well-bred of the ladies spent the earlier part of the visit craning round the knot of men to try for a better view of Joshua; the men, however, seemed unperturbed by anything they might have heard of the new man and swept him into the conversation. Whether he would or no, Joshua found him-self catapulted into the social stream, lending an ear to the problems of sheep infestation with one man, or hearing of the growing problem of bushrangers from another. There was a great deal of talk too about the whaling trade, which, together with sealing and timber, formed the mainstay of the New South Wales economy, but to that he could contribute little.

'I've been trying to persuade your wife to invest in the South Sea island trade,' said Hilton, a bluff man with a rolling gait who looked as though he had just this moment stepped off one of his own trading ships. 'Lacey invested very heavily in shipping; the maritime business has always been first in the colony.'

'Trade of the past,' said Hughes dismissively. 'More land – that's what you should be buying. It's there for the taking, now they've stopped the folly of land grants to the Emancipists. Mark my words, now the interior has been opened up, we'll be making even more of our money off the sheep's back.'

'Pooh, pooh!' said a third. 'You've been listening too long to old Macarthur. Wool may have its corner of the trade but I tell you, Delahaye, 'twill never overtake the sea trade in importance. The colony is naturally a maritime one. Newcastle, Port Macquarie ... want to get to any of 'em, you have to go by sea.'

'No one I know wants to get to 'em at all!' said Hughes. 'Damned holes, all on 'em, full of nothing but sand, ants and conv-, er, government men.'

'Some good timber there, though,' Hilton observed. 'Tropical up there – quite different conditions, they say. I tell you, Hughes, however far inland we spread, we'll always cling to the sea.'

Joshua knew a brief moment of panic as Garvey was taken off into a corner by two men to discuss the business of the Agricultural Society, but whenever matters threatened to become awkward, Kat was always at hand. 'My husband has scarce been here long enough to form an opinion, Mr Hilton,' she would say, or, 'We shall be eager to hear the new governor's opinions on that, Mr Edgar.'

In between eavesdropping on Joshua's conversations, Kat served tea and kept up her end of the conversation with the ladies. Sydney conversation was rarely demanding. Few of her female visitors would have been at ease at Bosingham House, where conversation might encompass politics, the latest novel, music or the theatre. In the colony there were no plays since Governor Darling had withdrawn Mr Levey's licence and little music apart from the military bands; politics was held to be fit only for the men to discuss. When the ladies had finished admiring her dress and quizzing her on the latest fashions at home in England, they moved on to their favourite topic: the difficulties of finding – and keeping – sober servants; once they had started on that, there was little more for her to do than make encouraging noises and leave them to rattle on. Cooks, with their ready access to the pantry and the cellar were the worst, and every woman present had a story to tell. Mrs Carter, a lady with die-away airs and a shabby-genteel accent that grated on the ear, whose chief preoccupation was ensuring that her husband, a meek little draper from Coventry who had made a fortune financing whaling ships in the Bass Straits, was not overlooked by Sydney society, returned to the story of her cook and Colonel O'Connell's Christmas visit, undeterred by the barely stifled yawns of those who had heard it all before.

'We were entertaining Sir Maurice and the Attorney and their wives, and as you know, I pride myself on my dinners, but the time went by and there was no sign of the food. At last I went to the kitchen and there was the goose and the beef a-charring in the oven. Everything scorched black, and no trace of the cook! I was like to have hee-sterics, my dear, *as* you can imagine, with the Attorney and his cousin, and his wife only just come from England. 'Twas the butler what salvaged the dinner in the end – though I vow and declare I did not know where to look when Lady Mary complimented me on the sauces. I found the cook hours after, flat on her back in the cellar, dead drunk and snoring fit to bring the house down.'

'That's convict servants for you!' agreed Mrs Hogarth.

It was Kat's experience that there were good and sober women to be found in the colony if you looked for them: women who had been brought down by adversity in England, too often compounded by their exploitation on the transports or by the overseers, but who would respond to any kindness shown them with honesty and hard

288

work. Jenny and Meggie were prime examples. She glanced nervously across at Joshua as she poured more tea, but she need not have worried, for Joshua was deep in a discussion with Nathaniel Brymer about the relative advantages of steam mills and tide mills.

'We have the same problems with our coachman,' lamented Mrs Brymer, in girlish tones that sat ill with her stout figure. 'Sober as a judge when he's with the horses, but he cannot be trusted to drive home from a party. Drunk on the box every time,' she went on, helping herself to another ratafia biscuit.

'Nothing is as bad as the housemaids,' said Mrs Hogarth with a sniff. 'Why, one of Lady Brisbane's maids was so addicted to spirits that she would drink camphorated spirits or a pint of hartshorn – even eau de Cologne or lavender water – if she couldn't get rum!'

'If only they would send us out some decent English emigrants!'

Kat could barely suppress a sigh of relief when Mrs Carter, who knew to the last second the proper timing of every social call, began the exodus, surging to her feet in a cloud of violet perfume and dragging her husband away in mid-speech. At last the knocker fell silent.

'Do you dine with the Carters?' asked Joshua as the door closed behind the last visitor. He lifted an eyebrow. 'Is their new cook an improvement on the old?'

Kat turned away from the window. 'She still has the same one.'

Joshua looked at her in astonishment.

'You don't realise the hold the servants have over their mistresses out here,' she explained. 'Few convict servants pay any regard to their mistresses; they can be as insolent as they please, even swear at them, knowing it will never come to the master's ears.'

'Why not?'

Kat primmed up her face behind her fan. '"My dea-ah, I could not *possibly* sully my lips with such words,"' she said, her die-away air a wickedly accurate parody of Mrs Carter. 'I promise you, three ladies at least have said as much to me! They won't punish their servants themselves – too unladylike – and they won't repeat their words to their husbands so that they can deal with it!'

'They can't handle their servants the way she does,' said Garvey when Kat had left the room to consult with the Chinese cook. 'We don't often get quality out here, as you'll maybe have noticed. It's the same with the administration – the colony is not seen as one of the prime appointments and so we get military men from the lesser regiments. Occasionally we strike lucky, as we did with Macquarie – someone who has talent, but can't afford to buy a decent commission at home. More often we get the incompetent officer whose career has ground to a halt in England – maybe because his wife thought herself grander than the colonel's lady. If it's a provincial miss giving herself airs and graces, the servants soon realise it.' He chuckled. 'Mind you, not many women could establish their authority the way the missus did. Thought we'd have a riot on our hands for sure once she took down the triangle, but she made her mark, by God she did!'

Joshua was intrigued, but before he could discover more, Garvey was called away, leaving Joshua with a handful of letters and some journals.

'Missus thought you should know what's been happening while you were on the high seas,' said the steward. 'And when you've finished them, there's Hall's *Monitor* and Wentworth's *Australian* to give you a notion of what concerns people out here.'

When he had read the letters from Leicestershire and put his mind at rest about those he had left behind, he turned to the *Times*, four months old, of course, full of details of Russell's long overdue proposals for a Reform Bill. There was news too of the countrywide agitation for pardon for the five hundred men transported after the previous year's troubles. Ironically, the calls for pardon were led very often by the very magistrates and farmers who had in the first place laid the charges. Perhaps the sight of five hundred broken and starving families had been too much, even for them.

When the bell rang to dress for dinner, Joshua followed the footman down the corridor, to be shown into a room far grander than the one he occupied at Lacey's Creek: the walls were panelled with cedar and hung with paintings in ornately carved and gilded frames and the large four-poster bed was draped with silk embroidered nets. A jug of hot water had been set out for him on the washstand in the dressing room, with a freshly stropped razor, and his evening clothes were laid out on the bed. A lingering hint of perfume suggested this was a shared dressing room and that Kat's bedchamber lay through the far door, in an arrangement similar to that at Lacey's Creek.

Anxious to avoid a repetition of the previous evening, Kat had bidden the steward dine with them and the evening passed fairly comfortably. As they ate the delicious food prepared by the Chinese cook, who had been transported for some dereliction of duty to an English master in Singapore, Kat and Garvey discussed Sydney politics, hopes for the new governor, and the slow progress they were making in recovering the furniture and plate which had been taken by Lacey's creditors from both the town house and the settlement.

'Someone said today that you had interests in shipping,' said Joshua.

'The lawyers are still working out just how many of Lacey's

interests passed to me, but apart from the land, this house and the ships, he had an interest in pearl-fishing, a mine in Van Diemen's Land, sandalwood cutting in the South Seas and some flax fields in New Zealand . . .'

'Then there's the factory extracting soda from seaweed and tannin from bark,' Garvey reminded her.

'Oh, and the rope manufactory.'

'So you see why she looked as dazed as you when she first came out,' said Garvey.

'She had good reason!' exclaimed Joshua.

'I thought she'd go into a decline in those first few days,' said the steward, 'until she drew the pistols on the servants.'

Of course Joshua demanded to hear the story and she related, reluctantly and with a deprecating smile, how she had assembled the servants and given them the demonstration of marksmanship.

'But you don't even know how to shoot!' he protested.

'Dickon always showed me anything he learned, so I had the rudiments. But he refused to book my passage until I had mastered firearms.' She turned her wide golden gaze on him. 'Oh, there were so many things I didn't know then. If it hadn't been for the riots, perhaps I would just have gone on as I was and never known any difference. But I'm not that girl any more, Joshua. I've grown up a great deal. I've had to.'

Soon after dinner, Kat rose from the table and shut herself in the library to write letters, leaving the two men to pore over Lacey's plans.

'I'm beginning to think I never knew her at all,' said Joshua sombrely, as the steward explained to him over a glass of brandy the alterations she wanted to make.

'In this country everyone changes,' said Garvey. 'Some for the better, others for the worse. Out here, with no family to look out for her, she'd to fight or go under.'

'But to draw a gun on the servants! Surely she would not have used it?'

'You'd know that better than me,' said Garvey with a sidelong glance. 'Mark you, I dare say the mistress would have won them over anyway in the end. She has the common touch. It generally succeeds.' With all but you, he added to himself.

Kat sat at the dressing table, her peignoir round her shoulders, brushing her hair as Meggie hung the discarded clothes in the dressing alcove.

She had been a fool to include Garvey in the dinner this evening, she told herself, pulling so vigorously at a tangle that she brought

291

tears to her eyes. Tomorrow was the soirée at Government House and how was she ever going to set everything right between her and Joshua if there was always someone else present?

The door slid open on well-oiled hinges and Joshua stood in the doorway with a look of anger on his face.

She laid down the ivory-backed brush with an unsteady hand. 'Leave that now, Meggie,' she said, struggling to keep her voice calm. 'I won't be needing you again. Good-night.' The sound of the door closing behind the maid echoed off the panelled walls and fell into the silence between them.

'There is some mistake?' said Joshua at last.

'No,' she said through stiff, dry lips. 'This is our room.'

His eyes raked the room and came to rest on the double bed on the far wall. 'Then I am to sleep here? Those are your orders?'

She willed herself not to cry out at the coldness in his voice. 'Joshua – please! Lacey's creditors stripped the house and the guest rooms are still unfurnished.'

'Then it seems I have little choice,' he said.

She rose in one swift movement and padded across the floor in her bare feet. He drew in his breath sharply as she stopped in front of him, her pale hair rippling over her shoulders and lying on the soft silk of her peignoir, which emphasised rather than hid the curves of her body. 'You have a choice,' she said through gritted teeth. 'A couch can be set up in the dressing room. Or in Garvey's room. Ring for a servant – if you want to humiliate me completely.'

'Ah, Kat, don't!' Instinctively he put his hand on her arm and felt the self-control slipping away from him at the sensation of warm flesh through the silk.

He dropped his hand as if he had been burned and leaned against the dressing table, eyes tightly closed, fighting down the desire to take her into his arms and carry her to the bed and make love to her as he had on that disastrous, drunken night in the filth and squalor of Aylesbury gaol. It would be so easy to throw his scruples to the wind, to accept her sacrifice and let her ruin her life to save his. As he unclenched his fists, his hand knocked aside the ivory brush; underneath, with bright strands of hair trailing across it, was a letter in Kat's spiky hand, addressed to Lord Godstowe.

'You must leave all this behind and go back to England.' The words were harsh; he had forced all emotion from his voice. 'I'll give you an annulment. You'll be able to start again.' He lifted the letter from the dressing table with a hand that seemed reluctant to do his bidding, an unbearable pain tearing through his heart. 'You could marry Godstowe,' he said, flinging the letter down on the bed. 'How long have you been writing to him?'

'Every week since I came out here.' She saw the contempt on his face and almost wished she had lied. 'But it's not what you think, Joshua. It's an official letter, not personal!'

'Don't treat me like a fool. You've not given up on him, nor he on you. Go back to England! Few here will have the entree to Godstowe's world, so you'll be able to pretend none of this ever happened.'

'There's nothing for me in England, Joshua! A father who has disowned me, a mother who can't even look after herself. At least here I can make some sort of life. And I will, Joshua,' she said, eyes flashing angrily. 'With or without you.' She shrugged the peignoir from her shoulders and slipped under the netting.

She heard him moving about the room, then the splash of water in the dressing room, and held her breath as she sensed rather than saw him at the side of the bed looking down at her. He snuffed out all but one of the candles. After a moment the mosquito netting trembled, the mattress dipped, and she felt him settle under the covers. She lay still, hoping against hope that he would reach out, if only to kiss her goodnight.

When he gave no sign of even acknowledging her presence she found herself frantically making excuses for him: He's still tired, still shocked, remember how you felt when you first stepped ashore after the voyage.

'Goodnight, Joshua,' she said at last.

Silence.

After a moment she risked a peep over her shoulder. Joshua was lying on the furthest edge of the mattress with his back to her. She stuffed her fingers into her mouth to stifle the howl of grief that welled up in her throat and the warm, bitter tears washed down her face and fell in little pools on the crisp embroidered linen.

He was still asleep the next morning when she woke; he had rolled a little further towards the centre, but still, even in sleep, held himself rigidly away from all contact. She would have given anything to be able to take him in her arms and smooth out the furrows between his eyes; her hand went out to him, but at the last moment she snatched it back.

They spent most of the day avoiding each other, only meeting up again in the bed-room. Walking in on Kat just as Meggie tightened the lacing on her satin under-robe, Joshua made to retreat.

'Meggie, ring for hot water for Mr Delahaye,' said Kat, barely looking up from buffing her nails. She rose to her feet in a cloud of cream satin held out over layers of stiffened muslin and leant towards the mirror to brush away an imagined speck. 'My robe, Meggie,' she said impatiently and the girl hurried back from the bell pull to pass the embroidered amber satin dress over her coiffure. 'I will see you downstairs, Joshua,' she said coolly, as Meggie straightened the low-cut bodice *à la coeur* over her bosom and puffed out the short blonde lace sleeves. 'The carriage comes in half an hour.'

The intention had been to welcome the new governor with a ball, but when General Sir Richard Bourke failed to arrive in time, it was decided to hold an entertainment anyway; although no one was bold enough to put it in words, it was widely felt to be as much a celebration of the departure of the unpopular Darling as of the arrival of Bourke. In case that was not reason enough, the colony recalled that it had not yet celebrated the King's coronation.

'Always supposin' the ould feller lived long enough to be crowned,' said Garvey with a smirk. 'It'll be months before we know for certain. Last year at the King's Birthday Ball they were toasting King George's health when he'd already been dead for weeks! Not that I was there, of course. Never an Emancipist to be seen at Governor Darling's entertainments.'

They rolled past the castellated stables, the only part of Greenway's grand design for a new Government House to have been built, and along the sandy road through the Domain. Despite the absence of the new governor – as far as anyone knew, still on the high seas on his way to the colony – no effort had been spared in decorating Government House for the ball. The long verandah where the guests alighted from their carriages was lined with colourful and sweet-scented flowers and shrubs, and lit by lanterns engraved and enamelled with Australian figures and landscapes and suspended from the ceiling. On the terrace in front of the verandah was an illuminated tent, with one of the regimental bands playing within. Some of the many partnerless men would spend their time drinking there, which was fortunate, for although the ballroom had been much enlarged, it was always very crowded. It had been a great disappointment to Darling that the rebuilding of the governor's residence had never progressed beyond the ballroom; it had been even more disappointing for Mrs Darling, who, to almost universal derision, had been awarded first prize in the competition for the new design.

A footman hurried forward to lower the step and Joshua handed Kat down from the carriage. There was no time for private speech: she had but a moment to shake out her skirts and gather her wits together before they were ushered through the doors. She stole a glance at Joshua, handsome in his coat of blue superfine, white waistcoat and jet-black trousers; his snowy-white cravat was well tied and anchored by a small plain brooch which Dickon had given her when they parted on the dockside. She wished Joshua would smile; the frozen expression he had worn since his arrival in Sydney gave him an appearance of aloofness that was at odds with his normally warm nature.

As they passed down the line of officials and dignitaries, it seemed as if dozens of pairs of eyes were boring into them; as they drew level with Colonel Sir Patrick Lindesay and his wife, the whispers swelled behind them. She could feel Joshua bristling at her side and tucked her hand into his arm. Perhaps it was not what he wanted, but it made her feel happier.

Sir Patrick, the acting governor, offered a few stilted words of greeting to her and then his eyes, passing over Joshua as if he were not there, had already moved on to Garvey and the couple behind him.

Etiquette dictated that she should now make way, but Kat, aware that this first appearance in Sydney society would make Joshua's position or break it, stood her ground.

'May I present my husband, Sir Patrick?' she said, her knees trembling. 'Joshua Delahaye, late of Wooburn, on the recommendation of – '

'Of Sir Anthony Cawfield,' said Sir Patrick curtly. 'I have read the correspondence from the Colonial Office.' He favoured Joshua with the smallest of bows, and the lady at his side inclined her head a fraction.

It was as much as she could hope for. Kat favoured them both with a brilliant smile and moved on. Next in line to the Acting Governor was Sir Maurice O'Connell, commander of the colony's military forces, and his wife, Mary, daughter to Bligh of the *Bounty*. Sir Maurice bowed warmly over Kat's hand, giving every appearance of welcoming the introduction to Joshua, and Lady Mary favoured them both with a weary smile. In swift succession, Kat presented her husband to the other leading figures in the colony, some in dress uniforms, their chests heavy with gold braid, others in formal dark coats. Only one, Dr Redfern, greeted Joshua with any great warmth, and only one, Archdeacon Scott, cut him dead.

Throughout the introductions, Joshua tried to hold his head high, keep his tongue between his teeth and a smile fixed to his lips. It helped that he knew a little about some of them from Kat and Garvey.

'You'll meet people there this evening who in England wouldn't be admitted to Bosingham House even for a political dinner, let alone a government reception,' she'd said in the carriage.

'But what if they ask me about my past? Whether or no it is true I was transported?'

'No one will. That Sir Patrick has commanded your attendance should be enough for them. Should anyone be so ill-bred as to ask you to your face, simply refer them to Sir Richard Bourke. No one will be fool enough to antagonise the new governor before he's even arrived! Beyond that, all you have to do is follow my lead.'

Joshua and Ned Garvey stood inside the door, halfway down the room, waiting for Kattrin, who had withdrawn to tidy her hair, to rejoin them.

'A few more Emancipists here than there have been for a while,' observed Garvey, who had not been invited to Government House since General Darling had taken over from Brisbane. 'It could be a good sign for the future. Though not if the Merinos have their way.' He looked down the room to where the Exclusives had gathered, the younger Macarthurs and the other great landowners frowning coldly on those they deemed unworthy of their attention. The introductions having been made, Sydney society was dividing, as it always did, into two distinct groupings. 'Will you look at those fine folk now, pulling their skirts aside from the great unwashed and looking down their noses?'

'And I've taken her from one end of the room to the other,' said Joshua gloomily.

'I think you'll find we can still go where we want,' said Garvey cheerfully. 'It helps that she was so much sought after before you came, though to be sure, among our leading citizens, *what has he*, rather than *what is he*, is all too often the test. And Lacey's Creek counts for a great deal, even before you consider the other aspects.'

Before Joshua had a chance to ask about these 'other aspects', Kat rejoined them on the arm of Wentworth, the editor of the *Australian*, who had also been conspicuously absent from Darling's table in recent years, owing to his talent for embracing everything that Darling opposed.

William Charles Wentworth was one of the most influential of Sydney's citizens; as a young man, along with Gregory and Blaxland, he had found the way across the previously impenetrable Blue Mountains to open up the rich grazing land of the interior. Son of D'Arcy Wentworth, surgeon and prosperous landowner who claimed kinship with the powerful Fitzwilliams, William had once dreamed of marrying John Macarthur's daughter, but his dreams had come to naught when word had got back to the Macarthurs that D'Arcy as a young man had escaped the gallows on charges of highway robbery only by informing the justices that he had already booked passage to Botany Bay; what was worse, he had fathered William on a convict woman on the voyage. Foiled in his ambitions to unite the two propertied families, and infuriated by the slur on his birth, William had promptly espoused the Emancipist cause against the Exclusives, and done his best to emulate his father by peopling Sydney with his bastards.

A powerful man with a large frame and leonine head, the editor seemed disposed to be gracious to Joshua, but though they exchanged polite greetings, there was something about the way Wentworth contrived to watch Kat out of the corner of his eye while he was talking to the others that put Joshua on his guard.

The introductions over, they were making their way with some difficulty across the crowded ballroom floor when the band, hidden behind an array of greenery and foliage in a large alcove, began to play. Kat was immediately solicited to dance by a fair-haired young man in scarlet regimentals.

'Nonsense!' came a voice behind them, and they turned to see the white-haired figure of Dr Redfern at their shoulder. 'What's the world coming to if a man can't have the first dance with his wife on his honeymoon?'

'Fie upon you, Dr Redfern,' said Kat, holding her fan before her face, 'would you make me blush? 'Tis nigh on ten months since we were wed!' She peeped flirtatiously up at Joshua from behind the fan.

'Follow my lead' she had said. 'Ten months!' said Joshua, gazing down on his wife with a sigh and trying not to think how much she reminded him at this moment of Philomena Bosingham. 'Though 'tis true that cruel fate has kept us apart for too long!'

'Quite!' Redfern smiled benevolently upon them. 'So we may consider you yet in your honeymoon month! You'll allow them the first dance together, Swinton, I hope?'

No man, convict or free, would willingly offend Dr Redfern, one of the most popular men in the colony. He was known for his ready humanity to any suffering soul who needed him, in the early years tending both governor's lady and convict family, yet he had an irascible temper which had not improved with age. The young officer bowed with an assumption of good grace and agreed to defer his request to the second set.

There was nothing for it but for Joshua to take Kat in his arms and lead her onto the floor. His heart was pounding as he placed his arm around her waist and glided around the room; though it was not the first time that they had danced together, it had always been for him a mixed blessing, reminding him of how much his body desired her, while his brain knew that he could never have her. And now that he had her, he knew he could not take her. Pride that would not let him see a ticket-of-leave man as an equal to a landowner, obstinacy that could not let him accept his freedom from her hands, and a twisted sense of honour that spurred him to drive her back into Godstowe's arms, still stood between them.

Kat had forgotten what a graceful dancer Joshua was. Her heart sang as she swept around the floor in his arms, and the pain and the hurt of the past year seemed to fade a little as his dark eyes gazed down at her. When they had danced down the room, an elderly man with a broad blue riband across his chest, somewhat the worse for drink, stumbled and lurched towards them, towing his hapless partner with him; Joshua tightened his grip on Kat and whisked her skilfully from under the drunkard's feet.

For a moment the swirling dancers around them seemed to freeze, the loud voices to cease, and while the band held a long, high note their eyes locked and they clung to each other so tightly that each could feel the other's heart beat. Kat dared not speak, dared not move, lest she break the spell; she wanted this moment to last for ever. Then Joshua's eyelids dropped over his dark eyes and when he opened them again the warmth had faded from his smile and that brief ecstatic moment was gone.

At the end of the dance he led her back to the little gilt chairs at the edge of the ballroom, but she had no chance to take her seat, for Swinton was there waiting for her, and after him a constant stream of men, young and old, all clamouring for a dance. She was young, she was pretty, and women were in very short supply.

The room grew hotter and hotter, the smell of the overheated bodies only slightly offset by the expensive imported perfumes from which Sir Patrick had had the sense to remove the heavy duties imposed by Darling. Joshua was debating whether anyone would notice if he slipped out to the verandah when he became aware that someone was watching him. Turning his head slightly he saw out of the corner of his eye two young ladies, rather overdressed even by Sydney's standards, sitting with an older woman; around them milled a group of younger officers and a few older civilians vying rather too loudly for the honour of leading the women into the set of quadrilles being formed up. The two younger women seemed to be discussing him, whispering to each other behind their fans; one, her pretty lilac robe marred by a profusion of knots and ribbons and silk flowers, caught his eye and winked boldly at him. Joshua turned his head away sharply and began to make his way around the edge of the ballroom to the verandah doors.

'You can't expect to have your wife to yourself all evening, Delahaye,' said Dr Redfern, appearing at his elbow with two cooling glasses of wine.

'I am aware – '

'Then wipe that scowl off your face, man, and lead someone else onto the floor.'

'I don't know anyone.'

'I'll introduce you.'

'You had better save your efforts, sir. I had rather not risk a rebuff.'

'My friend Garvey tells me you were somewhat reluctant to come this evening. I can sympathise with your predicament – '

'I doubt it,' growled Joshua.

Redfern's lips twitched. 'If you will not dance then let us drink,' he said, 'and I'll tell you who everyone is.' Joshua sat in silence, a scowl on his face, and Redfern craned round the dancers to see Kat in deep conversation with Wentworth. 'Oho! Not jealous of the Friend of the Emancipists, are you?'

'Is that what they call him? From what I've seen, he's a deal more interested in their wives than in their rights.'

'A little of both,' said Redfern, whose own friend, the Emanicipist lawyer Edward Eagar, had been cuckolded by the newspaper editor. 'But his appeal is to bored and foolish women. Your wife is not foolish and it is for you to see that she is not bored. That's Mackaness who's just joined them,' he continued. 'Good sound lawyer. He was sheriff until Wentworth dragged him into the quarrel with Governor Darling. Garvey told you about that?'

Joshua shook his head.

'We held a Turf Club dinner a few years back, when the troubles with General Darling were just beginning. Wentworth was holding forth about Darling's shortcomings, as usual. Then someone proposed a toast to 'Australian exports'. And someone else yelled, "And may Governor Darling be the first of 'em!" Well, you can imagine the uproar: cheers, jeers, hip-hurrahs! And then, to top it all, the band played "Over the Hills and Far Away". His shoulders shook at the memory. 'But Mackaness was chairman of the Turf Club and Darling blamed him for it. Couldn't rest till he'd closed down the club and turned out the sheriff. Pity.'

Wentworth moved on and Simeon Lord came to speak to Mackaness. Having been transported for theft, Lord now owned eighteen blocks of Sydney, a fleet of whalers and sealers and a mill at Botany Bay.

'Who's the man standing behind Lord?' asked Joshua.

'The swarthy fellow? That's Captain Rossi, chief of police. Fought for Napoleon in his youth, then came over to us when the British took Corsica.'

'Not him. The man next to him.' He frowned. 'I feel as though I know him.'

'I hope not!' said Redfern with a barking laugh. 'Augustus Miles is the last man an exile wants to get involved with.'

Joshua raised an eyebrow in question.

'Miles is commissioner for police. Only way for some men to get their freedom is to serve as constables or spies in the penal colonies,' said the doctor disapprovingly. 'And that's the best way to end up with an axe through your skull if the other men find out.'

'Nothing of that sort, I assure you!' said Joshua hastily. He looked long and hard at the man with the pineapple-shaped head and the bulging blue eyes. 'It's just that I have the strangest feeling I've met him before.'

'Ever met the Duke of Clarence?' said a voice over his shoulder. 'King William the Fourth, I *should* say.'

'Of course, that's it!' said Joshua, his mind flying back to the election dinner at Bosingham House. 'He looks just like the vicar of Mapledurham!'

Redfern introduced the striking dark man who had come to join them as Barnett Levey; he was a free emigrant, although he had come to Australia to join his brother Solomon, who had been transported for theft but had so prospered after his release that he had bought Henrietta Villa on Piper's Point when Piper went bankrupt.

'Aye. Just like Dora Jordan's brood, ain't he?' said Levey, looking at Miles. 'A bit older, though. One of Sailor Bill's earlier by-blows. Get Miles in his cups and he'll tell you he should have been William the Fifth, but for the minor point that his pa never married his ma. Mind you, if there was any justice in the world, our Colonel Gibbes of the Sydney Customs Service would have an even better claim. Mrs Fitzherbert's his mother. And George the Fourth was his father. And we all know George was married to the Fitzherbert long before Princess Caroline crossed the Channel.'

Levey lost interest in the Hanoverian brood as swiftly as he had found it. 'Your wife tells me that you play an instrument, Mr Delahaye,' he said, turning his brilliant gaze on Joshua. 'You'll maybe have heard of my At Homes. A little singing and recitation, an attempt to bring some culture to this somewhat benighted colony – '

'But I thought Darling withdrew your licence?' said Redfern.

'Ah, doctor, the pity of it!' sighed Levey, his head lowered and one hand laid theatrically upon his heart. He held the tragic pose a moment and then brightened up in an instant. 'But a new governor, sir, a new broom, as it were, to sweep the cobwebs from our fair city and bring back the Muses from their sad exile!' He paused, as if waiting for a round of applause. 'I trust, Mr Delahaye, that you will grant us the boon of your attendance, with aforesaid instrument, at one of our musical soirées?'

'I am not sure what plans – '

'Did you ever have the great blessing of seeing the divine Dora perform?' said Levey, sweeping on as if Joshua's agreement were a

300

foregone conclusion. 'Incomparable, my dear fellow. Incomparable. Now, you must excuse me, I am summoned to talk to dear Mrs Reiby.'

A flourishing bow and he was gone. With some amusement Joshua and the doctor watched him sway down the room to his next audience.

'Who is Mrs Reiby?' asked Joshua, intrigued in spite of himself to find out more about this strange society into which he had been so unexpectedly thrown.

'The little white-haired lady in the black silk robe and lace mantilla, talking to the Archdeacon. Transported at thirteen for horse-stealing – though she swore she only borrowed the mount from a neighbour, and how many young men of good family can you think of who have done the same in youthful high spirits?'

'Half the boys at Eton,' said Joshua with a smile.

'But no one ever suggested hanging *them* for horse-stealing. Just as no one calls it an unlawful gathering and reads the Riot Act when fifty landowners meet together to go a-hunting. One law for the rich, my boy, another for the poor. Mind you, Mary's prospered since she served out her sentence. Even Archdeacon Scott has to bow to her, for she's endowing one of the new churches. No doubt Levey hopes she'll endow a theatre to keep the balance!'

'I find it hard to believe that people associate so readily with convicts.'

'Not convicts, there's a good fellow,' said Redfern hastily. 'That's a fighting word around here. "Government man" sits much better. Or "exile".'

'Is not everyone here an exile?'

'In a way. Which is why those who come out of their own volition make the distinction by calling themselves Sterling, or Exclusives. Then they act as though they were still at home,' he said with a scornful laugh. 'But this land breeds different people, different virtues and vices, to the old country. Among the government men, fear may sometimes breed treachery; among Emancipists it may breed jealousy, false pride and sycophancy; but at its best it breeds an irresistible determination to win, to overcome the poor hand that fate has dealt. But enough philosophy. I see Dolores Rattigan and her daughters. Let me introduce you . . .'

Joshua danced a set of country dances with one of Mrs Rattigan's delightful daughters and a waltz with the other, then some more country dances with their friend Miss Tregorran, whose father plied him assiduously with drink in the hope that Joshua would reveal more about himself than Tregorran had yet been able to discover. In the event, however, Joshua ended up knowing far more than he wished to about Tregorran, his business schemes and his friends, including Dr Redfern.

Listening with only half an ear to Tregorran, he caught sight of Edward Deas Thomson, his head bent solicitously over Kat as if fearful of missing a word she said. As Deas Thomson offered her his arm, Joshua felt a wave of jealousy wash over him.

'If you'll excuse me...'

'Take your wife in to supper, my dear fellow, before Deas Thomson does,' said Tregorran, following his gaze. 'Edward's nose is quite out of joint since your arrival on the scene. Deal of disappointed young men wishful to give her their arm if you – ' But Joshua had already gone.

Taking Kat in to supper was a good move. It cut out the others, yet it was less painful than a dance, as he could keep himself busy fetching and carrying a plate, a dessert, a glass of lemonade to her.

'Glad to see you're looking after your wife,' growled Redfern, coming up behind him. 'Plenty of young men – '

'– willing to look after her if I don't,' said Joshua with the ghost of a smile. 'But I understand I owe you an apology, sir.'

Redfern gave him a sharp glance.

'I doubted you when you said you understood my plight.'

'And now you know that I understand perfectly? Who told you I'd been a government man?'

'Tregorran. He told me you had been caught up in the Nore mutiny and – '

Redfern's eyes twinkled beneath his craggy eyebrows. 'You, me and friend Garvey,' he said, 'we're all in the same boat. We showed sympathy to our fellow men when they struck out at the powers that oppressed them; we knew that they had gone outside the law, but we understood what had driven them to it. We tried to help and by helping, we became caught up in it ourselves.' He patted Joshua's arm. 'That we were sent into exile here may not have been justice, but it was the law.'

'Huh!'

'You have a wife who believes in you,' said Redfern kindly. 'She must have great influence with the Governor for you to be here tonight. If she has anything to do with it, your pardon – '

'What pardon?' said Joshua with a frown.

The doctor shifted uncomfortably in his seat. 'Forgive a foolish old man,' he said hastily. 'Not as young as I was... hear things amiss all the time.' He patted Joshua's arm. 'Don't be angry and bitter, young man. I was no older than you when I was sent out, but I found a role to play here in Australia. Some would hold that there was a divine purpose in it, although I'll allow I didn't see it that way when I first arrived! Australia needed physicians then; now we need engineers. This is a young country – only forty years ago there was nothing here but sand, soldiers and several shiploads of exiles! – but it's a land of great promise.' He grinned. 'How can she not succeed when her inhabitants were chosen by the best judges in England?'

Joshua made his way back to Kattrin's side, wondering whether to ask her about the pardon Redfern had spoken of, but the sight of Deas Thomson and Wentworth installed at her side, talking about the prospects for the colony under the new governor, checked him for long enough to realise that the Acting Governor's ball was not the place to discuss such matters.

Kat smiled as Joshua crossed the room to her side. It had been quite entertaining at first to listen to Wentworth holding forth with assumed modesty about how he was distantly related to the new governor, Sir Richard Bourke, but she was growing tired of the man and his efforts to impress her.

'The connection is through Edmund Burke, dear lady,' explained Wentworth, his eyes flickering across to Kattrin. 'A renowned philosopher who wrote – '

'*Reflections on the French Revolution*.' She revelled in the look of surprise on his face. 'You forget, sir, we are natives of Buckinghamshire, where Edmund Burke is held in high esteem. He is buried in Beaconsfield churchyard.'

How strange, thought Kat, that a man who had made his name as a friend of the convicts should be so eager to puff his own connections and establish himself as a pillar of society! What would he say if he knew of that secret dinner with Sir Richard and Sir Anthony? But it would not do to talk to Wentworth too long – his wife was already scowling this way.

'Poor Sarah!' whispered Carrie Rattigan, looking across the supper room at the woman who, like so many others, had been seduced by Wentworth's fine words. He had married her only days before she was brought to bed of his child, but within weeks he had begun to look elsewhere.

'Do you know Captain and Mrs Hurvine, Kattrin, my dear?' asked Mrs Rattigan, coming up behind them. Joshua, standing beside Kat, almost dropped his glass.

'Delighted to make your acquaintance. Miss Revel, is it not?'

'Mrs Delahaye,' said Kat, with a tremor in her voice. She laid her hand on Joshua's arm. 'I believe you have already met my husband.'

'Indeed.' Hurvine recovered his usual bluff composure after a moment and shook Joshua's hand heartily. If he was surprised to see his former servant at Government House, he hid it well.

Mrs Hurvine smiled at the little group. 'We had the pleasure of meeting Mr Delahaye in England,' she said, which was, after all, no more than the truth.

'We are in George Street at present,' said Kat, realising that Joshua wasn't going to speak. 'I hope you will call on us there or at Lacey's Creek.'

While Kat was exchanging polite remarks with the Hurvines, Joshua saw Lieutenant Marsfield, who had sailed with them on the *Perseus*, making his way across the room. A muscle twitched at the side of his mouth and his face turned grey.

Kat saw the agitation in his face and, knowing how great a strain he was under, pleaded tiredness. The little party from Lacey's Creek took their leave, amid much ribaldry on the subject of honeymoon couples.

The next morning, when the Hurvines had departed, full of horrified exclamations at the indignities of the auction, Joshua walked out into the stable yard and turned his face to the sun, already high in the sky. In the distance a bird shrieked and half a dozen more shrieked back at it; beyond the gates he could hear the rattle of chains as convict gangs marched out of the Barracks and along the street to their road-mending, but today was one of the rare and blessed days when there were no Hyde Park floggings. A large yellow and green bird settled on the roof of the stables and began its madwoman's cackle; Joshua sighed and wondered if he would ever become accustomed to this place.

They would be late departing, and that was not wholly due to Captain Hurvine's early morning visit; Kat had arranged to travel up the Parramatta on the new steamboat, only to find that it was, once again, out of commission. He loosened the knot of his cravat; it would be a relief to get out of Sydney and back to the farmstead: at least there he and Kat would not be forced to lie in the same bed.

He picked his way through a pile of wicker cases and casks to set his flute case on the carriage seat. Hearing a crash and a curse from one of the coach houses, he strolled across to find Garvey wrestling with the shaft of the cart. 'Where the hell have you been, Will?' asked the steward angrily as the shadow darkened the doorway. 'Give a hand here!' Joshua came up behind him and reached across to take the transverse piece from his hand.

'Why are you never here when you're needed?' muttered Garvey, wiping the sweat from his brow and leaving a dirty smudge across his forehead. He caught sight of the white shirt cuffs. 'Oh, it's you,' he said unenthusiastically.

'Aye, it's me. And I can hold the shaft as well as Will,' said Joshua tersely. 'Get on with it before you drop it.'

'Don't be tryin' to take the whole weight, though, or that shoulder o'yours will come out again and the missus'll have my hide.'

Joshua leaned across to hold the transverse piece in place and cursed as grease rubbed off on his fawn coat.

'Don't worry,' said Garvey, 'you've plenty more at Lacey's Creek. The missus got in a whole wardrobe for you.'

Joshua was tense and irritable. He'd endured yet another night of forced proximity with Kat, Garvey seemed to think him too weak and useless to do a simple task and, on top of all that, was now mocking him for being kept by his wife. 'Damn the stain,' he swore. 'Damn the wardrobe. And damn her interference too!'

Garvey raised his eyebrows. 'You seemed glad enough of both last evening,' he observed mildly.

'Did I?' He shifted his grip to ease his shoulder. 'Dressed up as a lie? No! I had rather have gone in my shipboard rags and been accepted for what I am than brook such interference,' he said irritably.

'Oh, they'd accept you for what you are, all right.' Garvey swung the hammer furiously and the shaft jammed in its socket. 'Oh, fine and dandy *that* acceptance would be!'

'What the devil?'

'You were due for Van Diemen's Land if it hadn't been for her *interference*, but perhaps she never told you that.' He swung the hammer again. 'Oh, very different is Van Diemen's Land, especially since Arthur went out there as lieutenant-governor. Over there you've to work out three quarters of your term before you can even apply for a ticket of leave, unless you've a mind to be an overseer and wield the lash yourself.' He crashed the hammer on to the shaft with a force fit to split it. 'Oh yes, that's where you'd be without her *interference*, like as not working down the mines or building Port Arthur penitentiary. And not in shipboard rags either. You'd be in the canary suit, grey and yellow, likely with broad arrows on it. Who'd accept you then?'

'But I –'

'They wouldn't care that you did it for a cause,' said Garvey, hitting the shaft with unwonted savagery. 'Tales like yours are ten a penny in Australia.' The hammer crashed down once more. 'So full of self-pity you are! D'ye think, now, that you're the only one has to suffer slights?'

Joshua looked a question.

'Oh, yes, she had her fair share last night.' Garvey scowled as he recalled the two young females, no better than they should be, who had been giving Joshua the eye. How desperate she must be for a man, they'd said in her hearing, that she'd chosen one who couldn't run away from her if he wanted! And then there were the priests, moralising fools that they were. But he'd promised not to mention them.

At his last blow the shaft squealed back into its socket and Garvey tossed the hammer aside and stalked off.

It was late when they arrived back at Lacey's Creek, for they had had more trouble with the cart. Two black women begging with their babies at the roadside had hurried across to offer help in the hope of a coin or two and Kat had insisted on offering them shelter for a few nights. 'Thank God we didn't come across a whole tribe of 'em,' grumbled Garvey as he set about finding a place well away from the livestock and the servants for the women to build a shelter.

'I've warned the men to keep away from them, missus,' said the steward when he returned at last to the house and the excellent dinner that Betsey had hurriedly prepared, 'but it's a lot to ask of them when women are so short. And you can see from the babes that they've been with white men before...'

'I doubt they had much choice,' she said crisply. She turned to Joshua to explain. 'Many of these young girls are kidnapped by the convict labour gangs or the whalers, and horribly abused. If they are unfortunate enough to have white men's babies, their tribes won't take them back. And in the dockside inns, they're treated even worse than the white women.'

'For God's sake,' said Joshua, almost choking on his food. 'Where do you get all this from? It's not suitable for a woman in your position –'

'It's because women in my position close their eyes to such things that they continue to happen!' she snapped. 'That's what Mrs Chandler says – and she's right.'

'Dr Redfern's housekeeper,' said Garvey. 'She's a Quaker. Runs a mission for convict women and another for the blacks.'

Joshua opened and closed his mouth several times. 'Whatever would Lady Isabelle – ?'

'Think of this? She'd be appalled. But I never thought you'd think like her,' she said crushingly.

'I don't. It's just that –'

'That it's scarce proper for Miss Revel of Clapton Revel? Of course not. Poor fool, she was so bereft of power or influence that she couldn't even save herself!' Her eyes glowed. 'But Mrs Delahaye of Lacey's Creek does have some power and some influence and, by God, she's going to use it!'

The three of them finished their dinner in silence, each caught up with their own thoughts. Joshua excused himself early, exhausted after two nights lying in the same bed as Kat. Not sleeping, even through the still small hours, for he dared not risk his body betraying him in sleep as it had done before in Aylesbury gaol; he feared that he might waken and find that his dreams of taking Kat in his arms had once more become reality.

But lying at last in his own solitary bed, sleep refused to come. He lay tossing and turning, trying to deal with the new Kat he had seen this evening, to see how what he had just learned affected his plans for her. Perhaps after all there could be a future here for them together; perhaps it was not necessary to persuade her to return to England. Tomorrow, he vowed, they would talk it all through. But sleep still would not come and after a wakeful hour he rose, slipped out from under the mosquito nets, drew on the embroidered slippers and the silken dressing robe that lay to hand and padded down the corridor to the dining room for a book to read. The slippers made no noise on the flagstones and he was at the door before anyone was aware of him.

'Have you Godstowe's letter ready to go?' asked Garvey. 'I've a meeting in Parramatta tomorrow, so I could take it in. Don't worry, I'll be sure and give it into safe hands. I know you wouldn't want anyone else to be reading it.'

Joshua stopped dead in his tracks, leaned against the wall and closed his eyes in anguish.

'I haven't had time to finish it.'

'Better hurry. You know how eagerly awaited it'll be. He hasn't heard from you for all of five days!'

Kat laughed and said something else to her steward, but Joshua didn't stay to hear it.

He'd meant to greet her politely, to say something pleasant, something uncontroversial, but when he came to the door of the dining room the next morning and heard her giving Betsey and Will their orders for the day, good intentions flew out of his mind and gentle words out of his mouth. As the echo of Will's heavy boots faded away down the corridor, he entered the room and stood where Will had stood, in front of the table, at a proper distance.

'What orders have you for *me* this morning?' he said.

He regretted the words the instant they left his lips, but before he could amend them she sprang to her feet, the blood quite drained from her face; the pile of tally books and account sheets at her elbow began to wobble and with one furious gesture she swept them aside. Books, papers and quills spilled onto the floor in disarray.

Cursing himself for his graceless words, Joshua bent to retrieve a handful of the papers, smudging the ink on one as he scooped it up.

He started to speak as he rose, trying at the same time to shuffle the papers into some sort of order. 'Kat, I'm – '

The apology was never made. Before he could straighten up, a book sang past his ear.

'I wish I had never begged your assignment!' she cried.

'Kat! I – '

He saw her hand move again and ducked just in time as another, heavier tome shot overhead, ruffling his hair as it went. 'I wish I had never asked for the ticket of leave! I should have let you rot in Van Diemen's Land!'

He ducked a third time, but a little too late. This time it was the brass ink pot, and it caught him a glancing blow on the side of his head before the porcelain liner smashed against the wall, spreading a blue-black stain over the peach-distempered wall.

'Oh God! Kat,' he said unsteadily. 'I never meant – '

The door flew back on its hinges and Garvey rushed in, a pugnacious look on his freckled face. In the opening behind him stood Betsey and Meggie.

Kattrin's fit of temper left her as swiftly as it had come and she collapsed back into her chair, burying her face in her hands in a paroxysm of weeping.

Joshua turned helplessly to Garvey. 'I never meant – '

'Do you ever?' said the steward furiously, crossing behind the table and raising Kat to her feet with surprising gentleness. 'Come on, lass, away from here now.' He raised his head. 'Meggie!' he shouted. 'Ah, there y'are. Take your mistress to her chamber, lass, and stay with her a while. Betsey, make her a cup of tea, good and strong now, none of your drawing-room cat-lap.' He caught sight of one of the men hovering in the corridor. 'And send someone in to clear up this mess.'

As the sobs faded away down the corridor he turned on Joshua, leaning against the wall and wiping a blend of ink and blood from his forehead.

'If you'd wait for me in my house, Mr Delahaye,' he said, his furious expression belying the polite words, 'I'd like the favour of a word with you.'

Garvey strode angrily across the yard to his house, where he found Joshua sitting in a chair in the kitchen, still clutching one of the books Kattrin had thrown at him, staring blindly at the whitewashed wall.

Joshua looked up at the sound of the door closing. 'It was my fault,' he said miserably.

'I never doubted that,' said the steward, crossing the room to an alcove and tapping two pewter tankards of ale from a barrel. 'You've pushed her too far, too often and 'twas clear one day she would be pushed no further.' He gave a half-laugh. 'You should be grateful 'twas only a pile of books she had to her hand and not the kitchen knife.'

'I know.' He looked at the steward. 'I've tried so hard, but I just can't come to terms with it.'

'What's to come to terms with? Being married to a good woman? One who has always stood your friend?'

'It's not that.' He dare not talk about his feelings for her. That way lay disaster, now he knew how she felt about Godstowe. 'I am a convict and no fit husband for anyone.'

'Do you not think she could be the judge of that?' Garvey had come over from the house determined to give the man a piece of his mind, but he could see Joshua's misery was genuine, and because he could understand the obstinate pride that drove him, he found his own anger dying.

'Kat? No. She's too soft-hearted. She is sorry for me and I would not trade on our old friendship for my salvation.' His mouth twisted with a wry smile. 'I'm a lost cause. She would be better by far to go home and marry ... someone who is not a branded criminal.' He picked up the book with RECIPES on the front cover. 'I – I don't know her any more. One minute turning guns on the servants, the next collecting recipes.' He shook his head in bewilderment. 'Baking drop cakes! Who would ever have thought Miss Kattrin of Clapton Revel would be reduced to such domest ...?' His voice tailed away and his jaw dropped as he opened the book and took in the contents.

'Mr Koop's recipe for making paper from thistles,' Kat had written in her spiky hand. He turned the page, eyes widening in astonishment.

'Mr Koop's recipe for extracting ink from old paper and the paper re-pulped' jostled with

> A consideration of paper made from old ropes and Mr Wm Delahaye's remembrances of a parcel of paper made from corn husks shown him by Mr Wm Cobbett. Mr Sprague of Fredonia, N.Yk, has following recipe:
> To 128 gallons water, 10 quarts of good lime or 6 pounds good alkalis put 110 pounds of clean corn husks or flag leaves; heat over moderate fire for two hours, will then be ready for the machines.
> Note: an alternative to the corn husks: 120 pounds of straw with the knobs cut off.

He looked up at Garvey in astonishment. '*Paper?* What the devil – ?'

'She thought you could work together,' he said harshly. 'Godstowe got her a licence from Howick – the Colonial Secretary – to

309

make paper. There's none been made in the colony since the old mill closed down about eight years ago. It's one way Darling had of keeping control of the press, being as the paper was all imported from the Cape Colony or from Bengal on government ships, and he had the say of who should have any.'

'A licence to make paper? Well, I'm damned!'

'There's a heap of packing cases in a shed down by the river. Fowdrin machine, or some such.'

'Fourdrinier?'

'That's the one. She's been waiting the moment to ask you to put the pieces together for a mill upriver. I've found a likely spot.'

'She arranged all that – for me?'

'Aye. Thought it would keep you busy while you waited for the pardon to come through.'

'What pardon?'

'She put in for a pardon for you; you know she has the ear of the new governor.'

His jaw jutted angrily. 'I never asked her to do so,' he ground out.

'Should she have waited for your permission?' Garvey was exasperated. 'It seems to me an eminently reasonable action for a wife to take. I dare say she even thought you might show her some gratitude!'

'If I spent the rest of my life grovelling I could never show enough gratitude for the sacrifices she has made,' said Joshua bitterly. 'And husband or no husband, I am no more than one of her servants; she has bought my service as she bought theirs.'

Garvey almost found himself pointing out that the service she wanted from the others was not the service she wanted from Joshua, but wisely bit his tongue on the words. 'I'm a government man, same as them, same as you,' he said after a moment, setting a tankard at Joshua's elbow and lowering himself into a chair opposite him. 'Like you I was sent out in chains for political crimes – though every Irishman in the colony will tell you that, as if there's never been an Irishman that stole or raped or murdered but he was doin' it for the cause of ould Ireland. However, I have me records, an' can prove it to any man,' he said fiercely. 'But I don't see meself as the same as Meggie an' Will an' all them.' He poked Joshua with his whip. 'Are ye listening to me?' he demanded.

'Yes, damn you!'

'What I can offer her is more the service of an equal. Anyone can wash and slop in the house; anyone can dig and sow and harvest the land. But not many can be a good steward. Sure, she's fortunate to have me, for there are many less honest than me might have fleeced her, her being a woman.' He put his head on one side. 'Though I'm no longer so certain of that, for she's a good head on her shoulders and now she knows what's what...' He took a deep draught of his ale. 'What was I sayin'? Ah yes. To be sure, I'm a good steward and that's the kind of service you should be doin' for her, though I'm probably cuttin' me own throat to say it, for she won't need two stewards and she'd be bound to favour her husband over me, stands to reason. She's kept those crates rottin' on the bank fer you to deal with, though I could have had 'em unpacked these months past. Still, if it's you she wants to build her mill, seems to me the least you could do is get off yer arse an' get on with it.'

# Chapter Sixteen

Kat returned from her tour of inspection with a heavy heart to match her aching muscles. She'd never been a natural horsewoman like Drusilla and any hope she'd had that a morning spent in the open air would blow the cobwebs from her mind and in a blinding flash show her the answer to all her domestic problems, had been shortlived. She could hardly breathe in the oppressive heat and felt so low-spirited that she was even berating herself for her folly in taking another group of useless mouths into the farm in the shape of the two black women and their children. The servants would object strongly if she brought them into the household – even the most miserable of convict servants had to have someone to look down on – and encumbered with the young children they could scarcely be set to work with the stock or in the fields. What the devil was she going to do with them now?

Her heart sank even further when she saw a carriage turn into the yard and the Reverend Samuel Marsden, chaplain of the Parramatta Female Factory and the greatest bigot in the colony, alighted at the door.

She ought not to have been surprised. His curate had spoken to her at the ball, promising that Marsden would call on her to discuss 'this appalling state of affairs', and men of the cloth would have to be true to their word. She would have to invite Marsden to eat with them; it was the rule of the bush, even though he had only come from Parramatta. Joshua in his present mood would be no help; she could only hope that he would stay away until she could get rid of the wretched man. Marsden was after all a magistrate, one who gloried in his reputation among the convicts as the flogging parson, and in the absence of the governor he could still make trouble for Joshua.

She found Marsden an unprepossessing figure. It wasn't just the bulbous nose and the thinning hair, nor the fact that his bulk sat ill with his lack of inches; it was much more the expression of ineffable righteousness, the conviction on his face and in his speech that when

312

it came to the Lord's right hand, Samuel Marsden would have no competition for the prime place.

'Watch your servants more closely, miss,' he said before he was even over the threshold. 'I saw them in the orchard eating as much fruit as they are picking.'

'I had rather they ate the fruit than leave it for the fruit bats,' she said mildly. She had set Lizzie and some of the other young girls to pick the fruit after the orchard had been plundered three nights in a row by a colony of fruit bats, hideously huge creatures, quite unlike the inoffensive English bats, resembling Buckland's drawings of the pterodactyls of the ancient world which Dickon had once shown her. The creatures had a great penchant for ripe fruit, particularly peaches, and what they didn't rob, they ruined by knocking it off the branches and imbuing it with the most unpleasant stink.

'Fallen fruit's good enough for convicts,' he went on, disapproval in every crease of his face as he handed his hat to Jenkins. 'There was plenty on the ground. Hardly bruised at all.'

But the fallen fruit, like anything touched, however slightly, by the fruit bats, stank. It wasn't even fit to feed to the pigs, for it would taint the pork with the same appalling stench.

'They tell me you've had no floggings since you arrived. Bad planning, miss. Very bad. Gives the convicts false notions. Hundred stripes every now and then will keep the rest of them on their toes!'

He stumped into the drawing room ahead of her and sat down without being asked, leaving her standing before him like a naughty scholar in front of the headmaster. With a mutinous set to her lip she took a seat to one side of him, so that he had to turn his head slightly backwards to address her.

'I shall speak bluntly and to the point, Miss Revel,' he said, settling his bulk in the upholstered chair and setting it creaking. 'I speak on behalf of Archdeacon Scott as well, who is conscious, as I am, that you have no male relative to advise you and set you on the right path.'

He looked sharply at her, as if daring her to comment, but she said nothing. He knew as well as she did that she had a husband.

'We are aware, of course, that you knew this Delahaye fellow before you came out here,' he went on. 'We understand how difficult it must be under those circumstances to keep a proper distance, particularly while the man is so blatantly received in society. But convicts are sent here to be punished, not pampered.' He scowled across the room at her. 'How may we keep the convicts in their place if they see one of their number being so cosseted?'

'I am not the first free woman to marry a convict,' she said, as calmly as she could. 'I've heard of many free-born women who have married their father's assigned servants and been granted a ticket of leave for their husbands upon the marriage.'

'Among the heathen out here it is not unknown.' If his voice had been cold before, it now grew icy. 'But then the Jews and Baptists and even the Papists in some of the smaller settlements have been somewhat limited in their choices. Not that one would consider them married at all, of course,' he hastened to add. 'Some heathen ritual spoken by a so-called priest or minister cannot count.'

'You are suggesting that I am not married?' Sweat prickled down her spine as she struggled to keep calm.

'Some mumbo-jumbo spoken by a Quaker? No more than a declaration of intent, no better than a de facto marriage.' She ground her teeth at the suggestion that she was no more than a common-law wife – in the eyes of the law, no wife at all. 'For someone in your position, a member of the Established Church, to consort with a convicted criminal – impossible.'

'You forget that Mr Delahaye is awaiting the outcome of an appeal!' she said coldly, determined not to let the chaplain goad her into losing her temper.

'A convict is a convict,' said Marsden harshly. 'At first we thought an annulment the only answer and the Archdeacon was willing to set the matter in hand, but the so-called ceremony was conducted by a dissenter, so of course there is nothing to annul. You may consider yourself not wed to the fellow at all.'

She swept to her feet and turned on him, high spots of colour on her cheeks standing out against a deathly pale face. 'I went through a perfectly legal ceremony, conducted before God and quite acceptable to the authorities!' she snapped. 'Pray thank the Archdeacon for his concern, but I believe I need not trouble him for an annulment of a wedding which I entered into quite willingly.'

Marsden rose from his chair like the wrath of God embodied. 'Then, Miss Revel, you are no better than all the harlots and whores and stinking drabs of the docks, and polite society will – must – turn its back upon you!'

'In that case you will not wish to sully yourself by remaining any longer under my roof!' She crossed to the door and called for the servant, who came running rather more swiftly than was his wont, in answer to the note of fury in his mistress's voice. 'Hugh, show Reverend Marsden to his carriage,' she said, ice in her voice. She picked up the minister's hat and thrust it at him. 'He is just leaving.'

She stood on the verandah grinding her teeth as the minister's carriage trundled away down the drive; sweat stood on her brow, as much from the effort of suppressing her rage for so long as from the heat, though it was more than usually oppressive. Lizzie and a couple

314

of the other young servant girls came from the orchard, swinging baskets of fruit that they had picked, calling to one another and laughing gaily. She had a sudden stabbing memory of Emmy and the rag girls coming out of the mill, arm in arm. Where was Emmy now, she wondered. Had the money she had sent come in time to save her and her family?

She felt an overwhelming urge to go down to the creek, to hear the sound of running water, to catch what little breeze there was against the heavy heat of midmorning, and wash away the contamination she felt after Marsden's visit. A chorus of musical laughter from the birds the natives called laughing jackasses rang out into the warm midday air, as if in response to Lizzie and her friends, but the sound failed on this occasion to raise an answering smile in Kattrin.

She didn't feel like singing as she walked through the thick grass of the paddock, but she forced herself. 'You've got to look at it this way, missus,' Garvey had said when she'd first heard about the poisonous snakes on her arrival and gone into a flat panic, 'if you were a skinny creature down at boot level that couldn't run, only slither, then you'd surely want to get out of the way of a clumpin' great human bein', if only you knew they were coming, wouldn't you? That's why the men always whistle.' But whistling was something she'd never been able to do, and Garvey had no more success in teaching her than Dickon. 'Well, and if you can't whistle, you'll just have to sing,' said Garvey. 'Anything so as not to creep up on 'em and take 'em by surprise. That's when they turn nasty.'

Singing a mournful song she wandered along the bank of the creek until she came to her favourite spot below the rushes, where the flow of the river had undercut the bank, leaving a flattened spot shaded by a clump of bushes and trees. The sharks and poisonous fish which made the waters of Port Jackson so treacherous, right up to Parramatta, never came as far as the creek so, after checking the undergrowth for snakes, she slipped off her shoes, hitched her skirts up around her waist and dangled her legs in the cool water.

The strong sunlight dappled the surface of the creek and gilded the scales of the fish darting about in the shallows; she had only to half-close her eyes and she could almost imagine they were the famed Wye trout glistening in the sparkling waters of the mill leat. But the similarities were deceptive and even a gentle creek like this could flood in a moment and wash away not only farmland but the very houses, and sometimes the sleeping people within. A number of the servants had had narrow escapes in the last floods, which was what had decided Lacey to build his new house higher up, away from the flood levels.

Something warm and soft rubbed against her hand and she

315

jumped. For a terrifying moment she thought of snakes and spiders, but looking down she saw with relief that it was Smoke, the little grey cat Dickon had brought to Aylesbury when Will Delahaye left Wooburn. She picked it up and hugged it to her while her heart slowed down once more to its customary beat. As Smoke purred at her she had a sudden memory of sitting on the bank of the Wye with the kitten in the basket while Joshua wiped the mud and dust from her face. It seemed half a lifetime away. That had been the first time she realised she felt more for him than just friendship; now it seemed he didn't even want to be friends.

The familiar smell of wet paper and size that hit him as he pushed open the door made his nostrils twitch. It was a smell like no other, and for a moment he was back at Clapton Revel, in the years before the troubles, when Kat and Dickon were not yet grown, the villagers still had work in the mills and the fields, and he and his father had lived happily together on the Green. He wondered how Will and Tom and Saul were getting along, not to mention Lucy Thornton. Kat had spoken of sending for Tom now they were all settled, but Joshua had no desire for the lad to see him like this, a common felon.

The ill-hung door closed on his fingers and he came back to the present with a curse. He blinked, pushed his hat back on his head and looked about him in amazement. On one long wall was ranged a series of packing cases, some of them with damaged corners, and on the wall opposite, under small and dusty windows, ran a rough-cut bench; above it at window height stretched several ropes with sheets of paper of varying hues and thicknesses draped over. At the far end of the hut stood heaps of shredded ropes, piles of chopped straw, sheaves of papery corn husks and bundles of brown and green rushes; to his left an old cauldron with a broken wooden paddle mechanism attached to it sat on top of a built-up stone hearth.

He mopped his brow and turned back to wedge the door open in the hope of disturbing the still air. It was scorching hot under the low roof; what must it have been like to have the fire going in here for two hours at a time?

He crossed to the bench and picked up a rough drawn-wire vat mould which lay among a scattering of deckles. A small selection of different types of paper was neatly stacked alongside.

He took a sheet off the first pile and held it up to the light. On the top sheet of each pile Kat had written notes on the method of manufacture, the sizing used, the tear resistance and absorbency, using pencil, charcoal and ink on each kind to test the quality.

'Straw cooked with milk of lime, drained and seasoned five days.

316

Washed four hours. Spreads ink. Packaging paper?' He rubbed it between his fingers, picked up a pencil and wrote below: 'Yes.'

He picked up a leaf from the second pile and held it up. It felt like good newspaper but he couldn't guess what it was made of and turned it over to read her notes. 'Bark from clearance trees – hard to drain – won't hold shape above this size – tears too easily.'

The third one had faults. 'Fibres settling one way – leads to tearing,' she had written. 'Vat needs agitator – see Joshua.' In spite of himself he smiled.

She had been most thorough, trying hand-vat forms of all the raw materials, and he examined each one closely: some of it was very good indeed.

She must have been holding the cat too tightly, caught up in her memories, for it began to scrabble free. 'No. Too dangerous for you here, kitty,' she said, picking it up and carrying it back to the house.

Caught up in her own thoughts she didn't hear the whistling; following the winding path she found herself face to face with Joshua, as if he had been conjured up from her memories. They stood stock still for a moment, gazing at each other, then:

'I've had a look at the machines and – '

'I wanted to speak to you about – '

They looked at each other and smiled.

'What did you want to say?' he asked.

'Nothing of any importance,' she lied.

'Some of that paper is very good,' he said, falling in step with her.

'You need not sound so surprised! After all, I did grow up in the mills.'

He bit his lip. It had not been his intention to offend. He passed his hand across his forehead. 'You shouldn't be out in the sun without a hat,' he said with a frown.

'You're already an expert on such matters?' she said, and then wished she had not been so shrewish.

They walked back to the house in silence and to her surprise he followed her in. 'Was the machinery still in good order?' she said at last. 'I had them pack it in straw and cotton waste but the boxes shifted at sea.'

'Nothing I can't mend,' said Joshua. 'I thought, with your permission, I'd make a start tomorrow. Unless you have other plans for me . . .?'

'I would not keep you here against your will,' said Kat, choosing her words carefully. 'Garvey thinks he has found a suitable site, but you know more about mills than he. If you find a better you have my authority to change it.'

317

'If that is your wish.'

'It is.' She moved impatiently across to the window, unable to look at his stony face a moment longer. 'There are few blacks left up there, and Garvey knows where their sacred sites are, so we shall not trouble them,' she said over her shoulder. 'Tell Garvey how many hands you need. Thomas can make stringy bark shelters for you all; the weather is warm enough.' There was so much more she wanted to say: *Take care, mind your shoulder, don't forget me.*

There was a sudden bustle in the yard, as men and women rushed out of the shacks. 'Southerly buster, missus!' cried Will, hurrying over to the window.

Joshua looked on in surprise as she began to wind up the blinds and fling open the windows. 'Don't just stand there!' she commanded. 'Open every door and window!'

'But the flies!'

'Just open them. It's a southerly buster!' she repeated, as if that explained everything.

Mystified, he did as he was bid. As he opened the last door on the corridor, he saw the trees at the far side of the yard bending in the wind and a sudden rush of icy-cold air struck him in the face.

Out in the yard the servants, having opened every door and window in the shacks and the kitchens, stood with their faces up-turned, revelling in the cold air. He hadn't realised just how many there were, and these were only the house and yard servants.

The icy blast whistled through the windows, shook the doors and insinuated itself into every nook and corner, driving the flying insects ahead of it and out of the house. Then, as quickly as it had come, the cold wind shuddered and died. Immediately everyone rushed around closing up all the doors and windows and trapping the cool air inside.

'So that's a southerly buster,' said Joshua, filling his lungs with the cool air.

'Isn't it wonderful? Icy winds straight up from the frozen south, just when you most need it. It's only the second one I've experienced,' she said, and he was reminded that she hadn't been out here that much longer than he.

She drew in a deep breath. 'I need Garvey back here as soon as you've settled in, so I shall have to name you overseer.'

'No!'

'I have to do it for the records. So many government men have escaped recently and turned to bushranging that it is forbidden for assigned men to travel into the bush without an overseer.' She drew a piece of paper towards her and dipped her pen into the inkwell. 'It's only a name on a paper, Joshua,' she said sharply. 'I'm not proposing to send whips and shackles into the bush with you.'

He looked at the paper with loathing, then with great reluctance took up the quill and scrawled his signature.

'You must stay on Lacey's Creek property. I cannot change the system,' she said as he cursed under his breath. 'It is the law through-out the nineteen counties and until we know whether there is to be a pardon or a retrial, you are subject to that law. I shall have to give my word on your behalf.'

'Very well,' he growled.

'I'll write you a pass to enable you to go into Sydney or Parramatta on Lacey's Creek business, but I beg of you not to go any further afield without my written warrant.'

He fixed his eyes on the top of the doorframe, as if he could no longer bear to look at her. 'I have your permission to go now?' he said, in tones as icy as the frozen southern wastes whence the wind had come.

The sooner he left, the better, she thought despairingly. She could not take much more of this.

When Garvey rode back to Lacey's Creek he found Kattrin where he had left her, sitting at the travelling desk in front of the window with the cat on her lap, looking blindly out into the yard where two days before Joshua had been supervising the loading of the machinery onto the bullock carts.

'Missus?' he said softly. 'Missus!' He laid his rough hand on her shoulder.

She jumped almost out of her seat and the cat leaped from her lap with a frightened mew.

'Thought you'd want to know all's well,' he said gruffly, averting his gaze from the tear-stained face and the red-rimmed eyes. 'We've agreed on a site, the shelters are made and they start work on the mill tomorrow.'

'Have I done the right thing, Ned?' she asked.

'You said yourself you had no real choice.' He frowned. 'Has that damned priest been upsettin' you?' She looked up at him in surprise. 'Ah, Betsey told me Lang has been here. What's he been sayin' to you? The same as Floggin' Sam, I don't doubt. When it comes to hypocrisy, that whimpering Scots bigot would be with Marsden all the way!' he exclaimed, for Lang had constituted himself the Low Church mentor of morals, as the Reverend Samuel Marsden was the High Church guardian.

'Strangely enough, no.'

'What?'

'Marsden was all for an annulment, but Lang demands that I marry Joshua at once. Put an end to the sinful example I'm setting.' She pressed her hands over her eyes. 'If only he knew...'

'You told him you were already married?'

'Of course. But I don't have my marriage papers – they had to go to the Colonial Office before Joshua could be released into my custody and I am still waiting for their return.'

'Your word should be enough for him!'

She shook her head. 'Lang says all the de facto wives say they've mislaid their marriage lines.'

'The insolence of the man! So what will you do?'

'I don't know. Wait for the Governor to arrive, I suppose. I've written to William Godstowe in the hope that he can set it all to rights, but that could take until next year.'

'What if you went through the ceremony again?' hazarded Garvey. 'Sure, 'twould do no harm, and might keep a deal of people happy.'

'Even if I could be sure Joshua would go through with it – which I'm not! – if I allow that I wasn't married in the first place, then how could Joshua have been freed into my custody?'

Garvey had to agree she had a point. 'Oh, it's a storm in a teacup, right enough,' he said with a mirthless laugh. 'Wouldn't you think they'd enough people to fret about without troublin' you? Half the couples in Sydney haven't been before a priest of any kind, and that's not just among the poor either. Look at Druitt, now, sits every Sunday in St James's in the Mount Druitt pew with his so-called wife Peggy and their daughters...'

Everyone in the colony knew the story of Miss Peggy Lynch of Cork: she'd followed her sweetheart, young Private Burns of the Forty-Eighth Foot, on board ship as a stowaway, and married him on the long voyage, with Captain Druitt of the Forty-Eighth standing witness to their shipboard marriage. Before the voyage was half over, however, the Captain had taken a fancy to Peggy himself and Mrs Burns left the ship on Druitt's arm to live with him and bear him children. Some years later the Captain, now the colony's chief engineer and inspector of public works, had simply declared the first ceremony invalid and married Peggy himself. What Private Burns thought of the matter no one had asked.

Kat shook her head. 'I don't begrudge the Druitts their position,' she said. 'What should it matter to me whether their marriage was lawful or no?'

If Joshua had still loved her, what would she care whether he and she were married or no? She could just as happily live with him out of wedlock, if only to throw it in the bigoted faces of Marsden and Lang

320

and their ilk. But they *were* lawfully married, and no hypocrite would make her say they weren't!

Time hung heavy on her hands after Joshua's departure. There was no longer any call to hurry into Sydney whenever a convict ship entered the Harbour and the papermaking no longer held the same attraction, depending as it did on Joshua and the mill.

Garvey and Will were making steady progress with the land clearance; the black women, settled for the moment in their lean-to shelters over by the river, were weaving rush baskets for the kitchen; everything appeared to be proceeding smoothly without her.

She wasn't short of social invitations – no one except the Macarthurs and Marsden's immediate circle had turned their back on her, so it seemed that the two grandees of Sydney society no longer had the influence they thought they had – but she hadn't the heart for dancing or gossiping. She drifted around the settlement and sketched out a few alterations to the plans for the new house, but she no longer felt the same enthusiasm for the improvements; her mind was constantly up in the hills with Joshua.

She hadn't even a visit to look forward to. 'No sense in riding back and forth all the time,' he'd said brusquely. 'I'll stay up there until the mill is built and running smoothly.'

'But there will be invitations...'

'You can make my excuses. If the Governor arrives, I'll come down. Then we can find out at last whether I can hope for a pardon or a retrial. Otherwise I'll stay where I am.'

She might have sat there for weeks, gazing dispiritedly out of the window, but one morning, several days after Garvey's return, while she was in the dining room, she saw something out of the window that brought her back to her senses.

Lizzie and Ben, whose arrival with Joshua had caused her such heartache, had slipped so easily into the way of life at Lacey's Creek that she had almost forgotten about them. Now she saw Lizzie hurrying out of the kitchen with Will behind her, shouting. She couldn't hear what he was saying, but the way he reached for her arm and the confusion on both their faces as she slapped him away, spoke volumes.

The relationships between some of the men and the few women on the farm had already been settled before she arrived and she had thought them none of her concern, preferring to leave them to Betsey, who spent more time in Garvey's house than in her own quarters. But Lizzie *was* her responsibility and she had been so caught up with her own troubles that she had left the girl to get into a difficult situation.

Racked with guilt she rang the bell, sent for Will and gave him orders that would take him away from the farm and out across the fields for the rest of the day. Then she rang for Betsey and asked her to send Lizzie to see her that afternoon.

'Time you was sortin' out what to do with that wench,' said the cook, banging plates of fruit and cold meat down on the table. 'All very well worritin' over a couple o' black bits, but it's me has to deal with the girl an' I'm none too happy about the way Will's waggin' his tail around her.'

'Pity you didn't mention it to me before now,' said Kat acidly. 'But since I've found out for myself, send her in to see me this afternoon and I'll see what's best to do.'


She looked across the table at Lizzie. She was a pretty little thing, with those huge grey eyes and dark curls, but still slightly gawky, beyond childhood but not quite a woman. And yet quite old enough to cause havoc in a household where there were too many men and not enough women.

Lizzie herself, when asked what she would like to do, was not very forthcoming. 'I could go and cook for Mr Joshua,' she said with a shrug of the shoulders.

'You couldn't go up to a bush camp, Lizzie,' said Kattrin, suppressing a pang of jealousy. 'It wouldn't be suitable. But if you like cooking you could work with Betsey.'

'I don't, missus. Not special, like. Never done much of it. Pa had an old cousin kept house after Ma died an' she done all the cooking.'

'I thought you had no family.'

'We don't. When Pa lost all his money, the old woman upped sticks and disappeared. Took me ma's ring and her brooch with her, she did, and the silver, what was left. That's why I had to go a-thievin', to feed me and Ben.'

'But wasn't there anyone who could help you?'

Lizzie shrugged. 'Most of Pa's friends, they lost money too when the bank collapsed. Only one who ever helped us was Mrs Porter. She caught me trying to steal a loaf one day and took us in.'

'Then why did you carry on stealing?'

'You don't understand, missus. We had to, if we wanted to stay with her. She taught all her kiddies to steal: difference was, she showed us how to pick things that brought the best price. Like reticules and silk han'kerchers.'

'She ran a thieves' den!' exclaimed Kat, a look of horror on her face.

Lizzie shrugged. 'I s'pose. I didn't care. She fed us both and kept us warm . . .'

But 'Never done it' or 'Never tried it' was her answer to every suggestion Kat made for her future occupation.

'Will's ticket of leave comes up soon,' she said, watching Lizzie carefully, 'and I'm thinking of setting him up across the valley, to take charge of the new cleared land. He'd have his own house, and he'll need someone to cook for him...'

Lizzie shivered. 'You're not goin' to send me away, missus?'

'Not if you don't want to go.'

'Not with Will, miss? Please?'

'Has he upset you?'

Lizzie blinked rapidly. 'I don't want to get no one into trouble.' She looked down at the floor. 'See, it was just a joke, missus. One o' the girls dared me to kiss him. It bein' his birthday. I didn't like it, an' I wisht I hadn't done it, an' now he won't leave me alone.'

Kat sighed. It was a difficult situation. So many in the colony, both Sterling and Currency, had accepted Marsden's view that every woman who came out on the convict ships was a prostitute – and many were, of course, shipped out as being 'of no trade', which it was all to easy to equate with 'on the town'; it had got so that even the most miserable of men thought he was doing a great favour by offering to make an honest woman of a female convict.

Lizzie looked at Kat with big, scared eyes. 'Only Will's not real bad, not like Calderson, an' I don't want he should get into trouble.'

'He won't. I'll speak to him. But Will isn't a young boy, and it isn't sensible to lead a man on if ... Well, 'tis done now and can't be undone,' she said as Lizzie gave a loud sniff. 'And we still don't know what to do with you.' She was struck by a sudden thought. 'Lizzie, did you ever work in your father's shop?'

'No, ma'am. See, by the time I was old enough, Pa'd made his pile o'money. Wouldn't have me in the shop; wouldn't even let me be prenticed.'

'You were to go for an apprentice?'

'Oh, yes, ma'am. I was to go prentice with the milliner. Same as Ma before me.'

'And would that have pleased you, Lizzie?'

'Oh, yes, ma'am.' Lizzie's face brightened up a little. 'When I was a little 'un, I used to sew the pretty ribbons on the hats Ma made.' For the first time the girl's face grew animated. 'Oh, she made all sorts. Real pretty ones. Lace, cloth, ribbon, straw hats, straw bonnets ... She had real quick fingers. I can follow a lace pattern, just like her. She taught me the straw work too. I showed Ben on the boat, just to pass the time. We had to use old bits o' rope, though.'

'You could teach others to make straw hats then?'

323

'There are some as are too clumsy, but if they got quick fingers, it's easy enough.'

Kat thought of the nimble-fingered black women weaving their rush mats and smiled. 'Lizzie,' she said, 'you and I are going to Parramatta tomorrow.'

She left it to Garvey to talk to Will, thinking it would come better from another man.

'I'm thinkin' 'tis time I took him on a visit to the Female Factory, missus,' said the steward, dropping by later that evening. 'Poor Will's that hot for a woman, he reckons he's even been eyein' up the black beggars, and that's frightened the lad half out of his senses.'

Smiling broadly, Kat came down the steps from Mrs Chandler's house on Dr Redfern's arm. Will tipped his hat as the doctor handed her up into the carriage, bowed, and walked off down the street with a jaunty step.

'I'm glad everyone's feelin' so cheery,' said Will gloomily.

'Oh, Will . . .'

'Lizzie staying there with Miz Chandler's orphans, then?' he said, pushing his hat back on his head and scowling up at the elegant façade.

'She'll help teach them a trade,' said Kat. 'Mrs Chandler is a kind woman; I think Lizzie will be comfortable there.'

'Could be she'll be lonely. Miss the company from Lacey's . . .'

'I'll bring Ben to visit whenever I come to town; if she doesn't settle, she can always come back to us.' Will's face brightened up and she wished she had chosen her words more carefully. 'Will, she's only fourteen.'

'Lots o' lasses that age get wed. Fourteen's old enough to – '

'How old are you, Will?'

'Twenty-six,' he said gruffly. 'I've served nigh on twelve year. Me father was a coin-shaver. The old feller was hanged an' I was transported.' He scratched his head. 'Don't know how it is, missus, but I ain't thought to look at a woman in all that time. Howsever, since Lizzie kissed me, seems I can't think of nothin' else. An' what with my time bein' nearly gone . . .'

'It's time you looked for a bride,' she agreed. 'But not one half your age.'

They drew up outside the Parramatta Female Factory. Housed in an elegant three-storey sandstone building topped with a clock and a cupola, Parramatta's penitentiary for female convicts looked from the outside not unlike the Assembly Rooms in any sleepy English market town. Greenway had built it for three hundred women, but there were often as many as five hundred crammed into it and a

324

hundred children besides. The convicts were divided into three classes: the first two were for the sick, for women who had been returned unsatisfactory or pregnant from assignment and those who could with good behaviour eventually earn their freedom, while the third class consisted of those who had committed new crimes in the colony or broken the Factory rules: they were kept in cells, their hair shorn, and set to break rocks or work the treadmill.

The door was opened by one of the first class, with a white cap and red calico jacket over her prison dress. Behind her the matron herself bustled out to meet them; it wasn't often they had quality visitors in carriages.

She was a hard-faced woman, none too certain that it was permitted to allow prisoners out on the say-so of Dr Redfern, being more accustomed to receiving a letter of permission from the chaplain, the Reverend Marsden. Her instinct was to mistrust anything that emanated from such as Redfern, who had led the campaign against the installation of the treadmill. She was perfectly appalled when Kat insisted on being taken into the rooms where the women convicts were working.

'You'll meet with a deal of bad language, ma'am,' she said disapprovingly, 'even among the general and merit class. And there are two bush farmers here already, looking for suitable wives among our merit women.'

A supervisor showed them into the main room where the women had been lined up, those interested in taking any offer from a bush bachelor busily primping themselves in their coarse flannel dresses, others scowling at being subjected to yet another indignity. There were women of all ages, some barely more than girls, others so old they could hardly stand. This was a daily humiliation which all had to undergo, whether they hoped to leave as wives or servants. At least these men were willing to marry the women they chose; she'd heard from Dr Redfern how all too often a wife would come in from a homestead in the bush to seek advice on her pregnancy while her lecherous husband went to the Female Factory to pick out a young servant girl to warm his bed in her place.

Kat and Will stood aside while the two Emancipist farmers from the outlying districts took their turn to pass along the line, to a great deal of teasing and taunting from the women. One farmer, his head surrounded by a cloud of smoke and his grey bushy beard and moustache stained with tobacco, sauntered along confidently, looking the women up and down; the other was a middle-aged, tongue-tied man with a cabbage-tree hat as large as an umbrella shading his face; he still had his stock whip in his hand and darted sideways glances at the women as he passed.

At last the tongue-tied man stopped in front of one rather blowsy woman, her hair hanging round her face and her lips slick and shining where she had bitten and licked them. 'A flash piece of mutton!' said the greybeard approvingly to Will.

'This one?' asked the tongue-tied man hesitantly, and the supervisor reeled off her religion, a list of convictions and a character which seemed to Kat most unlikely to belong to this particular example of womanhood.

'If she's willing,' he muttered.

'If he's a free man,' she simpered.

He nodded and the bargain was made, whereupon the bride-elect flew around her companions, bidding hasty adieus, and the groom-elect led her off. 'Give yer three months afore ye're returned!' cried one, and, as the elderly man went through the same procedure with a young woman in her twenties, 'You got a bargain there, old stringy-bark!' cried another. An assistant took them down to stores to change their prison dress for the slops they had worn when they landed from the transports. The two couples would then hurry off to the church to be wed, at which point the women, as they were marrying free husbands, would receive their ticket of leave as dowry. Whether either woman would stay in the bush, seizing the second chance and making the most of it, or whether she would quickly find an excuse to return to Sydney and more congenial company, was an open question.

While all this was going on, Will was looking about him, turning redder by the moment as first one convict woman, then another, winked at him, or suggestively ran a tongue around reddened lips. He was a well-set young man and a pleasing contrast to most who came to look. Suddenly the air was rent by a shriek from the supervisor. 'Why, you hussy!' she exclaimed, dragging one woman forward. 'You're breeding!'

'I done my time for my merit!' protested the young woman in a strong West Country accent. 'I goes out next week on assignment and you aren't goin' t'keep me here just 'cos I'm in the family way!'

'You stupid drab!' screeched the supervisor. 'Who'll want to take you on in that state?'

Kat felt a stirring at her side and saw Will open his mouth. She caught at his wrist, digging her nails in painfully. Will, whose ready sympathy had been stirred, quickly closed his mouth again.

'Who's the father?' hissed the woman, moderating her voice as she remembered her visitors. 'One of the convicts as brought you up-river, I'll be bound!' Male convicts manning the pinnaces from Sydney Cove to Parramatta were regularly flogged for the crime of 'taking four days to row convicts to the Female Factory where two would do'.

'Weren't any o' them,' she said, her nose in the air.

'So who's the father?' repeated the supervisor.

'Reverend Samuel Marsden,' she said defiantly and the room rang to shrieks of hysterical laughter at what was obviously a well-worn joke.

Gradually the women drifted back to their spinning and their looms, where they wove the grey and yellow canary cloth from which the male convicts' clothes were made, and Kat and Will walked about the weaving room, watching and listening. If Will was to prosper on his smallholding, he'd need a strong and healthy young woman, fit enough to work alongside him, but he was too stolid a character to deal well with a flighty wench. She pointed out several of the quieter ones to him. One had her hair bound into plaits, clearly not in the least desirous of attracting attention in the line-up. Kat watched her for a moment, chatting quietly with the old woman next to her, tying up an end for her when it broke.

Enquiry revealed that the woman, Mary, was twenty-two and had arrived in the colony six months ago, with a seven-year sentence for theft of a length of calico; she'd suffered a fever on board ship and being too weak to work, had been sent out to the Factory. She was the daughter of a farm worker in the Borders and announced herself willing to turn her hand to most things.

'Am I being taken for a servant, ma'am?' she enquired in a gentle Scottish lilt, looking speculatively at Will. 'Or a wife?'

'Whatever suits both parties,' said Kat, seeing that Will was at a loss for words. 'If you find you don't suit, I'll find you a good position. Be honest and hard-working and you'll never have to return here. My hand on it.'

Mary looked for a long moment at Kat's outstretched hand; scarcely able to believe her luck had turned after the horrors of the past year, she shook it. 'Bless ye, mistress,' she said with a trembling lip. 'If I'd had a few kind words like yours this past twelvemonth, 'stead of all the hard knocks, I'd ne'er have fallen in this trouble.' Then Will took her hand and shook it so vigorously that Mary didn't know where to look. At last he let her go and she went with the assistant to make her mark on the assignment papers.

Garvey stopped on the edge of the clearing and looked around him in satisfaction. To his left stood a cluster of stringy-bark shelters erected in the style of the wigwams of the North American Indians and nearby, a little higher up the valley, was a more substantial slab hut from which rose a plume of smoke and a welcome aroma of fried ham

327

and coffee. Over by the river a larger building was rising and through the unfilled framework he could see the small mill wheel turning and hear the sound of timber being sawn. In the distance a bellbird sang out its one-note call.

He dismounted and tethered his horse to a low branch. The door opened and one of the hands came out, wiping his mouth with the back of his hand. 'Mr Garvey! What brings you up here?' he asked.

'Come to see progress, Samuel.'

'Break your fast, sir, break your fast,' he said, flinging the door wide. 'I'll go and find the master.'

Delahaye must have made his mark, thought Garvey with a grim smile as he entered the slab hut and crossed to the stove. For a stubborn old lag like Samuel, a real pebble, to call Joshua 'master' was more than Garvey could have hoped for.

Joshua – a fitter, leaner, tanned Joshua with once more a full set of whiskers – was eager to show Garvey around the site.

Nature had provided a perfect setting for the mill in the form of a back stream at a point where the river dropped several feet over a rocky outcrop; only a small amount of digging-out had been needed. Wherever Garvey looked, the work seemed to flow to the same rhythm as the river, backed by the clacking and rushing of the wheel through the race. Two of the men were carrying sawn lengths of timber out of the sawmill and up the bank to the upper part of the framework where, under Thomas's guidance, they were nailed into place. Inside, two more men were laying thin split logs across the joists in the lower section of the mill to form a floor above the system of cogs and shafts that converted the revolutions of the water wheel to operate the saw.

Down by the river, under the supervision of Hugh Stevens, whose father had been a millwright, another two were trimming pieces to slot into a half-finished wheel, larger than the one already in use. The original plans had been to change the use from sawmill to paper mill once the main buildings were in place, but because of the terrain, Joshua had devised an alteration which would eventually incorporate two wheels and keep the sawmill wheel running in the tail race of the paper-mill wheel.

'In the dry season there may not be a strong enough flow to run both. But we'll have to have houses for the papermen, so we'll need the sawmill for some time yet.'

'Any trouble with the men?' asked Garvey.

'None. They work well.'

'So they should. They were all picked for the job.' He and Kat had deliberately chosen men who were near the end of their sentence, who wouldn't be likely to take to the bush.

'They moan a lot in the evenings, though,' said Joshua with a grin.

'Miss the women, I suppose? Unlike you.'

Joshua looked sideways at Garvey, started to say something, then changed his mind. They walked back to the slab hut in silence.

Joshua paused in the doorway, his hand tracing the knots in the wood. 'How is Kat?' he said at last. 'Is she well?'

'You could come down occasionally and find out.' Garvey's suggestion was greeted with silence. 'She keeps herself busy,' he went on, thinking back to the days after the men had left, when she'd been unable to turn her mind to anything. He sighed. What she was turning her mind to now with Hall, the editor of the *Monitor*, worried him a deal more than her inactivity had done then.

'There's always a great deal to do around the farm,' agreed Joshua. 'Have you made much progress building the new house?'

Garvey shook his head. 'We're no further forward than when you left. She seems to have lost heart,' he said pointedly.

'I've had some thoughts on the design,' said Joshua, holding the door open for Garvey to pass into the hut.

'Not a great deal else to do up here in the evenings,' said Garvey with a grin.

'All the old India hands complain that the heat here is harder to bear than in India,' said Joshua, crossing to the stove and setting the kettle to boil. 'I've talked to one or two and it seems to me that the buildings in India are better adapted to the heat. Here they build English houses, totally unsuited for the weather, with small windows and doors that only trap the heat.'

'Aye. So desperate they are not to lose touch with the fact that they're English.'

'What we need are French windows and broad doors to catch every breath of air we can.' Joshua drew back the curtain that divided the hut in two, pulled a saddlebag down from the hook above the sleeping platform and fished out a sketchbook. He flicked through the sketches of the mill buildings until he came to the page he sought.

'If we take – ' He corrected himself hastily. 'If the mistress takes the original plans, divides the rear section here and draws it out to form two wings to the main body, she can put a verandah all round, front and back, to catch the wind. And it might be possible to have a room on the corners – here – and here – with sections that can open or close according to the season: garden rooms for days when the sun is too fierce to sit outside. Kat – the mistress – told me the greatest fire risk is always from the kitchens, so they could be separated from the house and from the servants' quarters by a stone-flagged area. I've had an idea for the doors and windows too,' he went on, his enthusiasm showing through his customary reserve. 'Keep out the flies at the worst of the season but still allow the air to move through the house. Brymer's going to make the bed of the Fourdrinier machine at his mill. It requires a very fine mesh of drawn wire and I've asked him to make up an inner door and window in the same way – just one of each until we see whether it works.' He looked up at Garvey, his eyes bright. 'I hope Kat – the mistress – will like it.'

It occurred to Garvey that it was the first time he'd shown any enthusiasm since discovering it was Kat who had bought him.

'There's something I've never understood,' said Joshua later as they sat in the cookhouse over a brew of tea, made strong, black and sweet the way the men liked it. It was made from better leaves than the tea issued to most convicts – coarse green stuff so full of twigs that was known as posts-and-rails – but the men still liked to brew it up in the same pot as the sticky brown sugar they called coal tar. 'You've been your own man for some time now, and you must have been eligible for a land grant, so – '

'So why do I work for someone else?' Garvey set his cup down and refilled it from the pot. 'I had me own place, right enough, when I'd served me time: a sixty-acre grant, and a comfortable snug little place it was too, north of Sydney, but not far enough away. Two government men assigned to me, and I could have had more if I'd wanted them.' He chewed his lip. 'But I'd been fourteen years at someone else's service – it wasn't so easy to get a ticket in Van Diemen's Land, where they sent the politicals. Now in the early days we'd a shortage of currency in the colony – that's why we had the holey dollar, to make one coin work twice as hard – so back then, any work you did on your own time was paid for in rum. I'd got a taste for it and when I was me own man again I drank too much and gambled too much.'

'You lost it all?'

'Aye. If it hadn't been for meeting Betsey, I'd have carried on going downhill and likely ended up in chains again. She pulled me back from the abyss and begged Mr Lacey for work for us both, away from Sydney and the drink and the horses.' He sighed heavily. 'There was many a time in the early days at the Creek that I wanted to get on me horse and off to the races with me money, for that one lucky break to win me back all me land, but she kept me straight. I still give her all me money and she keeps it for me.' He looked sideways at Joshua. 'Oh, I'm not too proud to be dependent on my woman.'

'But surely Betsey would prefer to be her own mistress?'

'Maybe once she wanted that. She's never reproached me with it.' He shrugged. 'I had me opportunity and wasted it and now we're a bit old to be starting out fresh. That's for the young folk. No, we're quite content to work for the missus. And twice a year Betsey takes

330

me to the races and we have two small bets apiece.' He grinned wryly. 'It's as much excitement as we can take these days.'

While Garvey saddled up his horse for the journey back to Lacey's Creek, Joshua rolled the plans for the new house in a piece of canvas for the steward to take with him.

'Let's hope we can get her to turn her energies to these,' Garvey said heavily. 'At least 'twould take her mind off this newspaper nonsense.'

'Has she been talking to Hall?' said Joshua. 'He told me this mill will be the best thing that's happened since the first printing press arrived.'

'Lord bless us, is the man getting at you too?'

'I met him when I was at Brymer's mill last month, ordering the gearings; he says our paper will free the *Monitor* from government interference.' He looked at Garvey with a frown. 'You do not approve?'

'Would you expect me to? Oh, Hall is a good enough fellow and he's done some good with his newspaper, but – '

'I'm told he spoke out against Darling more bravely than ever Wentworth did.'

'Aye. And was thrown in gaol for his pains,' growled Garvey. 'Lost the use of the government printer and the government paper. Lost all his convict servants. Left his motherless daughters to fend for themselves. And now he's trying to get you and the missus involved in his work!'

'Kat? He never said.'

'He wouldn't, would he? It was one thing to promise him paper, but that's not enough for her any more. Nor for Hall. Not only does he want to see her reports to the Colonial Office, he wants her to publish them abroad in the newspapers! Dare say he won't be happy till they're both in prison for contempt!'

'Reports to the Colonial Office?' said Joshua. 'What reports?'

'Didn't she say?'

'No.'

'Then it's not for me to tell you.' He ran stubby fingers through his sandy hair. 'I shouldn't have got so heated – said more than I should.' He chewed on his lip. 'Best ask her yourself if you want to know more.'

'I will. When I see her.'

'An' that may be quicker than you thought.'

Joshua looked up, a question in his eyes.

'We're to dine with Lassiters, Wednesday next. 'Tis Brymer's brother-in-law. They've a property over the next ridge, not far.'

'I shan't be coming down. No.' He forestalled Garvey's protests.

331

'Until I hear whether or not I have a pardon or a retrial – and unlike your mistress, I don't hold out much hope for either – I intend to stay where I am. I'll go down to Brymer's for the parts I need, otherwise I don't stir from here.'

'You're a fool,' said Garvey roundly, 'but there's no arguing with you.' He unhitched his horse from the tree and climbed into the saddle. 'When you go to town, even if it's only to Brymer's, be sure to take your face fur off,' he said, looking pointedly at Joshua's beard. 'You look too like a convict for my taste.'

# Chapter Seventeen

'There's some more o' those bloody emigrants!' someone bellowed above Joshua's head. He reined in the horse at the mill yard gates as the weary procession of men, women and children trudged up from the quayside, watched by half a dozen redcoat sentries.

'Curse all Jemmy Grants!' shouted another of the men replacing shingles on the warehouse roof. 'Come to take the country from us!'

'Who'd ever ha' thought the day would come when the convicts thought they had more right to the land than law-abiding folk!' said the redcoat sergeant, spitting in the dust.

'Many more of these emigrant ships,' said Brymer, 'and the Exclusives and the Emancipists will forget their quarrels to stand together against the emigrants and say "We were here first!"'

The last of the emigrants had scuffled their way through the dust and up the road towards the town; Brymer and the sergeant seemed set to continue their light-hearted argument, so with a wave of the hand Joshua called to the horse to 'Walk on!'

He realised that he had been holding his breath. That moment when he left the safety of Brymer's mill and drove the cart past Campbell's warehouses, towards the cove where the convicts were being unloaded from the transports, was always the worst for him: at any moment, he was convinced, one of the redcoats was going to step out in front of him, musket levelled, order him down from the cart, clap him in chains and send him back to the degradation of the convict auction. He was eager to leave the town and make his way back to the hills, where he could breathe the fresh air and make believe he was a free man.

In spite of his fears, he had never had any trouble with the authorities. Not once on the several journeys from Prospect Creek to Brymer's mill had he been asked to show his pass, but Samuel had told him of a foot-loose free native lad, constantly on the wallaby track, swag roll on his shoulder, who as a consequence of the new Bushranging Act had been arrested a dozen times on suspicion of being an absconder, and brought in by farm constables, the 'trusty' convicts who hoped to shorten their sentence by bringing in bolters. The lad had carried no papers – being a free-born man he had no need in law to do so – but each time he had been dragged back to the town gaol to await proof of his status.

With this in mind, Joshua was always careful to wear one of the modish jackets Kat had bought for him, and a hat; he had even taken Garvey's advice and shaved off his beard. Obviously it had all to do with appearance: look like a gentleman and it would be assumed that you were one. It was a lesson that many of the Emancipists seemed unable to learn. On the way to Brymer's an expensive carriage with a prime pair of horses had overtaken him and drawn up in front of the smart shops on George Street. A family of Emancipists had stepped out, the mother and daughter smartly, if a little garishly, dressed; the father, wearing a grubby shirt and stained coat, looked as though he had just come from the fields while the son, his clothes almost as smart as a Bond Street dandy and his fingers covered with expensive rings, wore no socks or stockings between his rather too short trousers and highly polished shoes to which, in defiance of both fashion and reason, he had attached jingling spurs.

Once past the sentries, Joshua turned into the road that ran between the hovels, brothels and drinking dens of the Rocks, guiding the horse around potholes, pecking chickens and wandering goats, past dogs and pigs scavenging in the gutters. On every corner and step, alongside the animals, the drunken sailors and the rum-sodden black beggars, ragged and filthy children played in the gutters.

As he drew level with the Black Dog, a sailors' lodging house on the corner of the track that rose in jagged gradations to the uppermost part of the Rocks, a door flew open and a woman staggered out, followed by a large, heavily bearded man who gripped her by the arm and shook her violently. Joshua's first instinct was to go to her aid, but it was an instinct he hastily suppressed. This was no more than a brawl between a pimp and his woman, he reminded himself. Such fights were two a penny in the brothels and grog shops of the Rocks and the sentries at the end of the road would come down if matters grew out of hand.

He was almost past the pair when his brain registered that there was something different about them. Normally in this kind of fight, the air would be full of oaths and imprecations as the man cursed his woman to hell and back, and the woman gave back as good as she got, and probably paid back his blows by raking his face with her nails; but this woman was silent, giving no response to the curses raining down on her, lolling like a limp rag doll, her head snapping back and forth as the man shook her.

Self-preservation went to the wall. The sentries showed no sign of intervening so Joshua pulled up alongside the pair, shouting at the man to stop. As he looped the reins and jumped down from the seat, he saw that the woman was young and quite well-dressed for this area, with a cashmere shawl wrapped tightly over a rather old-fashioned dark-blue riding outfit so loose it must have been made for a much larger woman.

Within seconds a small crowd had gathered round them, hopeful of a good scrap for their entertainment. 'What's it to you, mate?' demanded the man, turning on Joshua. 'Ain't a man to get paid for board and lodging, hey? Fed the judy an' give 'er a place to sleep two nights now, I 'as, an' when I fanned 'er, she ain't a ring, nor a watch, nor even a holey dollar to 'er name. Well, I'll 'ave me money or the worth of it out of 'er.' The hand that had rained down blows on the woman caught at her chin and turned her face to Joshua. 'Fine-lookin' woman like 'er shouldn't 'ave no problems, wouldn't you agree, sir?' he leered. 'Per'aps you'd like to start 'er lodgin' fund?'

Joshua knew what he meant even if the woman did not. She seemed past caring, her face pale, her eyes bruised and wide and staring, as though she had not slept this twelvemonth.

'Lookee here,' wheedled the landlord. 'As good a bit of twang an' buttock as ever I seen in this port!'

Joshua resisted the temptation to punch the fellow in the face. 'Where is she from?' he demanded.

'From England,' she said in a voice so hoarse he had to strain to hear her. 'From Sussex.'

'You were transported?'

'I'm a free woman!' she said, for the first time showing some spirit. Then her head drooped again. 'I came to meet my husband. Only he's ... he's – '

'He don't 'ave no need of 'er no more,' guffawed a sailor who had emerged from the Black Dog to watch the fun.

'An' if he ain't goin' to pay 'er board,' said the landlord with a leer, 'then she shall 'ave to *work* it off. Won't you, darlin'?'

The look of terror on the woman's face was too much for Joshua. He groped in his pocket for a couple of coins and held them out to the man.

'This will amply cover her costs,' he said curtly. 'Now let her go.'

The man reached out greedily for the first coin and bit it, but as he made to grab the second, Joshua closed his fingers over it. 'She didn't sail from England with nothing but what she stands up in,' he said in steely tones. 'Fetch her gear.'

There was no more than a pair of worn boots and a small canvas bag, and when they had been handed over, Joshua relinquished the second coin. The woman herself looked fit to swoon, so Joshua caught her round the waist and lifted her up into the cart. It was fortunate that he had nothing in the cart beyond the pieces of metal from Brymer's, well-lashed down: the urchins of the Rocks crowded round them would think nothing of thieving anything they could sell.

'Have you nowhere to go?' he asked the woman as he flicked the reins and drove away. 'No family in Sydney?'

She shook her head. 'I thought I had a husband,' she said softly. She drew a letter out of her bag. 'He wrote to me, begging me to come out and join him. See? It took me two years,' she said fiercely, the words pouring out at last. 'But I told him I'd come. I *told* him. Me and the boy. As soon as we had permission from the government. The squire's lady give me good clothes, so's I wouldn't look like a convict. Wrote to the government to find it all out for me, she did. Me bein' free, she said I could have him assigned to me. It took me five months to get here – '

'You said, you and the boy?'

'Jack.' She bit her trembling lip. 'Four years old, our Jack was. I buried him at sea.'

He put his hand on her arm in ready sympathy.

'And when I got here – '

'Your husband had died too?'

She shook her head dumbly. 'They tell me he's got a ticket of leave,' she said after a moment.

'By servitude? Oh, but that's good. It means he – '

'Not by servitude, sir. By marriage. Oh, he was such a handsome man.' She put her hand over her mouth to stifle a sob. 'They said he was assigned to a widow with four children as runs an inn up at Newcastle. Three months ago he married her. About the time I was buryin' our boy.' She looked up at Joshua with bright-blue eyes drowned in tears. 'Funny that,' she said.

'*Funny?*'

'Him running an inn. Bein' as he was sent out here for smugglin' French brandy past the revenue men.'

Kat knew Joshua had declined the invitation to the Lassiters, so the sight of him driving into the yard came as something of a shock. When she saw him handing a woman down from the seat of the cart, she dropped her lace cushion and hurried out to the yard, a dozen questions on her lips, but before she could say anything, the woman swayed and almost fell; instead of giving way to her feelings, Kat found herself giving orders, sending one maid scurrying to the kitchen for Betsey, another to fetch the smelling salts.

The woman was carried off to the kitchens and Kat turned back to question Joshua more closely, only to find that he had taken the cart off to the stables. She started to follow him, then thought better of it.

A few minutes later Betsey put her head around the door. 'Nothing wrong with the wench that a good feed and a good night's rest won't cure,' she said reassuringly. 'And Mr Joshua's compliments and he'll be joining you at the Lassiters. Seems Seth Lassiter met him on the road,' she said with a grin, 'so he ain't got no excuse not to go.' She looked at the gilt clock on the mantel. 'Time you was dressing.'

After the initial stilted greetings, and a brief explanation from Joshua about Clara, the woman he'd rescued on the Rocks, the journey was undertaken in almost complete silence, though Garvey was aware that Kat and Joshua were each darting looks at the other whenever they thought themselves unobserved.

'Who'll be there tonight, I wonder?' asked the steward, trying to fill an overlong pause. He turned to Joshua. 'Most of 'em will be house guests,' he explained. 'We're probably the only ones who live close enough to travel there and back in one day.'

Kat rattled off a list of people, with an occasional aside to Joshua. 'Deas Thomson will be there, and as clerk of the Council he may be able to set enquiries in hand about poor Clara's husband. And the Rileys, of course, so if the talk's not all about horses and racing 'twill be about sheep and wool staple. Riley brought in Saxon merinos about half a dozen years ago and breeds them out at Yass,' she explained. 'He claims they are hardier than Macarthur's Spanish merinos and produce a better staple.'

''Tis to be hoped the ould feller's in a better mood than the last time I saw him,' said Garvey. 'Most of the time he can charm the birds off the trees, like his nephew, but when the blackness comes upon him, he can be as bad as old Macarthur. Must be something to do with living with sheep!'

'Then we must rely on Sir Harry to charm them out of their moods,' said Kat. 'They tell me he is expected.' She turned to Joshua. 'He was transported for kidnapping a fifteen-year-old heiress but I must confess I rather like the old reprobate.'

'A kidnapper?' Joshua was shocked.

'Oh, the heiress was nothing loth, they tell me. In truth 'twas an elopement, no more, but her family had influence. She lived with aged grandparents, and I can see that Sir Harry would have seemed a preferable companion. He has a droll way with him.'

Lassiter greeted them at the door. By the look of the house guests in the hall, they had been imbibing from Lassiter's excellent cellar for some hours.

A tall, dark-haired man with a hawklike profile pushed his way through. 'Lassiter, introduce me to the beautiful lady!' he said, enunciating his words carefully.

Lassiter shifted uncomfortably from one foot to the other. 'Mrs Delahaye – Mr Walter Ellis, newly arrived from – '

Ellis snatched at her hand and held it in his. 'Delighted to meet you, ma'am!' he said. 'First good-looking woman I've clapped eyes on since I came to this godforsaken spot! Sydney women – pah! Boot-faced, the lot of 'em!'

A ripple of indignation ran around the assembled guests and Mrs Lassiter controlled her temper with difficulty. Behind her, her sisters, Mrs Brymer and Mrs Thomas, bristled.

As Ellis showed every inclination to hold on to Kat's hand for the rest of the evening, Lassiter made one last attempt. 'Mr Ellis, I really think ... Mrs Delahaye, let me show you – '

Joshua, his patience sorely tested, stepped forward to intervene.

'See you've brought your musician,' said Ellis, catching sight of the flute under Joshua's arm. 'Play for us while we dine, will he?' He squeezed her hand and clasped it to his chest. 'Music to soothe the savage breast, hey?'

There was a sharp intake of breath from everyone within earshot: only convict servants played during the meal to entertain guests. Lassiter wondered who had been fool enough to let slip Joshua's situation to Ellis?

Sir Harry, bustling out of the card room with a young lieutenant in time to hear Ellis's insulting words, hurried to the rescue. 'Surely Mrs Lassiter won't desert us at table?' he said. 'No, no, Ellis. You'll see – time enough for music after we've dined.' He turned to Joshua, a smile on his cherubic face. 'Delahaye, isn't it? Been looking forward to meeting you.' He linked his arm in Kat's, forcing Ellis to release his grip on her. 'My dear Mrs Delahaye ... I do hope your husband will consent to join Mrs Lassiter in some musical entertainment after dinner?' he said, edging her away from Ellis and towards the drawing room. 'Our dear hostess is renowned for her talent on the pianoforte.'

Joshua's hands itched to take Ellis and throw him through the door, but seeing Mrs Lassiter's embarrassment, he took her hand and bowed over it with a flourish that brought a glow to his hostess's cheeks. 'I should be honoured, ma'am, to play a duet with you.'

That should have been the end of it, but as Kat passed among the guests, she heard Ellis say to Deas Thomson, 'No wonder the Macarthurs sent their excuses. They're very particular about the company they keep.' She ground her teeth in frustration; she could only hope that Joshua, further down the room, had not heard.

She could not remember a more uncomfortable evening. Ellis,

338

seated at the far end of the table from Kat after a hasty rearrangement, persisted in trying to converse with her across the other guests and Joshua, making stilted conversation with Amelia Lassiter, fresh out of the schoolroom, looked as though he would like to rend him with his bare hands.

'Ellis means no harm, my dear Mrs Delahaye,' said Lassiter, as the footman set a plate of mock-turtle soup in front of her. 'He's from Van Diemen's Land, you know.' As if being a Vandemonian should be considered sufficient excuse!

Esmé Lassiter was not having a very pleasant evening. What was supposed to have been a quiet soirée, introducing Amelia to adult society, was taking on all the aspects of a nightmare. Not only had Ellis been grossly offensive, but in the absence of further definite information on Joshua's status, she had to stay alert to head off all the usual topics of discussion, such as whether or not the tendency to crime was hereditary and the colony therefore condemned to an eternity of felonry, and whether the new governor would permit Emancipists to hold office in the colony. Fortunately Deas Thomson – such a gentleman! – was doing what he could to pour oil on troubled waters at his end of the table, admirably seconded by her brother-in-law Brymer, and by the time the desserts were served, much of the general irritation had disappeared under an avalanche of exotic dishes and an abundance of various wines.

Unfortunately, Ellis did not seem to have mellowed. 'New South Wales will never be a patch on Van Diemen's Land,' he said, belching gently. 'You're too soft on your convicts, for a start. And the damned printers! Look at the way they worried at Darling. Now, our Colonel Arthur, one whiff of libel from the Hobart printers and he throws them in gaol.'

'Darling threw Hall in gaol, after the Sudds case,' someone objected.

'But he let him out again! Then there's your ridiculous policy towards the blacks,' he said, motioning the convict servant to fill his glass again. 'You should do what Arthur did: herd all the blacks into one peninsula, away from the settled lands, and shoot them if they move away from it. We had five hundred troops and over a thousand settlers to net them – '

'Ah yes,' sneered Brymer. 'Colonel Arthur's Great Black Line. How many did he catch in his net? One black man and a small boy. That missionary fellow Robinson brought in more than that.'

'More than one way to catch a black,' said Ellis loftily. 'And it can't be denied, we've cleared Van Diemen's Land of 'em all. None left but what are on Flinders Island. Tell you what you should do – set your huntsmen on 'em.' He drained his glass again. 'Bugger all else to hunt round here. If you're goin' to put on yer huntin' pink, might as well have somethin' worthwhile to hunt. Can't beat a good chase after a fleet-footed black – '

Mrs Lassiter shuddered. 'Really, Mr Ellis,' she remonstrated feebly, 'I hardly think – '

'Nothing to beat a good ride after a fine buck kangaroo, Ellis,' said an elderly farmer who regularly donned hunting pink to ride through the scrub bush tally-hoing after dingoes. 'I remember when I first came out here, not long after the Rum Rebellion, it was . . . with just a couple of lads and a string of kangaroo hounds, we kept the table supplied with kangaroo and wild duck. Of course you have to go farther afield now if you want kangaroo . . .'

'I've bred some good coursers from my old kangaroo hounds,' said Sir Harry. 'Thought I'd put it to the new governor to bring out rabbits and hares from home. They'd breed well out here.'

'Good idea, old fellow,' said another farmer. 'There's nothing like a good coursing. Had some jolly fine runs at home . . .'

'If you're a true Englishman, then Hobart's where you want to be,' said Ellis with a sneer. 'The air's more like England, the hills are more like England, the huntin's more like England. Damn me, we can even grow apples there, which is more than you can here. Peach cider's all very well for the convicts, I say, but a true Englishman wants his apple cider – and only the Vandemonians can make it. Invite you to visit with me in Hobart, m'dear lady,' he shouted down the table to his hostess. 'Bring Miss Kattrin with you. Can promise you two fine ladies a delightful visit. No blacks to spear you or throw their firesticks on your roofs in Hobart.'

'Not a problem we have here either, Ellis,' said Lassiter curtly, his hospitality under severe strain.

'They killed poor old Logan up in Moreton Bay!' argued Ellis, becoming pugnacious with drink.

'If they hadn't, then the convicts would have,' said Brymer. 'The man's brutalities were beyond belief. Shall you be going to the Parramatta Races, Mrs Delahaye?' he asked, deliberately trying to change the conversation.

'I think not,' she said. 'I must ride out to see some of my tenants. But I understand 'tis a pleasant day's outing.'

'Allows the convicts too much freedom to get drunk and break heads,' said one man, rather sanctimoniously. He emptied his wine glass, belched softly and motioned impatiently to the footman to refill it. 'It's to be hoped the new governor will support the gentlemen's cricket team . . .'

His wife seconded him loyally. 'Cricket is so much more genteel than the hurly-burly of the race meetings.'

No one believed that cricket would ever match racing in its appeal; where was the excitement, after all, in gambling on a cricket match? The turf was a far more interesting topic and the general conversation returned to the chances of Deas Thomson's Tam O'Shanter against Williams's Thiefcatcher in the main race.

Mrs Lassiter heaved an almost audible sigh of relief when the time came to retire to the newly decorated drawing room. Having been starved of music until the recent arrival of her new instrument, she would not allow the gentlemen to sit too long over their port and rum, and they soon joined the ladies. Joshua, who had not touched his flute since his time on the *Perseus*, found that his fingers flew as swiftly as ever over the instrument. The music seemed to lift everyone's spirits and Mrs Lassiter, delighted to find a player who could meet her exacting standards, pronounced that she had not enjoyed herself so much for an age.

While Joshua and Esmé Lassiter searched through a pile of music which had come with the pianoforte, some of the men went out on the verandah with a bumper of rum, to smoke a pipe or a cigar. When Ellis came back in with a couple of young officers from Sir Maurice O'Connell's staff, he swaggered across to the group of young girls in the far corner, giggling with one another over their debut in polite society.

'Mish Lashter,' he said, 'in honour of your day-boo this evening, I have deshided to give you one of my mosht prized poshesh- posseshions.' He fumbled in his jacket pocket and drew out a string-necked purse made of some strange material.

'It is a most ... unusual purse, sir,' said Miss Amelia nervously, wishing her mother was by to support her. 'I am not sure that I – '

'Qui' righ', Mish Amelia,' said Ellis. 'Mosht unush'l. Had it made from a kangaroo's stone cashe,' he said with a leer.

One of the young lieutenants, whose advances to Miss Amelia had been firmly repulsed by her father, started to snigger.

'Stone case?' said Amelia with a frown. 'I don't understand.'

'The cashe, Mish Amelia, that the animal keeps hish shtones in,' said Ellis, cupping his hand suggestively in the region of his groin.

One of the young ladies shrieked and, as Miss Amelia realised his meaning, she coloured up and ran from the room, leaving Ellis and the young lieutenants shaking with laughter.

The Lacey's Creek party took its leave soon after the tea tray was brought in. Those who were not house guests could not stay late, in spite of the full moon which turned the landscape almost to day, for although Jack Donohoe had been killed a year or more before in a shoot-out with the law near Campbelltown, other bushrangers were

341

now active once more, preying on lone or late travellers who went in fear of hearing the dreaded cry of 'Bail up!'

Most of the men had drifted away to the card room. While the servant went for the carriage, Mrs Lassiter drew Joshua back into the drawing room to discuss what music they should choose for Barnett Levey's At Home recital to greet the new governor. Unless Sir Richard brought out with him a pardon or a retrial, Joshua had no intention of being there, but he couldn't bring himself to tell his hostess so: Esmé Lassiter had suffered enough already that evening.

By good fortune, only Kat and Edward Deas Thomson were in earshot of the card room when Ellis began to discuss her with the two drunken young lieutenants.

'Forget Mish Prim and Proper Amelia,' said Ellis. 'I tell you, the Delahaye wench ... only one worth making a play for.'

'Word is, she's devoted to that surly husband of hers,' said the first officer.

'Devoted marriage be damned!' said the other, slightly less inebriated. 'I saw him only this morning picking up a drab on the quayside. Where I come from they have a name for that. Begins with *whore* and ends with – '

'*-ing*' chorused his drinking companions.

Before Edward could stop her, she pushed wide the door. 'Really, Lieutenant Markham?' she said in ringing tones. 'Where I come from, helping a female in distress is called Christian charity.'

The officers goggled drunkenly at her as they staggered to their feet.

'And the widow of whom you spoke in such ungentlemanly fashion is a guest in my house.'

'Well said, ma'am,' said Edward, coming up behind her and fixing the two officers with an angry glare. 'A person foolish enough to spread such slander could well find himself in a great deal of trouble with his senior officers.'

The young officers, well aware of his influence with both government and military, were so unnerved by his attack that one of them dropped a winning hand.

Joshua, following them into the card room, became aware of the atmosphere as soon as he opened the door. 'Your shawl, Kattrin,' he said. He looked from her flushed face to the abashed expressions of the young officers. 'There is something amiss?'

'The gentlemen were just bidding the ladies adieu,' said Deas Thomson. 'A pleasure to make your acquaintance at last, Delahaye. Perhaps you'll dine with me when next you are in Sydney?'

'Poor Esmé,' said Kat, as the carriage wound its way back to the Parramatta road, down the curving track which ran between fenced paddocks and which Mrs Lassiter, in spite of the total absence of any trees, insisted on calling 'the Avenue'. 'Hardly the debut she would have wanted for Amelia.'

'But an excellent dinner,' said Garvey.

Joshua passed his tongue round his lips. 'I don't share the Australian taste for dried and smoked fish,' he said as the carriage bumped its way along the rough road. 'I've a terrible thirst.'

'Don't be tellin' them that, now,' said Garvey jovially, 'or you'll be settin' the tongues waggin' again! Convicts in their spare time go fishing to supplement their diet, y'see. So the gentry must prove they are different by importing dried and smoked fish and ignoring the riches on their doorstep.'

'Just as those who would happily sea-bathe in Brighton will not go near the sea shore here,' said Kat, who had been staring distractedly out of the window.

'I thought that was because of the sharks?'

'Only partly. For many of the convicts, particularly in Sydney, the sea is their only chance to get clean; the Currency lads and lasses have taken rather enthusiastically to swimming...'

'So the gentry won't be seen near it,' finished Garvey.

'Madness!' said Joshua.

The fresh air, damp from early morning rain, was soon laden with dust from the great numbers of horses and gigs heading down the turnpike to the Parramatta Races. The wife of the turnpike-keeper looked up from the table by the door where she sat with a cup and a half-gallon bottle of rum, nursing a black eye and a split lip. 'You'll need a ticket,' she said, her voice already slurred.

'But you know me,' Kattrin objected.

'Ah, but by the time you come back, missus, I shan't know anyone!' said the woman, shrieking with laughter.

'My God, is everyone drunk today?' exclaimed Joshua, watching a carriage weave erratically through the gate, the driver concentrating more on the contents of the bottle he was upending than on the road ahead.

She shrugged. 'Wages are high at present. A man can get by working scarcely half his day, and spend the rest drinking.'

'And the women,' he said grimly.

'Aye. The women are often as bad. Some say that's why Lang encourages the emigrants: more free labour will lower wages so the Emancipists will have to work harder and drink less.'

Once they had turned their horses off the Parramatta road towards Homebush the air was fresher, but the bush was denser and, with fewer houses and carriages, Joshua kept a wary eye out for bushrangers and his coat clear of his belt, where there was a serviceable pair of pistols. Kat still sat her horse very badly and he wouldn't like to have to make a run for it.

Joshua looked sideways at Kat, but her attention was fixed on a cloud of small blue and yellow parakeets wheeling above the eucalyptus trees ahead of them. He was as sure as he could be that she'd planned this deliberately, choosing today to inspect two properties on which the tenants had defaulted when she must have known that Garvey was to take Betsey to the Parramatta Races. It would have served her right if he had insisted on returning to the mill as he'd planned, but he knew her obstinacy of old: she was just as likely to ride out alone, in spite of all the rumours of bushrangers.

The first farm was tucked away off the Homebush road, down a little valley. The tenants had done their best to keep it smart: scrawny chickens picked and scratched in the yard, and in a fenced-off section by the kitchen door, pot herbs, small cabbages and a few colourful flowers struggled through the dust.

The house looked from the outside neat and tidy, with pretty chintz curtains at all the windows. A tired-looking woman in her early thirties opened the door to greet them. She urged them to come into the house and take refreshment, but they decided first to take a short ride around the farm, where the land told a different story, with fields badly cleared, vines and plants wilting. The maize cobs, which should by now have been plump and bursting, were dry and wizened. The farmer was still digging in the fields, working with his two small sons, but the look of defeat was in his face.

'We had such hopes when we came here, ma'am,' said the wife, blinking the tears back as she served them refreshments at the farmhouse. 'It weren't what we'd been used to in London, acourse, but we done our best, I swear we did. 'Tis the first time we've not paid our rent, but I – I don't know where to turn next. The pests got the crops an' when we tried stock, the sheep got the scab and the cattle failed to fatten. My man, he knows 'osses well, from bein' stableman at the inn, but he don't seem to do as well with other beasts.'

'Brews good ale, though,' said Joshua, wiping the foam from his lips.

'That's me, sir. Learned that from the landlady at the Talbot.'

'You were employed at the same inn?'

'I was, sir. Chambermaid I started as, then when the stagecoaches started a-calling, I helped in the brewhouse. Could turn my hand to most things in the trade. Indoor work that was, though.' She must have been attractive, he thought, before suffering ground her down and the pitiless sun lined her face. When she was turning down the sheets, there would have been guests aplenty to suggest she dispense

344

with the warming pan. 'I don't want to go back to the town,' said the woman tearfully. 'I've had my fill of that way of life, working for others and having to do their bidding no matter what. I've liked it that here we were our own masters.' She wiped her eyes on the corner of a spotlessly clean apron. 'I'm sorry, ma'am, I didn't mean to give way. We've been desperate to make a go of it, but for certain my man's not a good farmer. Even in good seasons he's made a hash of it. And 'tis a lone life for folk as has been used to company.'

Kat patted her on the shoulder and promised they'd take no action for the next three months, but as she rode away with Joshua, she had to agree with him that there was little hope that anything would change in that time.

The next property they were to inspect was a large, commodious building further up the Penrith road, not far from the ferry where people, carriages and horses heading into the interior were carried over the Nepean River on large punts.

There was a fine view of the Blue Mountains rising beyond the level Emu Plains on the other side, but the closer view was none too prepossessing.

Whereas the farmhouse had had a cheerful aspect, the large road-side house was close to turning into a wretched hovel to match the one behind, where the assigned man lived: that was no more than a pile of heaped turf and slabs, the rough pieces of split timber set on end like palings and thatched. If it had been plastered with mud it might have been weatherproof and comfortable, but here the slabs were falling asunder, the thatch was half off, the window stopped with wood. A door without hinges was propped against the wall.

In front of both cottage and house were heaps of ashes and wood chips; broken bottles, old casks, rags and bones and shoes were scattered everywhere, but there was not a herb nor a cabbage to be seen.

A dirt-coloured face topped with a mass of dark, matted hair appeared in the doorway as they dismounted. 'Wotcherwant?' said a slurred voice. Just inside the door a haunch of kangaroo hung from the ceiling, with a cloud of black flies swarming around it and a mangy cur snuffling at the dung-encrusted earth floor below. In the window a silent and dispirited mynah bird crouched in a cramped wicker cage.

Seeing Kat for the moment rendered speechless, Joshua explained that Mrs Delahaye, being the new owner of Lacey's Creek, had come to inspect her property and discuss the nonappearance of the land rent.

'I knows who you are,' said the drunken woman, her eyes narrowing to little slits. 'You're Delahaye, ain't you? You're the one as got – '

Her words were cut off as a brawny hand on the end of a hairy and grimy arm grabbed the neck of her dress and thrust her back into the Stygian gloom of the house. Thrown off balance, she slipped in one of the puddles in the earth floor and fell in an untidy heap, sending up a cloud of fleas as she sprawled on the ground, her skirts round her waist. 'Shut yer mouth, woman!' bellowed the man. After a swift altercation he emerged, wiping sticky rum from his moustache with the back of his hand, and straightening his shirt over his huge belly. All smiles, he enquired in oily tones what he might do for the gentleman and lady.

The slovenly couple proved quite indifferent to the prospect of losing their land, being concerned only to get as much as they could out of Kat 'for their interest in the property'. It went against the grain to pay them anything, but it was at least a way to guarantee that they would not burn the house down before they rushed back to Sydney, where no doubt they would swiftly be absorbed by the seething mass of drunken humanity clawing a living from each other in the hovels and grogshops of the Rocks. At Joshua's suggestion, Kat gave them a promissory note, insisting that the money would only be paid on application in Sydney once the house had been cleared of all but its original furniture and left fit for another tenant.

'Such a waste,' said Joshua, as they turned their horses back towards Parramatta.

'Garvey holds it all to be the fault of the government stroke,' said Kat, glancing back at the house, which from a distance appeared quite substantial and prosperous.

'The government – ?'

'Stroke. Just enough to keep the overseer happy. Garvey says that when they're free men, they can't break the habit, even for themselves.'

It had been a depressing morning and in their eagerness to get away from the squalor of the house by the river they found themselves riding back through the heat of the day. With relief they came upon a new, glaringly smart inn which appeared to be covered in twenty different shades of paint and gilding.

Blinking at the sight, dazzling in the bright midday sun, they dismounted from their horses, leading them into the shady yard in the absence of an ostler. Considering the hour and the heat of the day, the place seemed curiously empty of customers. Their footsteps echoed off the wooden boards as they went up the steps and into the public room. Here there were a few gaudily painted chairs and on the wall hung a small spotted mirror in a gilt frame; the cedar table was covered with tobacco ashes and liquor stains. Joshua looked around him in disgust and rang the hand bell. After a long interval there was a muffled shriek from down the corridor and a maid staggered into the public room so drunk that she could hardly stand. Blearily registering their presence, she reluctantly released her grip on the door handle, tottered across the room and began ineffectually to wipe the table with her grubby apron.

'We got mutton chops and damper, but no ham nor eggs,' she said in a singsong voice, revealing a mouth full of blackened stumps. 'But we got plenty ale an' sperrits, acourse.'

Kat and Joshua looked at each other and by mutual consent declined the offer, preferring to dip themselves some cool, sweet water from the covered well.

'Meat and ale seem to be the only things they care about here!' said Joshua in disgust as he helped Kat back into the saddle.

'Meat can run about and feed itself,' she said ruefully. 'Fruit and vegetables need more attention. Even bread – why it's folly to offer damper when they could easily do a proper baking!' Like Betsey, she held damper bread, made from unrisen dough and cooked in the ashes, to be the ruination of good flour, excusable only when travelling in the bush. 'Ned says it's because too many masters make their government men live on maize gruel, so that they value naught but meat when they've served their time.'

'Meat and rum!' he said as a burst of raucous singing followed them out of the yard.

'Not all of them, though. I hate the idea of taking the land away from the Watsons,' she said passionately. 'God knows they worked hard enough to get it.'

The idea struck them both at the same time. 'Why not move *them* – '

'– into the roadside house?'

'Yes!'

'They'll never be farmers, but they could run a respectable inn!'

'Something along the lines of the inn we stayed in at Parramatta.'

'The Red Cow?'

'Aye. Think what business they could take from places like this!'

It would be, they decided, ideally situated for the increasing number of travellers crossing the ferry on their way to Bathurst and the interior, somewhere they could be certain of a clean bed and food beyond the monotonous ham and eggs which was all that such establishments usually ran to. When they put the plan to the Watsons, their faces were a delight to see.

It was a brief moment of shared joy, quickly dispelled when Joshua parted from Kattrin to ride back to Prospect Creek.

347

'You'll be back for Levey's concert, won't you?' she asked, fighting the temptation to plead with him.

'I haven't changed my mind,' he said bleakly. 'I'll stay up in the hills until the new governor arrives.'

'And then?'

The shutters came down over his face once more. 'Then we'll see.'

That evening Garvey returned from the races with a letter for her. 'From that damned priest,' he said. 'Still insisting on a wedding, I suppose?'

'I told them I might consider having a blessing. That way I don't accept that the marriage was unlawful, so there can be no problems with Joshua's assignment.'

'A blessing? Hmm. And when would that take place?'

'After the new governor arrives,' she said, staring blindly out of the window. 'By then we should know whether there's anything worth blessing.'

# Chapter Eighteen

Kat looked across the table at the newspaper proprietor, wondering whether she'd misheard him over the clatter of the printing press.

'You are surely not serious, Mr Hall!' she exclaimed. 'Me? Sail to Port Macquarie?'

'There is no road, dear lady. One must travel by ship.'

'If one wishes to go at all. But I do not.'

'You must see, dear lady, that it would be quite impossible for me to go. It's a penal settlement and, as such, requires a pass to travel there.'

She frowned at him. Perhaps what Sydney society said of the man was true and he really had taken leave of his senses. Failure could do that to a man and he had failed quite comprehensively both as a farmer and as a banker. Not until he had started the *Monitor* did he really seem to have found his niche in life, and even there he had only succeeded in putting up the backs of everyone in any position of authority in the colony. She recalled what she had been told of the spectacular quarrels with Archdeacon Scott which had led to Hall's eviction from his pew in St James's and later from the church itself; while fighting that case through the courts, he had carried on his campaign against Governor Darling which had led to the loss of his convict servants, loss of the use of the government printer and ultimately loss of his liberty.

He looked at her anxiously. 'After my various spells of imprisonment, not to mention my position as editor of the *Monitor*, no one would contemplate giving *me* such a pass.'

'I don't understand why *anyone* should wish to go there. What purpose would be served by such a visit?'

'I have been told terrible tales about the settlement; if they are true, they must be made public. Upon my report on Moreton Bay, ma'am, I was vilified, called a liar to my face and thrown into gaol for libel, so I must have independent confirmation of the situation at Port Macquarie before I can publish.'

'But there must be a dozen people you could send, all much more suited than I to make your report for you.'

'None who are both detached from the military interest *and* influential with the new governor,' he said, fiddling absent-mindedly with a dog-eared letter on his desk.

'Besides which, a female would arouse fewer suspicions, I suppose.'

'That is a consideration.'

'But not the only one. Mr Hall, I have the feeling that there is more to this than meets the eye.'

'Ma'am?' He tried for a look of guileless innocence, but he was a poor dissembler.

'There is something here that you are not telling me.' She narrowed her eyes. 'What, for example, is there in that letter which so attaches your attention?'

Hall threw his hands up in a gesture of defeat. In the letter, he explained, was an account of the most appalling deprivation, of the blind, the sick and the insane being kept in disgraceful conditions at Port Macquarie, ill-fed and worked in chains. 'When this letter was smuggled out in August, the – ah – author warned that conditions were about to grow yet worse, if that can be imagined,' said Hall. 'You read last year's report in the *Monitor* on Logan's administration in Moreton Bay?'

'Yes.' She shuddered as she recalled the details. The commandant, Captain Logan, and one of his overseers, had been accused of beating and abusing the prisoners in the grossest manner, even murder had been alleged.

'There was to have been a commission of enquiry, but then Logan was murdered and the overseer disappeared, so nothing came of it.' He picked up the letter. 'Now there are rumours that the overseer, Trenand, has reappeared at Port Macquarie, under a new identity.'

'But why write to you?' she asked. 'Why not inform the commandant in Port Macquarie?'

Hall set his gold-wire spectacles on his nose and read out the letter.

They sent the blind and them with the eye sores down here, and the consumptives, and them as lost arms or legs, all down to Port Macquarie. They sent a new overseer down too and it's him. There was three of us was at Moreton Bay and we knew the villain. We cast lots as to which would tell to the Commandant. Him as drew the short straw was found dead with a snake in his bed. We drew again. The second was picked out at muster, they says he stole a Hawkesbury duck.

Hall looked up at Kat. 'Which incidentally is not a duck at all, but a cob of corn.'

> They found it in his bedroll. It took the flogger two days to give all, three hundred lashes it was. They had to bring him back in a wheelbarrow for the second lot, but he didn't last it.

Hall folded up the letter. 'Man's inhumanity to man,' he said softly. 'So you see there's not a great deal of incentive for the remaining witness to go to the Commandant.'

She sat staring at him, bereft of the power of speech.

'Now if the new governor were to read the account of an eye-witness, it might persuade him to do something at last about these living hells that mar our land. We cannot alter the lot of every convict,' he said sombrely, regarding her over the top of his spectacles, 'but to stand by while the halt and the lame, the blind and the insane are so treated is more than I can stomach.'

She was weakening. The bargain she had made with the Colonial Office in return for Joshua's assignment had been that she should make as full a report on the state of the colony as she could. It was hardly fair to back out now.

'But what clerk in his right mind would believe that I wanted to go to Port Macquarie?' she asked.

A slow smile spread across Hall's face. 'Your licence to manufacture paper . . .' he said. 'I believe there is a method to manufacture from sugar cane?'

She nodded.

'And the nearest place to Sydney to grow sugar cane in any quantity is Port Macquarie.'

Will was to take the bullock cart up to the valley next day, laden with equipment and fresh supplies, and in spite of his warnings about the danger of bushrangers so far from the main roads, Kat donned her dungaree skirts and announced her intention of travelling with him. 'You drive the bullocks,' she said, 'and I'll ride shotgun! I want to see how work is progressing.' Only to herself could she admit the need to see Joshua in private – or at least as private as it was possible to get with several dozen workmen around. The Governor was expected to be here soon, in time for Christmas, and she would not leave Lacey's Creek without one more attempt to talk Joshua around.

The green valley was a hive of activity as they emerged from the dense bush. As it was a Saturday, when government men were on their own time to wash and mend their clothes and take their rest, most of the men were in the pools below the falls scrubbing their clothes, or in the bush trying to catch colourful birds to cage and tame, ready to sell when they next went to town; some, however, were still at work, up on the mill roof, securing the last of the wooden shingles over the stringy bark, or daubing a mixture of cut grass and loam onto the green wood walls of the sturdy huts that had replaced their lean-to shelters.

The nearest group of men dropped their tools and hurried down the dirt track to meet the heavily laden bullock cart. Surrounding them, jostling for the honour of handing the mistress down, they eagerly fired questions at her and Will: How was Sydney? Had the new governor arrived yet? And back at Lacey's Creek, how was Meggie? Jenny? Jess?

Joshua hurried up from the river and elbowed his way through the group with difficulty. Kat turned to find him standing close behind her; she caught her breath as he took her arm, and wished her heart would not betray her every time she saw him. And he, damn him, looked quite unmoved.

She had been prepared to make allowances for the mill, considering the difficulties under which it had been built, but none were needed. The building was solid and well planned and every contingency had been thought of. Joshua led her from the cutting room, where he had set up something like a chaff cutter to deal with the straw or bark and the old split ropes Garvey had been buying up from the docks and the whaling ships, into the dusting room where the chloride of lime would be stored, ready to be mixed with the water from the cistern above, to the kettles and breakers where the mixture would be cooked, bleached, washed and drained and the half-stuff taken off to the beaters. Hugh Stevens, the millwright's son, had a team still working inside, attending to the last details: making adjustments to the second wheel, manhandling a stuff chest into place or in the salle testing out the gearings that connected the Fourdrinier to the main shaft.

'We should be able to start the machines before long,' said Joshua proudly. 'The pharmacist in King Street thinks he has found a way to make size from some of the gum trees and it may be possible to apply the size to the paper in the machine itself.'

'It would never have got this far without you, Joshua,' she said. 'Truly, you have worked wonders.'

It wasn't just in the mill that progress had been made. Scattered over the hillside between the mill and the cookhouse were a number of sturdy two-room huts, each with a rough-hewn table, benches, and bunks set like shelves into the wall. Hollowed out logs were already in position to bring water from above the mill to a reservoir closer to the houses and in a shady hollow, Seth, the simple boy who tended the bullocks, had begun to scratch out a truck garden. Before long they would be able to move men and stock up here and the settlement would run independently.

It was an oppressively hot afternoon and the men congregated beneath a stand of trees above the mill, where it was a little cooler, to drink tea and smoke some of the tobacco that had come up with the cart.

'It felt very strange to be in a mill again,' she said, sipping cautiously at the sweet and sticky brew. 'Discussing the processes with the men – it was quite like old times.'

Joshua picked up a twig and began to trace patterns in the dust with it. 'You seemed somewhat agitated,' he said, not looking at her.

'Old habits die hard: I quite expected Father to come in and shout at me!' She looked at him from under her lashes. 'It's only the second time I've thought about him since I came out here,' she confessed. 'The first time was a few weeks ago, when all this finally became mine.'

He looked up at her with a frown. 'Was it not before?'

'Ye-es. But if he had ever found out where I was, then as long as I was underage, I dare say he could have taken it away.'

He buried his head in his hands. 'Your birthday,' he said with a groan. 'You were one and twenty. And I forgot.' As he had forgotten her twentieth, hurrying off to Wycombe to deal with the troubles at Ash Mill, unaware that she was locked, bruised and beaten, in her room at Clapton Revel, instead of being safe in London.

'The mill is a fine birthday present, Joshua,' she said. 'But the best present of all was to be able to lift my glass to his cursed memory and know that there is nothing he can ever do to hurt me again.'

'I too have been thinking a great deal since I've been here. When I first arrived, I felt such anger, such frustration, knowing that my freedom and my good name had been snatched away so unjustly...' He looked about him at the tree-covered valley, with the smoke of the cooking fires rising gently to hang in the blue, blue sky. 'But here in the wilderness, that's all so irrelevant. I thought, Kat, that if – '

'Would ye have another fill, missus?' said Samuel. 'The boys are – '

'No!' She spoke more harshly than she had intended. 'No, I thank you, Samuel. Mr Delahaye and I – '

Joshua shook his head, a confused expression in his eyes as if his thoughts were coming back from somewhere far away. He set down his tin mug. 'I thought I'd show the mistress our newest building, Samuel,' he said, leaping briskly to his feet.

'Aye. I'll wager she's not even noticed it's there, so neatly tucked away it is,' said Samuel with a grin.

As Joshua strode ahead of her up the slope, Kat could have

screamed out loud. It had been the closest that Joshua had come to pouring out his innermost thoughts and feelings to her, and it had all gone for nothing. Now he was cool and distant once more as he led her up the slope. As if to mirror her despair, clouds moved across the sun, shadowing the ground.

The house was considerably larger than the shack which had doubled as cook house and Joshua's own abode; tucked away behind a handsome stand of trees it stood a little apart from the rest of the dwellings.

A frame had been made from the abundant hardwood trees that grew in profusion over the hills, lathed inside and out with thin split logs, and the walls plastered with two coats of sand and loam mixed with the finely ground contents of the local ant hills; in the summer heat the plaster had already dried to a pale stucco. The roof of pliant stringy bark had been extended out in the front and lashed down onto two rooted tree trunks with the inner fibres of the kurrajong tree to form a shady verandah and lengths of bark had been rolled above the window apertures to keep out the heat of the day and the cool of the night, with shutters for severe weather. A thin spiral of smoke rose from the rear chimney to dissipate itself against the metallic grey sky.

'It's not Clapton Revel,' said Joshua, watching her face for a reaction, 'but I think it will do for the mill manager.'

The door from the verandah opened into one room with a rough table and a couple of benches in it; across a small hall was a second room with a rope-based bed frame tented with coarse insect netting. Joshua's few possessions were neatly stacked or hung on the walls and it struck Kat that he had made himself more at home here than he ever had in Lacey's Creek.

'Any mill manager would think himself fortunate to have such a well-appointed house,' she said, swallowing a lump in her throat as he led her through the covered way to show her round the detached kitchen, where Will had stacked the rest of the supplies they had brought up from Lacey's Creek: pork, Brazilian tobacco, half a case of green tea, sacks of flour and Mauritius sugar, hogsheads of small ale and a parcel of cotton shirts.

'Best be making tracks, missus,' said Will, squinting up into the hills. 'I don't like the colour of that sky overmuch. I'll send Seth to harness up the bullocks and we'll be on our way.'

She hesitated, weighing up the chance of a brief moment with Joshua against the likelihood of a wetting, but before she could speak there was a flash of brilliant lightning and a crack of thunder that shook the walls, and the wind whistled down the valley seemingly out

354

of nowhere, bringing with it a driving, howling summer storm that lashed rain in torrents upon the little settlement.

The rain and the screaming wind persisted for the rest of the day, the lightning flickering and thunder rolling and echoing across the valley; however sure-footed the bullocks might be, there would be no chance of returning to Lacey's Creek that day.

Any hope Kat had cherished of a fine opportunity to talk matters through with Joshua was soon dashed: when he was not airing his bedroll for her to sleep on, or carrying blankets to the main room where he proposed to sleep on one of the benches and Will on the other, he was scurrying about, in spite of Will's protests, cooking food for them to eat, Will being notoriously unhandy in such matters. With a sigh she battened the shutters and lit the candles.

'The raising liquid's down in the cookhouse, so you'll have to make do with damper,' said Joshua, raking out the ashes before putting the large thick disc of unleavened dough on the hearthstone and piling embers back over. He grinned at her over his shoulder. 'But it's good damper – I'm a dab hand at it now.' Before she could answer, he started a light-hearted discussion about whether it really had been invented by Dampier, the great circumnavigator from Somerset. Every time that she showed any inclination to move the conversation onto a more personal plane, Will being out of the room, he introduced another inconsequential topic, whether it be the races, her plans for the new house at Lacey's Creek or the likelihood of the river rising too high for the wheel – anything, it seemed, rather than open himself up to her as he had almost done earlier.

They ate in silence, caught up with their own thoughts, but when Joshua lit Kat to her door, he did not immediately bid her the anticipated curt goodnight.

For a moment her heart began to race at the sight of his handsome figure leaning against the doorframe, but when she bade him come in, he shook his head. It was not romance that he had in mind.

'It seems I owe you an apology,' he said, the muscle in his cheek twitching as she crossed to the bed where she had earlier lowered the rough netting, having first driven out the mosquitoes.

She looked at him warily, but said nothing.

'Garvey told me that you had been asked to send reports back to England.'

'Yes. Those letters to William . . .' A look of pain crossed his face, but she forced herself to carry on. 'I've been writing them ever since I arrived out here. But Godstowe is just a staging post; from him my letters go straight to Cawfield at the Colonial Office.'

He straightened up, a look of surprise on his face. 'But what can you write about that would interest the Colonial Office?'

'I write about anything,' she said, sitting on the edge of her bed and unpinning her hair. 'Politics, the economy, the press, illegal things like those auctions, the awful way the women convicts are treated, how Darling's cronies picked any convicts they wanted before they even got to the Barracks...'

'But surely the Colonial Office has its own representatives for that?' he said, struggling to keep his mind on business as her nimble fingers unpinned her fall of pale hair.

'It was quite impossible for anyone to know what was really going on, particularly when Darling dismissed some officials and appointed his cronies in their place.' She picked up the fly swat and flattened an unsuspecting insect against the wall. 'I do wish you'd come in or go out, Joshua,' she said briskly. 'I've swatted all the insects in here once already, and you're just letting more in.'

He shook his head. 'I can't believe you're writing reports to the Colonial Office,' he said once more.

'Copies are also sent on to Sir Richard,' she said over her shoulder. 'Although there's no certainty he will receive them all on ship.'

'To the Governor? Kat, if you hope by such services to persuade him to give me a pardon, I fear you delude yourself. I know that the Governor seems to have more power out here than the King but – '

'Oh, he has. Far more.' She picked up the silver-backed brush she had given Joshua at Lacey's Creek and began to draw it through her hair, tugging at the tangles. 'After all, there's no parliament and he has the King's warrant to do precisely as he pleases. If anyone chooses to complain, it takes eight months to get back the answer!'

'But any pardon would have to come from England,' he said, returning doggedly to the point. 'And when Sir Richard gets out here and finds you've deceived him...'

'But I haven't!'

'When do you propose to tell him your husband's a convict?' he said sarcastically.

'He already knows.'

'What?'

'I told him the first evening that I met him. Did I not say?' she said insouciantly, well aware that she had *not* said. 'William and Dickon and I dined with Sir Richard shortly before I took ship. We passed a most pleasant evening with him and Sir Anthony Cawfield of the Colonial Office. We found so much to talk about.'

'You did?' Joshua was by now completely mystified.

'He spent the early years of his marriage in High Wycombe, after he was wounded. He was shot through the jaw, you know. It still gives him great pain.' She looked up at Joshua. 'I wonder whether Betsey could give him something for that?'

356

'Very likely, but – never mind that now,' said Joshua, rubbing his eyes. 'You surely don't write to him about Wycombe?'

'Of course not! I write about anything that is of concern to the colony.'

Joshua shook his head as if he was having difficulty taking it all in. 'But why you? You're only – '

'Only a woman?'

'Yes. No. What I meant was – well, what do you know of politics? Or economics? Or agriculture or industry? Perhaps now you know more than you did, but at first, when you were new in the colony – '

'I could listen. That's what they wanted, don't you see? Someone unconnected to all the factions that had sprung up under General Darling; someone who was a landowner but not an Exclusive, who sympathised with the Emancipists but wasn't one; they wanted to know what life was like for the new convicts, the new settlers. I do believe that Earl Grey's new government truly wants to make things better out here. And I can tell them what's really happening.'

'What do you know of the convicts' life?' he said scornfully.

'I went to Hyde Park Barracks every time a new convict ship came in.' The bile rose in her throat at the memory of the seething, fighting mass, where new convicts were robbed of what little they possessed and where the business of assignment was conducted to a constant litany of young boys sobbing. 'But you're right; until I have visited the penal colonies, like Port Macquarie, I won't have given a true report. And I gave my word that I would.'

Joshua went to bed with his head spinning.

Joshua was called out to the mill before breakfast to deal with a problem with the gearings and only emerged in time to see the back of the bullock cart disappearing down the track.

He stood at the head of the valley in his shirtsleeves, cursing himself. He should have spoken to her last night, but he had needed time to think through everything that she had said to him. He had been a fool to believe that Kat loved Godstowe. He wondered whether she might still harbour warm feelings in her heart for the man she had married, or whether he had driven her away with his anger and bitterness.

Tomorrow, he told himself, tomorrow or the next day, he would go to Lacey's Creek and talk to her.

Down the hill Hugh Stevens and Michael Shanley were taking turns to read to the men from the Bible; Joshua turned back, realising he was in no mood for homilies. He crossed to the rocks above the river where someone had set a billy can to boil over a little fire, and leaned back, turning his face to the sun. Closing his eyes, he sniffed at

357

the fragrant air and listened to the sounds of the bush which had once seemed so alien to him. If the Governor were indeed to bring out with him a pardon, then he would be free to return to England. Yet as he looked around him at the splendours of the countryside, which in these last months had taken a curious hold on his heart, he wondered whether England was really home to him any more.

As he sat whittling a stick, Samuel came out of the bush, whistling some tune about a bold highwayman, the kind of thing which, under a harsher overseer, could have earned him a taste of the cat.

'You're not at the Bible reading?' asked Joshua, still intent on his carving.

Samuel shook his head. 'That's not for me, sir. Mebbe the meek will inherit the earth, but I never seen no sign of it in any of the places I been in.'

Joshua looked up with a frown. 'I thought you had always been at Lacey's Creek.'

'No. If I had, mebbe I'd feel different.' He looked around him appreciatively. 'Good food and good shelter for a good day's work. That's what I calls fair going. But it's hard to believe in a God in heaven when you've been in a penal colony. And I been through the lot, mister. Every one of 'em from Newcastle and all points north to Moreton Bay – barring Norfolk Island, acourse, but no one ever comes back from there to tell the tale...'

'Except poor broken souls like young Jenny.'

'Aye.'

'You were assigned direct to Newcastle?'

Samuel shook his head. 'Had a sweet little posting not far from here, down Liverpool way. Comfortable town 'twas then, though working on the land was no holiday, for there was a terrible drought back then. Drought an' bush fires. On'y a few years ago we had bush fires all over, right up to the edge of Sydney town. I was in town with the old master, Lacey, and we could hear the flames cracklin' at the end of Macquarie Street.' He drew on his pipe. 'But like I say, I started assignment in Liverpool. Thought I'd drawn a good master, too. For six years all but a day I'd worked hard, said not a word out of place to any. They didn't come no meeker than Samuel. Then the day before my ticket was due the master told me to my face I was too good a man to lose and he wouldn't put me forward for my ticket.'

'Could he do that?'

'Master can do what he wants with his government men. They say you can complain to a magistrate, but the few as dares are marked men from that day. Well, we had words and I lost my temper. I napped twenty-five lashes for insolence, and was put back a year in gaining my ticket. I swallowed my anger and set myself back to work.

The next year he done the very same thing and I, like a fool, took him by the throat and cursed him for a villain. I was hauled before the magistrates, but 'stead of setting my ticket back again, as my master had hoped, they sent me to land clearance in Emu Plains.'

'That's terrible!'

Samuel shrugged. 'I could find you a half dozen with stories as bad.'

He told Joshua how the overseers of the cutting gangs, often convicts themselves, were set up against each other by the superintendent; each gang had to clear a certain acreage in a given time, so the overseers tended to harsh stratagems to keep their gang ahead, and harsher punishments when they failed. A favourite trick was to have twelve men raise a huge trunk above their heads with spikes and then command six of them to step out, leaving the rest of the team to struggle or have their brains knocked out. 'And if you dropped the log, or fell foul of the overseer in any way, you'd be chained up in the stockade in the open sun, no food or water. Sometimes they'd chain your arms above your head and when they took you down, your wrists 'ud be twice their proper size; no feelin' in your hands or arms for days after. Sometimes the constables would pick out a man and offer him supplies if he'd run, so they could claim the reward for recapturing him; some of the men took the chance just for the sake of a few days of freedom, even though they knew there'd be a flogging at the end of it, but I wouldn't take the bait. Not me. I still had hopes of keeping my clean record.'

'What went wrong?' asked Joshua as Samuel fell silent.

'One of the older men, he couldn't move for the pain in his belly – the food being so bad, we all had dysentery most o' the time. The overseer said he'd have him flogged for a crawler. He kicked the old fellow while he was on the ground – '

'And you went for the overseer.'

'Aye. Fifty lashes and sent to Newcastle, chained up below decks. Till then I'd thought I was bad done by, but there was a man on the transport had napped three hundred lashes in two days.' He rubbed his eyes. 'You could see the bones in his back, like those skeleton drawings the blacks does. And he had maggots crawlin' in the wounds, eatin' him away. We all had to piss in a puddle for him to lie in, so's to kill 'em off. That's a sight I won't never forget.' He pushed some more tobacco into his pipe with shaking hands. 'I was for the cedar cutting gangs, but by the time I got there, the cedar forests was all but gone. So they sent me down the coal mines. That were a cruel place. King of Coal River, they called the Commander; dawn every Sunday he'd ride up in his dress uniform, all gold braid – his fighting coat, the men called it. He'd inspect the triangles and the whips and

359

call for the punishment roster: no oaths, no hearing of charges, no defence. I've known the day he handed out four thousand lashes and the worst of it was the pleasure he seemed to take in it. At the triangles you were a sandstone man or a pebble – you crumbled under the punishment or you stayed solid.'

He stirred the ashes of the fire with his boot, gazing into the flames that leaped up. 'That Commander, the only thing he liked better than gold braid was to break an iron man, turn a pebble into a sandstone. I heard tell they did send him on to Norfolk Island. Well, I vowed to keep my own concerns this time, but the work was very punishing and the overseer within a month gave me a canary for idleness – that's a hundred lashes – and had me sent across the Hunter River to the lime-burners' camp.'

Joshua shook his head in disbelief. Samuel was one of the steadiest workers he had known.

'I'd never seen anywhere as bad as that place, sir. Line of hovels inside a palisade of cabbage-palm wood and some of the most vicious men you ever saw, inside and outside of the fence. We was set to carry seashells to the lime kilns and baskets of burned lime from the kilns to the boats, all of us with two sets of leg-irons rubbing our flesh raw and some poor beggars with four sets.' He laughed. 'Put iron in your blood, that's what the men said. I asked the overseer if he could set me to another task first day, as my back was raw from the flogging. He tore my shirt from me – for the lime-burners wore nothing but rag aprons for decency – and the bastard flung a handful of quicklime into the wounds and drove me into the waves.' He chewed his lip. 'Well, sir, you know what quicklime does in the water, it sizzles in the flesh.'

Joshua pressed his hand to his mouth. 'Oh, for pity's sake...'

'Weren't none o' that, sir,' said Samuel with mordant humour. 'Got the holes in me back still. And that was my life, sir, for sixteen hours a day, summer and winter. I thought they'd fed us ill at Emu Plains, and worse at the Coal River, but the lime-burners they starve.'

'But there's a standard issue of food for all prisoners. The Commissary – '

'The Commissary?' Samuel spat into the flames. 'The more hands the food goes through, the less there is for the men. Everyone takes their bit, see. Some of the best fortunes in Sydney was made that way. You got to remember, all the clerkin' jobs go to the Specials and barrin' a few politicals like Mr Garvey, Specials are mostly forgers. They can change the record to read whatever you like. Mark it as a sack of flour when they know half of it's been thieved and somethin' else put in to make up the weight. Prison bread has more straw than flour in it – we called a loaf a scrubbing brush, for what it did to your guts. When you're starvin', food's all you can think about. I've seen a man split another man's skull open with a shell-rake for the sake of a bone, and boast as they took him away that he was for Sydney and the hangman; he'd rather dance the Newgate hornpipe than stay in such misery any longer. And there were many as envied him the escape. I've seen men deliberately throw themselves into the waves with the baskets on their backs to drown themselves rather than put up with any more.'

Joshua opened his mouth to speak but the words died in his throat.

'I might have done the same as them, but it being thought that Newcastle was ready now for settlers, we was sent away north to Port Macquarie.'

Joshua recognised the name that Kat had mentioned the previous day. 'But Port Macquarie is surely not as bad as Newcastle?' he said anxiously.

'No better nor worse than any other penal settlement, I'd say. Only thing in its favour was that it had some women. But they, poor devils, they had it even worse than the men: they were at the mercy of the officers *and* the government men. Prisoners of prisoners. But I didn't stay there long; got sent on to Moreton Bay, on the Brisbane River. That's a place as'll never prosper, sir. Ticks, snakes and scorpions and everyone with infected eyes. And ground so hard it breaks the hoe. Very little grows there.' He looked round him at the lush greenness of the little valley. 'Hard to think it's the same country as this. We lived on little but snakes and leaves; there's no manure to rich up the soil, for they won't have horses nor bullocks, but puts the prisoners to pull the carts, barefoot and naked in the sun, with twenty-pound leg irons for those as steps out of line. Captain Logan of the Fifty-Seventh was the commandant of the camp and he told us to our faces that it was his task to drive scum like us off the face of the earth. Exterminate us, he would, 'cos we were vermin, lower than the snakes. Men died in their hundreds under Logan's reign,' he said. 'In the fields, in the cells, in the hospital. One day he and Trenand, the gaol-gang overseer, they decides everyone in the hospital's malingering – though God knows who'd want to put themselves in the surgeon's hands, for he was stark mad. Had 'em all dragged out and flogged, they did, even the blind men and the cripples in their crutches ... I was glad when I heard Logan had been killed, sir!' he said, his voice rising. 'I know it ain't Christian to say so, but I was hearty glad. I only wish the blacks had murdered Trenand the same way. They could have gone together to hell.'

He paused a while to tap his pipe out on the heel of his boot.

'Me and Blind Bob, he'd lost his sight in the lime-burning, we

361

settled to make a break for it,' he said when he had grown a little calmer.

'From Moreton Bay? But where is there to go to?'

'Oh, you'd be surprised, sir! Most o' the explorin' up there has been done by men bolting north from Port Macquarie and south from Moreton Bay. If you're caught, you bargains off some of the punishment for a few days with the mapmakers! They do say some o' the first bolters thought if you went north, you'd end up in China, but we weren't so green! Blind Bob, he remembered seein' a chart years afore, with all these islands on a great reef to the north, and hearin' how some shipwrecked sailors had survived there for years. He told me stories about some Robinson fellow what had survived on an island; well, we reckoned if he could do it on his own, two of us couldn't hardly fail. Anyways, half a chance was better than none and we'd determined to take it. We didn't care if the snakes or the heat got us, nor even the blacks. A spear would ha' been welcome. We'd gone past the point where we cared.'

'But you're in line for your ticket – I thought bolters lost all hope of a ticket?'

'We never made it. See, they put Seth in our gang.'

'The boy who looks after the stock?'

'The very same, sir.' He looked up at Joshua sharply. 'I wouldn't want you should take me amiss, sir. There's many men as takes young boys under their wing, there bein' so few women, specially in the penal settlements, if you follow my meaning, but me an' Blind Bob, we never – '

'You don't need to tell me.'

Samuel shook his head. 'Poor Seth, poor beggar, he never deserved the treatment he got. Now me and Blind Bob, at least we knows what sent us out in the first place was thievin' and forgin', but Seth never done no wrong. Powder-monkey in the navy, he was, and had his brains addled in an explosion. Get him really riled up and he'd lose all control: break things, hit out at folk as were troublin' him. Well, the men at Moreton Bay, they picked on him, tormented him till he couldn't take no more. Blind Bob and me, we did what we could to shield the lad, and before we realised it, he was followin' us round like a little puppy dog. Well, there wasn't no one wanted to cross Blind Bob; he'd put a tiger snake in your bed or your boots, fangs up, if you fell out with him, so whiles Seth was with us, the others left him alone.'

'And your plans?'

'We carried on talkin' about it for a while, me and Blind Bob. But I guess we knew we could never go. Seth was too slow to take with us, but we couldn't turn our backs on him.'

362

'Then how did you get away?'

'By the strangest of chances, sir.' He shook his head at the memory. 'There was a ship come down from India, calling at the prison settlements with letters an' such like from home. We rowed the Captain out to the ship in the whaleboat, to dine with some officer on board as was on his way to Port Macquarie. I saw his wife and daughter at the rail – sweet little thing the child were, no more than eight or nine. An' I looked at her with the sun in her golden curls and thought, That's what my Sophia looks like, as I'll never see no more.' He passed his hands over his eyes at the memory. 'The mother moved away to where Logan was bein' piped on board and the child must have clambered up, like children do, to see over the edge a bit better. Well, there was a sudden swell an' she went over the rail, straight into the sea. I never thought twice about it. I dropped the oar and went straight over after her and brought her to the boat.' He scratched his head. 'Only afterwards I thought, Thank God they'd taken our leg irons off!'

When the child was safely back on board and all the hysteria had died down, Samuel had been summoned to her father's cabin. Looking for a magnanimous gesture to commemorate Miss Amy's safe deliverance from drowning and sharks, the officer had commuted Samuel's internal exile and sent him back to Sydney to work out the rest of his original sentence in more congenial surroundings; he'd even agreed to grant the same boon to one of Samuel's companions, overriding Logan's protests by insisting that his daughter was worth ten – no twenty! – convicts to him.

'And you chose Seth.'

'Aye. Poor lad. Thought he deserved a better go in life. Often wonder whether Blind Bob ever took off into the bush. There were plenty of others would have made a break for it with him.' He sighed. 'Either way, he'll be well out of that hell now.'

# Part IV

# Port Macquarie

I was the convict
        Sent to hell,
To make in the desert
        The living well:
I split the rock,
        I felled the tree –
The nation was
        Because of me.

# Chapter Nineteen

Kat groaned and lifted her throbbing head carefully from the pillow, wishing that whoever was making all the noise would stop at once, before her head split. The screaming reverberated around the room, drowning out even the booming surf and the noisy hiss and chirrup of the insects in the tall pines.

'If I want to wear my new dress, I will!' came the shrill voice. 'I'll do what I want and you can't stop me!'

'But it's not come back from the laundry maid yet and – '

'Then go and get it back! Tell the idle hussy to have it ready within the hour!'

'But Miss Amy, here's your lovely dress with the pink ribbons and – '

'I *hate* pink ribbons. Jed Bannister's daughter wears pink ribbons and he's just a poor settler! I tell you I want my new dress, and I won't wear anything else!'

'Oh, miss!' wailed the maid.

'Well, what are you waiting for?' The shrill little voice was rising higher yet. 'Fetch it for me and be quick about it, Mullins, or I'll have the flogger give you twenty-five lashes!'

'Give over, Miss Amy, now do! You'll have your pa coming to see what all the fuss is about, and you know he don't like to be troubled.'

'Fetch me my dress, then. Or I'll stand at the bottom of the stairs and scream and scream till Mama wakes and – '

'Oh, miss, you wouldn't! And her bein' so poorly!'

'I will! And when Pa wants to know why I'm so upset, I'll tell him about you going across the river to meet Mr Curtis,' she said malevolently.

There was a sharp intake of breath. 'You been spyin' on me?'

'So it was you!' said the girl with glee. 'I was sure it was! Well, you won't go to meet him today, because I want you here. I suppose it's him I hear on the stairs when Papa's away, too?'

'Oh, miss, I'm sure I don't know what – '

'Never mind that. Just fetch me my dress. Oh, and Mullins?'

'Yes, miss?'

'There'll be no piano practice today. See you tell the tutor. And when you fetch me my dress, be sure to call in at the kitchens and tell cook to make me some more comfits.'

Kat sat up with a sigh; mind and body were exhausted, but she knew she would not get back to sleep again now. She rang for water, enquiring after her hosts from the maid who brought it.

'Missus is no better, ma'am,' said the woman with a barely suppressed smirk. 'The master sends his compliments, he hopes you're quite over the sickness and he'll see you tomorrow evening. He's a-goin' upriver on business. You're to make yourself free of the house, your meals will be brought to your room and Miss Amy's maid will see to your needs.'

The master's actual words to the convict maid who had warmed his bed ever since his wife had taken to hers had been: 'Damned female? Whoever heard of a governor sending a damned female to look at our cane fields, hey? Still, got to keep in with the new fellow, eh, Tess? Or I'll never be promoted out of this pest-house!'

When she had breakfasted, Kat walked across to the window and breathed in the fresh sea air, tinged with the scent of the aniseed tree in the garden below, where blind gardeners were hoeing between the melon vines. Her gaze moved on, past the whitewashed palisade. A man with a wooden leg was stumping up the road from the Hastings River with a heavy package; beyond the estuary, out in the white-fringed surf, a line of chained men moved slowly forward, gathering shells for the lime kilns; an officer stood by a pile of stones close to the watch house, sketching plans for the new jetty; inland a gang of one-armed stone-breakers was crushing rock for a new road that would serve the shacks that had sprung up beneath the towering pines, housing the new settlers who were beginning to trickle into Port Macquarie.

From the Old Barracks came the wailing of a soul in torment and Kat quickly closed the window. Downstairs Miss Amy was screeching that Cook had made the wrong sort of comfits. In spite of the appalling heat Kat shivered: she would as soon move a family into a plague pit as bring them to live in this grotesque mixture of prison and asylum.

She didn't want to stay in this terrible spot a minute longer than necessary; she'd already lost two days from being so dreadfully sick when she arrived, not an uncommon reaction, the governor had told her. What with the sandflies and the snakes and the dysentery ... why, his wife had scarcely spent more than two days in a row out of her bed since they'd been sent here! Port Macquarie, he'd said sternly, was no place for a lady.

Kat wiped the dampness from her face and throat as she crossed to her trunk and drew out the log book and her travelling desk from within the folds of her clothes. Scratching absently at an inflamed insect bite, she cast her eye over what she had written the previous day.

The sugar cane had proved to be a perfect excuse, as Hall had said it would be. Two of the overseers, far more alarming in their appearance than any of the convicts, and Mr Curtis, the tall, hawk-nosed commissary of supplies, had walked out to the cane fields with her the previous day, but only one of the overseers really seemed to know anything about the crop and it had been simple enough to convince him of her purpose. What had not been so simple had been holding her tongue when she saw how the workers in the cane fields were treated, and keeping her distance from Curtis, whom she had found a little oversolicitous of her. She told herself that this must be a harsh posting for one who was so obviously a ladies' man, with none but a handful of female convicts left in Port Macquarie, but she hadn't liked the gleam in his eye when he looked at her, nor the familiar way he had put his arm round her waist when they crossed the rough ground, even though she was wearing perfectly stout and sensible boots. She wished, uneasily, that she had at least told Garvey where she was going.

From that first trip to the cane fields she had brought back with her sugar cane leaves and stalks which were dissolving in jars in the little shack the governor had set aside for her. She had returned to her room with her hands covered in bites from the sandflies and wanting nothing more than her bed, but before she retired to sleep she had written up in her journal everything she had seen and heard that day.

'Delahaye!' exclaimed Brymer, catching at his reins. 'Thought it was you. Saw you come out of Hall's office as though a tribe of blacks was at your heels.'

'If that were all!' said Joshua ruefully. He looked around him with a frown. 'What the devil are all these people doing on the quayside?'

'Haven't you heard? The Governor's ship has been sighted off the Heads. They've determined to give him a rousing welcome.' He looked curiously at Joshua. 'You look a bit flushed, old fellow. Come over to my office and have a bumper with me.'

'I regret, I can't stop. Have to get on my way.'

'What's so urgent?'

He was almost tempted to tell him, but what could he say? *My wife's gone to Port Macquarie.* Brymer wouldn't believe him. He

369

could scarcely believe it himself. 'Pressing business for my wife,' he said at last.

'Then I won't hold you up. My compliments to her.'

Joshua pushed his horse through the crowds, racked with fear and barely contained rage. He'd raced down to Lacey's Creek the previous day, only to find that Kat had gone into Sydney.

'She'll be wantin' to visit the shops, with Christmas so close,' said Betsey, looking up briefly from the cakes and puddings she was stirring, to direct Ben and Jenny where to put the scarlet shrub in a large pot that they had just carried in. In the peace and solitude of the hills, Joshua hadn't even realised that it was December. 'There are two merchant ships come in this week and I know she was waitin' on some music for you.'

With that Joshua had to be content, but in the still small hours of the night the doubts began to creep back in and he found himself tossing and turning restlessly. He'd been away from Lacey's Creek before dawn and ridden into Sydney with fear in his heart.

Jenkins had opened the door half in and half out of his livery. 'I hadn't expected to see you, sir,' he said with a look of surprise. 'I thought you had gone on the voyage with Mrs Delahaye.'

In Kat's desk Joshua found the latest letter from the Colonial Office, in which someone had written how 'awfully useful' it would be for them to have a first-hand report from one of the penal colonies 'for one cannot depend on the veracity of the newspaper reports'. He cursed the ignorant fool who had so casually sent her into danger, then cursed himself for an uncaring villain. He should have been there, at her side, instead of nursing his wounded pride up in the hills. She had sacrificed everything to come to the other side of the world for him, and he had turned his back on her.

What made him call in on Hall on his way to the quays he couldn't say, but when the editor admitted that he had had a hand in her mad voyage, Joshua could hardly keep his hands from the man's throat. Even before Kattrin reached Port Macquarie, there was the ever present danger of shipwreck: only the previous year many Sydney families had lost loved ones when a sturdy fifteen-tonner bound for Newcastle had gone down with all hands.

It took him an hour to find a ship travelling north, and he went on board to try to persuade the captain to stand to off Port Macquarie on his way to Java.

'Only government ships go to the penal stations,' said the captain brusquely. 'Sail with one of them.'

'I don't have time to wait for a transport!'

'You might be a government man for all I know,' said the captain, raising his eyes briefly from the cargo manifest. 'Might be a bolter.

Wasn't so long ago you could have your ship seized and scuttled if you stood to off Port Macquarie without permission.'

Joshua remembered what Garvey had said about looking the part. He drew himself up to his full height and looked down on the captain with a haughty expression. 'Do I look like a convict?' he demanded.

'I'm bound to say you look like a gentleman that's ridden a long way and not stopped to wash off the dust,' said the captain, eyeing him. 'But then I've seen a-many Specials who can look more like a gentleman than just about any in Sydney. Hey, bos'un! Tell 'em to go steady with those crates or I'll have their hides!' He turned back to Joshua. 'There's only two ways I'll take you to Port Macquarie, sir, an' that's with a pass from the Governor's Office, or if you charter my ship.' He squinted up at the sun. 'But you'd have to hurry. We'll be loaded in a couple of hours and I sail directly.'

Joshua had no luck with the authorities. 'Sir Patrick really is far too busy to see you, Mr Delahaye,' said the young officer who served as his secretary. 'The Governor's just passed through the Heads and we must have everything ready for his reception.'

'Then I'll see Deas Thomson!'

'He's gone out with the pilot to meet the Governor. We hear that Sir Richard's wife has been very ill on the voyage.'

'But it's most urgent!' said Joshua in despair. 'I have to go to Port Macquarie and –'

'Port Macquarie?' Sir Patrick had come through the door behind them. 'Why the devil do you want to go there?'

As briefly as possible, Joshua explained the situation.

'For God's sake, man!' Sir Patrick exploded. 'A lady in a penal settlement? It's unheard of! What fool sent her?'

Joshua, not wishing to bring more trouble on Hall, showed Sir Patrick the letter he had found in the Sydney house.

'None of these fellows at the Colonial Office have any notion what life is like in these stations!' said the Commander in exasperation.

'You must see, sir, that I have to go after her.'

'Understand your agitation, Delahaye.'

'But my situation is difficult, sir, . . . well, I have no papers.'

'Then, sir, you must not go. I will send after her.'

'When?'

'When I have a moment.' A messenger hurried into the room with a piece of paper in his hand. Sir Patrick read it swiftly and turned on his heel. 'Now if you will excuse me . . .'

After that Joshua knew he was on his own. He lathered his horse back to the Sydney house, from there to the Bank of New South Wales, where the clerk, accustomed to serving him on Lacey's Creek business, merely smiled and cashed the order, then down to the quayside where he handed over a large sum of money to the captain.

'At your disposal, sir,' said the captain with a smile. 'Barring the sailing side of things, you're in charge. And if we sail into trouble, then, by God, sir, it's your trouble, not mine!'

Just after they left the Cove they passed the Governor's ship, the trading vessel *Margaret*, surrounded by ships and skiffs and whale-boats jostling for the honour of escorting her in.

'You want to stop, sir, and pay our respects?' asked the captain.

'No,' said Joshua curtly. 'We've wasted too much time already. Cram on all sail. There's another hundred for you if you can get me there within two days.'

Once they had left the Harbour and passed through the Heads, the sea freshened and Joshua went below to his cabin. It was only then that the implications of what he had done struck home. He, a ticket-of-leave convict, had forged a signature. He sank his head in his hands. If anyone found out, he might never come back from Port Macquarie again.

Kattrin made her way across the parched garden to the shack which the prison governor had offered for her to make her experiments, and there, dozing in the shade of a handsome cedar wattle, was the Special who had been sent to assist her.

'Good day to you, Mr Kellow,' she said.

He leaped to his feet, brushing yellow flowers off his coat, and made her an elaborate bow, holding the door open for her to pass into the shack ahead of him.

'The Commandant will have explained to you my requirements. I understand you have some knowledge in science.'

He bowed once more, bleating about his superior education being wasted – quite wasted! – in this cultural desert. As she explained to him what assistance she required in cooking the stalks and leaves, he was constantly bowing and wiping his hands together.

'Pray be still, Mr Kellow,' she beseeched him, 'or you will overset the experiment jars.'

'Your pardon, ma'am,' he whined, looking down at her with the attitude of a goose looking down the neck of a bottle. 'Naturally I will do my poor best to assist you. Perhaps I may dare to hope that you will take pity on the miserable soul you see before you ... quite broken down by my sufferings...'

'I am sorry for it. If, however, you would cut up those leaves and stalks to about four-inch lengths, keeping leaves and stalks separate, then we may proceed with the experiment.'

While he cut up the stalks and leaves with an air of injured dignity, he proceeded to tell her his sorry tale in which everyone had con-spired against him to rob him of his inheritance and banish him to a land of criminals. Arriving at a time when Darling was trying to rid Sydney of the Specials, who as educated convicts might be tempted to side with Hall and Wentworth, Kellow had been sent direct to a penal settlement which was supposed to be only for those with second convictions in the colony. Simply for being an educated man he had been doubly punished. She wanted to sympathise, but he was so patently self-pitying and recounted his tale so like a very bad actor that he made an almost comic figure of himself. 'If you could use your influence to have me transferred to Sydney, my gratitude would be eternally yours.' She looked up from her examination of the various pulps to find he had dropped the cutter and was clutching his hand to his heart. 'My soul pines for society and culture,' he said. 'For such as I to waste away in the desert wastes of this antipodean Sodom and Gomorrah . . .'

She tried to close her ears to him, but eventually her patience began to wane and while her hands were transferring the soaked fibres into the sieve and washing them, her mind was seeking ways to be rid of him.

She explained to him that the next step would be to prepare the milk of lime, mix it in various strengths and observe its effects on the leaves, the stalks and the bagasse – the refuse left after the juice had been pressed from the cane – in the third vat.

He goggled at the bubbling mixture in one of the pots. 'Oh, I don't like to handle such stuff,' he said nervously. 'I'm sure I should drop it and burn myself, or blow us all to kingdom come. And working with lime can be so damaging to the eyes. I already have such weak eyes – '

'But I must have someone to help with the boiling and beating.' She knew full well that it was a job she could quite well do alone; from the look of the fibres, it was probably a waste of time anyway, because they didn't look regular enough to make decent paper and were proving hard to drain.

She had a sudden inspiration.

'This is not like the cane I was sent from Moreton Bay,' she said with a frown. 'The fibres seem to be of a different thickness.'

'I'm sure I don't know,' he said. 'But there's a fellow here who was at Moreton Bay.'

'Pray send him to the house, Mr Kellow, with all speed. I'll wait on his arrival.'

Almost an hour later a sweating young ensign appeared at the house; over his shoulder she could see two men standing in the shade of the huge Moreton Bay fig tree in the courtyard.

She had to give the ensign a note of hand for his officer, to cover the removal from the muster of the two men who were to assist her. As the young soldier marched off down the path in the noonday heat, she tied her bonnet on her head and went out to see what she had been given this time.

It was not just the motion of the *Java* as she ploughed her way through the heavy seas that caused Joshua's stomach to churn; as he forced his reluctant hands to turn another page in the bundle of depositions which Hall had pressed on him, detailing the torments that Logan and the overseer Trenand had inflicted on the wretched prisoners of Moreton Bay, he felt the bile rise in his throat, threatening to part him from his dinner. The more he read, the more he cursed himself for turning his back on Kat.

Neither the chaplain at Moreton Bay nor the surgeon, who from his rambling deposition seemed to be quite mad, had been willing to testify against either Logan or Trenand. Only the young surgeon's assistant, at the hearing into his request to be relieved of his post on the grounds of ill health, had been willing to speak out. 'I often saw him – Trenand – flog the cripples and the lunatics. He'd stand there like a vulture, picking out the weakest. He is an evil man.'

Someone had put a note at the bottom of the page: 'On the voyage home the assistant descended into a melancholy, escaped restraint and threw himself overboard.' Another, more clerical hand had added: 'Deposition unreliable – balance of mind disturbed.'

Kat looked in astonishment at the two helpers: one was an undersized youth with the pale curls and wide blue eyes of an angel, who looked scarcely old enough to be out of the schoolroom, let alone in a penal colony; the other was a white-haired man with skin grown leathery by long exposure to the relentless sun, and the pale, staring eyes of the blind.

The older man turned to the boy. 'The lady is gazing at my face with an anxious look, wondering how a blind man is ever to be of assistance,' he said. 'Am I correct, Cornelius?'

'Quite correct,' said the young man in a voice barely above a whisper.

'Explain to her, Cornelius,' said the blind man.

'Robert will handle the lime for you, ma'am...'

'Eyes past damaging, you see,' said the man with a wheezy laugh.

'And we can do anything else you require. Robert has worked in the cane fields here and in Moreton Bay.'

She took in a sharp breath. This must be the third man, the one who had written – or at least dictated – the letter to Hall. But how could a blind man possibly identify anyone?

374

The man turned his sightless eyes to her. 'There is something amiss, ma'am?' he asked.

'No.' She let the tension drain from her. 'You were also sent down from Moreton Bay, Cornelius?' she asked.

'He was never in any other station but Port Macquarie, ma'am,' said the man. 'Sent straight here, for he has the falling sickness. Why do you ask?' His voice was sharp and suspicious and she had the feeling that she was being closely scrutinised. She told herself she was being foolish. Closely scrutinised by a blind man?

'No reason,' she said quickly. 'I just wondered whether he knew Moreton Bay cane too.'

'Cornelius is quite new out here,' said Robert, relaxing his guard a little. 'He acts as my eyes.'

'We can help you, miss!' said Cornelius, fearful lest they be sent back to the overseer with a complaint against them. 'We're more use than you might think. Between us we fetch and carry for everyone. Robert knows the area like the back of his hand. Better than anyone, for all he's only been here a year.'

She took a deep breath. 'Cornelius, would you go to the well and draw some fresh water?' she asked.

In spite of the heat the boy seemed to freeze. 'B-by myself?' he asked nervously.

'There's only housemaids about in the yard at this hour,' said Robert. 'They'll do you no harm, boy. Go.'

'He's very nervous,' she said, as the boy moved out of the shack and made his reluctant way back to the garden.

'Aye. He's had some cause.'

'He's been badly treated?' she said, tipping the half-stuff into clean trays and looking at it through a magnifying glass.

'Aye. Like many another young boy before him. But it's not a tale for ladies' ears.' He groped for the trays and ran the pads of his fingers lightly over the fibres. 'This is from the leaves and that from the stalk?'

She nodded.

'Ma'am?'

'Yes,' she said, berating herself for her folly in nodding at a blind man.

'The leaves produce the better fibre, I think,' he said. 'Will it be suitable for your purposes?'

'No. I fear Mr Hall will be disappointed this time.'

Robert stiffened. 'Mr Hall?'

'You have heard of Hall of the *Monitor*?' she asked casually. 'I've promised to supply him with paper.'

'I believe I may have heard the name,' said the man uncertainly.

'I think you know it better than that,' she said. 'I think you wrote to him.'

'In God's name, lady, would you put a noose around my neck? I wrote to no one. How could I? I'm blind. I – '

'Quietly, I beg of you,' she said, putting her hand on his arm. 'I imagine you dictated it – to Cornelius?'

'Keep him out of this! Neither he nor I wrote any letter.'

'But it said, three who had been at Moreton Bay...'

'There were four here from Moreton Bay. The other three are dead. When I went into the hospital they were alive; when I came out they were gone.'

And with them the only chance of identifying the overseer from Moreton Bay, she thought, realising that the three wouldn't have counted the blind man among their number – for obvious reasons.

'I don't understand what it is you want with me, ma'am,' he said after a moment.

'I need someone who knows his way around and is willing to show me what's going on, so that I may make my report.'

'This report – it's for the newspaper editor?'

'And for the new governor, Sir Richard Bourke.'

'What? Forgive me, ma'am, but why should the Governor listen to you?'

'I know him,' she said simply.

'You'll tell him the truth of it?' he said, his face lightening. 'What this terrible place is really like?'

'I swear it. That's why I need – '

'A special tour?' He cocked his head on one side 'Not the kind of tour laid on by the Commandant?'

'Most definitely not.'

She could see the conflict within him as expressions of hope and anguish battled for supremacy in his face. At last he reached a decision.

'I'll put my fate in your hands, ma'am, but the boy stays out of this.' He gave a savage laugh. 'I've had eighteen years of misery in just about every one of this country's stations and it's a long time since I've put any value on my life – but I won't have the boy put at risk.'

'Eighteen years? You were transported for life?'

'Seven year sentence, ma'am, for forging five-pound notes.'

'Then how – ?'

'It's simple, ma'am. A word out of place here, a falling-out with a crooked overseer there, and before you know it, you're serving three sentences on top of the one you brought with you from England. But enough of that.' He crossed to the door and listened, head on one

376

side. 'I'll show you how things are,' he said, turning back into the room. 'It was bad under Morrisett in Newcastle, worse under Logan in Moreton Bay, but at least most of them started out whole there. Here they chain the sick and the crippled and still expect them to do the work of a fit man. What chance do they stand? Now the Commissary's halved our rations. Not that they were that generous before . . . And they say the new man, Curtis, is a worse flogger than the Commandant, though I've not come across him yet.'

'Will you take me to see all this? I promise 1 will do my best to bring it all before the authorities.'

'You'll see sights not fit for a lady,' he said harshly. 'If you faint on me, I could get flogged, or sent to Norfolk Island.'

'I want to see it all,' she said, taking a deep breath. 'No blame can attach to you. I am a guest of the Commandant who insisted on being shown around. Who are you to argue with the Commandant's honoured guest?'

'Who indeed?'


In the cool of the early evening she walked out onto the verandah. The blind gardeners were hoeing the weeds again while a chain of men – in ragged shirts, in deference to the Commandant's ladies – hauled buckets of water up from the river to water the flowerbeds. She spotted Cornelius among the gardeners and gazed out to sea while he edged up to the verandah.

'See that clump of trees over there?' said Cornelius, looking nervously over his shoulder. 'Heat of the day, when all the officers and the flash morts are resting up, Blind Bob will be waiting for you.' He looked anxious. 'I hope you're not gammoning us, lady. You're straight up?'

'Straight up,' she promised, but he had already gone.

Footsteps echoed through the room behind her and she turned away to see Mr Curtis, the tall, hawk-nosed commissary, emerging onto the verandah. He seemed to be very much at home here, she thought, seeing that he had not waited to be shown in by the maids.

'I understand that the Commandant will not be back this evening,' he said, with a smile that twisted his mouth. 'Shameful of him to leave you to dine alone.'

This is the man who has cut the convicts' rations, she thought. The man that Mullins crosses the river to see on the sly – and sometimes brings to the house when the Commandant is away. She wondered what the maid saw in him.

'Will you do me the honour of dining with me, ma'am?' he asked with a bow.

It would scarcely be proper for her to dine with a single gentleman without a chaperone, but she was not going to say so. Somehow she felt that to see her go all missish would give him great pleasure.

She gathered her skirts around her and drew herself up, wishing she had Lady Isabelle's inches. 'If you will excuse me, Mr Curtis,' she said with a smile, 'the Commandant's wife is expecting me.'

'Then you'll join me after dinner.' It was not a question.

She swayed on her feet, catching at the balustrade. 'I am a little fatigued,' she said, fanning herself vigorously. 'Quite unaccustomed to this terrible heat.'

He insisted on giving her his arm to the foot of the stairs where, to her relief, they found Tess, the parlour maid. Kattrin hooked her free arm in the maid's, and as the stairs were barely wide enough for two, Curtis was left with no alternative but to fall back. She felt his eyes burning into her as she staggered up the stairs.

When she arrived in her room she was so nervous that she could scarcely hold her pen to write her notes. She had the strangest feeling that Curtis's eyes were still on her, that if she turned he would be there, looking at her as though she were his next course. She shivered, scolded herself for being fanciful, blotted the log and tucked it away in her trunk beneath her chemise.

# Chapter Twenty

The bed creaked as the man eased himself off the crumpled body and crossed to the chest, buttoning his breeches as he went.

'Coming ... to tell you,' gasped the woman through bruised lips. 'Swear it ...'

'You were too slow, my dear,' he said, bending to rearrange his cravat and stock and watching in the mirror the huddled shape on the bed. He ran his hand over the leather cover of the logbook. 'Why isn't she here? In the heat of the day ...'

She moved with difficulty, groaning at the pain in her ribs as she raised her arm to pull the folds of her dress away from her face. With a sob she rolled onto her side; blood dripped from her mouth and spread like a blot on the crisp linen sheets.

He looked up from the spiky handwriting. 'I won't ask again,' he said softly.

'Shed,' she whimpered. 'Experiments ...'

'Good' He brushed a speck off his dark stock and flashed his teeth in the mirror. 'When she returns I may even have a little experiment of my own for her. As for you,' he said, not turning round, 'next time you have something for me, you'll be a little more prompt in bringing it, won't you?'

'Only found ... this morning,' she said, stifling another groan. 'Couldn't leave ... the brat.'

'I take no excuses,' he said, crossing the room to her side. He looked down on her with a smile and bent to twine his fingers in her glossy brown hair. 'What do I take?' he asked softly as he drew her head up and twisted it back.

'Ahhh!'

'What do I take?'

'No excuses,' she gasped.

'That's right.' He let her head fall back on the pillows. 'Try not to forget it,' he said, turning away and picking up Kat's brush to smooth his crisp dark curls.

'Thought you'd ... gone upriver,' she muttered. 'Usually go ... with the flogger.'

'You don't learn, do you?' he said, crossing back to the bed. He jerked her head up by the hair once more and slapped her hard across the mouth, once for each word. 'No excuses.' He released her, brushing his hands contemptuously, and crossed back to the mirror. 'I wonder if it would be entertaining to set *you* to the triangles? I'm certain your fellow convicts would enjoy the spectacle.' As she whimpered again, a smile played over his lips. 'Major Foveaux on Norfolk Island used to take twenty-five off the flogging if the woman went naked to the triangles. Perhaps next time the Commandant goes upriver ...?'

'Land ho!' cried the look-out, and Joshua crawled out of his bunk and made his way, pale-faced, up the companionway.

'There's Port Macquarie,' said the captain when his passenger emerged into the dazzling sunlight.

Joshua shaded his eyes and squinted at the land. Against a back-drop of huge Norfolk pines, a small settlement of whitewashed houses could be seen huddled around the estuary of the Hastings River. He borrowed the glass from the captain and surveyed the station a little more closely, making out the Commandant's house and another large building which the captain told him was the prison barracks.

'What now?' he asked.

The captain shrugged. 'Now we just wait on them,' he said fatalistically.

'Whaleboat being launched!' called the mate, and Joshua moved the glass along the shore until he saw a team of men draw a boat out of a long shed on the beach, close by a wooden watch-house, and push it out into the booming surf.

The captain took back his glass. 'This'll be the military,' he said. 'I only hope you've got your story right. It's a long row back to Sydney.'

Kattrin was glad of the maid's bonnet, with the veil to draw over her face and hide her eyes as horror vied with horror. She had seen sights this past hour that would stay with her for the rest of her life, etched in blood on her memory. She had seen men wading barefoot in the estuary, their suppurating feet cut to ribbons on the sharp oyster shells they had been sent to collect; she had watched in appalled silence as a group of overseers on the foreshore selected two legless men from their gangs and propped them up on overturned boats within arm's length of each other, placing bets in rum on which would punch the other to a pulp. She had stood at the edge of the land clearance while a gang of half-starved men fought over a mouldering cabbage stalk snatched from a filthy pigsty and then, barely able to hold herself in check, she had watched a poor dribbling lunatic being flogged at the barracks triangle until his boots brimmed over with blood, for some misdemeanour he could never have comprehended.

She put back her veil and mopped the sweat from her face.

'Miss?' Cornelius tapped her tentatively on the shoulder.

She was glad of an excuse to turn away from the stomach-turning sight of a gang of emaciated workers in the cane fields, the halt, the lame and the simple, greedily cutting up a snake they had caught in the cane, and split and dried in the scorching heat of the midday sun.

'Miss?' A hand on her arm drew her back into the nearest stand of sugar cane. 'There's someone watching us.'

She dropped the veil and drew Mullins's cloak around her before she peeped out; she looked back across the settlement, but she could see no one.

'Over there, miss.' He pointed across towards the Commandant's house. 'See?'

There was a flash of light as the sun winked on metal and she could just make out a man.

'Got a spyglass to his eye,' said Cornelius.

'That merchant ship still there?' asked Blind Bob, turning his head towards the sea and then back to Cornelius.

'Yes. The whaleboat went out this morning,' said the boy. 'And a longboat came on shore not long since, over by the watch house. But this one's not looking out to sea. He's looking over here.'

'An officer?' asked Bob.

The boy raised his hand to shield his eyes from the dazzle of the sun on the white foreshore. 'Coat looks dark blue or black. Can't see any gold braid.'

There was a scuffling in the field behind them as the cane workers, hearing the approach of the overseer who had been dozing the midday hour away with a bottle of rum under a shady pine, kicked the snakeskin into the thicket of mature canes and turned back to their planting.

'Any leaves lying around?' asked Robert.

'Heap of them over there.'

'Pick up an armful, Cornelius,' advised Robert. 'Watch out for snakes, though. In the noonday heat they go anywhere for shade.'

'Perhaps I should speak to the overseer,' said Kat anxiously. 'Explain why we're here...'

'Best avoid explanations if we can. Ten to one the man was

watching the cane fields, not us.' Robert thought a moment. 'We'll make our way back by the beach path.'

Amy opened her eyes reluctantly, confused by the blackness around her; her heart was beating painfully fast, as though it would burst into her throat, and she couldn't remember where she was or how she came to be there. She was lying on the floor, something sharp, wet and smelling of leather digging into her cheek. The air was heavy with the smell of lavender, overlaid with a bitter, acrid odour.

After a moment she shifted, and as sensation returned to her extremities, she became aware of a bag of comfits squashed under her left hand, while her right was clenched into a fist. She sat up tentatively, shaking her head, and flexed her fingers. The string slipped from her grasp and the door of the wardrobe creaked slowly open.

She cowered back among the clothes as the terrifying images flooded back into her brain, almost swooning once more for fear, but after several long moments, she realised that Curtis was no longer in the room. An insect buzzed insistently against the lowered holland blind and there was a sound like the last fat drip of the pump when the handle was released. Slowly, trembling in every limb, she raised herself to her feet and stepped cautiously out into the sunlight, blinking.

They were not even halfway to the beach when Cornelius, emerging from the cane ahead of the other two, spotted two figures passing through the stand of trees behind the beach and heading directly towards them.

'Is it the watcher?' asked the blind man anxiously.

'No. One of the beach overseers and a man in a brown coat. There's usually not a soul about at this time of day, apart from the work gangs,' he said, his voice shaking.

'There's nothing to fear,' said Kat soothingly. 'You are out here because I commanded it.'

'We'll turn back and go by the pressing house,' said Robert. 'Then if we do meet anyone, at least we'll be where we should be. We'll collect some bagasse for the lady. For the experiments.' He turned his face to Kattrin. 'Cool and calm if explanations are required, ma'am. Remember, I beg, that our wellbeing depends on you.'

They made their way back through the canes, taking care to keep away from the overseer and his gang and watching where they set their feet, for the searing midday heat had passed its height and the bright-green cane frogs and black snakes were beginning to come out from the shelter of the stalks. Emerging from the tall sugar cane onto the path that led past the pressing house, through a thicket of trees and on to the edge of the settlement, they stopped for Robert to pick up an armful of the pressed stalks.

'Someone coming,' said the boy, seeing a movement in the trees.

Robert came to an abrupt halt, his head on one side, listening intently. 'One man, in a great hurry,' he said. 'And there's something about him that...' He bit his lip and shook his head, as if in some great internal debate. 'I had rather meet this man in the open than in the bush,' he said at last. 'Perhaps your boot is untied, ma'am?'

Kat was on her knees fumbling with her bootlace when the man in the dark coat emerged from the trees, a stout cane held threateningly in his hands.

'It's only Mr Curtis,' she whispered, peering up through the veil.

'It's the Commissary,' said Cornelius.

'Mullins? What the devil, you scum! How dare you trouble this woman?'

'Oh, God!' groaned Robert, dropping the armful of bagasse.

'What!' bellowed Curtis as he advanced on them. 'Harass one of the Commandant's servants, would you? He shall hear of this, I promise you!'

Kat, realising that in the borrowed clothes he had mistaken her for his paramour, the nursery maid, opened her mouth to protest.

'Trenand!' panted Robert, his sightless face turned towards the advancing figure. 'You're not Curtis!' His voice rose to a crescendo. 'You're Trenand from Moreton Bay! Trenand the murderer!'

The man she knew as Curtis stopped in his tracks, the rage in his eyes replaced for a brief moment by fear.

'By God! It's Blind Bob!' he hissed, recovering himself swiftly. 'Always were too clever for your own good.' He drew a pistol. 'You've just signed your own death warrant.' And before Kat could rise to her feet or utter a word, he cocked the gun and aimed it.

'No!' screamed Kat as the pistol fired, but her scream was drowned out by a bellow as Cornelius pushed her aside to fling himself in front of his friend.

Cornelius took the ball in his chest and staggered back into Bob's arms. They fell together in a heap.

Trenand dropped the smoking pistol into his pocket and stepped forward, smiling evilly. Ignoring Kat, sprawled in the middle of the path, he drew out a second pistol and fired into the tangled bodies. Blind Bob twitched and lay still.

There was a burst of shouting from a cluster of shacks down towards the mouth of the river and a group of settlers, alarmed by the shots, started hurrying up the track towards the cane fields.

Cursing, Trenand reached down and hauled Kat up by the front of her cloak until her face was within inches of his and her feet were barely touching the floor. 'Not a word of this,' he snarled. 'If you value your life . . .' She drew her breath in sharply, knowing she must keep up the masquerade until the others reached them. 'I shot these scum to save you from them, didn't I? Saved your *honour*,' he said with a sneer. 'D'ye hear me?' She nodded, not daring to speak. 'I said, d'ye hear me, you bitch!' With a growl he struck her full across the face, his fist tangling in the veil and pulling it off.

'My God!' he exclaimed. '*You!*'

She could feel a trickle of warm blood where his signet ring had caught the side of her face, but she forced herself not to cry out. 'If you would be so good as to let me go, Mr Curtis,' she said carefully, 'I should like to return to the Commandant's house.'

'So you can add this little nugget to your hoard of lies?' he demanded. Fear flickered across her face and he laughed out loud. 'Oh, there's nothing happens in Port Macquarie without I know about it,' he gloated. 'Mullins found your log and brought it to me. Stupid bitch, but she has her uses. Made fascinating reading before it went on the fire. Pity we'll have to deprive the Governor of his entertainment.'

She risked a glance over his shoulder. The figures hurrying up from the settlement had disappeared into the belt of trees and she had no way of knowing when they would emerge. If only she could keep Curtis – no, Trenand – talking . . . But her mind was frozen. All she could think of was that she didn't want to die without seeing Joshua again.

'I can't possibly let you go back to Sydney now,' he said, and his arm clamped her slender body to him like an iron bar. She opened her mouth to try to reason with him, and his free hand slid up under the cloak and over her breast. 'Pity. I was looking forward to getting to know you better.' His hand moved up and he gripped her slender neck in strong fingers, cutting off the scream. 'Unfortunate that I wasn't in time to stop the boy from strangling you. I told the Commandant it was a mistake to let women loose around so many desperate men . . .'

The sky was whirling in front of her and she was going to die. She felt fiercely angry that she was going to die in this plague spot. If she had to die, let it be at home, in Lacey's Creek, with the sound of the river and the blue haze of the mountains beyond. And Joshua beside her, his hand in hers.

Trenand's face was fading before her eyes and for a moment she could see only blackness; after what seemed like an eternity the face swam into view again, but this time it was Louis in front of her. One of her dangling feet brushed against Trenand's shoe and she steadied herself on his instep long enough to smash her other knee into

Trenand's groin. He staggered back, temporarily loosening his grip on her throat and as she whooped air into her starved lungs, she brought her hand up and raked at his face, exulting at the sensation of the welling blood beneath her nails. She knew she was going to die, but she would ruin his story and save the prisoners' good name before she expired.

There was a harsh cry as the first pursuers shot out of the trees and on towards them; Trenand realised with a furious oath that his story would no longer stand. Whoever would have thought there could be so much fight in such a slender body?

'Stay back, curse you!' he shouted, locking his arm across her throat and swinging her round to hang between him and the pursuers, their numbers swollen as the rest of the settlers emerged, breathless, from the trees.

Lights were dancing before her eyes as he hauled her past the fallen bodies, and she gasped as she felt the rim of his pistol grind into her temple.

'Move back!' he commanded. The crowd hesitated. 'Move back, I say, or she dies!'

The crowd moved back at last with an angry mutter. 'That's better.' He turned to the cane workers huddling at the edge of the cane fields, eager to see what was afoot without getting involved. 'You – Armitage!' He picked out a convict who had recently been demoted from overseer for alleged insolence to the Commandant's wife and now lived in daily fear of his life from the men he had previously mistreated. Such a man had nothing to lose.

'I'm with you, sir!' cried Armitage, snatching a whip from one of the overseers and cracking it threateningly in front of the men. Overseers and convicts alike backed away, eager to avoid any contact with trouble which experience had taught would make their miserable lives even more miserable, and disappeared into the cane. One of them dropped one of the wicked curved cane-cutting knives in his haste and Armitage picked it up and thrust it into his belt.

'Watch my back, Armitage, and I'll see you safely away. When we get to the beach, you go on ahead and get the boat ready.' He smiled. 'Tell 'em it's Mr Curtis's orders.'

There was a rasping noise from behind them. 'Not Curtis!' croaked Cornelius. 'Trenand!'

'Trenand!' The whisper of horror ran round the circle and one or two of the settlers made to step between them.

The gun ground into Kattrin's head once more and she winced. 'The Commandant would be very angry if you people were the cause of his guest coming to harm,' said Trenand, the softness of his voice strangely more threatening than bellowed curses.

To Kattrin's despair the little group of settlers fell back.

'Just remember!' said the Commissary quietly. 'Follow us and she dies.'

He turned towards the sea and the pressure on her throat eased a little; as she gasped air into her tortured lungs she thought for one mad moment that she saw Joshua's face.

Amy ran down the road, her shiny little black dancing shoes coated in dust and scratched by the stones, her beautiful dress stained with vomit and shredded on the low scrub. There was a terrible burning pain in her gut but she tried to ignore it as she ran on.

She blinked hard, trying to push out of her mind the sight of Mullins's battered body sprawled across the bed, the only movement the trickle of blood falling from the corner of her mouth and spreading its starry points on the soft white rug. But worse still were the sounds that haunted her: the sounds Mullins had made when she was still alive, when Mr Curtis had slammed his fists into her soft body and then –

It had seemed such a simple dare. When the dancing master – a handsome Special, transported for his skill in glemming diamonds in jeweller's shops onto fingers sticky with dried beer – was out of the room, she'd told Laura Bannister how Mullins always took Mr Curtis, the commissary officer, up to the guest bedroom whenever her father went upriver. She'd wondered out loud whether Mullins would still take him there now that the room was occupied. Laura boasted that she knew all about what men and women did to each other when they were in bed, and then she'd dared Amy to hide in the wardrobe and see if she could find out. But surely *that* wasn't what Laura knew? Surely knowing about *that* was nothing to boast of, rather it was the stuff of nightmares! Images came flashing back into her mind and the sounds filled her ears and she had to stop to be sick again.

The armed constables and overseers had melted away into the sugar cane at the first sign of trouble and there was no help to be had from the little group of settlers, armed only with stout sticks. Most of them were Emancipists and reluctant to get involved with anything that might bring them into conflict with the military.

'At least send someone across to the barracks!' Joshua demanded.

'Have to cross their path to get there and Armitage will pick us off.'

'Besides, most o' the military has gone upriver with the Commandant. One o' his magistrate tours.'

'We could signal to the ship to up anchor!'

'Then what?' said a woman who was staunching Cornelius's wound with her petticoats. 'He'll kill the wench, sure as anythin'.'

'Surely there's another path to the beach?' said Joshua. 'Can't anyone get me to the beach without them seeing us?'

'Aye.' Bannister looked at him stolidly, taking in the white shirt, the neatly tied cravat and the close-fitting coat. 'But it's a fair run and you don't look fit for it, if you don't mind my saying so.'

'Boat watch is armed, ain't it, Bannister?' said one man.

'Aye. But not fit for much.'

'The villain will be slowed right down with the woman,' observed another man.

'It's my wife he's holding at pistol point,' said Joshua harshly. 'Don't doubt me, man: I'll match you step for step.'

'Your wife? Oh, for pity's sake,' said one of the women, putting her hand on Joshua's arm. 'Show him the path, Jed Bannister. And if ye're not man enough, then I'll show him meself!'


'Why, Miss Amy!' said the voice above her. 'Whatever be you doin' out here so far from home?'

She caught her breath on a sob and turned her head to see a boot and a wooden stump.

''Tis me, Miss Amy,' said the man. 'Ben the Porter. Don't be afeared. I'll see you straight home.'

'There's no one there can do anything, you fool!' she snapped, staggering to her feet and stepping back out of his reach. She wiped her mouth with the tattered hem of her best dancing dress. 'Got to get Jed Bannister,' she muttered.

Before he could move she was off again, heading for the river, hoping that the pain in her side would not get any worse.

She'd known when she found the body that there would be no purpose in alerting Cook, or the other maid, still less her mother: she had seen a strength and an evil in Curtis that none of them could deal with. And there was no one in authority to help her: in her father's absence, Curtis was in charge. She was unsure what Jed Bannister could do to help, but she could think of no one else to turn to.


Joshua, stripped of his coat and with his shirt rolled in mud to stop it gleaming through the pines, ran at Bannister's side as they skirted the settlement and headed for the sand dunes on the far side of the watch house.

'Slow down?' Bannister offered as Joshua's breathing grew more laboured.

'No!' he gasped. How could he slow down when he was haunted by

387

the look of terror on Kat's face? If they were to have any chance of saving her from Trenand, they *had* to get to the beach and the watch house before them – though God alone knew what they'd do once they got there. As they crested the slope and saw the sea sparkling at the end of the track, he fixed his eyes on the *Java*, riding at anchor offshore, and tried to close his mind to the thought of Trenand with Kat in his clutches. Life couldn't be so unfair as to snatch her away from him again!

Since his time on the hulks he'd told himself he no longer believed in a just God, but as he stumbled down the sandy track towards the beach he found himself bargaining with Him in his head. Never mind me, he said. I deserve no favours. I turned my back on her when she most needed me, all because of my cursed pride. But what has Kattrin ever done to deserve this? She's always been on the side of right and justice, even when it rebounded against her. Even as a child she took more than her share of punishment just to protect Dickon and Lucy from her father's wrath; she came to King's Mead to warn the men about her father's cannon; she went to Beaconsfield to clear my name – for pity's sake, she even came to the other side of the world to save me! All that deserves something, surely?

They waited in the trees, watching Armitage, all swagger gone from his step, stand before the master of the boat watch, eyes lowered, and pass on the message that Mr Curtis wanted the boat ready, with all speed, to row out to the visiting ship.

Trenand ran the muzzle of the pistol almost lovingly down the side of her face. 'We'll go to Tahiti,' he whispered in her ear. 'If Bligh could make Timor in an open boat, we'll have no trouble in a fine ship like that.' The pistol slipped down her throat and pressed painfully against her breast. He smiled as she winced. 'Or maybe the Friendly Isles. The women wear grass skirts there,' he said throatily. 'Just grass skirts. You'd look good like that.'

There was a rustling in the trees and the pistol moved swiftly back to her temple. She squeezed her eyes tight shut, convinced that her last moment had come.

'Or perhaps Chile would be more to your taste,' said Trenand, burying his face in the side of her neck. 'You've as much spirit as any haughty Spanish wench and I'm sure you're as hot-blooded. What do you say to Santiago, or Valparaiso?'

She opened her eyes to see Armitage coming up through the tree line to join them and breathed again.

'They do say the *Cyprus* sailed all the way to China and on to Japan,' said Armitage, putting the blade and the whip in his belt and arranging her cloak over his arm to cover them. He looked down at

388

Kat with narrowed eyes. 'You goin' to send her back in the whale-boat once we've taken the ship?' he asked.

'We'll need to keep her until we're out of sight of the coast,' said Trenand. 'Too many navy ships in these waters.'

'But once we reach the islands...'

'I'm sure we can find some use for her,' said Trenand, nuzzling her neck. She wanted desperately to evade his lips, but with one arm around her throat and the other holding the gun, she had to force herself to stay still. She couldn't remember whether the pistol was cocked; to jog his arm might be to sign her own death warrant.

The pistol. As she struggled to think whether he had cocked the pistol, an insistent voice in her exhausted, air-starved brain was trying to tell her something else. Something else about the gun...

'Plenty of use for her,' said Armitage, grinning as Trenand stood up and tightened his grip on her throat, leaving her little feet in their dainty boots dancing several inches off the ground. He drew the whip through his fingers and licked his lips in eager anticipation.

'I think she'll prove her worth,' Trenand went on, 'if only to barter our way through the islands.'

The watch master, dragging his lame leg behind him, turned back to the watch house for his whistle. Three short blasts and one long one and a line of shackled men with double leg irons turned to and pulled the boat out of the shed. They shuffled back to stand in line as the vessel was inspected, then five oarsmen stepped forward to have the shackles knocked off their ankles.

Behind the watch house Bannister frantically wound the strips of stinking rags around Joshua's feet and locked the chains in place round his wrists and ankles while the deputy watch master smeared something stinking out of a bucket onto Joshua's face.

'You know your duties?' whispered Joshua.

'Aye,' said Bannister. 'It's a risk, though. If you don't get right between them as he takes his seat, the gun could go off and – '

'Do you think I don't know that?' hissed Joshua. It was a desperate enough venture and if it failed, then Kat could die. Unbidden, the memories of what he had read on the *Java* about Trenand and his evil activities flooded into his mind and he knew he would take any risk to keep her out of that devil's clutches.

He made a conscious effort to slow his breathing down and forced himself to put all thought of failure out of his mind. 'You take out Armitage, Bannister,' he said calmly. 'That's all I ask.'

Bannister checked the priming on the watch master's pistol. 'Trust me for that,' he said confidently.

'Here they come!' hissed the watchman. Through a chink in the latrine fence they watched the little procession make its way down the beach while the settler smeared sand and dust onto Joshua's face, sticking it on to the filth as it dried in the hot sun. From a distance it looked as though Trenand had his arm draped in loving fashion around Kat's shoulders, but he was slightly behind and to one side of her and Joshua knew that his other arm would be holding the gun at her head. It was a desperate chance that they would be taking, but what choice was there?

'What's amiss with her arms?' asked the watch man.

'Her arms?' echoed Joshua. 'Nothing amiss with her arms when we saw her.'

'Here.' He passed Joshua the spyglass.

Freeing himself from Bannister, who had threaded him into a grubby greying shirt and was about to clap a round hat on his head, Joshua focused on the figure of Kat. Her head was held high, her eyes wide as Trenand tightened his arm. He dared not linger on her pale face with the thin trickle of blood running down her hairline, not if he hoped to stay calm. He dropped the glass down until he could see her hands. They were held slightly out from her sides, the thumb and forefinger of each hand forming a round 'O'.

'What the devil?' He turned to Bannister. 'An "O",' he said. 'What would she mean by an "O"? Somebody's name?'

'No. A destination?'

They looked at the watch master. He shook his head as he retrieved the glass. 'If he's going anywhere it'll be Tahiti or China. An "O" means nothing to me,' he said.

Bannister seized Joshua by the arm, eyes blazing. 'That's what it means, don't you see? *Nothing*. By Jesus, *twice* nothing.' He saw the blank expressions of the other two men. 'The pistols,' he said urgently. 'Two bodies. One shot for each. Ever known someone go out with more than a brace of pistols?'

'And if he's had no opportunity to reload ...?' said Joshua in a shaking voice. 'By God, Bannister, you may be right.'

'Better pray that I am.'

The five oarsmen were already seated in the boat, holding their long oars clear of the sides, blades up, when the sixth staggered round the side of the latrine, hat pulled low over his eyes and clutching his stomach.

'Got the gripe in his belly,' said the bo'sun, taking up his position behind the rowers and shaking out the cat-o'-nine-tails with which he'd keep the oarsmen up to the mark on the short passage out to the *Java* and back. The last oarsman's chains were struck off and he hurried round to the vacant place, reaching it just as Trenand altered his grip on Kat for her to step up.

The bo'sun stood up. 'Come on, you cur!' he yelled at the tardy oarsman, just as Trenand pushed Kat forward to step into the boat. 'Pick your feet up, or I'll have your hide!' Kat seemed to hang above the thwart, with Trenand glued to her side, not leaving an inch of space between them.

No one noticed the little figure stumbling down the path towards the boat until she was almost on top of them.

'Murderer!' screamed Amy as she caught sight of Trenand. All heads turned as if manipulated by some celestial puppet master. 'You horrid, beastly man! You murdered poor Mullins!'

For a split second Trenand's grip loosened. It was all the time they would ever have; it was all the time they would ever need. Kat went slack in Trenand's arms, her dead weight almost slipping through his grip. As the smallest of spaces opened up between them, the last oarsman dropped to the sand and the bo'sun cracked the cat, sending the thong flying through the air above Kat and catching Trenand on the side of his head.

Trenand staggered back, cursing, the hand that had been around Kat clasped to the long bleeding gash that had opened up across his cheek and scalp; Joshua bounced back up, snatched up his oar and, as Kat threw herself into the bottom of the boat, brought it down with precision on Trenand's gun arm.

The pistol flew out of his hand, the oarsmen cowering away as it struck the side of the boat, but there was no discharge. Kat had been right and the gun had been empty. Reeling from the blow, Trenand staggered again, retaining his precarious position half in and half out of the boat with difficulty. With a triumphant cry Joshua lifted the oar to finish him off but Armitage, seeing all hope of escape evaporating before him in the hot sun, leaped forward and grabbed at Trenand's arm. As Trenand teetered on the gunwale, arms and legs flailing as he tried to keep his balance, a pistol shot rang out and hit Armitage in the shoulder. The big man recoiled, his grip on Trenand tightening, and the two men fell in a tangle on the beach. The oar was too long and heavy to stop in mid-swing; it swished through the empty space where Trenand had been, struck the gunwale and bounced back up, wrenching Joshua's shoulder and throwing him to the ground.

The shock of the impact made him release the oar, leaving him defenceless. He lay a moment half stunned, hearing only the cries of the sea birds above the boom of the surf. As he raised his head, he saw to his horror that though Trenand was lying still on the sand, Armitage was on his feet, blood oozing from his shoulder, but otherwise seemingly unaffected by the bullet wound. As Joshua

391

shook his head to clear it, Armitage drew the long curved cane knife from his belt and lunged at him with a blood-curdling cry.

Joshua only just managed to roll aside in time, drawing in a sobbing breath as he felt the blade whistling past his ear; it buried itself in the sand, which gave him a moment to rise to his feet before Armitage was upon him again. They grappled and fell, rolling over and over; again the blade whistled past Joshua's face, trimming his hair as it went; this time it buried itself so deeply in the sand that after what seemed an eternity Joshua managed to break Armitage's grip on it. Above him he heard a gun discharge; he could only hope Kat would have the sense to stay in the bottom of the boat and keep her head down.

The two men rolled away from the boat, across the sand, pounding at each other with more instinct than science. Joshua wondered how long he could keep going. His breath was coming in short, stabbing bursts and his shoulder felt as though it were on fire. His opponent, a much bulkier man, seemed to have no such problems: it was as if the bullet, far from handicapping Armitage, had given him new strength. He was on top of Joshua, jabbing his fists into his face, when suddenly the world went black. Just as Joshua began to think it was the end, the smothering dead weight was pulled off him and he felt gentle hands on his face.

His eyes flickered open and he saw Kat's anxious face only inches away from his. Before he could reach out for her, strong hands drew him to his feet and held him steady while he filled his lungs with the fresh salt air. After a moment he put aside the supporting arms and stumbled towards Kat, wrapping her in his arms as if he could never let her go again. Over the top of her head he could see Armitage's body with the carved ivory handle of a seaman's knife sticking up between the shoulder blades.

After a moment he eased his grip on Kat. There was something wrong; he could sense it in the people around him. He looked anxiously around and realised he could see only the one body.

'Trenand?' he said sharply.

'Got away in all the confusion,' said the bo'sun, pointing across the cane fields to a figure on the edge of the bush, with the men in pursuit being gradually left behind. 'He won't last long in the bush; if we don't get him, the blacks will.'

'The watch master is the worst shot I've ever seen,' said Kat, stamping her foot in frustration. 'If only he'd let me have the gun!'

'Don't fret, ma'am,' said the watch master, turning his head to the top of the beach where a whole column of men had appeared, bayonets fixed, at the tree line. 'There's the Commandant, fresh back from his trip upriver. I'll warrant he was furious when he heard what's been happenin', specially with Miss Amy bein' involved. He'll turn the guard out to hunt him down. And there's nowhere for the bastard to run.'

# Epilogue

They stopped the cart on the crest of the hill overlooking Lacey's Creek.

'We could start work on the new house,' said Joshua, gazing down into the sunlit valley. 'Would you like that?'

Kat could think of little that would give her more joy than to work side by side with him, planning and building the home that they would share. 'But what about the mill?' she found herself asking, lips dry and heart skipping nervously at the fear of how he might answer.

'It's running well enough,' he said. 'Hugh can take over now, unless...'

'Unless?' she prompted him gently.

'I thought, while I was on board the *Java*, that if the papermaking is successful, we might have to move it down to Botany Bay,' he said. 'Garvey mentioned a mill down there.'

'And – you would go down there and – '

'Not me. Hugh knows enough now to set it up.'

'Then why – ?'

'It was the sea that gave me the idea,' he said. 'I found it hard to think of that beautiful valley scarred by stinking settling ponds. Better surely to put it where the tides will wash all the filth away?'

'I thought perhaps you wanted somewhere further away...'

'From you?' He looped the reins and took her in his arms, smiling down at her. Catching her chin, he tilted her face up to his and as he spoke he kissed her eyelids, her nose, her cheeks, her chin, the solemn corners of her soft mouth. 'I thought – that we had sorted all that out – before we took ship. I told you then – and I'll tell you now – that I plan to spend – as much of my life – as is humanly possible – in your arms.'

'I know that's what you said, but – '

'But me no buts,' he said, in a fair imitation of Lady Isabelle. 'If I didn't convince you on our honeymoon that all that nonsense is in the past, then I don't know what else I can do.'

'I think you'll just have to persuade me again,' she said, suppressing a smile. 'As you did before we took ship.'

It had been a strange honeymoon. Perhaps it would have been more seemly for them to have waited until they got away from Port Macquarie, but the tension of acknowledging his love for Kat and then nearly losing her had proved too great a strain for Joshua; besides, the surgeon had ordered them both to rest before embarking on another sea voyage. The Commandant had at least had the decency to move them to another room, leaving poor Mullins to recover in the bed where she had so nearly died. With a very subdued Miss Amy playing quietly with her dolls in her mother's bedroom and the Commandant out every day with the soldiers hunting Trenand, Kat and Joshua had had a few days to get to know each other rather better than before. Time had passed swiftly; if it hadn't been for the roast goose, they wouldn't have known that Christmas had come and gone.

He slid his arm around her and lowered his lips to hers. 'How shall I persuade you?' he said. 'Like this?' He kissed her gently. 'Or like this?' He tightened his embrace and his mouth became more demanding. She returned his fervour, her lips answering his urgency and her soft breasts pressed against his chest. He dropped the reins and ran his hand up her spine and the horses shuffled nervously forward, almost tipping them out of the wagon.

'Don't go away,' he breathed, reaching for the reins without taking his eyes off her.

'I don't think it's just the horses who are getting – '

'Restless?'

'Excited.'

Reluctantly he released his hand from hers and jumped down from the board, leading the horses down to a clearing near a stand of scented myrtles, whistling loudly as he went. He came back to the cart and took the plaid rug from under the seat; he spread it on the ground, placed his jacket in the centre and then came back to lift her down.

Their hands were all over each other, as if they could never make up for the time they had lost and soon questing hands were replaced by questing mouths and questing bodies and then there was nothing to be heard but the one note song of a bellbird calling to its mate in the nearby flame trees.

When at last they lay exhausted in each other's arms, he reached out idly, caught at a handful of dried grass, shook it and placed it in her hands.

She eased herself up onto her elbow and looked down at him. 'What's that for?' she asked.

'Nearest thing I could find to straw,' he said, a smile quirking the corner of his mouth. 'Thought it might remind you of our first time. When you seduced me in the straw in Aylesbury gaol.'

She giggled and rolled into his embrace. They kissed again, but this time they were fleeting butterfly kisses.

'Aylesbury,' she said at last, snuggling into his arms. 'It all seems so long ago.'

'A year ago. A lifetime ago. We were very different people then.'

'Different in some ways. But I loved you long before that.'

'And I you. Even when you were still a gangling girl and I a not much less gangling youth.'

'Then why – '

'Why did it take so long for me to admit it? Because you were the mill owner's daughter, and I just the mill manager.'

'I didn't care about that.'

'I know. Any more than you cared about marrying a convict.'

'But you're not any more.'

'No.' He smiled a triumphant smile. 'And I've the papers to prove it.' He patted the jacket pocket beneath her head.

'You could go back to England,' she said sombrely.

'And wreak my revenge on Tarquin and Youngman?' He shrugged. 'I can't even remember what they look like. No, I think I'll stay here. There's a great deal of work here for an energetic man to do.'

'And you're a very energetic man, aren't you?'

'Very energetic,' he said, burying his face in her hair. 'An enthusiast. An amateur, a lover of fine things...'

'A doer. That's what Hall called you.' She wriggled as his tongue found the sensitive spot just below her ear. 'Did I tell you,' she said, controlling her speech with some difficulty, 'that Hall wants us to go to Van Diemen's Land to write a report on – '

'Hall can go hang!' exclaimed Joshua indignantly. Then, more gently, 'I could tell you that Governor Bourke has asked me to serve on his committee for the reform of the convict settlements, which might be even more influential than one of Hall's reports, but I wouldn't dream of discussing such matters ... when I'm trying to seduce my wife...'

She reached over and handed him the bunch of dried grass. 'To remind you of the first time,' she said with a giggle. Somewhere in the bush a kookaburra laughed, and the other birds joined in the chorus.

Later, much later, they stirred, to find that the summer sun had dipped low in the sky; reluctantly they agreed that it was time move on.

A few minutes later the cart rumbled into the yard and Ned Garvey strode out to meet them, the anxious look on his face swiftly replaced by a smile. He was followed out by Jenny and Betsey and Meggie, while Mary stood in the kitchen doorway, her hand on Will's arm. Kat felt a warm surge of affection for them all, and for Lacey's Creek. She looked up at Joshua and knew that he was feeling the same way.

'Do you think Tom would be happy here?' he murmured.

'I'm sure of it.'

'Then let us write to him tonight.'

As he swung her down from the board his hand lingered on the worn wedding ring that he had placed on her finger just over a year ago in Aylesbury gaol.

'When next we go to Sydney I shall buy you a new ring,' he said.

'Buy me all the rings you like,' she answered with a smile, 'but for a wedding band, this is all I've ever wanted.'

You have been reading a novel published by Piatkus Books. We hope you have enjoyed it and that you would like to read more of our titles. Please ask for them in your local library or bookshop.

If you would like to be put on our mailing list to receive details of new publications, please send a large stamped addressed envelope (UK only) to:

Piatkus Books: 5 Windmill Street
London W1P  1HF

The sign of a good book